While Angels Slept

A Medieval Romance

By Kathryn Le Veque

Copyright © 2012, 2014 by Kathryn Le Veque
Print Edition

All rights reserved. No part of this book may be used or reproduced in any manner whatsoever without written permission, except in the case of brief quotations embodied in critical articles or reviews.

Printed by Dragonblade Publishing in the United States of America

Text copyright © 2012, 2014 by Kathryn Le Veque
Cover copyright © 2012, 2014 by Kathryn Le Veque

Library of Congress Control Number 2014-020
ISBN 9781495231476

Kathryn Le Veque Novels

Medieval Romance:

The de Russe Legacy:
The White Lord of Wellesbourne
The Dark One: Dark Knight
Beast
Lord of War: Black Angel
The Falls of Erith
The Iron Knight

The de Lohr Dynasty:
While Angels Slept (Lords of East Anglia)
Rise of the Defender
Steelheart
Spectre of the Sword
Archangel
Unending Love
Shadowmoor
Silversword

Great Lords of le Bec:
Great Protector
To the Lady Born (House of de Royans)

Lords of Eire:
The Darkland (Master Knights of Connaught)
Black Sword
Echoes of Ancient Dreams (time travel)

De Wolfe Pack Series:
The Wolfe
Serpent
Scorpion (Saxon Lords of Hage – Also related to The Questing)
Walls of Babylon
The Lion of the North
Dark Destroyer

Ancient Kings of Anglecynn:
The Whispering Night
Netherworld

Battle Lords of de Velt:
The Dark Lord
Devil's Dominion

Reign of the House of de Winter:
Lespada
Swords and Shields (also related to The Questing, While Angels Slept)

De Reyne Domination:
Guardian of Darkness
The Fallen One (part of Dragonblade Series)

Unrelated characters or family groups:
The Gorgon (Also related to Lords of Thunder)
The Warrior Poet (St. John and de Gare)
Tender is the Knight (House of d'Vant)
Lord of Light
The Questing (related to The Dark Lord, Scorpion)
The Legend (House of Summerlin)

The Dragonblade Series: (Great Marcher Lords of de Lara)
Dragonblade
Island of Glass (House of St. Hever)
The Savage Curtain (Lords of Pembury)
The Fallen One (De Reyne Domination)
Fragments of Grace (House of St. Hever)
Lord of the Shadows
Queen of Lost Stars (House of St. Hever)

Lords of Thunder: The de Shera Brotherhood Trilogy
The Thunder Lord
The Thunder Warrior
The Thunder Knight

Highland Warriors of Munro
The Red Lion

Time Travel Romance: (Saxon Lords of Hage)
The Crusader
Kingdom Come

Contemporary Romance:

Kathlyn Trent/Marcus Burton Series:
Valley of the Shadow
The Eden Factor
Canyon of the Sphinx

The American Heroes Series:
The Lucius Robe
Fires of Autumn
Evenshade
Sea of Dreams
Purgatory

Other Contemporary Romance:
Lady of Heaven
Darkling, I Listen

Multi-author Collections/Anthologies:
With Dreams Only of You (USA Today bestseller)
Sirens of the Northern Seas (Viking romance)
Ever My Love (sequel to With Dreams Only Of You) July 2016

Note: All Kathryn's novels are designed to be read as stand-alones, although many have cross-over characters or cross-over family groups. Novels that are grouped together have related characters or family groups.

Series are clearly marked. All series contain the same characters or family groups except the American Heroes Series, which is an anthology with unrelated characters.

There is NO particular chronological order for any of the novels because they can all be read as stand-alones, even the series.

For more information, find it in **A Reader's Guide to the Medieval World of Le Veque.**

Table of Contents

Chapter One 1
Chapter Two 9
Chapter Three 22
Chapter Four 36
Chapter Five 61
Chapter Six 72
Chapter Seven 99
Chapter Eight 125
Chapter Nine 140
Chapter Ten 153
Chapter Eleven 164
Chapter Twelve 176
Chapter Thirteen 195
Chapter Fourteen 205
Chapter Fifteen 217
Chapter Sixteen 228
Chapter Seventeen 244
Chapter Eighteen 253
Chapter Nineteen 264
Chapter Twenty 284
Chapter Twenty-One 295

Chapter Twenty-Two	305
Epilogue	315
Author Note	322
Excerpt from Rise of the Defender	325
About Kathryn Le Veque	351

"And so it lasted for nineteen years while Stephen was King, till the land was all undone and darkened with such deeds, and men said openly that Christ and his angels slept."

~ Anglo-Saxon Chronicle

CHAPTER ONE

Rochester Castle
Kent, England
September, 1139 A.D.

*T*HE SUNRISE IS *bloody.*
It was her first thought as she looked to the east with its hazy splashes of red and orange across the horizon. As dawn approached, black turned to dark blue and dark blue to azure. She could hear her husband behind her, rattling about their smoky bower, dropping a gauntlet here or a piece of armor there. But there was more to the clumsiness than met the eye or the ear. The wife slowly began to realize that he was dropping things purely to annoy her.

She did not want him to believe that he had rattled her, though he had. It was a game they played sometimes to see who could hold out the longest. He would annoy her until she took a swipe at him, though it was all in good fun. Such was the playful banter that they so often had. She finally turned away from the lancet window only to find him grinning at her.

"I was wondering when you were going to put your attention back on me where it belongs," he said. "Or is the sunrise too lovely to tear yourself away?"

Her lavender gaze traveled over him, indeed, her irises were lavender. A shade of blue so pure that that it was nearly purple. Surrounded by a hedge of dusky lashes that mirrored the titian color of her hair, Cantia du Bexley Penden was all shades of loveliness. *A thousand degrees of beautiful*, her husband called her. But eyes so lovely could go from passionate to furious faster that the human mind could track. Her husband both feared and revered that particularly gift.

"Why do you stare at me so?" Brac Penden held out his hands with mock confusion. "Have you never seen a man dressed for battle before?"

She lifted a well-shaped eyebrow and sauntered in his general direction. "I've seen you dressed for battle more times than I can count," she replied.

"That would stand to reason since, as son of the Steward of Rochester, I have been in more battles than I can count."

"Such was my misfortune for marrying into the heirs of Rochester. You're a warring bunch."

His grin broadened. "Such is the price of privileged servitude. We are stewards of the bishops of Rochester and, by this privilege, we go where we are told to go and fight whomever we are told to fight. Of course, in payment we are allowed to live in this fine castle…."

"A cold, howling mess of stone and mortar."

He held up a finger to hush her so he could finish his sentence. "And we are granted the lordship of Gillingham, of which you enjoy the status. Now, have you any further complaints to voice before I quiet you?"

He said it lightly, as it was meant. She approached from his right, coming to rest just out of arm's reach. "Nay," she said softly. "I've become accustomed to the way of things though I must voice my concerns once in a while or I will surely go mad. More often than not I have the utmost confidence in your return from these skirmishes. But today seems… different."

"Why? Because of a red dawn?"

"Perhaps."

Brac was a tall man with an equally long reach, yet he did not grab for her. There was something in her expression that did not invite it. Well built, with a battle-conditioned body and shaggy blond hair that curled and poked in every direction, he was handsome in a way that men often are who have achieved wisdom and character. It was more than his appearance. It was his heart and soul beneath. There was a gentle humor about him, so easy to laugh, so easy to become emotional. It was a time when men seldom showed their emotion. But Brac wore his on his sleeve. And he obviously, insanely, doted on his lovely wife and small son as few men would allow themselves to.

"We more than likely will not see any action today," he said to be of some reassurance. "Some of the king's forces have taken control of the bridge at Dartford and we must retake it. They will not risk an assault on the bridge that Rochester protects along the Medway, so they go further west to attack the larger crossing that has no such local protection. But I am sure that I shall be home before nightfall."

"Who has issued this call for aid?"

"Viscount Winterton," Brac replied. "Tevin du Reims. You have heard his name."

"Aye," she said quietly, remembering the implication that name brought about. "You have fought for him before."

"I have."

"You said the man is more formidable than anyone on the field of battle and that his own men have been known to fear him. Is he so terrible, then?"

Brac fussed with a strap on his shoulder protection. "You have only to see the man to understand why such things are said about him. He looks like a barbarian and fights like Lucifer himself." He leaned down and picked his gauntlet off the floor. He held it out to her with a gentle smile on his face. "Help me, please."

After a brief hesitation, she took the gauntlet and held it firm as he shoved his big hand into it. Then she helped him with the other. A perusal of his body showed that he already wore his mail coat, the hood of his hauberk still draped down the back of his neck, and his greaves. His legs had taken a beating over the years as the scarred leather armor on his legs showed that clearly. She was disappointed that there was nothing else she could assist him with.

"Your squire has you well dressed," she said, almost sadly. "There is nothing more I can do."

Her husband read her expression. It wasn't like her to be so melancholy at this time. While other women threw themselves into fits with weeping as their men departed for war, Cantia would smile and pretend that all would be well. He depended on that to see him through these struggles that were consuming their new nation. It was King Stephen against Empress Matilda, ripping the country to shreds with their demands for the throne. Everything the Duke of Normandy had fought for was in jeopardy and the new country that was England threatened to collapse on itself.

And the barons were caught in the maelstrom, Brac along with them. It was his duty as heir to Stewardship of Rochester. *But no,* he shook himself inwardly. His duty was to Cantia and their son, Hunt. His duty was to provide a safe country in which to raise his family.

He gazed down into that sweet face he knew so well. She was slender and strong, of average height that appeared short against his tall stature. To be with her, to touch her, balanced his entire world. He had known her since she had been a small child, when he knew that he would marry her someday. He'd never been without her.

"What is the matter with you?" he murmured. "You are usually far better company than this."

She gazed up at him, unsure how to answer. His normal manner was to jest until she was nearly crazy with it. Today she had no patience for his levity.

"I cannot say," she said. "All I know is that the sky is filled with blood. It gives me a feeling of doom."

"Are you a prophet, then?" he lifted his eyebrows.

"Of course not."

He grinned and kissed her forehead. "Nay, you are not. And I will hear no more of this foolishness. My men are waiting for me in the courtyard, growing fat and lazy as we speak."

She reached out to grasp his hand even as he moved for the door. She could not explain why she did not want to let him go, only that she did not. As Brac lifted the latch, a small boy suddenly came rushing in.

Robust and tow-headed, he held a small wooden sword in his hand and thrust it at his father.

"Die, fool!" the child cried. When the man didn't react fast enough, he threw up his arms. "Fall down already. I've kilt you!"

Brac grabbed his gut as if mortally wounded and fell to one knee. "Mighty Sir Hunt," he grunted. "Could you not have spared my life, O Great One? Must you kill me in front of my wife?"

The little boy pointed at him with his imperious sword. "Die and be done with it. I would bury you now with a grand funeral."

"How grand?"

"The grandesth!"

Brac sprawled out on the floor, but not without a tremendously painful and overly-dramatic scene of death. Even his death throes had death throes. His son grinned triumphantly then pounced on his father's stomach. Brac grunted loudly and put his arms around the leaping child. His booming laughter filled the room.

"You should not encourage his unhealthy preoccupation with funerals," Cantia scolded softly. "He buries everything he comes across: mice, bugs, animals…."

Father and son continued to tussle. "I see nothing unhealthy with a grand funeral other than the fact that someone has to die in order to have one," Brac said.

"That is not the least bit humorous."

"Aye, it is."

"Can I go into battle with you, Father?" Hunt ignored his mother completely. "I can fight. I have weaponths!"

Brac sat up. "Soon, little man," he rose to his feet, gingerly rubbing his stomach where the boy had leapt on him. "When you are old enough, I should be proud to ride into battle with you."

Huntington Penden had turned five years old last week and, with his latest birthday, was convinced he was man enough to do just about anything his father did. Brac's answer did not please him, but he did his best not to argue. Knights did not argue. They simply followed orders.

"Nexth time?" he asked.

Brac's blue eyes twinkled at the boy. "I shall consider it. But until then, I will leave you here to take care of your mother. That is the most important task of all."

Hunt nodded seriously. "Aye."

"Do not let her come to harm. I am depending on you."

"I won't."

Hunt had a thick tongue and a bit of a lisp. But it was part of his charm. Brac ruffled the child's downy head. "Good lad." Glancing at the boy's mother once again, he could see right through her thin smile. She was still worried. He put his arm around her as he led her out the door. "I would have beef tonight for sup. And none of those turnips you and the cook harvested last week, they're bitter and foul. But I will have some of those honey cakes with the nuts on them."

Cantia nodded, memorizing his wishes. "It shall be done, my lord."

They descended the narrow steps to the great central room below. It was bitterly cold outside and Brac did not want her out in the midst of it. So he faced her at the bottom of the steps while Hunt stood beside them, more interested in his sword than his parents' farewell.

"Your weapon?" Cantia asked.

"My squire has it outside."

She nodded, satisfied. But the longer she stared at him, the more anxious she became. "Oh, Brac," she whispered. "Please... perhaps you could not go, just this once."

He kissed her to silence her, drawing a snort of disgust from his son. "I shall see you again before the sun sets," he whispered against her mouth. "Have you no faith in my abilities?"

"Of course I do. You're a magnificent knight. But you cannot always control...."

"You are damaging my confidence. Tell me you have faith in me."

She could see that he would not take her seriously. Or, at least, he wanted her to think that. Looking deep into his blue eyes, she could see a flicker of longing and a shadow of fear.

"I have faith in you," she whispered.

"Swear it."

"I do."

His easy grin was back. He blew a kiss at her as Hunt chased him out the door, slapping his wooden sword against his father's mail coat. Cantia's last vision of her husband was as he grinned at his son, descending the steps into the bailey and leaving her line of sight. She stood there for a moment staring at the empty doorway as if hoping he'd make a sudden reappearance. But the doorway remained open, yawning and empty. She could hear noise wafting up from the bailey below, the sounds of men and war horses mobilizing for battle. It was a smelly, frenzied, disorienting sound.

A bulky figure hastily blew down the stairs from the upper floor, nearly knocking her over. She stepped aside as Brac's father adjusted his too-tight armor against his lumpy body.

"Damn pieces," he growled. "I must speak with the armorer. Someone has switched mail with me."

Cantia didn't say what she was thinking. Perhaps Charles Penden had simply grown too fat with his enormous appetite. The man could eat half a sheep at one sitting.

"We'll make sure to right it when you return," she said patiently. "Brac awaits you in the bailey, my lord."

Charles response was to grunt as he tightened the strap on his gauntlet. He was a big man, his graying hair long and unkempt past his shoulders. He was gruff and rarely smiled, and most of that was done in the presence of his beloved grandson. He loved the boy almost more than he loved his own son. When Hunt turned away from watching the activity in the ward and saw his grandfather, he attacked the man with his wooden sword.

"See here!" Charles said as Hunt smacked him with the weapon. "I am not the enemy, boy."

Hunt whacked him again on the thigh. "Fight me!"

Charles fought off a smile. "When I return, perhaps I will," he said.

"For now, I must save my skill and my strength for those I face today."

"If you die, can we have a grand funeral?"

"The largest the land has ever seen."

Hunt barred his teeth menacingly and his grandfather broke down into soft laughter. "You'll make a fine knight someday." Mussing the boy's blond hair just as his father had done, he disappeared through the open door that led to the ward.

As Hunt raced to the archway to watch his father and grandfather depart for the conflict that await them today, Cantia continued to stand where Brac had left her. She wasn't like the boy, eager to watch the men drain from the bailey in search of blood and glory. She certainly wasn't eager for any grand funerals. It was difficult to stomach the departure of Rochester's army from the safe confines of the castle. War was never a simple thing and they had seen more than their fair share over the past few years. Every time Brac returned to her safe, she thanked God profusely for his grace. But she couldn't help but wonder how long His grace would hold. Brac and Charles tempted it almost daily.

She had things to attend to for the day. It was best that she focus on her tasks and not her husband's mortal situation. Herding Hunt away from the door and closing the massive panel behind him, she diverted her warring son by tempting him with the morning meal. Hunt had a good appetite like his father and grandfather. From the shadows, a lanky yellow dog appeared and joined the lad as he raced into the great hall with his wooden sword held high. George the dog was the recipient of a wooden sword to the neck as Hunt sparred with his constant companion. But the dog was used to the abuse. He settled at the foot of the table while Hunt took a seat on the long, well-worn bench to await his food. His mother brought bread and last night's meat and Hunt fed the dog scraps before he fed himself. George was a glutton like the rest of the Penden men.

Cantia took a seat opposite her son, her morose thoughts on the army as it marched westward towards the Dartford Crossing Bridge.

CHAPTER TWO

She didn't remember much of that night other than it was dark and there were many torches illuminating the rectangular-shaped bailey of Rochester Castle. The army had returned long after Brac had promised. There were many wounded. There were also several dead. One look at her husband lying upon the cold, hard ground with two arrows in his chest and one in his abdomen, and Cantia ceased to see anything else. At that moment, she passed into a world that she had never hoped to be in.

It was a ghastly, dark place where she existed between denial and hope. She could hear the noise of the ward around her but it sounded strange and muffled. Her heart was pounding so hard that soon she could only hear the blood coursing through her head. She stared at her husband's supine form, wondering why he was simply lying there with no one to help him. It took several long moments for her to realize that he was beyond help.

She took a step closer to him. Brac looked as if he was sleeping except for the ugly projectiles sticking out of his body. She didn't even notice the host of knights now standing around, like vultures on a death vigil, watching her react to life's greatest tragedy. They had all seen this before. It never grew easier. But what Cantia felt was far beyond pain. Slowly, her knees gave way as she attempted to kneel beside her husband. Someone grabbed her elbow to help her to the ground.

"Nay," she moaned, reaching out to touch the spiny arrows but recoiling as she drew too close. "This cannot be."

"We were ambushed, my lady." A voice beside her spoke. "Brac was at the front of the column and took the worst of it."

She absorbed the words. Strangely, she felt no anguish at the knowledge, only peculiar numbness. She reached out and touched his neck, feeling for the blood that should be pumping through his body. There was none. His skin was strangely cold and moist. She took hold of one of the arrows.

"I shall heal him," she said decisively. "We must remove the arrows. Come, someone help me."

The men surrounding her glanced at each other. "There will be no healing, Lady Penden." Another disembodied voice spoke. "Your husband is dead."

She had begun to pull at the arrow, stopping when she heard the word. *Dead*. It was the spoken confirmation of what she already knew, but still, it was excruciating to hear. Her arms suddenly went weak, as if her blood had just drained from her body. She could feel the cries bubbling in her throat as she gazed down at her husband's peaceful face.

There was a body kneeling next to her. She could see his armored knees. She reached out, grasping the hand that happened to be there. She didn't even know who it belonged to. She squeezed the hand as if to break it.

"He's dead?" she whispered tightly.

"Aye, my lady."

She swallowed hard, forcing down the ferocious sobs. "He felt no pain?"

The man next to her, whose hand she clutched, spoke softly. "He was at peace with his passing. His last thoughts were of you."

She was too stunned to know if she felt better or worse by that statement. "Did you comfort him?"

"We held him, my lady," the man's voice was low and gentle. "We called him brother and told him of our love."

A sob escaped her lips no matter how hard she tried to control it. She slapped a hand over her mouth, the back of her fingers shoved into her teeth.

"But… he was at peace, was he not?" she was starting to lose control. "He was soothed in those last moments?"

"Aye," the man repeated himself quietly. "He asked that we look after you. He asked that we tell you that he was honored to have been your husband."

The horrid sobs broke through again, one after another. Soon she could not control them and she pitched forward onto Brac's lifeless body. He was so cold and stiff. His arms did not go around her as they usually did. But she could smell his scent, the comforting musk that told her without sight or sound that he was her husband. She pushed her face into his linen shirt, now exposed as the armor had been removed. She inhaled deeply, smelling of him. She thought it would bring her consolation but it did not. It only added to her pain. She held on fast and wept deeply into his battered, cooling flesh.

Someone tried to raise her but the hands were abruptly removed. She could hear voices behind her. One of them was the voice that had so gently told her of Brac's last minutes.

"Give her a moment to grieve." The soft, deep voice was now laced with threat. "'Twill be the last time she will see her husband in this life. At least give her that courtesy."

Another voice could be heard in response. It was Charles. "Not out here in the ward for all to see." His tone was dangerously unstable. "I will not have my family show weakness for the world to know."

More arguing voices. Someone was pulling Charles away. The man was crazed with grief over his son's death. Seeing Cantia sobbing over Brac's body only inflamed the madness. Cantia wept deeply, alternately cursing God and begging for a miracle. She had no idea how long she lay there, spread over her husband's body. All she knew was that the torture she felt consumed every fiber of her being. It hurt simply to live, to be left behind like a forgotten memory. In the midst of her torment, calming hands touched her and there were lips by her ear.

"My lady," a gentle male voice spoke. "Let me get you inside. 'Tis far too cold out here and you must rest."

She opened a wet, swollen eye and glanced up, seeing her husband's second in command. Myles de Lohr's familiar features were lined with grief. She put up a hand and grabbed him as if afraid she would fall if she did not cling.

"He must be taken care of," her voice was a hoarse whisper.

"He shall," he reassured her, ever so gently pulling her away from the body. "I will tend him myself, I swear it."

"God was not listening to my prayers this night, Myles. He and his angels must be sleeping, for surely, they would have protected my husband had they been at their posts."

"This I cannot know, my lady. I am sorry that we failed to protect him since God could not."

She continued to stare into his face, the scruffy man with the haunting beauty whose skills were so capable. "Tell me again that he did not suffer," she begged.

"He did not," Myles lied. Brac had lived for several long, agonizing minutes as he bled to death. "He was at peace."

As Myles helped her stand, Cantia realized that she was still holding on to the hand that she had gripped so tightly whilst kneeling. She had held it the entire time she had wept over her husband's body. She looked up at the man who had spoken so soothingly in his soft, deep voice.

She did not recognize him but that did not matter. Brac's death was a bonding experience. Everyone in that worried, tight circle of men was participating with her and she felt akin to them.

"Did he speak of Hunt?" she asked him.

The man patted her hand as she clutched him. "He spoke of his family, my lady, of a little boy who would one day bear his father's weapon."

Tears anew sprang to her eyes as she was reminded of a son who was now fatherless. "I do not know you."

"Tevin du Reims, my lady."

Her eyes widened slightly, the tears momentarily halted. "You…," she breathed. "You are Viscount Winterton."

"I am."

"You issued the call to take the bridge."

His piercing dark eyes gazed steadily at her. "I did, my lady."

Her first reaction was to become irate and curse him, but she could not muster the strength. Somewhere in the logical part of her mind that still remained, she knew he was not at fault.

Her gaze turned back to Brac, lying white and bloody on the ground. She tried to pull away from Myles to return to her husband, but the knight held her fast. He would not let her return to death. They tried to help her walk back to the donjon, but her legs would not function. Myles lifted her into his arms and carried her back to the massive four-story keep that dominated Rochester Castle.

It was very late, well after midnight as the knights supporting the return of Empress Matilda watched de Lohr return the lady to the keep. They were saddened by the waste of Brac Penden, an unnecessary death in this dark and evil time. They were equally saddened for the anguish brought upon Lady Penden.

Some of Penden's men led Charles away. The Steward of Rochester was still muttering to himself madly, refusing to leave his son until his men forcibly removed him. Those still crowded around Brac's body gradually left, filtering away into the night to take care of their horses or console each other with drink. Aye, they had retaken the bridge on this day, but the cost had been too high.

Viscount Winterton and his knights were the only men remaining with Brac's corpse when the others had faded into oblivion. They knew that Myles would be back once he settled Lady Penden and did not want to leave Brac's body unattended. Du Reims and his men stood around, quiet moments of conversation between them, waiting for this hellish night to be over.

"He was a good man," a burly, red-haired knight approached the viscount. "He was well-liked. This will be hard on his men."

Tevin glanced at one of his four most trusted knights. Sir Simon Horley was a ferocious fighter, not given to fits of sentiment that he was currently displaying.

"I fear this will be harder on his father and wife," Tevin's dark eyes glanced up at Rochester's keep. "We've lost a fine knight, but they've lost considerably more."

Simon wandered away, pacing around Brac's body like a guard dog. Tevin's gaze moved to the three other knights who served him personally. Each man was worth his weight in gold, skilled and powerful fighters. They all stood around Brac's body, protecting it, showing respect for Brac and his family. Soon enough, they would put him in the ground and move beyond the grieving. But not tonight.

Tonight belonged to Brac.

ೞ

"We have a problem."

Settled in Rochester's warm, smoky solar with a cartographer's drawing of England spread out before him, Tevin glanced up at the two knights standing in the doorway. Sir John Swantey had uttered the ominous words and Tevin focused his attention on the lanky, slender man.

"What problem is that?" he asked.

The knight sighed. "Charles Penden. He refuses to let us bury his son. He wants to burn him instead."

"What does the wife say?"

"She's nearly gone to blows with him."

Tevin stared at him a moment before slowly rising from the massive table that held the well-worn map. His expression was pensive. "We have more of a problem than that. I received word this morning that Dartford Crossing has been reclaimed by the opposition."

John's eyebrows lifted, perhaps in disbelief and some frustration. "Then we retake it, my lord?"

Tevin shrugged as if John had just made the most obvious statement in the world. "We've no choice. That bridge is our link to London and regions beyond." He thumped the vellum beside him. "But what I cannot figure out is if the king's forces, specifically Worcester, is trying to separate me from my seat or if by taking control of the crossing, they're trying to separate the Empress' concentration of forces. To separate Kent from London would be a great feat."

"And to take Thunderbey Castle would be a stroke of excellent fortune." The second knight spoke, although it was not in a tone that one would have expected from a warrior. This knight was smaller, wearing heavy mail that seemed absurd on such a slight frame.

At second glance, one would notice that the knight was, in fact, a woman. Lady Valeria du Reims had been fighting with her older brother since she had been a very young woman. She was fierce in battle, though Tevin knew he should not allow it. Still, he had never been able to deny her. Val did as she pleased and Tevin was weak enough to let her. If he'd tried to stop her, she'd only go fight for someone else. It was a pity as well. She was a lovely girl with pale red hair and luminous dark eyes. She would have made an excellent match as Viscount Winterton's sister. But in her current state, she would only make some man an excellent knight instead of a wife, and there was no market for that sort of thing.

No matter how Tevin approved or disapproved of her behavior, one thing was for certain; her advice was always sage and he valued it. He felt all the more guilty for his selfishness.

"They'll not take my seat, no matter how they try," he said. "Thunderbey is well fortified. She'll hold against any onslaught. But they could separate us from it." He picked up his gauntlets and shoved them on his fingers. "All that aside, we must bury Brac Penden before his body begins to rot. It's been nearly three days that he's lain in that tiny chapel across the ward. I do not believe his wife has left his side."

"She hasn't," Val said. "Nor has that little boy."

Tevin knew that. He'd been kept abreast of the behavior of the Penden family. Other than the breakdown in the ward the night they had brought Brac home, Lady Penden had shown remarkable control. She remained quiet and calm, praying for endless hours over the body of her husband. Tevin respected that. What he did not respect was Charles Penden's mad ravings day and night about the fate of his dynasty. He'd had them all on edge. Lady Penden had ignored him for the most part. John's report of the conflict between the two was the first he had heard in three days. If Charles were incapable of making the decision to bury his son, then as his liege, Tevin would be forced to do it.

"Brac will be buried before sunset," Tevin tightened the last strap of his expensive gauntlet and headed out the door. "Inform the men of our plans and tell them that we move out before dawn. I will go speak with the family."

"The Steward is dangerously brittle," Val said. "He does not think clearly."

"Where is he?"

"The last I saw, standing outside of the chapel."

The solar was off the great hall. Tevin, Val and John marched through the empty room, listening to their boots echo off the plank floor. The hall was eerily still. They moved through the front door, the same door that Brac had quit days before when it had been his last day on earth. The wooden steps, made portable so they could be raised in case the ward was breached, creaked under their combined weight as they descended. Once on the solid dirt of the bailey, Tevin turned to the right and headed to the chapel.

Had he not been so focused on the task at hand, he would have noticed that it was a spectacular fall day. The sun was shining and a soft breeze fluttered the banners that flew high upon the parapets. Days like this were rare. But the weather remained unnoticed as the chapel came within sight and Charles Penden with it. The man was standing outside the door of the tiny, wooden structure built within Rochester's great walls. His appearance was unkempt, his graying hair long and dirty as he worried his hands through it nervously. Tevin knew he was in for trouble before he even reached him.

☙

CANTIA HEARD THE VOICES from the bailey. One was soft, deep and calm, while the other was unsteady and tense. She recognized the second voice as that of Brac's father, but did not immediately identify the second. Whoever it was, he was not succumbing to Charles' psychosis. She could sense that the situation was escalating.

Excusing herself from her kneeling position next to her husband's lifeless body, she went to the door and opened it. Charles was pacing back and forth in front of the chapel, kicking up clods of dirt with his emotional stomping. Several feet away, evenly planted, stood Viscount Winterton.

Cantia took a moment to study the man who had been in command when Brac had met his death. She'd not given him another thought until this very moment. He was tall, extremely broad shouldered, with enormous hands that rested comfortably at his sides. She had remembered the size of his hands from the night of Brac's death when she had clutched one of them so very tightly.

She looked closely at his face. He wasn't young, nor was he old. He had piercing dark eyes, so dark that they were nearly black, and a decisively square jaw. He wasn't unattractive in the least. In fact, he was extremely handsome if she thought about it. But the one thing that she noticed about him above all else was that he did not groom himself in the Norman fashion. While knights of the realm shaved their faces clean and wore their hair in various lengths of short, the Viscount Winterton's hair was long, well past his shoulders. It was the color of tarnished copper, dark and glittery, tumbling in spiral tendrils across his shoulders. He pulled the front of it back behind his head to keep it out of his eyes, but the rest of it was wild and free. And upon his face he wore a well-trimmed beard and mustache, evidence that he did indeed take some stock in his appearance.

Aye, he was a bit of a curiosity at first glance, like a beautiful untamed horse. Yet she did not sense cruelty or unkindness from him. That had never been her first impression. He may have looked like a barbarian, but he had the manners of a gentle knight. When he caught her looking at him, he bowed his head in greeting and acknowledgement. The action jolted her from her thoughts. Slightly embarrassed that she had been caught staring at him, she spoke.

"What goes on here?" she said to him, to Charles. "I could hear your voices inside."

Tevin's dark eyes appraised her for a moment before answering. He'd first seen the woman that horrible night of her husband's passing when she had not been at her best. Now, in the sunlight and properly dressed, he was rather struck with the fact that she was an exquisite creature. Her rich brown hair with flame-colored highlights was caught in a simple braid, yet on her, it was like wearing a strand of rubies. Her figure, slender in the middle yet round in all of the right places, wore a simple broadcloth gown like a goddess. Aye, she was a unique example of a woman. He'd never seen finer. But he realized he'd been staring at her too long, so he answered.

"The Steward seems to believe that cremating his son is in everyone's best interests," he said. "I was simply telling him that civilized people do not burn their dead like yesterday's rubbish."

Cantia's lavender eyes flew to her father-in-law. "Indeed they do not," her voice was strong. "Brac will be buried with his ancestors in the crypt at Rochester."

Charles' pacing came to a stop. He glowered at her. "Cremation is an honorable burial," he growled. "I intend to go with him."

Tevin had heard that part earlier in their conversation, hoping that he would not restate it for the lady. It was the madness speaking. He glanced at Cantia to gauge her reaction. As he'd come to expect from the lady, she did not outwardly respond. But her spectacular eyes did, in fact, narrow.

"Would that I could let you," she growled back at him. "But you have a position to upkeep and a grandson who looks up to you. Do you think it would be easy on Hunt were he to lose his grandfather and father at the same time? Did you stop to think of that, you old fool?"

A bit ferocious, but Tevin was impressed. The lady wasn't about to let a madman march all over her. A lesser woman would have simply succumbed, but not Lady Penden. In those few short moments, his respect for her grew.

"Speak not to me of sons, lady," Charles snapped, "for I have lost mine. You still have yours."

"But your son was my husband," she bit back. "I have lost all that is dear to me in this world. Aye, I still have Hunt and for that I am deeply grateful, but never again will I know the warmth that was my dear Brac. Stop acting as if you are the only person at Rochester who is feeling pain with all of this. Cease this madness and act like an honorable man."

Charles puffed out his chest as if preparing to come back at her, but he suddenly slumped. It was as if all of the wind had left him. He turned away from Cantia, his tired old gaze moving over the lines of Rochester's massive keep. His pale face grew even more ashen.

"My son is gone," he half-whispered, half cried. "I would join him, I swear it."

Cantia did not know what more to say. She glanced at Tevin, still standing strong and silent several feet away. His piercing eyes, focused on Charles as the old man wandered away, turned to her.

"I fear that my duties have taken me away from being of complete service to you, Lady Penden," he took a few steps towards her. "I've left you alone in all of this and for that, I deeply apologize. Is there anything I can do for you?"

She gazed up at him, her lavender eyes glistening with unshed tears. Tevin could see that the strength she had exhibited against Charles was purely for appearance. Inside, she was dying.

"Aye, my lord, there is," she said softly. "You can help me bury my husband in a manner befitting his distinction."

"It would be my honor, my lady. I will see to it personally."

Her lovely face seemed to relax. Before she could reply, a small boy exited the chapel, his blue eyes blinking at the brightness of the sun.

Seeing his mother, he scurried over to her.

"Mama?" he slipped his hand into hers. "I've given Da my sword. He isth holding it now. Would you like to see? I think we should bury him with it. He would like that, don't you think?"

Cantia very nearly lost her fragile control. Her other hand went to her chest, pressing against it as if to hold in all of the emotion that was threatening to burst out. As she struggled to form a reply, Tevin could see the turmoil in her face. He quickly thought to give her time to compose herself.

"Little man," he addressed Hunt. "What is your name?"

Hunt's enormous blue eyes focused on him. "Huntington Penden. What isth yours?"

It was a bold question. "Tevin du Reims," he replied, fighting off a grin.

"Viscount Winterton," Cantia whispered hoarsely to her son. Tevin could see the tears were still very much on the surface. "Show him all due respect, Hunt. He is your liege."

Hunt's expression didn't change. He continued to size the big man up. "You are a viscount?"

"Aye."

"But I thought viscounts were mean, gluttonous men?"

Tevin cracked a smile while his mother nearly choked. "Hunt," she snapped softly. "You will apologize immediately."

The child had no idea what he had said wrong. "But you said that the nobility of England wasth full of fat, gluttonous old men who live off the life and death of their vassals. Didn't you…?"

She slapped a hand over Hunt's mouth and quickly turned him in the direction of the chapel. Tevin watched her nearly pull the child's arm out of his socket in her haste to remove him.

"My lady?" he called after her. "A word, please."

Cantia paused. Practically shoving Hunt back inside the chapel, she retraced her steps back to Tevin. When she forced herself to look at him, she swore the black eyes were twinkling.

"We will bury your husband at dusk," he said quietly. "Since I will take care of all of the arrangements, perhaps you will go and rest until the time comes. Will there be anything else I can do for you?"

She shook her head, perhaps a bit too hard. "Nay, milord, you have already shown us far too much grace and generosity."

Tevin stood there a moment, gazing at her. He wanted to talk to her more. He didn't know why, but he did. Yet the situation did not warrant it, and he felt a bit caddish for even entertaining the thought. No matter how lovely the lady was, or how much he respected her character, she was a newly made widow and his thoughts were inappropriate. Besides… her status as a widow was at his doing.

He silently excused himself from her presence and turned away. He hadn't taken three steps when shouts from the kitchen yard off to his left suddenly caught his attention. The servants were in an uproar. He caught two words: fire and steward. Before he realized it, he was off and running in that direction with Lady Penden close on his heels.

She had heard the screaming, too.

CHAPTER THREE

STANDING IN THE MIDDLE of the kitchen yards, Charles had covered himself with oil and was holding a torch at arm's length. Several frightened servants hovered in the yard, unsure what to do. By the time Tevin and Cantia got there, the Steward of Rochester was in the full stages of dementia, falling apart before their eyes.

"My God, my God," the man yelled to the heavens. "Can you not take me instead? I give myself to you freely. Can you not leave my son here to finish his life?"

Cantia was horrified. Some of the other knights had heard the yelling and soon, Tevin was joined by Val, John, and his two remaining knights, Dagan Sutton and Gavril de Reigate. Tevin held out his arm to stop them as the men began to spread out behind him, fearful that their presence would cause Charles to light himself immediately. Myles was the last one to arrive, his strong face tinged with shock. He went to stand next to Cantia, hoping to take her away from this. Tevin saw what the knight was up to and encouraged him.

"Get her out of here, de Lohr," he whispered loudly. "Her presence will only inflame him."

Cantia thought to resist, but something in Tevin's dark eyes told her that he would not tolerate disobedience. She allowed Myles to turn her for the yard gate just as Hunt raced through it. Neither one of them was fast enough to stop him as he broke through and headed straight for Charles. He grabbed the old man around the legs, holding him fast.

"Grandfather!" the little boy wailed. "What are you doing? I would come, too!"

"No!" Cantia screamed.

She broke away from Myles but made it only a few feet before Tevin caught her. He ensnared her in his massive arms and there was no way to break free.

"Stop," his mouth was by her ear. "You may only provoke him with whatever you say. The emotions between the two of you are raw. Let me deal with this."

"But... *Hunt!*"

"I know." His lips were on her flesh, his hot breath permeating her brain. "Trust me, Lady Penden. Please."

She was bordering on panic. Her hand was at her mouth, holding in the hysterics, but she finally nodded. She had little choice but to trust him. Slowly, very slowly, Tevin released her back to Myles, his mind focused on the next step in his life. The Steward of Rochester was ready to die, that much was certain. But his five-year-old grandson did not understand any of this, and the child was in peril.

He had to get the boy.

"Penden," Tevin moved towards him, very cautiously. "Look at what has happened. The lad knows nothing of what is going on. He is innocent. If you torch yourself and take him with you, God will make sure you spend all of eternity far away from Brac. You will never see him again, tucked away in the depths of hell only reserved for those who take their own life. And what of the boy? You would take his life with your selfishness. Does he not deserve to live?"

Dripping with the oil that he poured all over his head, Charles put his hand on the boy clinging to him. He struggled to hang onto the madness, now in conflict with his common sense.

"Someone come and claim the boy," he said loudly. "He does not belong here."

Tevin moved closer. "I will claim him. Throw the torch away and I will come near."

That apparently wasn't good enough. Charles looked down at his grandson, now slimy with oil. "Go," he whispered huskily. "Go to your mother, boy. Give me a grand funeral, as grand as your father's."

Hunt shook his head. "Nay, grandfather. Pleath let me come with you."

"You cannot. I go to be with your father."

"But my father ith dead. I do not want you to be dead, too. You are my only father left. Why do you want to leave me?"

Charles stared at him. The determination of his actions began to slip away, fading until he could no longer hold onto it. But he wanted badly to maintain his focus. Still, Hunt's soft words drilled into him as harshly as those arrows that had killed his son. They weakened him until he could no longer stand it. With a sob, high-pitched and uncontrolled, the torch tumbled from his fingers. Tevin dove for it before it could hit the ground and ignite the oil surrounding them.

The flame blew out before Tevin caught it. He lay in the dirt and oil, looking up to see Charles throw his arms around Hunt and weep like a woman. It was a heart-wrenching scene, the grief for Brac finally pouring out through every vein. But it did not erase the terror he had just put them all through. It was a struggle for Tevin not to become infuriated. While Charles held his grandson and wept, Tevin picked himself up and dusted off the dirt.

Cantia could hardly hold back the sobs. She was livid at what Charles had just put them all through, yet she could see his naked anguish at the loss of Brac. He'd held it in as long as he could and called it strength of character. But the strength would not hold, and the grief demanded to be felt. As she walked towards them, she thought to snatch Hunt away to punish Charles for his uncontrolled lunacy. But she hadn't the heart. Instead, she went to Tevin.

"My lord," she said, her voice quivering with emotion. "I have not the words to adequately thank you for what you have done for us. I fear that you will leave Rochester believing we are a foolish bunch. Believe me when I say that we are not. We are simply… shattered at the moment. Please forgive us our weakness."

His dark eyes were intense. "There is nothing to forgive, Lady Penden. You and your family have suffered a great tragedy. Your emotions are understandable."

"You are far too kind, my lord."

He lifted a dark eyebrow at her. "Nay, I am not." He handed Myles the torch when the knight came up behind Lady Penden. "In fact, I must ask your forgiveness for what I am about to do."

"What is that?"

Tevin's gaze moved between Cantia and Myles. "I must rally the men of Rochester once again. We ride at dawn."

"My lord?" Myles asked, somewhat surprised.

"Dartford Crossing has been captured once again by Stephen's forces," Tevin told him. "We must retake it."

Cantia drew in a sharp breath and lowered her gaze, unwilling to let them see her fear. Tevin waited for more of a response, but she gave none. He focused on Myles.

"Rally your men, de Lohr," he said. "Make them ready to ride before sun up. Tell them of our destination. I would have them understand that we must retake this bridge at all costs. Let Brac Penden's death be the rally cry. I refuse to let that man die in vain."

Myles bowed swiftly and was gone, but not before casting a long glance at Charles, still huddled on the ground with Hunt in his arms. Tevin would never forget the look of disgust on the man's face. It was difficult to have such little respect for those you served. He watched de Lohr quit the yard before emitting a low, sharp whistle between his teeth. It was the signal for his knights, like one would whistle for a horse or a dog. The knights knew that sound and knew it well. The five of them were still in the yard, near the gate, and immediately looked over at Tevin when they heard the shrill sign. All he had to do was nod and they disappeared through the gate to carry out their liege's wishes.

The servants had drifted away when the crisis was over, leaving the kitchen yard essentially empty. Tevin stood a few feet away from Cantia, watching her as she struggled with her emotions. He took a few steps and stood next to her.

"I will take the Steward with me," he said quietly. "Perhaps taking him back to battle, to the same place where his son fell, will give him a sense of vengeance. Perhaps it will end this madness he displays."

She looked up at him, those magnificent lavender eyes full of tears that she quickly blinked away. "I would be grateful, my lord."

He almost reached out to pat her arm, an innocent gesture of reassurance, but he stopped himself. It was not appropriate, harmless as it was. But it did not prevent him from giving her a tight smile, one full of regret and pity, as he left her side. Charles was still on his knees and Tevin paused a few moments beside him, speaking low words that Cantia could not hear. Very soon, Charles stiffly stood up and released Hunt. Woodenly, he followed his liege from the yard.

Hunt's sweet face watched his grandfather go. He was wracked with confusion, with grief, as only a youngster could understand it. He looked up at his mother when she walked up beside him and took his little hand.

"Isth Grandfather going to be all right?" he asked.

Cantia did the only thing she could do, she nodded. "Aye, he will." She touched his face, so very grateful that he was unharmed. "You were very brave, Hunt. I am sorry if your grandfather frightened you."

They started to leave the yard. "I wathn't scared," he declared boldly. "But I wath afraid that Grandfather would hurt himself."

"You saved your grandfather. I am proud of you."

Hunt didn't understand the all of that statement so he shrugged. He looked at the gate where his grandfather and the viscount had just disappeared. "Where are they going now?"

"To prepare for your father's funeral."

"Isth it going to be grand?"

"The grandest."

Hunt fell silent as they crossed the threshold of the yard gate and continued out into the bailey.

"Mam?"

"Aye, my love?"

"Can we bury my father with my sword?"

The ever-present tears sprang to Cantia's eyes but she held them back. She would not let Hunt see her devastation at the poignancy of his sweet question.

"Aye, my darling," she said tightly. "I think he would like that."

☙

As Tevin had told her, the funeral commenced at dusk. Every man, woman and child at Rochester held a single taper that, when lit, created an unearthly glow that illuminated the entire ward. Shadows danced against the massive stone walls, undulating shades of grays and blacks. The knights were in full armor, their mail coats glistening wickedly in the candlelight, as the mood of the place lay heavy in the air. It was Brac Penden's final time and all were appropriately somber.

The populace moved from the gates of the castle, heading down the road for the great cathedral of Rochester. It was a long, slow procession, full of bleak grief and the uncertainty of the times. Down the road went the ghostly wraiths, some on horseback, most walking, all of them carrying the light of hundreds of candles. The illumination gave the procession a surreal glow, as grand as Hunt could have ever hoped. Once inside the massive house of worship built by Bishop Gundulf in the year ten hundred eighty, the cavernous hall filled quickly to capacity.

Brac had been placed near the altar, dressed in his finest and draped with flowers from his wife's garden. Stalks of foxgloves mingled with roses from the vine. Myles and the knights from Viscount Winterton's army had carefully cleaned and dressed Brac for his viewing. Lady Penden had been enormously thankful for their care of him. He looked peaceful and ready for eternal sleep.

The cathedral was lit with dozens of fat tapers as the soft wail of the monks droned in the background. The Archbishop of Rochester had been called to preside over the funeral, but the messenger had not been able to get through to London where the Bishop was in residence. Therefore, a local clergyman from Northaven was summoned to do the duty.

After the lament of the monks ceased, the priest began the funeral liturgy. Cantia stood in the front of the cathedral with Hunt to one side and Charles to the other. She knew that Viscount Winterton and the other knights were standing directly behind her, as she had seen them upon entering the chapel. Myles de Lohr was as somber as she had ever seen him, nearly close to tears, she thought. He and Brac had known each other since they had been squires, a long friendship that had seen life and death together. Though his blue eyes were watery, his appearance was neat and his collar-length blond hair was combed. He had forced a smile when their eyes met, but there was no warmth to it. He was as miserable as she was.

The funeral mass was in Latin. Cantia's father had taught her the language at a young age, when it was a rarity for a female to know how to read or speak it. It was a male language, reserved only for the educated. But she knew it, and she understood everything the priest said as he spoke his low, soothing words.

Hunt kept asking her if the funeral was grand enough. She finally had to hush him so that she could concentrate on her prayers. Over her shoulder, Myles finally motioned to the boy and Hunt left his mother to go stand with the knights. Myles was something of an uncle to him, sometimes to the point of conflict. In very rare times when his father would deny him something, perhaps a toy or an activity, Hunt would run straight to Myles, who would more often than not make him feel better with some manner of distraction. Now, with Brac gone, Myles felt more protective of the lad than ever. The situation earlier in the kitchen yard had strained every ounce of his self-control. Had he possessed any less, he would have throttled Charles. But his was a peculiar position in life. As a substitute father to Hunt, yet a servant to him as well. When the fidgeting child left his mother to come to him, Myles picked him up so that he could see where his father lay.

Too soon, the liturgy was over. Too soon did they want to put Brac in the crypt. Cantia realized that she wasn't ready for that moment as the knights broke rank to collect the body of their liege and deposit it in the crypt next to his long-passed mother. The monks began their lament again and Cantia could hear the blood pulsing in her ears. Her control began to slip. Pushing her way through the knights bearing her husband's body, she took one last look at Brac's handsome face, fighting the torment and anguish that was roiling up inside her.

She picked a rose from the vine that was draped across him, pricking her finger and sending a drop of blood onto the blue and gold colors of Rochester he wore across his chest. Unnerved by the sight of her blood on his clean tunic, she tried to wipe it off, but it absorbed into the fabric. The harder she wiped, the more it would not come out. Big hands suddenly grabbed her wrists and pulled her gently but firmly away from Brac's body.

"If I had a wife who loved me very much, I should be greatly comforted to have a spot of her blood on my tunic that would soon be laid to rest with me in my grave," Tevin's low voice was in her ear. "It would be as if I took a part of her to my grave with me. A greater honor I could not imagine."

The tears welling in Cantia's eyes because she had mussed Brac's tunic now welled for another reason. She looked at Tevin, the lavender eyes glowing with humble gratitude. "I did not think on it that way," she whispered. "What a beautiful thing to say."

He allowed himself to smile at her, a reassuring gesture. "I think Brac would say the same thing, don't you?"

She was greatly comforted by his words. "He would."

"May I stand with you?"

"I would be honored, my lord."

They put Brac in the great stone crypt and closed the lid as she stood there. His effigy would be added later after the stonemasons finished it. For now, it was a plain crypt, strong and solid as Brac had been. Cantia stood there as Charles paid his final respects and as the cathedral cleared out of all those in attendance. Myles took Hunt with him and she could hear the little boy proclaim his approval at the grand funeral as the knight escorted him from the room. At some point, the

Viscount Winterton left her, too, until she was the only person left in the warm, candle-lit chapel. It was peculiar sensation, empty and wrought with finality.

It was the same cathedral she and Brac had been married in, the same place where Hunt had been christened. Now it was the place where her husband was buried. Standing there, gazing down at the sealed crypt, Cantia felt as if her life was over. She put her hand against the icy stone sepulcher.

"I first saw you when I was eleven years old," she murmured. "But from the time I was old enough to understand, I knew that I would be your wife. When I met you, I was not sorry. You were tall and skinny and you teased me about my missing front teeth, but deep down, I knew I loved you. I have always loved you. And now that you are gone, I do not know what shall become of me. I never imagined that I would be without you."

Her hands were rubbing the stone, the calm she had been able to achieve now suddenly overtaken with grief again. The tears came and she laid her cheek against the cold stone, wishing with all of her heart that it was Brac she was laying against.

"Oh... God," she sobbed. "Please do not leave me, Brac. Please do not go."

Her soft sobs filled the church, an empty room now as empty as her broken heart.

ೞ

TEVIN STOOD JUST outside the doors of the noble cathedral, waiting for Lady Penden to come out. Val and John waited with him, though they stood several feet away and huddled in quiet conversation. Since Myles had charge of the Steward and the young boy, Tevin appointed himself the lady's escort. The entire Penden family needed tending this night and it was their duty, as knights and vassals, to see to it.

In hindsight, it probably hadn't been the best idea to leave her alone with her husband in the cavernous cathedral, so cold and devoid of hope. It wasn't long before he could hear weeping. He glanced over at Val, who merely shrugged her shoulders. Val felt more emotion than she let on at times, and he knew that she was intuitively sympathetic to Lady Penden. It was difficult not to be.

"You should not let her weep overlong," Val said. "She has had three days of constant grieving. At some point, she must come to terms with it."

"Three days for a lifetime of marriage hardly seems an outrageous price," Tevin replied. "We have all known Brac Penden for many years, though we were not particularly close to him. He was a good man. Allow him his due, especially from his wife."

"She will make herself ill," Val said, more strongly. "You must remove her from the cathedral without further delay."

The weeping was not easing. He thought it was getting worse. His sister had a point in not allowing Lady Penden to make herself ill. He didn't need that on his conscience, too. In the distance, the funeral party was moving back down the road to the castle, anticipating the feast that was sure to follow. It would last all night. With some regret at having to force Lady Penden back to the event that would, in essence, be a celebration her husband's death, Tevin pushed himself off the wall he was leaning against and turned for the cathedral entrance. He was surprised to see Lady Penden already standing there waiting for him, completely composed.

"My lady," he greeted. "My knights and I have waited to escort you home."

"My thanks," she said, her tone slightly stuffed from all of the crying. "Where is my son?"

"De Lohr took him back to Rochester."

She took a deep breath, looking up into the new night sky. A million stars winked back at her.

"Such a lovely night," she murmured. "'Tis hard to believe the night could be so lovely during a time like this."

Tevin motioned to his men, one of whom brought around the lady's small gray palfrey. Cantia continued to stare up into the night as if oblivious to all else. She was struggling to put the tears aside, struggling to conduct herself as the wife of Brac Penden would. She finally glanced down, noticing the horse.

"If you do not mind, my lord, I would rather walk," she said.

His eyebrows lifted. "Walk?" he repeated. "If it would not be too taxing on you."

"Not at all. I love to walk."

"My lord," came a stern voice from one of the knights. "'Tis not safe to walk these roads. We must make haste back to…"

Another flick of the wrist from Tevin not only silenced the knight, but had the horse disappear. It was blatantly clear who was in command. Without another word, his knights spread out around them, staying to the edges of the road, in front and behind, well out of earshot of the viscount and Lady Penden. They were silent protection for the apprehensive walk back to the castle. During uncertain times like this, the night could harbor all manner of threats and there wasn't one man who did not take this lightly. To walk out in the open, with enemy conflicts all around them, bordered on the foolhardy.

But Tevin said nothing to that effect. The lady had been through enough and if walking brought her comfort, so be it. One of his men brought up his charger, a red beast with flaming eyes, but he waved the horse away. He would walk, too.

"Thank you for your kindness in arranging my husband's funeral," she said as their steps fell in unison along the dirt road. "I am most grateful."

"It was the very least I could do, my lady," he said. "Warring times are hard on us all, but not too hard that we should forget our civility and manners."

She was silent as they continued to walk. The three-quarters moon overhead cast an eerie glow over the landscape, ghostly beams shimmering off the River Medway in the distance. It was, in fact, a lovely night.

"May I ask a question, my lord?" she asked.

"Of course."

She started to speak but caught herself. He looked down at her to see what was causing her such difficulty.

"What is it?"

She shrugged. "I want to phrase this correctly so that you will not take offense."

"My lady, nothing you can say would offend me. What is it?"

She looked at him, then, her lavender eyes haunting in the moonlight. "If I ask you this question, will you promise me a completely truthful answer, my lord?"

"I am always truthful."

She cocked her head slightly as if debating the validity of that statement. "Very well," she said. "This is something I must ask, for my own sake. I fear that I have been lied to in order to spare my feelings."

"Why would you think that?"

"I want to know of my husband's last moments. And I do not want to be spared any detail. Were you with him when he died?"

Tevin hadn't expected that question, but he wasn't surprised by it. "I was, my lady."

Her lovely features tightened. "Then you spoke to him before... before he passed on?"

"I did, my lady."

Her jaw began to tick and her expression turned to one of frustration, sorrow. "Perhaps I am being foolish, my lord, but one of my biggest regrets is the fact that I did not have a chance to say farewell to my husband before he died. Certainly, I saw him off from the castle the day of the engagement, but I was not at his side when he died and...." Her lower lip began to tremble and she wrestled for her composure yet again. "You were there when he died. Perhaps you can tell me how he looked, what he said. To hear it from you would be to have been there."

Tevin didn't dare look at her. He could feel himself folding like an idiot, succumbing to both her tears and her wishes. Usually he was far more resolute, a paragon of strength when all else around him crumbled. But there was something inanely pathetic and touching about Lady Penden and he could not help himself.

"My lady," he said after a moment. "This has been a trying day. Perhaps this is something we should discuss at a later time."

She shook her head, firmly. "Nay, my lord. I would discuss it now. I... I cannot explain why I must know this, but I believe I must hear it in order to overcome my sorrow. Or at least deal with it. As it is, everything feels open and hanging and... meaningless. Will you not tell me?"

He thought a moment, looking off into the night, mulling over the intelligence of such a move on his part. He tried to phrase it as delicately as he could, as honestly as he could.

"As we were riding up on the Dartford Crossing, we were ambushed," he said quietly. "I do not believe there were many men, just enough to do damage. They stayed to the trees and fled once their arrows had been fired. Brac took two arrows right away, both to the chest. But he stayed mounted, giving orders and following his men into the woods. By the time he reached the perimeter of the trees, the enemy unleashed another barrage of arrows and he was struck in the belly. That one was enough to topple him from his horse, and that was where we caught up to him."

Cantia remained silent, staring at the ground as they walked. When she did not reply, he continued.

"It was clear that his wounds were mortal," his voice grew softer. "Myles was the first one to him, with the rest of us close behind. He tried to remove the arrows, but Brac would not let him. He knew it was hopeless and did not want to waste the energy fighting the inevitable. When it was evident that his time was short, Myles collected him into his arms and called him brother. We reaffirmed our love and respect for him. Brac spoke of the greatness of England he would never live to see, and of the beautiful wife and son he would leave behind."

She emitted a noise that sounded suspiciously like a sob, but she held her ground. "I know all of that," she said hoarsely. "Were the wounds painful?"

"He was shot in the chest and in the belly. I would imagine so."

"Was it really hopeless? Had he allowed Myles to remove the arrows, do you think he would have lived?"

Tevin came to a halt, facing her in the moonlight. She was an exquisite creature, even in the dark. "Nay, my lady, I do not," he said quietly. "The wounds were mortal the minute the arrows pierced him. There was never any chance."

She gazed at him, steadily, her lavender eyes filled with tears. "Tell me the truth," she whispered. "Was it horrible? Did he suffer greatly?"

Tevin stared at her. He should have stopped himself from telling her, but he didn't. Until the day he died, he did not know why he simply didn't shut his mouth. "It was horrible."

She sobbed and the tears fell. Filled with remorse at his lack of control, he reached out to grasp her arm in a comforting gesture. But she shook her head sharply and pulled away before he could touch her.

"Nay," she whispered. "I... I am all right. I will be fine. Thank you for telling me the truth. It means a great deal."

He watched her resume her walk down the road. With a heavy heart, he followed.

CHAPTER FOUR

THE VISCOUNT'S ARMY rode out before sunrise. Cantia knew this because she had been awake all night, staring into the hearth of her bower and wondering how she was going to survive the rest of her life. It wasn't simply grief she felt. It was loneliness for her husband's presence. His clothes were still strewn around the room where he had last left them. An old pair of boots lay haphazardly at the side of the bed. She missed his teasing, his joy of life, and his tenderness when he touched her. She missed everything.

Hunt had slept in her bed, placed there by Myles an hour or two before dawn. The boy had fallen asleep in the knight's arms, sitting in the great hall with him and the other warriors and listening to them tell great stories of battle. It had been the perfect diversion for him and a chance for Cantia to collect her thoughts. But instead of bringing comfort, her thoughts turned dark and miserable. Life was an ugly thing now. If only for Hunt, she would have to do her best to struggle through it.

It was still dark outside when she watched the army depart from the bailey. There were a few soldiers left behind to man the gates and the watchtowers, but for the most part, the castle was empty. It was less than ten miles to the Dartford Crossing, an area once controlled by her father before his passing two years prior. Now the fiefdoms of Dartford and Gravesham had passed to the baronetcy of Gillingham and, consequently, Charles Penden. Someday they would belong to Hunt. She hoped he would be as fine a baron as his father would have been.

She remained in her chamber as the day progressed. Hunt ran in and out with George on his heels, hurting with his father's passing but displaying the resilience only children are capable of. Brac's death would not set in for a long time yet, when the days and months passed and Hunt realized his father was never coming home. That was the finality of death. Right now, it was a concept and nothing more.

Time seemed to have little meaning as the sun moved across the sky. Cantia's gaze was fixed outside of the lancet window, her thoughts lingering on the past where Brac was the center of her world. She was not yet ready to accept that her world was forever changed. Perhaps it was still too soon. Perhaps she was not a good, sensible wife in not accepting that change immediately. She didn't know. All she knew was that she was living in limbo, dulled by grief and uninterested in what went on around her.

Hunt's chamber was across the hall. The doors to both bowers were open, allowing the child to flow between the two. He was hungry at some point and Cantia left her chair to take him down to the hall to request food. The servants moved around her quietly, whispering in the shadows of their sorrowful lady. She knew that they were speaking of her in hushed tones and it inflamed her, but there was naught she could do about it. Most of the servants had been at Rochester since before she had arrived and they had watched her and Brac's life together. They knew how badly this was affecting her.

One of the older serving women finally took pity on her and took Hunt outside in the yard to play. Between Hunt's shouts and the dog barking, the hall was abruptly silent as soon as the child left the keep. It was, in fact, dissonantly quiet. Cantia sat at the table she had shared with Brac so many times, feeling his ghost all around her. Instead of comforting her, it brought anxiety. She fled the hall for the safety of her bower.

She had sought peace. Instead, she found even greater ghosts. In the large chamber she had once shared with her husband, the sensations were heady and cloying. The room smelled of him and she couldn't shake the sensation of desolation. She had tried so hard to keep the agony at bay, but it was stronger than she was. It began to overtake her. Small sobs turned into body wracking sobs, which transformed into physical pain. Eventually there was so much pain that she couldn't stand it. Gasping for air, she caught sight of the small, lady-like dagger that Brac had purchased for her when he had visited York. It sat with some of her other valuables on her dressing table. She stumbled over to it, picking it up to examine the delicately bejeweled handle, remembering how Brac had taught her how to wield it.

Sobbing, she dragged the razor-sharp tip across her wrist lightly. It was enough to create a small red line across her flesh. She had hardly felt it. She wondered if a deeper cut would hurt more. She wondered if Brac would be angry with her for being so weak.

She pointed the tip at her wrist again. At the precise moment she planned to thrust it deep, a herald sounded from the parapet of Rochester's walls and the small crew of soldiers began to run about in a frenzy. The noise distracted her. Cantia forgot about the dagger and went to the window, watching the returning army approach from the west. The sight should have brought her joy, but it did not. The last time the army returned, it was with Brac's body.

She went back and found the dagger.

03

THE CONTINGENT HOLDING the bridge at Dartford had been considerably larger this time around. Consequently, there were quite a few injured, some of them severely. The battle had been brutal and close-quartered, hand-to-hand combat that had exhausted everyone.

The returning army made haste to get inside the ward of Rochester so that the gates could be closed and fortified. A few hundred exhausted men functioning as archers were sent to the walls. Rochester was under lockdown with the opposing army on the approach. A battle was in the air, though the men in charge of Rochester's defenses were confident in her abilities to hold fast. No one had ever breached her.

Myles had command of the walls, while Simon Horley had charge of the ward and men on the ground. Charles wandered between the two locales creating more trouble than helping. The man still wasn't right in the head and most everyone ignored him. But the command of Rochester had to be divided because Tevin was else occupied. Val had been knocked from her charger and had taken a serious blow to the ribs. Tevin had carried his sister, literally, the entire way back to Rochester. He was, at the moment, only concerned for her and little else. He had to trust the defense of the castle to his dependable men.

The great hall was quickly transformed into a surgeon's ward, though they had no surgeon. Cantia had always performed most of the healing duties with the exception of when she gave birth to Hunt and Brac had summoned a physic from Canterbury. Even then, she thought to tell the man how to do his job because healing was a skill she had worked to acquire. When Tevin burst into the hall supporting an injured knight, the servants moved into action. It took some coaxing, but they managed to take the wounded comrade from the viscount and lay him upon the ground. The next step was to find Lady Penden.

When the servants vacated in search of water, medicaments and the lady of the keep, Tevin was left crouched next to his sister. He tried to remove her mail but didn't get very far. He had to lift it over her head but couldn't manage to do so without causing her excruciating pain. So he gave up for the moment, waiting for Lady Penden to appear. Several long minutes passed until his anxiety was at a splitting level. He could no longer wait. He turned to go and find the lady himself but ran straight into Hunt.

The boy had been standing silently next to him, a wooden cart in one hand and something that looked like a toy ballista in the other. His blue eyes were wide on the knight lying on the floor.

"Ith he hurt?" he asked.

Tevin nodded. "Aye," he didn't want to have a conversation with the boy. He wanted action. "Where is your mother?"

"In her room," the lad replied. "How bad ith he hurt?"

"Bad enough," Tevin snapped before thinking. He saw Hunt's expression at his tone but he could not manage to calm himself. "I must go find your mother."

"She hath locked the door," Hunt said, almost casually. Then his voice picked up. "Do not worry. We shall give the knight a grand funeral if he dies."

More wounded were being brought in all around them. The more serious were placed near the hearth, while those who were still conscious were moved to the walls to be out of the way. Tevin left the boy standing there and made his way to the narrow stairs that led to the third floor. Just as he mounted the bottom step, a frail-looking servant came barreling down as if to knock him down. The old woman's face was taut.

"My lord," she said. "The lady… she does not answer. Her door is locked and I cannot get in."

Tevin did not understand why that was so urgent, but he moved around the woman and took the stairs to the next level. There was a small landing and two doors. One was open, with a small bed inside and toys strewn about. A big yellow dog lay sleeping on the bed. Tevin tried to lift the latch of the second door, which was indeed locked.

"She never locks her door," the worried servant was behind him. "She was weeping this morn… I am afraid for her, my lord. She's not been right since the lord passed."

That was Tevin's first inkling as to why the servant seemed to be so worried. It also clarified the boy's statement of the mother's door being locked. He rattled the door latch.

"Lady Penden?" he called gently. "Please open the door. We have a good deal of wounded that require your attention."

He received no reply. Rattling the lock once more, he again spoke softly, asking her to come forth. Still no answer. When the servant began to whine with fear, he took action. There was no time for pensive ponderings or sweet pleas. Something was wrong. Even if there was not, the lady was required in the hall and he would not tolerate her stubbornness.

Tevin was a broad man; though he may not have possessed the lanky height that Brac had, he was nearly twice as wide. The width of his shoulders was the first thing anyone noticed about him. Lowering a massive shoulder, he took a large lead before ramming the left side of his body into the door. The panel creaked and shook, but remained fast. Standing back, he lashed out an enormous booted foot and kicked the latch. The iron twisted. With another kick, it bent further and splintered the wood around it. Tevin gave one last kick, with a grunt this time, and the door swung open.

The room was large and cluttered, but comfortable. Tevin's dark eyes darted around the room in search of the lady, finally coming to rest on a titian-colored head on the opposite side of the bed. He rounded the furniture, seeing that Lady Penden was sitting upright on the floor, leaning against the bed. Her head was down, staring at her lap. She was unmoving, like stone.

That was enough for Tevin. With a growl, he chased the vexed servant from the room. He did not want anyone else to view the scene.

When the damaged door slammed shut and they were alone, he knelt beside her, trying to assess her state. With all of his other worries, he could have easily become angry that she had added to them. But all he could manage to feel at the moment was extreme concern.

"My lady?" he said quietly. "Can you hear me?"

Her luscious reddish-brown head bobbed slightly. Her hair was askew, covering her features. "Are you injured?" he asked gently.

After an eternal pause, she shook her head sluggishly. "I could not do it."

He barely heard her. "Do what?"

Her head came up then, the lavender eyes red from crying. There was such pain in the cool depths that it literally reached out to strike him. Then he noticed the dagger in her hand. Tevin gazed back at her, realizing what she meant, feeling more horror and guilt than he had ever imagined possible. He reached down and tossed the dagger to the other side of the room. An examination of her wrists showed that she had slightly cut herself across one of them, hardly enough to draw blood. But the intent was obvious.

"No, no…," he murmured. His self-control, fed by his emotions, left him and he encircled her in his massive arms. "No, my lady, not like this. You will not meet your end like this."

She was tense in his embrace, stiff as he held her. But after a moment, it was as if all of the sorrow and confusion she was feeling suddenly vanished when she realized that warm, comforting arms held her. Her arms went around his neck and horrid, deep sobs bubbled out of her chest. Tevin held her so tightly that he was sure he was crushing her. He felt so horribly guilty that this woman felt she had no hope, no comfort, and nothing left that death was her only escape. He shouldn't have felt responsible, but he did.

She wept like a child as he held her. Though Val was downstairs and in need of help, Tevin felt that he had to spare these few moments for Lady Penden. He'd spared her little else.

"I am so sorry," Tevin whispered into her hair, not knowing what else to say. "I do not know much, my lady, but I do know death. I have seen much of it. All I can tell you is that this too shall pass, and these dark days will seem less so. You have your son and a host of knights that serve only you. I know that we are a weak substitute for your husband, but we nonetheless support you. The sun will shine again, my lady. You must have faith."

She couldn't answer. Everything from the past few days was coming out in torrents of grief. Tevin let her cry, hoping he was at least bringing some comfort by simply being there. He tried to ignore the growing sensation of the pleasant feel of her in his arms. Since that moment when he'd seen her at the chapel yesterday, he'd done nothing but think on her. He'd known other women. He'd even married one. But he couldn't ever remember a woman that stuck with him the way Lady Penden did. She had a nameless charm that went beyond normal attraction. He was starting to feel like a fiend.

He ended up sitting on his buttocks with the lady clutched against him until the tears would no longer come. It really hadn't been that long, but to him, it had seemed like an eternity of warmth and compassion. Even when she was silent and quivering, he continued to hold her. It began to occur to him that he wanted nothing more at this moment than to hold her. But that was wrong, and his conscience wreaked havoc within his mind. Had his motives been pure, he would not have been so torn. The fact that he felt guilty for holding her told him that his motives went beyond normal comfort. He was finding some distorted gratification in it. He liked it.

"My lady," his lips were against the side of her head. "I realize that this is more than likely not the most opportune time to speak on this subject, but we have many wounded in the hall that require attention. Though we can hardly expect our needs to supersede your own, I would consider it a personal favor if you could find the strength to tend the men. They are in great need of you."

Her arms were still around his neck, her face in the crook between his neck and shoulder. When she lifted her head to look at him, Tevin felt a jolt run through him as their eyes met.

"How selfish of me." Unhappily for him, she slowly unwound her arms from his neck. As he watched her, she struggled for composure. "Your men are injured and all I can do is think of myself. Forgive me."

"There is nothing to forgive."

She smiled weakly. "I doubt that is the case, but you are kind to say so." She wiped at her face, erasing the last of the tears. "I am not usually the dramatic type, but it seems that all you have witnessed since coming to Rochester are dramatics and hysterics."

It was an effort for him to keep his hands to himself. She was so deeply filled with sorrow and his natural compassion begged to wipe away a tear, or squeeze her hand to ensure some measure of comfort. But he would not. He'd done more than he should have already.

"As I told you yesterday, there is no need for any apology," he said quietly. "You and your family have suffered a great loss. Your grief is natural."

Her lavender eyes grew steady. As he watched, she seemed to draw on the last reserves of strength she must have held. But it was a fragile composure. "Grief, indeed. But madness… surely there is no excuse."

She suddenly stood up, prompting him to also rise. The contrasts in their sizes were pronounced. Tevin was easily twice as wide as the diminutive lady and a head and a half taller. It seemed that she had something more to say to him but could not seem to bring forth the words. After a moment, she simply moved for the door and he followed. But she abruptly paused before opening it and he nearly ran into the back of her.

"May I ask a question, my lord?" she asked.

He was hesitant. The last time she asked a question, he divulged details that had almost driven her to insanity. But he nodded. "Aye."

"Have you ever lost someone close to you?"

"Many people, my lady."

"May I ask who?"

"My father, my uncle, my older brother."

"In battle?"

"I lost my father and brother in the same battle."

She digested those facts. "When you said that these dark days will pass… will they indeed?"

He nodded, slowly, his dark eyes studying every curve, every delightful contour of her face. "They will appear less so in time."

"It does not seem like it."

"I know. But you must trust me."

She took a deep breath, for strength and for courage, and lifted those magnificent eyes to him. "Your comforting presence has meant more than you can know to me and my family and to that end, I am eternally grateful. To thank you seems wholly insufficient."

He smiled weakly, feeling humbled. "Your thanks is more than adequate, I assure you." Then his smile faded. "But you must promise me one thing."

"Anything, my lord."

He began to look around as if he'd lost something. Cantia watched as he took a few steps towards the massive wardrobe and reached down to collect the dagger he had thrown. His dark eyes were fixed on her.

"You will never try anything like this again."

She nodded, embarrassed and ashamed. Opening the chamber door, they made their way down to the hall in complete silence.

Tevin didn't take any chances. He kept the dirk.

༄

THOUGH THERE WERE OTHERS who were more severely wounded, Cantia's first patient was Val simply because she happened to be the closest to the door. It took Cantia a matter of seconds to figure out that Val was, in fact, a woman, and her features registered the surprise.

But she said nothing as she examined the patient, determining that she had a few broken ribs and a broken collarbone. Tevin held his sister steady as Cantia and a serving woman bandaged up the ribs and then secured the left arm into a permanent, wrapped position so that the collarbone would heal. It was a relatively simple procedure that had taken less than an hour. But the relief Val, and Tevin felt, was immeasurable.

Cantia had Val moved into the small solar, away from the bulk of the wounded, for the sheer fact that she was female. It was not proper for her to convalesce in a room full of men, even if the woman was dressed like a knight. Oddly enough, Cantia asked no questions of Tevin as to the identity of the female knight. She simply accepted it on face value and moved on to her next patient.

Though Tevin's attention was focused on settling his sister, he could not help but be distracted by Lady Penden as she moved among the wounded. He was impressed by the fact that she was able to put the needs of others over her formidable grief. It must have been exceptionally wrenching for her to tend men with arrow wounds, knowing her husband had died days earlier in the same manner. But she said nothing, focused on helping those who needed her. From what he'd seen over the past few days from her, he'd expected nothing less.

Tevin eventually accompanied Val into the solar and saw to her comfort there on a bed that the servants had placed near the fire. He was glad that the result of her having been slammed off her charger was just a few cracked bones. In the heat of the battle, it could have been much worse. Val had been given a brew of willow bark that eventually caused her to drift off to sleep somewhere near dusk, at which time Tevin left her alone. He had many others wounded and would use the time to see to them.

The great hall was darkening as evening fell. A fire burned brightly in the hearth, sending ribbons of smoke into the air. As Tevin entered the hall, the first thing he saw was Hunt and his big yellow dog sitting near the fire. The boy had a big piece of bread in his hand and the dog licked at the crumbs on the floor.

"My lord," Simon Horley somehow had snuck up behind him and he'd never heard him. "How fares Val?"

"She is sleeping," Tevin replied. "Do you have a casualty report?"

"Nine dead, twenty-seven wounded," Simon replied. "Considering the fierceness of the battle, I had expected worse."

Tevin nodded. "Is everyone attended to?"

"Aye," Simon replied. "Your knights are in the knight's quarters, awaiting your debriefing."

Tevin usually gave a small talk after every battle. It was usually to discuss the battle as a whole, how well it was managed, and if there could be any improvements made with skill or manpower or weapons. But tonight, he didn't feel much like talking about it. Perhaps it was because he had been preoccupied with Val, or perhaps it was because he was too spent. The past few days had been inordinately draining, both physically and emotionally.

"Tell the men to get some rest and we shall speak on the morrow," he said. "I shall sleep with Val in case she needs anything."

Simon nodded. "Very good, my lord."

With a wave of his hand, Tevin dismissed him. At some point, he realized that Hunt was walking over to him, winding his way amongst the wounded on the floor. The yellow dog followed behind. When Hunt reached him, he stood there looking up at him, chewing on his bread.

"Are you hungry?" the child asked.

Tevin shook his head. "Nay, boy. I am here to look after my wounded."

Hunt took another big bite of bread. "Mam already did that."

"Where is your mother?"

"In the yard."

Tevin nodded his thanks for the information and proceeded to the exit of the keep. The kitchens and yard were on the opposite side of the bailey. It took him a moment to realize that Hunt and the dog were trailing after him.

"I thaw the dead men," Hunt said as they crossed the dusty ward. "Are you going to give them grand funerals?"

Tevin looked down at him, a disapproving expression across his brow. "Why did your mother allow you to see dead men?"

Hunt had finished his bread, but there were crumbs all over his face. He gazed up at Tevin with blue-eyed innocence. "They were in the ward. I thaw them. One of them had arrowth sticking out of him."

Just like Brac. Tevin didn't know what to say so it was best that he say nothing. As they neared the kitchen enclosure, he spied a few women in the yard, bent over a large iron cauldron. It was steaming furiously and they were removing pieces of cloth from the boiling brew with big sticks. Even in the darkness of the bailey, he could see great clotheslines of boiled rags strewn all over the yard.

As he stood at the threshold to the enclosure, Cantia suddenly emerged from the warm, moist kitchen with a tray in her hands. She spoke to the servants stirring the pot, asking them to add more lye to the mixture. The bandages were for the wounded and she wanted to make sure that they were clean. Then she spied Tevin and Hunt at the yard gate.

"My lord," she headed straight for him. "I was just coming to find you. I thought perhaps you might like something to eat."

As Tevin gazed at her, he quickly realized one thing; he was glad to see her. "And I was coming to find you to discover the state of my wounded," he said steadily.

"Perhaps we should go into the keep and discuss it while you eat."

He merely nodded, allowing her to lead the way. Hunt raced to his mother's side, holding her hand as they retraced their steps across the bailey. Tevin followed along behind, his eyes alternately scanning the ward and scanning Cantia. He tried not to watch her, the smooth sway of her slender backside, instead focusing on their surroundings. It had long been a habit, as it was the habit of most knights, to be constantly aware of his surroundings. Threats often lingered in the shadows. But no threat this night could capture his attention more than Cantia's graceful figure.

Somewhere during the day, she had donned a heavy linen apron and tied a kerchief around her head to keep her gorgeous hair out of her eyes. The garments were simple, course even, but she still wore them like a goddess. The woman could wear nothing that made her look bad. But more than that, her spirit seemed much improved. She had greeted him with a clear, even expression and had even smiled, however faint. He was pleased to see that she appeared in a better state of mind.

Entering the cool, dark keep, she took the food into a small alcove directly off the entry. It was barely large enough for three people, but there was a small table and an even smaller hearth that smoked and sparked as she set the food down. Tevin stood just outside of the doorway until he realized that she wanted him to come in and sit down. He did so, silently, as she removed the cloth covering the contents of the tray. A large piece of bread, butter, a pitcher of wine and a knuckle of beef await him.

"I thought you said you weren't hungry," Hunt was standing beside him, puzzled, as he eyed the food.

He looked at the boy. "Your mother had gone to much effort to feed me. The least I can do is eat."

Hunt looked up at his mother. "I'm hungry, too."

She put her hand on his head. "You ate enough for three people earlier this eve."

"But I'm still hungry!"

Before Cantia could reply, Tevin tore his bread in two and handed the boy a chunk. "Here."

"Butter, too?"

Tevin indicated the butter and knife, to which Hunt helped himself generously. The lad pulled up a chair and sat next to Tevin, eventually picking at the beef knuckle. Cantia pulled his hand back the first time he tried.

"Nay, Hunt," she admonished. "This is his lord's meal. Consider yourself honored that he has shared his bread with you. Do not ask for more."

Tevin tore a big piece of beef off the bone and handed it to the boy. His dark eyes looked up at her. "The worst I can tell him is no. There is no harm in asking for more. Most ambitious men do that, and then some."

She smiled, properly contrite. She put her hands on Hunt's little shoulders. "Thank you for being so kind to him."

Mouth full, Tevin watched Hunt stuff his mouth with the beef. "He is easy to be kind to. You have raised your son well."

"Thank you," she said softly. "His father deserves a good deal of the credit."

Tevin's gaze returned to her, watching a melancholy cloud suddenly drift across her face. He moved to another subject quickly. He said the first thing than came to mind.

"Cantia," he said, pouring himself more wine. "That is an unusual name."

She struggled not to linger on thoughts of Brac, focusing on Tevin's statement instead. "It is the ancient name for Kent."

"Your family has been in Kent for many generations?"

There was a small three-legged stool in the corner and she pulled it near the table, sitting. "For hundreds of years. In fact, my family had a very specific role in the ancient Kingdom of Kent, something that still carries through to this day."

"What is that?"

She looked at him, her lavender eyes reflecting the weak firelight. "The firstborn female in my family always married the heir to the throne of Kent. Though the nobility title was passed down through the males, the first born female had the most important role. When *William le Bâtard* conquered these shores in the days of my grandfather, our role became no less important. But because there is no future king of Kent, I have married into the Stewards of Rochester, traditionally the family that serves the king as the protector of the throne."

Tevin realized he was watching her mouth as she spoke. It was delightful and captivating. He further realized that she had the same lisp that her son had, though it was barely detectable. He'd never noticed before, but it was something that made her all the more charming. He shoved another piece of meat into his mouth, praying his growing interest in her wasn't obvious.

"Most interesting," he said. "In that respect, your family and mine share something in common. We are both of noble lineage predating William's conquest."

"May I beg you to tell me of your family's line, my lord?"

He swallowed the bite in his mouth. "It is rather complicated, but suffice it to say that my grandsire, several generations back, was the second son of the last king of East Anglia. My father held the title Viscount Winterton, heir apparent to the Earldom of East Anglia."

"How are you related to the seated Earl of East Anglia, then?"

"Geoffrey de Gael, the current earl, is my cousin. My father's mother was Geoff's father's sister. My father inherited the heir apparent title through his mother, as the next eligible male in the line. When he died, I inherited it."

"I see," she nodded thoughtfully. "Noble lineages are often very confusing. For example, there is no seated Earl of Kent, which is why I married the stewards of the ancient throne."

"I know."

He understood the progression of lineage better than she did but he found it rather touching that she felt the need to explain her position as if he would not have understood the workings of Anglo-Saxon nobility. Reflexively, he smiled at her and she smiled back. It brought him such a feeling of warmth that he just as quickly quelled the gesture by shoving more food in his mouth.

"Something to consider now is the fact that your son has inherited any titles that your husband may have held." He couldn't believe he'd brought Brac into the conversation when he'd tried so hard to keep away from the subject. He watched her reaction carefully.

Surprisingly, she didn't seem to dampen. She merely nodded her head. "Charles holds all of the titles for the time being," she said. "Hunt will inherit them upon his death."

"Speaking of which, where is Charles?"

She shook her head. "I've not seen him all day. But I am sure he is well, else we would have heard otherwise."

Tevin eyed her as he finished the remainder of his beef. "You do not get on well with him, do you?"

She shrugged, careful of what she said with little ears present. "We have always accepted one another."

Tevin let it go. He could see there was more to it but it frankly wasn't any of his business. He turned back to the remainder of his food, nodding his head in thanks when Cantia poured what was left of the wine into his cup.

"What is to happen now, my lord?" she asked as she reclaimed her stool. "Are there to be more battles?"

Tevin drained his cup, wiping his mouth with the back of his hand. "I do not know, my lady," he said honestly. "Since Rochester is closer to Dartford than my own castle, I suspect I will stay here for the time being to protect the crossing. Beyond that, however, I do not know."

"Do you not have a family that will miss you?" she asked. "Perhaps you should bring them here for the duration of your stay."

He looked at her, strangely startled by the question. It was a personal inquiry, though he could see by the look on her face that she'd not meant it as such. For the first time since he'd met her, he actually felt uncomfortable.

"No need," he said shortly, wanting very much off the subject. He abruptly stood up. "My lady, I thank you very much for the meal and conversation. If it would not be too much to ask, I would visit the wounded and be apprised of their conditions."

He seemed edgy and Cantia stood up with him, wondering what she said to upset him so. Without another word, she led him out of the alcove and into the great hall, full of miserable men lying upon the floor. It smelled of smoke and blood.

As they visited the wounded one by one and discussed their condition, Tevin found himself paying more attention to the sheer grace and beauty of the lady rather than listening to what she was saying. Too soon, they were finished discussing the condition of the men and their purpose for conversation was over. It was growing late.

"If there is nothing else, my lord, then I shall put my son to bed," Cantia said, glancing over at the boy as he inspected a soldier with a splint on his leg. "It has been a busy day for him."

Tevin nodded. "I thank you for your attention to my men." He eyed her as she bowed slightly to him, to excuse herself, and moved away. "My lady?"

She paused. "Aye, my lord?"

"Will you be all right tonight?" he lifted an eyebrow. "Should I check on you later to make sure?"

She knew what he meant and her embarrassment returned. She averted her gaze. "I will be quite well, my lord," she assured him softly. "Moreover, you took the only weapon I had."

"You can always obtain another one if the will is strong enough."

She shook her head, firmly. "No need, my lord. But I thank you for your concern."

Taking Hunt by the hand, she quit the hall with the big yellow dog in tow. Tevin swore that when she left, all of the light went out of the room.

~ ☙ ~

CANTIA AWOKE ON the floor of her bower. The bed was right over her head but she realized that she couldn't bear to sleep on it any longer. The bed reminded her of her husband and it brought more distress than she could handle to sleep upon it. So she had slept on the floor, just as she had done since his death. She didn't know if she would ever be able to sleep on the bed again.

She was slow to rise and even slower to dress. Shades of dawn were beginning to spread across the sky, growing brighter by the moment. But Cantia saw no magic in the sunrise. The last time she had gazed upon such a thing had been the day her husband had perished. She did not believe she would ever be able to gaze upon another sunrise as long as she lived and not think of that ominous morning.

After a brisk wash in the rosewater that the old servant woman had brought her, she donned a simple blue sheath and surcoat, securing it fast with a black broadcloth girdle. She rightly suspected she would be busy with wounded for the day and did not want to muss a finer garment.

Securing her magnificent hair in a thick braid that draped over her shoulder, she gazed at herself in the polished bronze mirror and thought that there was something different about her this morning. She didn't look like a happy young girl any longer. She looked like a woman whose grief had matured her. She stared at herself until tears came to her eyes and then she put the mirror down. She couldn't bear the reflection any longer.

Hunt was in the small landing outside when she came out of her chamber. He had his toys spread out all over the landing and top stairs, something that Brac had repeatedly admonished him against. Cantia found herself doing the same thing. Hunt made the effort to put a couple of wooden soldiers back in his room but then he began begging for food. Taking her son down to the living level, she passed by the solar on her way to the great hall and caught a glimpse of bodies in the small room. Pausing, she peered inside.

The lady knight was on her cot, sitting up against the wall. The lady knight looked at Cantia, nodding her head slightly as their eyes met. Cantia was about to say something to the women when movement caught her attention further off to her right. She had to step into the room to see who it was.

Charles Penden sat at the large table so often used by his son over the course of the years. She'd not seen the man for two days and now, he had appeared. He looked disheveled and she could smell his stench from where she stood. When his gaze found her, she instinctively tensed. She did not like the expression on his face.

He grunted at her. "This is not an infirmary," he said. "Move this woman out."

It was an order. Cantia's mood was rapidly darkening. "She is injured. It would be painful and difficult thing to move her to the upper floors. 'Tis best that she recuperates down here where she can be watched with the rest of the wounded."

She wasn't being combative in the least, but Charles flew out of his chair and grabbed her by the neck. Hunt was shoved back out of the way with his grandfather's swift moment, ending up on his backside. Startled, but not hurt, he burst into loud sobs.

Charles smelled of alcohol and sweat. His foul breath was in her face, his hand squeezing her neck. "I will not be challenged in my own house," he snarled. "You will do as I say or I will turn you out. Do you hear me?"

He was hurting her, but more than that, she was angry. "Let go of me," she hissed. "Have you gone completely mad?"

He struck her, then. Cantia's head jerked with the force and she could taste the blood in her mouth. Lifting her hand, she was fully prepared to strike back to defend herself when Charles suddenly grunted and fell backwards. Cantia pushed the hair out of her eyes in time to see Tevin descending on the old man, moving in for a mortal blow with his enormously balled fist. She shrieked.

"No," she grabbed his arm before he could strike again. "Please... no more, not in front of Hunt."

The little boy was crying loudly on the ground. Cantia went to her son and swept him into her arms, whispering comfort to him as Tevin, exerting the greatest self-control, stepped away from the sprawled old man. His dark eyes were as hard as obsidian as he gazed at her.

"Are you all right?" he asked.

She nodded, more concerned for Hunt's state of mind than her own. But she tasted her blood and wiped at the trickle on her lip. "He did not hurt me."

Tevin lifted an eyebrow. His entire face was taut with rage, so much so that his flared nostrils were white. He looked back down at Charles, still in a heap on the floor.

"Next time," he growled at the old man. "I will kill you."

Hunt wailed louder. Cantia shushed him gently. "Please, my lord," she said to Tevin. "He... he is not himself. You must make allowances."

"I make no allowances for a man that would strike a woman," he said coldly. He stepped around Charles, circling him as a vulture would circle its prey. "You will remove yourself from this keep, Penden. I do not want to see your face again today."

Charles gazed up at him, his eyes red and unfocused. Somehow, he managed to get to his feet and walk unsteadily from the room. He didn't even look at Cantia. When he was gone, Tevin and Cantia focused on one another.

"What happened that he would do that to you?" he demanded quietly.

Cantia opened her mouth, but the lady knight in the corner spoke first. "She did nothing, Tevin. He attacked her for no reason at all."

Cantia looked at the lady in the corner. She did not know what to say, ashamed that this stranger should witness such a scene. "He is not himself," she said with some remorse.

Tevin took her chin between his thumb and forefinger, tilting her head up to get a better look at Charles' handiwork. Her lip was split, but she would heal. He held her face much longer than necessary, simply for the fact that he couldn't seem to let go.

"Has he done this before?" his voice was low.

She shook her head. "Never," she replied honestly. "Brac would have...."

When she refused to finish, Tevin lifted an eyebrow at her. "What would he have done?"

She wasn't going to answer him, but he shook her chin gently to prod her. Eyes averted, he barely heard her words. "Brac would have killed him," she whispered.

Tevin let her go. Hunt was calming and she set the boy on his feet, wiped the remainder of his tears, and instructed him to go to the kitchens and get some watered wine for the lady knight. When the boy ran off with the dog close behind, she looked at Tevin.

"Charles was always a gruff, hard man, but he was never cruel," she said. "I fear that Brac's passing may have changed him. This madness shows no sign of letting up."

Tevin put his hands on his hips, his dark eyebrows furrowed for effect. "I'll not let him take his grief out on you if that is what you mean," he said. "If I have to lock him in the vault for the safety of you and your son, I shall do it without hesitation."

"I am sure there will be no more transgressions, my lord."

He just stood there, looking at her as if he didn't believe her. In the corner, the lady knight shifted slightly, grunting when her ribs pained her. It was enough of a noise so that Tevin and Cantia took their attention away from each other and focused on her.

"Are you in pain?" Tevin asked her.

Val tried to shrug, but with a broken collarbone, it was not a simple gesture. "As much as is to be expected, I suppose."

"I shall bring you more willow bark," Cantia turned for the door.

"Wait," Val stopped her. "Though I appreciate your kindness, my lady, that brew makes me exceedingly tired. I find the pain tolerable."

"As you wish, my la…lady."

Cantia wasn't quite sure how to address the lady knight and the room fell into an awkward silence. Tevin lifted his hand in Val's direction.

"Lady Cantia, this is my sister, the Lady Valeria du Reims," he introduced them. "I apologize that I am so late with introductions, but it did not seem the appropriate time yesterday. Please know that we are both very grateful for your delicate care of her injuries."

Cantia dipped her head in Val's direction. "A pleasure, my lady."

"My pleasure as well, Lady Penden. And my thanks."

Cantia gazed at the red haired lady knight, feeling foolish for staring at her and realizing that they both knew that she was staring at her. It wasn't hard to read her thoughts. Val smiled a toothy grin that was both impish and charming.

"I know, it's not usual to see a woman in armor," she said. "Blame my brother. He would swordplay with me as a child and I grew to love it."

Cantia looked at Tevin, an eyebrow lifted in mock reproach. "You turned this lovely woman into a warrior? How dastardly."

He pursed his lips, knowing this was a battle he could not win but willing to make the attempt. "Do not believe everything she tells you. I had no hand in this. She would blame me when the truth is that I cannot get rid of her."

As Val burst out in giggles, Cantia went on the attack, however in jest. "She should be married to a fine lord and have many children about her. Why are you so selfish that you would force her to bear arms? Haven't you enough men at your disposal that you do not need to force your sister into armed servitude?"

As Val hooted, Tevin threw up his hands as if to defend himself. "My lady, if you have any ideas on how to get my sister out of armor and into feminine garments, I am at your mercy. Perhaps you can succeed where I have failed."

Cantia fought off a grin, winking at Val as the woman stifled her snorts in her hand. "You are a wicked brother, my lord. See how your sister suffers because of you."

Tevin, too, was fighting off a grin. He simply shook his head and turned away knowing that any further words from him would only be twisted by Cantia's humorous tirade. On the other hand, he was perfectly willing to be a target if it would help her forget Charles Penden's brutality. Moreover, this was the first light moment they'd had since his arrival to Rochester. He was discovering that she had a delightful sense of humor.

Cantia, for her part, had indeed forgotten her cut lip. The levity of the moment was helping her mood for the first time in days. And she was pleased to see that the viscount also possessed a sense of humor, a surprising factor given the man's warring nature. As he walked away from her, smirking, she found herself admiring his broad back. It was a rather nice back. But the uninvited thought shocked her, sickened her, and she abruptly lost her humor. She suddenly felt very ill at ease, desperate to get out of the room and away from the inappropriate thought that had unexpectedly entered her mind.

"I will fetch your meal, my lady."

Val watched her nearly run from the room, her own humor fading at the swift departure. She looked at Tevin, who himself had only caught the tail end of Cantia's garments as she fled from the door. He met Val's gaze.

"Why did she leave so swiftly?" he asked.

Val shook her head. "I do not know."

Tevin nodded his head, wondering if he should go after her. Val, not surprisingly, could read it in his eyes. And having known her brother her entire life, she could read something else, something she had never seen before. But just as quickly, she chased those thoughts away. It was impossible. Still…

"Why don't you go after her," she suggested, watching his expression carefully. "If we somehow offended her, then we should apologize."

Tevin didn't say a word. He merely nodded his head and left the solar. Val sat there for several long moments, entertaining thoughts that she had never before considered. There had never been any need. If she hadn't known better, she would have thought her brother held some interest in the lovely, grieving Lady Penden. For Tevin's sake, she sincerely hoped not.

Tevin caught up to Cantia just as she exited the keep into the kitchen yard. Dogs scattered in front of her and much activity went on all around them. Hunt was running in her direction, splashing the contents of the wooden pitcher he held, and Cantia directed her son to take the liquid to the lady knight. As the boy ran on, Tevin came up beside her.

"Is something amiss, my lady?" he asked.

Startled at his voice, she nearly tripped on her skirts. He had to grab her to keep her from falling. "Nay, my lord," she said.

"You left rather quickly. We were afraid we had offended you somehow."

So she had made a fool of herself yet again. Cantia thought she was the only one who had noticed her swift flight. It seemed that all she did was make a fool of herself in front of her liege. Gazing up into his dark eyes, she began to feel extremely foolish.

"Of course you did not," she said. "You could not possibly do anything to offend me. Even if you did, I would forgive you. But I am truly sorry if I seemed rude or abrupt. I did not mean to."

Tevin gazed into her beautiful face, feeling a pull he'd never felt before. It was enough to seriously disturb him, for whatever pity or compassion he had been feeling for the lady over the past few days was transforming into something that seemed to be affecting his mind as well as his tongue. He should have fought it with all his strength, but at the moment, he couldn't seem to. All he knew was that any time he spent with Lady Penden, however brief or trivial or emotional, was unlike any time he'd ever spent before, with anyone.

"Say no more," he said. "As long as all is well, I shall leave you to your duties."

She nodded, watching as he excused himself. Cantia stood there a moment, observing his powerful form stroll across the yard and back into the keep. She'd never seen a man move with such strength before, with such commanding presence. It was interesting to compare it to Brac's presence, which was by far more relaxed and easy. Brac had never radiated the power that Tevin did. It was curious. Turning for the kitchen once again, she went about her business with a good deal on her already-strained mind.

CHAPTER FIVE

MYLES HAD BEEN on duty constantly since Brac's passing. Though he rode with Viscount Winterton on the second raid to retake the Dartford Crossing Bridge, he'd spent the majority of his time patrolling the walls of Rochester and trying to keep an eye on Charles. With Brac's passing, Myles would assume what responsibility he could. He owed it to Brac, and to Cantia, to do so.

Now, he was taking a much deserved rest in the knight's quarters. All of Viscount Winterton's men had temporary quarters here, and he knew them all from the past years of battle. He knew and liked Simon Horley; the man was fierce, bold and, strangely, thoughtful. John Swantey was also a reputable man that he was comfortable with. Dagan Sutton and Gavril de Reigate were latecomers to the viscount's corps, having been gifted to the viscount from the Earl of Norfolk for services in battle. They were a quiet pair and he did not know much about them, but he had seen that they were courageous fighters.

Myles sat at the table in the small gathering room of the knight's quarters, contemplating the last of his wine and thinking he should probably try to get some sleep. But he seriously wondered if he should check on Lady Penden and her son first. Though the lady's outward grief had not reached the fevered pitch that Charles' had, still, he could see how devastated she was. Myles knew very well that Cantia and Brac had been fond of each other.

As he contemplated his thoughts, the door to the knight's quarters flew open and Charles stomped in. Myles looked up to see that the man was in a serious degree of madness, mumbling to himself and looking around the room as he was searching for something. It seemed that he didn't even see Myles until the knight spoke.

"Is there something I can do for you, my lord?"

Charles froze, looking at Myles as if startled to see him. Then he marched straight to him and slammed his hands on the table.

"A weapon," he growled. "I need a weapon."

Myles did not like the sound of the request. "Why?"

Charles threw up his arms. "Must everyone disobey me at my own house?" he cried. "Give me your weapon, de Lohr. Give it to me now."

Myles broadsword was lying on his bed in the next room, thankfully. Myles set his wine down and stood up.

"I am sworn to you, my lord," he said steadily. "If there is any defending to be done, I will do it in your stead."

Charles grabbed him as if to shake him, but Myles was too big a man to shake. "I do not defend anything. I will kill him."

"Kill who?"

Charles' expression was beyond madness. It was obsession and impulse, blended into an elixir of pure psychosis. "The viscount. He has shamed me. He has killed my son. He must pay."

Now it was Myles' turn to grab Charles. "You speak treason, my lord," he said quietly, firmly. "I will hear no more of this. Should the viscount catch wind of what you have said, it would mean great danger for you and possibly your family. You must keep yourself in check, my lord, or all will be lost. Do you understand me?"

Charles' lips curled back in a sneer that just as quickly faded. "I understand that he has invaded my home. Rochester is no longer mine."

"Rochester will always belong to the stewards," Myles assured him, praying that the man would get a grip on himself. "Get some sleep, my lord. You've not slept for days and your exhaustion is weighing heavily. Come to the next room and..."

Charles yanked away from Myles, pacing sloppily across the floor. "She did this," he muttered. "That foolish wench has caused this. She sides with him, you know."

"Who?"

"The viscount," Charles insisted. "She sides with him. He protects her. They are going to take Rochester away from me. Well, that will not happen. It cannot. I forbid it!"

He suddenly bolted from the room before Myles could catch him. He stood in the doorway, watching Charles lose himself in the bustle of the ward. He could only shake his head. So much for the idea of sleep.

Myles went in search of Tevin.

ଔ

THE SEPTEMBER DAY was cool and rainy. Clouds had moved in off the sea and a steady rain had pounded the land since late morning. Cantia was in the solar with Val, feeling obligated to give special attention to the sister of her liege. After the meal that the injured lady so delicately ate, for even swallowing seemed to be painful, Cantia had the fire stoked and proceeded to warm some water to wash the lady with.

Val didn't protest as Cantia ran a warm, wet cloth over her one good shoulder and one good arm, and then moved to clean the dirt off her face. Val really was a pretty woman, even prettier without all of the grime associated with battle. Cantia said little as she bathed her patient and made every effort to insure the woman's comfort. Val had been watching her closely, however, thinking that she had never before seen such a lovely woman. She could understand her brother's fascination with her.

At some point, Hunt entered the solar with the ever-present dog on his heels. Hunt was used to coming and going as he pleased, for his father never admonished him for anything. Brac had always been unusually lenient with the child and though Hunt wasn't spoiled, he was bold. He walked right up to Val as Cantia tightened the bandages that braced her bad shoulder.

His big blue eyes focused on the lady knight. "You are not a real knight," he said flatly.

Cantia looked at her son with displeasure. "Hunt, you are rude to address the lady so," she admonished firmly. "Please apologize."

But Val grinned, waving off the motherly scolding. "Nay, my lady, he is quite right," she said. "I am not a man and, therefore, not a real knight. But I fight as one anyway."

"Why?" Hunt asked innocently.

"Because that is my calling."

Hunt cocked his head. "You are called? Called what?"

Val's grin broadened. "I simply mean that this is what I do. I was born to do it."

"But…" his little nose scrunched in confusion. "How can you fight if you are not a real knight?"

"Enough," Cantia turned her son around and faced him towards the door. "Take George outside and play with him. Throw him the balls. He likes that."

Hunt dug his heels in. "But I'm hungry!"

"Then go to the kitchen," she slapped him lightly on the buttocks. "Cook will give you something to eat. Go now and leave me in peace."

Hunt did as he was told, but not before he walked a wide circle around the room, touching everything within his reach, all the while watching his mother finish tending the lady knight. Only when Cantia shot him a threatening look did he leave the room completely. When he was gone, she dared meet Val's amused gaze.

"I must apologize for my son's behavior," she said. "He is, unfortunately, quite stubborn and not quick to obey."

Val merely grinned. "He is still very young. But that will change when you send him to foster. He'll have to obey swiftly or risk a beating."

Cantia's delicate fingers froze for a moment, then resumed tightening the bandage. Val glanced at the woman, noting that her expression seemed distressed. She wrongly guessed at the trouble.

"Do not worry, Lady Penden," she said. "He will learn to obey. Have you selected his foster house yet?"

When Cantia looked at her, Val swore she saw tears. But Cantia quickly lowered her gaze, refocusing on the wrappings. "Nay," her voice was strangely tight. "He... he is still too young to foster."

"Not necessarily," Val said. "My brother was about Hunt's age when he left for Kenilworth Castle to foster. Our father arranged for that when he was born. Tevin was gone for many years... I did not truly even come to know my brother until his return as a fully-fledged knight. He was eighteen years of age."

Cantia's head came up again. "He was gone for thirteen years?"

"Aye."

Cantia left the bandages. Head hung, she went back over to the table and collected the things she had brought with her – more bandages, a bowl, a small knife to cut the cloth with. She piled them all in the bowl and moved for the door. But as she left, Val heard the distinct sound of stifled sobs. They only grew louder when the woman quit the room and thought she could no longer be heard. Val called out to her, twice, but the lady apparently did not hear her.

When Tevin entered the solar a short time later, he got an earful.

෪

"My sister is afraid that she has upset you."

Cantia was sitting at the well-scrubbed table in the great hall, alone up until Tevin walked into the room. He walked towards the table, slowly, his massive body moving with grace and ease. Cantia watched his approach, hoping there were no tears left on her cheeks but not wanting to be obvious by checking.

"She did not, my lord," she said, eyes downcast. "I simply... that is to say, I am..."

Tevin plopped his enormous body on the tabletop right next to her. His right thigh was next to her arm and she instinctively pulled away. When she looked up, it was into glittering dark eyes.

"This evasiveness simply will not do," he said flatly. "If you are upset, I would very much prefer you told me so that it is out in the open. You have been most kind and accommodating to us and I will not see you distressed over things that I would do all in my power to right. What did my sister do that upset you so?"

Cantia shook her head, struggling for courage. She even smiled, weak though it might be. "Any number of things can upset me these days, my lord. It matters not. I am a silly woman."

"You are not," his voice grew softer. "You have a great many things on your mind, and rightfully so. What was it my sister said that sent you from the room in tears?"

Cantia struggled with her brave front. "Nothing, my lord. We were simply speaking of my son and she asked me where he was to foster. I said… I said that we had not yet petitioned to foster him because…."

So much for the brave front. The tears returned and she struggled not to fall apart. Tevin was careful to resist his natural urge to physically comfort her in some way. Instead, he sat beside her on the bench, very close, and watched her wrestle with her composure.

"Because why?" he asked gently.

She sniffled into her hand. "Because he's too young," she finally blurted. "I have just lost my husband. I cannot fathom the thought of losing my son."

So there it was. Against his better judgment, he took her free hand in his massive one, rubbing the fingers gently. He knew he shouldn't, but he couldn't help himself.

"How old is Hunt?"

She squeaked as she spoke. "Five years."

He fought off a smile. "Aye, he's far too young still. You do not have to worry about sending him to foster for two more years at least."

The hand came away from her eyes, the wet lavender orbs shimmering with emotion. "Why must I send him away at all? Why can he not stay here, with me, and learn to be a knight? Where is it written in law that he must be sent away?"

She was growing more grieved with each passing word. For lack of a better action, Tevin put his enormous arm around her shoulders and pulled her close, his cheek on the top of her head. *I would do this for anyone rightfully distressed*, he told himself. But he knew, deep down, that he would not. He had, in fact, never done it before. Now it seemed as if he was looking for any excuse to pull Lady Penden into his arms.

"There is no law that says a child must be sent away," he said quietly. "But the purpose of being sent away to foster is to learn skills and knowledge from those who are not your family. It is a sharing of wealth and knowledge that builds strength of character in men. Wouldn't you like your son to learn to be a knight from men who have traveled the world doing just that?"

She sniffled. "I don't like it. I will not do it."

He gave her a squeeze before he realized he did it. "Hush, now. There is no use in working yourself up over something that is a few years away. You'll not lose your son any time soon, I promise."

Her head came up, gazing at him with those magnificent eyes. "If I do not want to send him away, I do not have to, do I?"

"Nay."

Only then did she seem to relax. Tevin realized almost too late that she was far too close. He could feel her breath on his face. With her wet eyes and sweet lips, he felt an overwhelming urge to kiss her. The very thought startled him, distressed him, causing a violent outburst of contention within him. The woman was a new widow, grieving over the loss of her beloved husband. She was not a woman to be trifled with. Much to his dismay, however, she put her head back down, right onto his shoulder. He swore he felt her nestle against him. It was a damn sweet feeling.

"Thank you, my lord," she said. "Your words bring me great comfort."

"It is right that they should," he said quietly. "I tell you the truth."

Her reply was to lift her head, put a soft hand on his jaw, and tenderly kiss his cheek. Then she rose and was gone.

Tevin sat there for several long minutes, his heart thumping against his ribs and the spot on his face where she had kissed him blazing with sensation. As small a gesture as it was, as perfectly innocent, it was the most significant kiss of his life. He felt it down to his soul. And he knew, at that moment, that he was in a good deal of trouble.

But thoughts of trouble quickly fled when Myles entered the hall, his blue eyes fixing on his liege. He made straight for the table.

"I saw Lady Penden in the solar," he said to Tevin. "She looks much better today. Have you spoken with her at all?"

Oh... yes, Tevin thought. "I have," he said evenly. "She does seem much better, though now her distress seems to be with the thought of sending her son to foster."

Myles brow furrowed. "What?" he sat down opposite Tevin. "What brought that up?"

"A conversation with someone apparently broached the subject," Tevin replied. "I have spent the past several minutes attempting to convince her that it was far too soon to worry about sending her son away."

Myles snorted, looking around the table to see if there was any ale or wine available. Seeing none, he summoned a servant. As the man went to do his bidding, Myles turned back to Tevin.

"I believe we may have more trouble on our hands, my lord," he said. "I have just come from a most distressing exchange with Charles."

Tevin was glad for the change in subject, even if it was about Charles. "What happened?"

Myles shook his head, with regret. "I fear his madness is gaining," he said. "He was in the knight's quarters not a half hour ago asking for a weapon."

Tevin found he had little tolerance when it came to the madness of Charles Penden. "Before you continue, you should know that he struck Lady Cantia this morning. I was witness to it. I ordered him from the keep, not to return until my anger had cooled."

Myles stared at him a moment in disbelief. "He *struck* her?" he repeated. "My God... Brac would have had his head. His father had always been inordinately jealous of Lady Cantia, mostly because she held Brac's attention captive. Charles could never come to terms with the fact that he was not the center of his son's world, just as Brac was the center of his. There are years of contention between Charles and Lady Cantia, all of it Charles' fault."

Tevin's jaw flexed. "Then it would seem that the Lady Cantia needs to be protected from her father-in-law, for clearly, with Brac gone, he feels no need to hide his hostile feelings for her."

A steward brought some wine and Myles poured himself a healthy measure. "I will be vigilant, my lord, have no doubt."

"He does not resent the boy, does he?"

Myles took a large swallow of the tart red liquid. "He adores Hunt. He would never harm him."

Though it was one less thing to worry over, Tevin was still disturbed that Lady Cantia would need protection from Brac's insane father. "Back to your statement, then. Why was Charles asking for a weapon?"

Myles cast him a long glance. "He's not in his right mind, my lord. He says much that he does not mean."

"Why does he want a weapon?"

Myles sighed heavily, toying with his cup. "I am not sure if he feels the need to protect himself or the need to commit murder. He seems to think that you and Lady Cantia are conspiring to take Rochester from him. He further blames you for Brac's death."

Tevin scratched his head, absorbing the information. "His lunacy grows," he insisted. "I suspect the man needs to be locked in the vault for his own protection as well as the lady's. I do not need the added element of a madman running amuck at Rochester, not when there is much else that requires my attention."

"Agreed," Myles said. "Would you have me corral him, my lord?"

Tevin shook his head. "You should not be the one to arrest your liege. My men will do it."

Myles downed the last of his wine. He found that his fatigue was catching up with him. "Shall I shadow the lady until Charles can be put away?"

"Nay," Tevin said. "You have enough to do with the command of

Rochester. I shall make sure the lady is well protected until Charles can be caged."

"Very good, my lord. If there is nothing else, I shall retire for a time."

Tevin waved him off, mulling over the conversation as Myles quit the hall. He thought to find Sir Dagan and order the imprisonment of Charles Penden until the man could get himself under control, but as he rose from the bench, Lady Penden passed within his line of sight, emerging from the solar and mounting the steps to the upper floors. A second later, Hunt and the big yellow dog also emerged and ran after her. He could hear the dog barks echo in the stairwell.

Now he was thinking on Cantia again. With a sigh of frustration, mostly at himself, he went about his business.

CB

CHARLES PENDEN, AS suspected, did not react well to being imprisoned. He shouted conspiracy and murder as Dagan and Gavril practically carried him to the gatehouse, dragging him down the narrow steps and incarcerating him in the bottle prison. The name of the prison was derived from the shape of the cell. The door was in the ceiling and the room was literally shaped like a bottle; wide at the bottom and narrowed up towards the top. It was virtually impossible to escape from. They left Charles screaming at the bottom of it.

They stood over the cell, looking into the hole that showed Charles at the bottom. The man was distraught, incoherently shouting. The two knights shook their heads.

"Crazy man," Dagan growled.

Gavril nodded in agreement. Shorter and darker than his cousin, he was also the oldest man in the viscount's service at nearly forty years of age. He had seen much, done much. He did not have much patience for a mad baron.

"We've duties on the wall," he told his cousin. "Come along now. Let's leave the baron to his hell."

When they began to move, Charles started yelling louder. "Wait!" he called. "Wait, I say! Do not leave me here alone!"

Dagan called down to him. "Cease your struggles, baron," he advised. "A show of sanity may very well see you released."

Charles was trying to climb up the sides of the prison, only managing a few feet before sliding back down to the floor. "Release me and you shall be well rewarded," he clawed into the brick so hard that his fingers came away bloodied. "Let me out of here and I shall give you all that I have. Let me out!"

Gavril shook his head, jabbing his finger in Dagan's arm to prompt the man to follow him. But Dagan was finding a weird fascination out of watching Charles struggle.

"This is what I mean, baron," he said. "You sound like a madman. Calm yourself and the viscount may take pity on you."

Charles had stopped trying to scale the walls. He sat at the bottom of the pit, gazing up into the only opening that provided both light and air.

"Release me and I shall give you the lady and her dowry," he offered, though there was defeat in his tone. "She came to my son with a large dowry. Release me and I shall give it, and her, to you. You could live like a king."

"I'm sure I could," Dagan said with mock patience. "And whereby would you get the power to do such a thing?"

"She belongs to me now." Spit flew from Charles' lips as he spoke. "She and the boy are mine, to do with as I please. Release me and I give her to you."

Gavril continued to walk away, up the steps that led to the gatehouse. But Dagan stood there a moment, looking down at the crazed baron and entertaining possibilities that he just as quickly chased away. *A madman's desperate plea*, he told himself. But he had seen the lady and she was quite lovely. An interesting thought, but not a realistic one. 'Twas a madman's desperate plea.

He followed his cousin from the vault.

CHAPTER SIX

THE NEXT TWO WEEKS passed in relative peace. Charles stayed in the vault, which gave Tevin one less worry. Val was up and about, having been moved by Cantia to the third floor of the keep now that she was able to maneuver the stairs, and life in general seemed to be settling down for the first time since the death of Brac Penden. For the most part, there had been no more battles for the bridge, though a week after Brac's death there had been a minor skirmish. Tevin and his knights had ridden to battle, but the enemy had quickly fled and the scuffle was over almost before it began. After that, it was eerily peaceful. Tevin couldn't decide if he was grateful or suspicious.

He kept telling himself that he needed to stay at Rochester due to its close proximity to the bridge. It was the same story he told everyone. But two weeks after Brac's death, with the country relatively quiet, that excuse wasn't holding much weight. Truth be told, Tevin didn't want to leave. He was coming to be comfortable here and more than that, he did not like the thought of leaving Cantia. In fact, it was almost a desperate situation.

Since the day that Charles struck her, she had kept her distance from him. He had seen her daily, ate with her almost every night in the great hall, but she was silent and reserved around him. It was almost as if she were afraid of him somehow. Yet when she was with Val, she would relax and smile and laugh. He was coming to feel very jealous that his sister could elicit such a reaction from the lovely lady. It made him more determined than ever not to leave Rochester. For some reason, it was becoming a fascination with him. He did not want to leave her and he could not clearly discern why.

On the morning of the first day of the new month, Tevin and a few of his men escorted Cantia to mass at the massive cathedral in the village. Val tried to suit up in her armor, but it was still too painful for her, so Cantia had loaned her a soft linen sheath and yellow surcoat. With her flowing reddish gold hair, she made a striking picture.

It was a cool day, with puffy white clouds riding the gentle breezes. The sky was as brilliant as any of them had ever seen it and even though it was close to winter, there were birds about. It seemed that every living creature was determined to enjoy the day, including Cantia. She finally felt as if she was finally emerging from her destructive grief and a day like today was not only welcome, it was necessary. She needed to feel strong again.

The colossal cathedral loomed before them. Though it was not unexpected, the sight threatened to bring back memories of Brac's funeral, but Cantia fought them. She would not allow herself to digress, not when her new-found strength was so hard won. As they entered the cavernous, cool sanctuary of Rochester Cathedral, Tevin spoke softly to Cantia as she walked past him.

"I am at your mercy, my lady," he said quietly.

She paused to look at him, her lavender eyes filled with curiosity. "What do you mean, my lord?"

Tevin nodded his head in the direction of his sister, now entering the cathedral in the company of Simon and Myles. "You have done what no one has yet been able to accomplish," he said. "You convinced my sister to dress in feminine garments."

Cantia grinned, watching Val move stiffly across the cathedral floor. "It wasn't difficult, I assure you. She cannot wear anything with weight or restriction right now. It is a matter of pure comfort."

It was as much of a conversation as they had had for a week. He intended to keep it going. "Comfort or not, I promised that I would be in your debt if you were to accomplish such a thing. How can I repay you?"

Her grin broadened and she lowered her gaze. "You were so kind and thoughtful after my husband's death that I felt I owed you a great deal. I've done nothing at all for Val, in spite of what you say, but if you like, I will call our scores even."

Tevin extended an elbow to her, meaning to escort her into the church. He held his breath as she looked at the arm, perhaps thought to refuse, but reconsidered. He could feel her warm hand through the linen of his tunic. It was a marvelous feeling.

"Whatever I may have done for you upon Brac's passing was my duty," he said quietly. His voice was naturally very deep and booming and he did not want it echoing off the walls of the great stone church. "What you have done for Val is not. I have not seen my sister so light of mood in quite some time. She enjoys spending time with you."

"And I, her," Cantia replied. "She has become my friend."

"I know she feels the same about you."

"Then may speak boldly?"

"Of course."

Cantia came to a halt, her eyes on Val in the distance, standing with Simon, Myles, and now John. "Your sister is far too lovely to be a warrior. You must find her a husband."

Tevin glanced over his shoulder at his sister, a dark eyebrow raised. "I have said the very same thing to her many times. She had no interest in a husband. Besides, who wants to marry a woman that can lick you in a fight?"

In spite of herself, Cantia giggled. Tevin had the joy of being the one to cause it. She had a big dimple in her left cheek, something he found captivating. Even her teeth were pretty, straight and white. The more he saw of her, the more he wanted.

"Surely there is a man who will appreciate her for who she is," Cantia said. "Why, look at Myles. Do you know that he has spent a great deal of time with her?"

"De Lohr?" Tevin snorted. "He has known Val for years. He considers her a fellow warrior."

Cantia lifted a knowing eyebrow. "Does he? I wonder."

Her comment made Tevin turn and stare hard at the tall knight with the shoulder length blond hair. "Why do you say that? What do you know that I do not?"

Cantia shook her head. "Nothing in particular. Call it a feeling."

He looked at her. "What *kind* of a feeling?"

"That Myles would perhaps like his association with Val to be something more. Perhaps it already is something more."

Tevin looked at her as if she had gone mad. "What on earth would make you say that?"

Cantia's gaze moved to Val and Myles, talking softly between them. "I do not know for certain. Perhaps it is the way he looks at her. He looks at her with such... longing and hope."

He snorted. "I look at you the same way, though no one can say there is anything more between us than propriety allows." Appalled that, in trying to prove his point, he had said what he was thinking, he hastened to change the subject. "Speaking of my sister, I understand that Rochester has a large merchant district. I would be grateful if you would help my sister select material for a few feminine garments. She knows very few women of taste and culture that would offer such assistance."

Cantia was staring at him, still lingering on his earlier words. *I look at you the same way.* Did he really? She had spent many days attempting to avoid him, allowing only necessary contact, but still, she had been unable to shake the sensations his presence gave her. Her affection was still Brac's. That would probably never change. But in a completely different context, Tevin brought something into her heart and mind that she could not define. Her heart leapt at the sight of him, her limbs grew warm and shaky when he came near.

Even now, she held his elbow and relished the feel of it. Once, she had felt the same thing with Brac, but those days had vanished long before his death. What remained between them was warm comfort and little more. The fires of impetuous passion had banked long ago. What she felt when Tevin came around was like lightning bolts.

Lost to her thoughts, she realized he was looking for an answer. "I would be honored, if that is Val's wish." Her eyes suddenly narrowed at him. "You're not going to force her, are you?"

He shook his head, pursing his lips so that the massive dimples in each cheek carved deep ruts, disappearing into the well-manicured beard on his jaw line. "I will not force her, but you could do me a favor and make the gentle suggestion. She may take it better from you than from me."

She nodded, her gaze again moving to Val, who was now gazing up into Myles' face with a serene, interested expression. Cantia tipped her head in Val's direction. "Look at your sister," she said knowingly. "See the expression on her face when she looks at Myles? She feels something for him. I can see it."

"I think you are imagining things."

Her eyebrows lifted. "Is that so?" she was forced to contradict him. "And just what would you think if I looked at you like that? You would think I was a silly, besotted girl."

Tevin's dark gaze moved to his sister several feet away. "I would think that I was the most fortunate man alive."

Cantia suddenly couldn't breathe. She had asked the question to prove her point of a potential romance between Val and Myles. She wasn't hunting for a personal response from Tevin. She yanked her hand from his elbow but he reclaimed it firmly, tucking it into the crook and holding it fast with his free hand. He was without his armor this day and he wore no gloves. His flesh against hers was the sweetest thing he could have imagined.

"Nay, lady, you'll keep your hand right here," his voice was hardly above a whisper. "You've ignored me for days and I'll not let you retreat again."

Cantia's heart was thumping madly against her ribs. Tears sprang to her eyes and she lowered her head so he wouldn't see. There was such confusion in her mind, such exhilaration and such guilt. She didn't know what to think.

Tevin looked down at her lowered head. "Surely you've sensed that my interest in you goes beyond normal concern," he said quietly.

A lone tear trickled down her cheek. He saw it. Not wanting her to burst into tears in front of everyone, he led her to a small alcove off the main sanctuary where hundreds of tallow prayer candles burned. It was out of eyeshot and earshot as he faced her.

The room was warm and glowing, giving her beauty an even more ethereal look. His thumbs came up to wipe away the tear, but more followed and he found himself fighting off a flood.

"I am sorry to make you weep," he said sincerely. "I don't know why I said that. I should not have. Forgive me."

She shook her head, wiping at her face. "There is nothing to forgive," she whispered. "I simply do not know what to say."

"Say nothing," he told her. "I will never say anything so bold to you again. It was wrong of me."

He started to leave but she put her hand on his arm, stopping him. "Nay, do not go," she whispered. "I did not mean it the way it sounded. I simply meant that I wish I could say the same thing to you."

He patted her hand. "You are a truthful woman. You will not say what you do not feel simply to gratify me. I respect that."

"Nay," she said, more strongly. The lavender eyes gazed up at him. "You do not understand. I would say the same to you, my lord, only… only I cannot possibly say it because my husband is barely cold in his grave and to do so would be wrong. If I were to tell you that your presence brings me more comfort than you can possibly know, then it would sound as if I am merely saying so because I just lost my husband and am desperate to find someone to cling to. I do not know myself if that is the case. But I do know one thing; I respect you far too much to treat you so carelessly."

He looked down at her. His gentle expression turned into something of regret. "I can see that my extended presence at Rochester has only brought you more pain," he said. "To stay any longer would only bring us both anguish."

"Why?"

He suddenly took her face between his two massive hands. He had the biggest hands of any man alive.

"Because I stay only to be near you," he whispered emotionally. "But I fear my presence has been selfish. I've not thought of the effect it might have on you. You need to come to terms with your grief over Brac before you can move on with your life. I fear I have added to your burden more than I realized and for that, you must forgive me. I have been horribly selfish. You are such a sweet, pretty thing. I simply wanted to be near you."

Cantia closed her eyes to his touch. His hands were powerful and warm, something so different than what she had ever experienced with Brac. It was wrong, she knew it, but she didn't care at the moment. She found herself leaning into his grip, rubbing her cheek against his rough palm. It was instinctive, flesh against flesh, feeling something she had not felt in ages.

Tevin's hands moved from her cheeks and into her hair. He could hardly believe she was responding to him but he wasn't about to question it. It was selfish of him but he did not care. Now that he had her, he knew what he wanted to do. Without any further words, he guided her sweet lips to his mouth for a kiss.

It was tentative at first, as if both of them knew the wrongness of what they were doing. But the moment he tasted her, a ferocious passion took over and he pulled her to him so forcefully that he drove his teeth into her soft upper lip. He tasted her blood along with the sweetness of her flesh and it drove him wild. He tongue probed deep into her mouth, gorging himself on something he had never before known.

He licked and suckled, bit and kissed. Through it all, Cantia was collapsed against him as if rendered boneless by his touch. She let him ravage her, forgetting her guilt and confusion for the moment. What she was experiencing with him, was no bad reflection on Brac, was something she had never before felt. Brac had been like the warmth of the afternoon sun. Tevin was like the scorch from the fires of hell.

When he finally removed his mouth from hers, it was with great reluctance. Her mouth was red from his attention, the small cut on her lip oozing with a drop of red. Tevin saw the blood and licked it hungrily. Cantia responded to his probing mouth and they lost themselves in yet another powerful kiss. He was aggressive and, surprisingly, so was she. In the process, Tevin backed into the candles and promptly lit his tunic on fire.

He smelled the smoke, felt the flame, and quickly quelled it, leaving the hem of his tunic scorched. Cantia's eyes were wide with concerned until she saw the fire was out completely. Then she burst out in laughter so strong that she had to cover her mouth to quiet the guffaws. Tevin struggled against his own laughter for a half second before erupting in deep chuckles. Cantia was laughing so hard she could barely stand. They must have created something of a commotion because Val, Myles and Simon came rushing to the threshold of the alcove, concern written all over their faces. One look at Cantia with her hands over her mouth and Val thought something horrible had happened.

"What's wrong?" she demanded. "What's happened to her?"

Tevin was wiping tears from his eyes. "Nothing," he turned to show them his singed tunic. "But I almost went up in flames."

Val's concern turned to understanding. Cantia took her hand away from her mouth, unable to speak for the laughter that was bubbling forth. Val grinned her toothy, charming grin.

"I see," she lifted a pale eyebrow. "You are most entertaining, brother."

"Damn near burned the place down," he mumbled, taking Cantia gently by the arm and steering her towards the door.

With Cantia still sputtering with laughter, they re-emerged into the sanctuary. Val had Cantia by one hand while Cantia's other hand was tucked into Tevin's elbow. A priest moved towards the group, also alerted by the sounds in the alcove. He was a pudgy man in dirty robes.

"Is all well, my lord?" he asked Tevin, though his eyes were on Cantia. He knew Lady Penden and knew of her recent loss. At the moment, it rather looked like she was being supported.

"Indeed it is," Tevin answered, faking his composure.

The priest looked as if he didn't believe him. "But I heard...."

"You heard nothing unusual," Tevin assured him in his deep voice. He looked at Simon, standing a few feet away. "Give the priest a donation on Brac Penden's behalf. We wish a mass said for him."

Simon dug into the change purse he carried, producing a few coins for the priest. The pudgy man accepted them graciously. "A pleasure, my lord."

As the priest turned away to prepare for the mass, Tevin wriggled his eyebrows at the group. "I would suggest we conduct our business quickly and leave before we wreak any more havoc."

"Keep him away from the candles," Cantia muttered to Val.

Val nodded in agreement, biting her lip to fight off the giggles as Tevin cast her a threatening look. Cantia, too, struggled to compose herself. It was difficult to look at Tevin, however, and not break into laughter. So she kept her gaze forward, moving for the pedestal of holy water that was near the western wall. Dipping her fingers in it, she made the sign of the cross across her body and murmured a prayer. She wasn't sure if she should pray for Brac, or for herself for having allowed such a carnal display with Tevin in the cathedral. It was wicked and she knew it. But at the moment, she almost didn't care. She had felt more alive in his arms, more vital, than she had in quite some time. It wasn't wrong to want to feel alive when she'd suffered through so much death.

As she knelt in preparation for the rosary, she could feel Tevin's dark eyes upon her. He wasn't kneeling in prayer as she was, but was rather standing behind her respectfully. When she should be praying, all she could think of was the blaze he had ignited within her the moment he had touched her. The memory of those massive arms, the pure passion of his kiss, caused her heart to start racing all over again. She forgot about the prayers. With her eyes closed, she imagined their kiss over and over again in her mind.

Tevin, too, was having a good deal of trouble concentrating. He stood there, staring at the back of her luscious head, wondering just how long he was going to spend in Purgatory for ravaging the new widow. He'd never felt more evil and he was not, by nature, an evil man. But he knew that, whatever the cost to his soul, his brief encounter with her had been worth the price. He could never have imagined anything sweeter. His eyes trailed from her head to her torso, studying the curve of her waist and the gentle flare of her hips through her emerald surcoat. She had a delicious figure. He'd noticed it from the first. He was so wrapped up in his thoughts of her that he barely felt the first tap from Simon. But he felt the second stronger one.

He looked at his knight, who was pointing at the entrance to the cathedral. Several Winterton men stood in the doorway, waiting for their lord's attention. Tevin left the ladies on their knees, moving to the entrance accompanied by Simon, John and Myles.

"What is it?" he asked his men.

The first soldier, an older man who had seen service with Tevin's father, spoke. "A missive, my lord," he handed him the cylinder of yellowed vellum. "It came a short time ago."

Tevin cocked a dark brow, noting the seal. "It's from East Anglia," he said in a low voice.

He moved outside the cathedral with his men in tow. Several kept watch around them while Tevin broke the seal of the missive and unrolled it. Very carefully scripted letters met his gaze as he read the contents. Simon, though he couldn't read, looked over his shoulder while Myles, who could read, read slowly of the first few words. But Tevin was finished before he was and rolled the vellum up quickly.

"We must return to Rochester immediately," he said to his knights. "Get the men moving. I shall gather the ladies."

"What does the missive say, my lord?" Simon asked.

Tevin's jaw ticked. "Not here. Send John back to Rochester immediately to summon the rest of my knights. I would speak with everyone upon my return."

Simon moved to carry out his liege's orders, readying the soldiers who had accompanied them and bringing about the wagon that had carried the ladies. John mounted his big brown destrier and took off in the direction of the castle. Tevin went back inside where the ladies were still kneeling. He moved to them swiftly.

"I am truly sorry, Lady Penden," he said quietly, "but we must return immediately."

Startled, she looked up into his dark eyes and saw hardness to them. Something was amiss, though she could not imagine what. Somehow it frightened her. Without a word, she followed him from the cathedral and to the wagon waiting outside. Tevin helped Val in first, being careful of her ribs, but when it came to Cantia, his enormous hands encircled her waist and he gently lifted her into the cab. His hands lingered a moment and she smiled faintly at him. He winked in response. And then he was gone.

03

"DE GAEL IS on his way to Rochester. It would seem that the man has had a change of loyalties."

Clustered in the musty solar of Rochester Castle, Tevin made the grim announcement. While the knights of his corps remained quiet and calm, Myles eyebrows lifted dramatically.

"Change of loyalties?" de Lohr repeated. "What does that mean?"

Tevin had been through this before with his cousin. The man was an opportunist and a scoundrel. He'd already betrayed Stephen of Blois some time back, pretending to support the man when what he really wanted was to confiscate some of his English holdings. Now it would appear he was doing the same thing to Matilda.

"It means precisely that," Tevin said steadily. When de Lohr looked flustered, he continued. "These are lawless times, de Lohr. England has no true monarch. Anarchy has been reigning for thirteen years now, ever since Henry passed away and declared Matilda his heir. While she hides in France, the nobles of the country have basically created their own dark worlds in which to govern and murder. Geoffrey is no different, though he is more clever than most. He supported Stephen for a time until he betrayed the man and stole some of his holdings. Now he betrays Matilda by claiming the fiefdom from Dartford to Canterbury in the name of Stephen."

Myles was beside himself. "And you accept this?"

Tevin lifted an eyebrow. "He is my liege as well as my cousin. I have little choice in the matter."

There was more passion in Myles than was healthy. "So you change your own loyalties at the whim of your cousin?" he growled. "You now support the same faction that killed Brac Penden. Now you side with the enemy."

"There are no enemies during this time. There is only survival."

"They killed Brac!"

Fortunately, Tevin was not quick to anger. He never had been. He understood Myles' distress. "What would you suggest I do?"

"Resist him," Myles snapped. "Support the true empress and deny the usurper."

Tevin paused in thought. "Let me ask you something, de Lohr, and be honest. If you were in my position, heir apparent to the earldom of East Anglia, and owing all of your power and wealth to the man, would you so easily create a battle that cannot be won?"

Myles stopped pacing. He looked at Tevin, knowing there was some truth to his words but still angered over the changing of tides. He ran his fingers through his blond hair. "You do not know that. You command fifteen hundred men."

"And East Anglia commands three or four times that. I could not win this battle, Myles. It would be a futile gesture and a lost cause."

"So you support his change in loyalties without question?"

"Without question."

"Why would you do this?"

"When you are in a position of power during these evil times, you will understand."

Myles shut his mouth. He had nothing more to say. With a lingering glance, Tevin turned back to his men. He noted the varying expressions, some supportive, some doubtful. Val sat in a padded chair to support her healing ribs, her expression somewhat veiled. She would do whatever her brother commanded, but he could see that she was distressed.

"Lord East Anglia should be here in a few days," Tevin said with some resignation in his voice. "We must show him all of the support he requires. I do not know what he will demand of me, but we must be ready."

The knights of his corps merely nodded. They did as they were told. Myles didn't reply, but he didn't protest, either. When Tevin dismissed his men to go about their business, Myles was the last man from the room. Tevin called after him.

"I trust that I have your loyalty, de Lohr," he said quietly. "If not, then you and I have more to discuss."

Myles' gaze move from Tevin to Val and back again. After a moment, he shook his head, perhaps understanding more of Tevin's position than he let on. "You have always had my loyalty, my lord," he said. "I suppose I fear for Lady Penden's reaction when she realizes that her husband died in vain. Had we received this news a month ago, there would have been no bridge to retake. Brac would still be with us."

"Life is full of choices and what could have been," Tevin replied. "And I would appreciate it if you would not stress that point to the lady. It will do her no good to anguish over something that cannot be changed."

Myles nodded and left the solar, leaving Tevin and Val sitting alone. Val watched her brother's tense brow.

"You are displeased," she said knowingly.

He shrugged. "I am always displeased when Geoff comes around. Surely a more immoral man has never existed."

"Keep Cantia away from him," Val said. "He has no control when it comes to women. I am afraid what he will do when he sees her. And I fear what you will do should he touch her."

His head snapped in her direction, the dark eyes piercing. "What do you mean?"

Val shook her head. "Do not pretend with me, brother. It is of no use. I see how you look at her. I know your thoughts, though I must say that I am surprised. I thought you well beyond any lady's charms."

Tevin was fully prepared to protest but thought better of it. Val wasn't an idiot. And she wasn't judgmental, either. With a sigh, he sat in the nearest chair, easing his massive body down wearily. He knew he could confide in her and it would go no further. He felt the sudden need to do so.

"I thought myself well beyond that, too, but it seems I was wrong," he muttered. "I've tried to tell myself how wrong it is, how inappropriate my thoughts are, but it does no good. I see the woman and feel myself turn to putty."

Val smiled sadly. "I know. I've seen it."

"Has anyone else?"

"I doubt it. Your knights are not as intuitive as I am." Her gaze lingered on him a moment. "Have you told her how you feel?"

He snorted. "Aye, I have."

"How did she react?"

He lifted his hands in a helpless gesture. "It caused her more distress than she needs. The woman is still grieving over her husband. I have no right to demand her attention."

Val fell silent a moment, listening to the sounds of the bailey as they drifted in through the lancet window. Then she looked at her brother pointedly. "Does she know everything?"

He looked at her. "About what?"

"About Louisa?"

He abruptly stood up, shaking his head. "There is no need to tell her that."

"No need?" Val repeated, incredulous. "Tevin, just what do you plan to do with Cantia? Toy with her feelings and then leave her in despair? What exactly are your intentions?"

Tevin, having strolled halfway across the solar, suddenly stopped and looked at his sister. "I...I do not know," he snapped in frustration. "All I know is that the woman makes me feel something I have never felt before. She has awakened a part of me that I thought was long dead. I cannot go a moment of the day without thinking of her. So you tell me what my intentions are, for truly, I do not know."

Val wasn't trying to agitate him, but she needed for him to think clearly. "You are not a man given to whims, Tevin. Make sure that what you feel for the lady is not simply opportunistic. She is a beautiful, grieving widow and you have felt responsible since the day of Brac's death. Do not confuse passion with pity. You will do more damage to her if you do."

His features flickered with hurt. "That is a cruel thing to say."

Val lifted an eyebrow. "Is it? Or is it the truth and you cannot admit it?"

He sighed heavily, wandering over to where she sat. He sat down beside her heavily, his dark eyes dulled with bewilderment. Val put her hand over his.

"It's not as if you can marry her," she said softly.

He hung his head, staring at the floor. "It's strange," he muttered. "But that fact never bothered me until you just said it. Louisa has been gone so many years now that I do not feel married. I haven't since the day she ran off."

Val hated bringing up the old shame, but given Tevin's train of thought, she had to. "She may very well be alive," she said. "But then again, she may not. We simply do not know. But you cannot take the chance that she is still alive, somewhere."

Tevin grunted, still staring at the floor. "The woman is not a part of my life, yet I am married to her." He lifted his gaze from the ground, staring off across the room. "Until this moment, it never bothered me."

Val squeezed his hand. "Then you feel something more for Lady Penden than simple pity," she confirmed. "But whatever it is, you must stop. It is not fair to the lady. She is still young and beautiful and will make some man a fine wife. You cannot let her fall for a man who will never be able to marry her."

Tevin looked sharply at his sister. She could read the turmoil in the dark eyes and it pulled at her heart. She could already see that he was far gone for the lady. She put her hands on his face.

"Tevin, for her sake, you must stop this," she whispered. "The death of her husband has already broken her heart. You cannot possibly think to destroy it further."

He opened his mouth to argue with her, but just as quickly closed it. A sardonic smile creased his lips. "Louisa and I were so young when we married. I never even knew her until the day we said our vows. And after she left… I just forgot about her. I didn't care. She left Arabel with me and that was all that mattered. Just so long as she did not take my daughter, I did not care where she went. But now… now I have, in the most unexpected of places, found a woman I would give up the entire world for and I cannot have her. The irony of the situation is unfathomable."

"I know."

"Nay, you do not. I want her, Val. I cannot stomach living the rest of my life without her."

"Then it would be only as your mistress, not your wife."

"She is far too worthy to be a mistress. She comes from a long line of consorts to kings. She deserves more."

"More than you can give her," Val said.

His gaze was piercing. "I can give her everything but marriage."

Val didn't say any more. She had said her piece and the rest was up to her brother. Mostly, she couldn't say any more because she could see the pain in his eyes. Whatever he was feeling was consuming him. He needed time to sort it out.

"Well," she stood up stiffly, favoring her torso. "We can talk about this at another time. I fear you have much on your mind with the approach of Geoff."

He stood up next to her. "You and Cantia must leave before Geoff gets here. I do not want either of you here with him around."

Val nodded in agreement. Her cousin could not control himself around women, even a blood relative. "Where shall we go?"

Tevin thought a moment. "Rochester has other holdings, including the fiefdom of Gillingham. I shall ask Lady Penden about it. Perhaps she knows of a place you can go until the storm blows over. In fact, I'll send Myles with you. I'm not sure he should be here when Geoff arrives, either."

They moved towards the door of the solar. "Then we should probably start making some manner of preparation," Val said, not entirely upset by the prospect of going into seclusion with de Lohr.

"I'll know more after I talk to Lady Penden," Tevin said. Noting his sister's expression, he held up his hands in supplication. "I'm simply going to talk to her about Gillingham and nothing more. And stop looking at me like that."

Val stuck her tongue out at him and made her way to the stairwell that led to the second floor. Tevin stood at the base of the steps, making sure she didn't falter as she mounted then. When he was sure she was safely on her way to her chamber, he went to seek out Lady Penden. While the knights had gathered in the solar, she had taken her son out into the kitchen yard. He would start looking for her there.

ଓଃ

TEVIN FOUND CANTIA far beyond the kitchen walls. Far beyond Rochester's walls, in fact. It seemed that Hunt wished to chase rabbits and she had followed her son out into the flat, vast plain just to the west of the castle. His momentary annoyance at her leaving the safety of the castle was dashed when he saw her face. She was laughing as her son would run after a rabbit and then trip over himself in his efforts. She was having a marvelous time.

Cantia noticed him approach and she turned to him just as her son fell flat on his face when a rabbit slipped away from him. Before she could speak, Hunt waved and called out.

"My lord," he picked himself up off the grass. "I am catching rabbiths!"

Tevin gave him a short wave. "I can see that," he said, turning his focus to the boy's radiant mother. "Why aren't you helping him?"

She smiled. "Because he and the rabbit are much faster than I am." She watched him snort. "Is there something I can do for you, my lord?"

Tevin's dark gaze lingered over the topography before settling on her. "I need to speak with you when you are free of rabbits," he said. "Something has come up and I require your assistance."

"Oh?" she cocked her head, shading her eyes from the sun overhead. "Is it serious?"

He nodded faintly. "It could be. My cousin, the Earl of East Anglia, is coming to Rochester."

Her eyes widened. "How marvelous," she said. "When is he due? I must make all necessary preparations for the...."

He cut her off. "'Tis not a grand occasion, I assure you." Hunt was off after another rabbit and Tevin lowered his voice as he watched the lad leap over the tall grass. "I do not want you or your son here when my cousin arrives. I would ask your advice on where to send the two of you for the duration of his visit."

She gazed at him a long moment before lowering her hand from her face. She seemed to lose her good spirits. "Of course," her voice was strangely cold. "We would not want to be underfoot. We will certainly go away for the duration of the earl's visit if that is your wish."

He sensed that perhaps she had taken his meaning wrong. "Cantia," he said gently. "It is not that I wish you to go away. It is a necessity. My cousin is, shall we say, a less than scrupulous man. I am even sending Val with you because I do not trust him where women are concerned. Especially around you."

Her momentary offense at what she thought he had been trying to tell her vanished with his quiet explanation. She should have known better.

"Why especially around me?" she asked.

Tevin's dark eyes glimmered warmly at her. "Because you are the most beautiful woman in England, if not the world, and my cousin would not be blind to that. He might very well try to make you another one of his conquests and I would not stand for that."

She gazed up at him, her lavender eyes luminous. A hint of pink crept into her cheeks. "You wouldn't?"

He frowned. "I do not wish to commit murder, which is exactly what would happen were he to so much as look in your direction. You are not a woman to be trifled with."

She lowered her gaze, humbled with his words. Or so he thought. As Tevin watched, she slowly reached out and took his fingers in her small, warm hand.

"How fortunate I am to have a protector such as you, my lord."

He gripped her hand strongly, bringing it to his lips for a tender kiss. "In private you will call me Tevin," he rumbled. "And I will protect you, always."

Cantia felt the heat from his kiss course down her arm like a river of fire. She remembered the kiss in the church, the force of his passion, and it made her knees weak.

"Because it is your duty?" she asked breathlessly.

He shook his head. "Because I want to."

She smiled at him, a dazzling gesture that sent bolts of exhilaration pulsing through Tevin's big body. He kissed her hand again, forgetting about the boy chasing rabbits or the fortress behind him. There could have been eyes watching them at that moment and he could have cared less. All he cared about was that beautiful face.

"God, I wish I could kiss you again as I did at the cathedral," he admitted, his mouth against her fingers.

She put her hand on his head as he bent over her hand, feeling the soft copper tendrils beneath her fingers. "As do I," she whispered. "Yet I suspect this is not the place for it. But at least there are no candles."

He lifted his head, fighting off a grin. "You will never let me forget that, will you?"

She shook her head, an impish grin on her lips. At that moment, Hunt suddenly popped up with a tiny rabbit in his arms. He struggled with the little creature as he made his way to his mother.

"Mam!" he called. "Look, I have one!"

Cantia discreetly took her hand away from Tevin as Hunt approached. "My, he is a little one," she said to her son as he drew near. "Perhaps he needs to go back to his mother."

But Hunt was firm. "I will take care of him. I will be his mam."

"He is too young, Hunt," she insisted gently. "He will be missing his mother. Would you not miss me if you were taken away?"

Hunt cocked his head just as Brac used to. Squinting in the sunlight, he looked curiously at his mother. "But I will go away, some day. I will go away to learn to be a great knight."

Cantia's heart just about broke. Tevin eyed her, remembering their conversation on fostering and knowing how she had reacted to it. Hunt had unknowingly reopened the tender wound. He took control of the conversation before Cantia could react.

"You do not have to go away to be a great knight," he said, moving for the boy and pretending to inspect the little brown bunny. "But your mother is right, Hunt. This rabbit is too small to be away from its mother. You had better let it go and try your luck with another."

Hunt hesitated for a split second before doing as he was told. He brushed his little hands off on his breeches as he watched the rabbit hop away.

"Can I go with you to learn to be a great knight?" he asked. "I could live with you."

"But what of your mother?"

His little brow furrowed thoughtfully. "Can't she come, too?"

Tevin fought off a smile. "Mothers do not usually follow their sons to foster."

Now Hunt's little mouth twisted as he thought of a solution to the situation. He didn't particularly want to leave his mother, but he wanted to be a great knight. His turmoil was evident and Tevin laid an enormous hand on his downy head. "We do not have to decide this today," he told the boy. "Now, if you're going to catch another rabbit, you'd better hurry up. The day grows late."

Hunt turned around and went in search of his prey. Cantia watched her son, her gaze moving between the little blond head and the massive dark knight. When Tevin turned to look at her, she smiled sweetly.

"You are very good with children," she said. "I think he likes you."

"And I like him," his dark eyes were on her, "as well as his mother."

Cantia didn't know what to say. She simply smiled. Tevin moved back to stand next to her and the two of them stood in silence as Hunt went off on another chase. Eventually, Tevin moved close enough to hold her hand. He tucked it into the crook of his elbow, his fingers playing gently with hers.

"How did you come to be so comfortable with children?" she asked, simply making conversation. "Most men are not so practiced."

But it was not idle conversation to Tevin. He had been dreading a line of discussion just like this one. He could be evasive, but that would only delay the inevitable. Val had been correct. Cantia had to know, right from the start before things got out of control and it would be increasingly difficult to tell her. He felt so strongly about her that he would not disrespect her by lying or withholding the truth. He could only pray that she understood, for this was a situation he'd never before faced and he was unsure how adequately he could explain it.

"I am comfortable with them because I have one," he said simply.

Cantia's head snapped to him. "You have a child?"

He looked down at her. "Aye."

A look of bafflement swept her. "But if you have a child…," her eyes suddenly widened. "You must have a wife."

He sighed heavily, holding her hand firmly as she tried to pull it away. The more he held on, the harder she pulled. "Stop, madam," he commanded softly. "It is far more complicated than that."

For too many reasons to guess, her eyes began to well. She lowered her head, but she also stopped pulling. "Please let me go," she whispered.

"Nay, not until you hear me," he sounded strangely as if he was begging.

"There is nothing to hear," she hissed through clenched teeth. "You have a wife, yet you have openly displayed feeling for me and...."

She suddenly yanked hard and dislodged her hand. As she quickly walked away in the direction that Hunt had been leaping, Tevin followed.

"Cantia," he called after her quietly.

She whirled to him, still walking, almost tripping over her skirts as they became entangled in the grass. "No," she jabbed a finger at him angrily. "No more. Never again will you say those things to me. I will not hear you."

He took two giant strides and grabbed her. She struggled against him but she was no match for his strength. "Cantia, please hear me," he very nearly pleaded. "It is not what it seems."

She looked at him as if he were pure evil. "How can you say that? You are married."

"By law, yes. But it is not that simple."

She looked as if she wanted to punch him, her little fists balled up as she struggled. "You have toyed with me. I shall never forgive you for that."

He spoke steadily, firmly, hoping she would hear his words above her outrage. "My wife has not been a part of my life since my daughter was born," he said. "She was a noble of Teutonic birth and we were betrothed as children. We were married at a very young age and my daughter was born less than a year later. But Arabel was born with defects and my wife refused to accept the child. She blamed me for everything. She abandoned the baby and she abandoned our marriage. She ran off with one of the German knights who had escorted her to our marriage from her homeland and I've not seen her since."

By this time, Cantia had stopped struggling. She gazed up at Tevin with a mixture of disbelief and anger. "The baby," she said. "What is wrong with her?"

Tevin's tight grip on her loosened, his hands beginning to caress her. "She was born with her spine exposed," he said. "She is a cripple who cannot walk and can barely move her arms. But she is fifteen years old now and the most brilliant woman I have ever known. I am not sorry she was born, not in the least. Though I am sorry every day that her mother left her, I am not sorry that her mother left *me*, if that makes any sense. Louisa was proud, arrogant, and cruel. She has been gone these fifteen years and until a few weeks ago, I'd not thought of her in almost as long. And then I met you and began to wonder if the woman still lived. For as long as she lives, I can never remarry. You have made me think of such things and be concerned for them. But that does not stop me from adoring you, Cantia. It does not stop these feelings growing inside of me."

Cantia just stared at him. He suddenly became so human in her eyes, so fragile. The viscount who commanded thousands was a man with a heavy heart and a humiliating past. She lifted a timid hand to his cheek.

"Oh… my poor Tevin," she said softly. "Your wife ran off and left you with an ill child."

He shrugged. It was an old wound, long since healed. "Arabel is a beautiful, intelligent girl. She has been my one joy in life until now. Since I met you, it is as if an entirely new world has opened up to me, something I never knew to exist. I don't want to lose this, Cantia, but it all seems horribly unfair to you."

"How do you mean?"

"Because nothing can ever become of it. I cannot marry you, and you should most definitely remarry. You will make some man a very fine wife."

He hated uttering those words, for they were like daggers to his heart. Cantia removed her hand from his face and lowered her gaze, obviously contemplating all he had just told her. She resumed her walk, following the path of her son. They could see him in the distance, throwing himself on the ground in an attempt to trap his quarry. She came to a halt on the crest of a small hill, about fifteen feet from Tevin. He still stood there, watching the breeze gently blow her hair about, wondering if all of the joy and excitement of the past few weeks had come to a tragic end.

That was more than likely the case. Cantia stood far from him, unmoving and silent. Tevin stood there a nominal amount of time before turning away from her with the intention of returning to the castle. But her soft voice stopped him.

"Tevin," she called quietly.

He turned to her. "Aye?"

"Your wife," she began. "Have you ever tried to find her?"

He paused, retracing his steps back in her direction. "Right after she left. But her father told me what she had done. Apparently, she had been in love with this knight since childhood and did not see her marriage to me as an obstacle to their happiness. Her father thought she was living in Paris with this man but he was not sure. I did not pursue it beyond that."

He was within a few feet of her when she turned to look at him. "I must ask you a serious question."

"By all means."

"If your wife was dead, would you want to marry me?"

"Tomorrow, if I could."

"Do you feel so strongly, then?"

He snorted at the irony of the question. "I believe that I do. Do you?"

She fell silent, her lavender eyes watching her son in the distance. As he watched her, he could see the tears returning. "No, Cantia," he comforted. "No tears, not now."

His words only made her burst into soft sobs. With a sigh, Tevin put his arms around her, holding her tightly against him. She clung to him, her soft body pressed close.

"I have felt so guilty for these feelings I harbor for you, thinking them very disrespectful to Brac's memory," she wept. "At first I thought I felt them because you had been kind to me and I was grieving and lonely, but as time passed, I realized these feelings had nothing to do with Brac's passing. They were strong on their own. Now I cannot deny them no matter how hard I try."

His face was buried in the top of her head as he rocked her gently. "As I have harbored the same guilt, only worse. I thought perhaps I was taking advantage of your vulnerability."

She pulled her face out of his chest, looking up at him. "Never have you done that. You are a man of too much honor."

He gazed down at her, feeling that uncontrollable pull again. It was a supreme struggle not to kiss her, out in the open to the shock of her son. A massive hand came up, smoothing her hair away from her face as he absorbed her lovely features.

"My cousin will be here for a week or two," he said quietly. "You and I will be separated for as long. Perhaps… perhaps it will give us time to discover what we really feel, if it is something more than pity or convenience or lust."

She knew he was right, though she did not want to be separated from him, not even for a moment. "And if we discover they are true?"

He pulled her closer. "Then I will go to Paris. I will not stop until I have discovered what has become of Louisa."

Cantia swallowed hard. "And if she is alive?"

"I will petition the pope to annul the marriage on the grounds of abandonment and cruelty. And then I will marry you, we will have a dozen sons just like Hunt, and we will grow old in each other's arms."

She smiled, loving the feel of him against her, loving the glorious handsomeness of his masculine face. The wind was kicking up, blowing his copper curls into her face. "But what if you cannot obtain an annulment? What then?"

"I will still adore you for the rest of my life. You and no other."

Her smile faded. "And I will still bear you a dozen strong sons and we will still grow old in each other's arms."

"I cannot ask that of you."

"You did not. If it is the only way I can have you, then I am happy to make that choice."

His dark eyes glittered like shards of obsidian, hard and unyielding and powerful. "Madam, I cannot imagine a greater honor, but you should think carefully about that statement while we are apart. I may hold you to it."

"I would hope you do."

He wanted to kiss her so badly that he began to shake. Unable to control himself, he lifted both of her hands and hungrily kissed them, devouring her flesh, sucking on her fingers until Cantia gasped softly. He nibbled her palms, her wrists, even her fingernails. In his grasp, Cantia was breathing heavily.

"Oh, Tevin," she gasped. "When you do that...."

"I know," he moaned, his lips against the back of her right hand. "If you could only feel my need for you now, madam, you would know how badly I want you. All of you."

Shockingly strong words, but she was not surprised or offended. She was not a maiden and Brac's want for her had been insatiable. She knew what it meant to have a man make love to her. She wondered what it would be like when Tevin did. And she had no doubt that he soon would.

She moved close to him, taking his face between her hands. "I will take Hunt back to the castle so that he may play with his dog in the yard," she whispered, her face an inch from his. "And then I will retreat to my chamber. You may find me there in one hour. Alone."

He stared at her a moment, unsure if he heard correctly. He knew what she meant simply by the look in her eye. "Are you sure?"

"Verily."

"But... Cantia, I do not want you to think that I am only interested in conquest. I do not take this lightly."

"Nor do I," she whispered. With that, she pressed her open mouth against him, her tongue engaging in a delicate dance with his. The blaze between them flared like a fire with too much dry kindling and, for a brief moment, Tevin was in danger of swallowing up her entire face. He couldn't get enough of her. But just as quickly, she pulled away, walking hastily in the direction of her frolicking son.

Heart thumping painfully against his ribs, Tevin watched her go. He put his hand on his chest as if to stop the crazy beating. He couldn't breathe. But she said she would be waiting for him in an hour.

It was the longest hour of his life.

CHAPTER SEVEN

With her healing ribs, Val couldn't seem to find a comfortable position. The sling back chairs did not provide enough support and the benches were too awkward. The only way she could find even moderate relief was if she pushed a sling back chair against a wall and propped herself up with a pillow.

Ever since their return from the cathedral that morning, she had been seated in the solar in precisely that upright position. Though she hated needlework and wasn't any good at it, she was giving it a moderate try. One of the serving women had given her a clean piece of linen on Lady Cantia's old frame and several colors of silk thread. So, like a true lady, Val was attempting to do something other than shoot arrows and thrust swords. Truth was that she couldn't do much else.

It was turning out to be a horrendous piece of work over the past few hours she had been attempting it. And it was difficult to focus, too, considering the solar door was near the entry of the keep and she could see all manner of traffic passing in and out. Cantia and Hunt came in at one point, the boy rushing into the great hall while his mother mounted the steps to the upper levels. Then Myles came in a short time later and parked himself in a chair next to Val just to pass the time. Val had always liked Myles. He was handsome, wise and good of character. But he only spoke of the weather and a new charger or the price of a good sword. Never anything she might like to hear, though she wasn't sure what, in fact, she might like to hear from him. Still, she wished he would speak to her of something other than warring.

Tevin came in a short time after Myles' arrival, entered the solar, and engaged Myles in talk of de Gael's arrival. Myles seemed to have calmed after his initial outburst. In fact, he showed his reluctance when

Tevin asked him to escort the ladies to another location for the duration of the earl's visit. He wanted to stay, but Tevin convinced him that escorting the ladies was far more important. Val was secretly glad he would be going. Maybe she could coerce him into speaking on the color of her eyes instead of the color of battle.

But thoughts of Myles aside, Val sensed something in Tevin. Outwardly, her brother was cool and collected, as usual. But an odd flicker in his eyes gave him an almost edgy expression. When he spoke with Myles, it was obvious his mind was elsewhere. Val wondered if it had something to do with Cantia. Tevin just didn't seem like himself since they had returned from the cathedral.

To make the situation even stranger, he lingered so long in the solar that it almost seemed like he was killing time. Tevin was a man perpetually busy, which made it seem odd for him to loiter over meaningless conversation. But that was exactly what he appeared to be doing. Val was becoming suspicious. Just as she was preparing to ask him why he seemed so solicitous, Hunt entered the solar with a stick in one hand and the big yellow dog on his heels. The blue-eyed boy looked up at Tevin.

"My lord," he tugged on Tevin's tunic. "Have you theen my grandfather?"

Tevin looked down at the child. The question surprised him. Hunt had been displaying the resilience of a child in the wake of his father's death and his grandfather's subsequent madness, which made the question seem odd. It was the first the boy had mentioned his grandfather in two days.

"Your grandfather is safe, Hunt," he said evenly. "You will see him soon, I am sure."

Hunt's little brow was furrowed. "But he promisthed to make me a new sword. I buried my other sword with my father. Where is grandfather?"

Tevin glanced at Val. Her pale eyes were wide. She was wondering how Tevin was going to handle this delicate situation. Tevin crouched down so he was nearly eye to eye with the child.

"Your grandfather is not feeling well," he said honestly. "He is very sad that your father has died. He needs a few days to rest and then I am sure he will be well again."

Hunt's eyes were the shape of Cantia's, even if they weren't the same color. But Tevin also saw a good deal of Brac in the little face.

"But where ith he?" Hunt persisted. "Can I go and see him?"

"Nay, lad," Tevin did not want the boy visiting his hysterical grandfather in the vault. "Not today. Perhaps tomorrow."

Hunt didn't protest, though it was obvious he was disappointed. He looked at his stick and then looked back at Tevin. He raised the stick. "Will you fight me, then?"

Tevin had spent nearly an hour in the solar, marking time until the magical hour was up. Cantia had told him one hour in her chamber, and he planned to be there right on the mark. But gazing into Hunt's sweet little face, he felt that he could not refuse the lonely little boy. To have lost his father, and now his grandfather, was coming to take a toll on him.

"I will fight you," he agreed quietly. "But you cannot fight with a stick. We will find the smithy and see if he cannot fashion you a sword suitable for a young man."

Hunt's eyes widened. "You will?" He beamed a big smile, complete with two missing bottom teeth. "Can we go now?"

If he took him now, he would miss his date with Cantia. But gazing into her son's face, he suspected that she would understand. He put his hand on the boy's blond head and turned him for the door. "We shall," he said.

He hadn't taken a step when Myles spoke. "I shall take him, my lord. I am sure you have more pressing duties."

Tevin almost took the excuse. He could still make it to Cantia at the appointed time. But gazing down at the child, something deep inside would not let him be so selfish.

"I have no more pressing duties than to properly arm Master Penden," he said. "Come along if you like."

Myles took a few steps after him, then suddenly turned to Val as if he had just remembered she was in the room. He held out a hand to her. "Val? Come with us?"

She smiled. Tevin thought she actually blushed and he thought on Cantia's earlier observations. *Maybe she was right*, he thought. Stiffly, Val rose, taking Myles' outstretched hand. Happily, Hunt led them all from the solar and out into the yard.

The smithy had been at Rochester for years and was happy to help with Hunt's first weapon. He set aside what he was working on, measured Hunt's arm, and went to work. Frankly, with Viscount Winterton's massive presence hanging over him, there wasn't much else he could do. But it was a long process, certainly not one that could be accomplished in a few hours.

As the sun dipped into the late afternoon, Tevin had never felt so restless. All he could think of was Cantia waiting for him, and here he was playing with her son. But he remained nonetheless, leaning back against the support beam of the smithy's lean-to and watching the ruddy man heat the steel, pound it, cool it, and repeat the process. More than once he had to pull Hunt out of the man's way. The child was so excited he could hardly stand it.

During the course of the afternoon, Val and Myles stood in quiet conversation as the smithy worked. Eventually, Val's ribs ached too much from standing around and Myles escorted her back into the keep. Tevin watched his sister go, paying closer attention to the pair than he had before purely based on Cantia's observations. If there was something going on, he wanted to be aware of it. Val was his only sister and he was understandably protective over her, even with a suitor as mild as Myles de Lohr. Moreover, he was quite pleased with the prospect.

When the sun began to set, he was forced to swallow his impatience and resign himself to the fact that he would not be seeing Cantia alone this day. As much as he had been looking forward to it, more than he had looked forward to anything in years, somehow he was not entirely disturbed. Spending the afternoon with a very excited five year old had been a most rewarding substitute. Hunt was a wonderful little boy and he was coming to like him a great deal. He congratulated Brac Penden on fathering such a fine son and he was also quite sorry that Brac would never see the boy live to adulthood. It would have been a proud thing.

Lost to his thoughts as he watched the hypnotizing rhythm of the smithy, he was surprised to see Cantia enter the lean-to. She went straight for her son and put her hand on the boy's shoulder, asking him his business with the smithy. Hunt promptly turned around and pointed at Tevin, still leaning up against the support column. Partially hidden in the shadows, Cantia hadn't seen him when she entered the shelter. Tevin unfolded his arms and pushed himself off the beam.

"Your son came to me a few hours ago with a serious problem, my lady," he told her as he moved in her direction. "Since he was generous enough to bury his sword with his father, he had no weapon. I told him we would remedy the situation immediately and have been here ever since."

A light of understanding flickered in her big eyes. He saw it. She looked down at her son. "So that's it," she grumbled, ruffling the blond hair. "I was wondering where you went. Both of you."

Hunt was beside himself with excitement. He held his mother's hand tightly as he showed her the sword the smithy was working on. Tevin watched her the entire time, the shape of her exquisite face, the expressions that creased her brow. He couldn't look at anything else. But at some point he became aware that she did not look entirely pleased and when the smithy gave the boy the sword to test the weight, he moved up beside her.

"Did I do wrong?" he asked softly.

She turned to look at him, her sweet face gently illuminated in the dusk. "What do you mean?"

"You do not seem entirely pleased about the sword."

She lifted an eyebrow, though there was no anger behind it. "Brac always wanted to give him a metal sword but I would not allow it. He can hurt himself, or others, with it."

He wriggled his eyebrows. "Then perhaps I should have asked you first. Your son came to me in the solar a few hours ago and asked where his grandfather was. I gave him an evasive answer that somehow led to the statement that Charles had promised your son another sword in place of the one he buried with Brac. So I ended up down here with the smithy."

She nodded in understanding, her gaze moving back to the little boy as he swung the sword about under the smithy's watchful eye. "I assumed that something came up when you did not come to my bower," she said softly. "Clearly, I cannot fault you your noble deeds on behalf of my son. And for that, I thank you."

He took another step so that the right side of his body brushed up against her. "Know that I would not have missed any opportunity to spend time with you unless it was undeniably important," he muttered. "I thought perhaps a lonely little boy qualified as such."

"It does," she looked at him again, her beautiful face serene. "Given the choice, I would have made the same one."

"I would still like to see you alone."

"There will be more opportunity."

"Are you sure? You have not reconsidered our earlier conversation, have you?"

She smiled faintly, studying the lines of his strong face. "No, Tevin. I have not."

He smiled back at her but dare not touch her. He forced himself to change the subject lest he lose his self-control. It seemed as if the more time he spent around her, the more he wanted to touch her.

"Have you given any thought to where you and Hunt would like to go for the duration of my cousin's visit?" he asked.

She nodded. "My father's fortified home in Gillingham sits empty, as does a larger fortified manor in Darland a few miles to the southwest. Either one of them would be acceptable."

"Which would you prefer?"

She thought a moment. "I was born at Darland. I have always liked it there. The village even has an outdoor theatre where they give entertainment."

He lifted an eyebrow at her. "You are not going to go cavorting about the town while you're out from under my watchful eye, are you?"

She grinned. "Of course not. And even if I do, it is none of your affair. You'll be here wildly entertaining your cousin and you'll never even miss me."

He put his massive hand on the overhead beam, leaning over her in a rather dominating and provocative stance.

"That, madam, is an untrue statement," he rumbled. "I cannot go a moment of the day without thinking of you. When you are out of my sight, I shall miss you all the more."

She gazed up at him, feeling his breath on her face. Her heart began to race. "Do you think that you shall be able to come and visit us while we are there?" she asked intimately.

"I doubt it," he replied. "All of my focus will be on Geoff. He's like a naughty child that needs constant attention."

"Then this parting will not be a particularly pleasant thing," she said.

"Nay, it will not."

Hunt interrupted their increasingly passionate conversation as he ran into the lean-to with his weapon aloft. "Mam!" he shouted as only a five year old can. "My sword ith good for fighting. Did you thee?"

"I did," she put her hand on his head affectionately. "You must thank Lord Tevin for his generosity. It was most kind of him."

The little boy had his sword in two hands. He looked up at Tevin with such naked joy that Tevin instinctively smiled. "Thank you, my lord," he said. "Will you fight me now?"

Tevin cocked an eyebrow, though not unkind. "Perhaps tomorrow, lad. I suspect the evening meal is fast on the approach. There will be time for swordplay tomorrow."

Though disappointed, Hunt didn't argue. He kept staring at his new sword, perhaps the length from his elbow to his wrist, and admired it. It was a nice little weapon, purposely left dull at Tevin's request. Hunt couldn't have hurt himself, or someone else, if he tried. As the sun dipped below the horizon, Cantia took her son by the hand and led him back to Rochester's massive keep. Tevin kept pace with them, though at a respectable distance.

Inside, the great hall was filled with smells of fresh bread and smoke from the hearth. The servants were bringing bowls of food to the tables and the hall was already half full with senior soldiers and a few knights. John Swantey, Sir Simon, Sir Dagan and Sir Gavril were already seated and eating. Val and Myles sat next to one another, conversing quietly.

Hunt raced to his usual place at the table and elbowed his way in next to Sir John, demanding to be fed. The old serving woman that helped watch over him was at his side, trencher in hand and admonishment for his manners on her lips. Cantia made sure her son was well tended before leaving the hall with the intention of changing her clothes. In the process, she had lost sight of Tevin but gave it no particular mind.

The emerald surcoat she wore was slightly torn from her trip to the cathedral and she did not want it to tear further. It was a small tear, near the fastens at her waist, but she would rather put on a more stable garment. Strange she hadn't changed it the entire time she was in her bower waiting for Tevin. Her mind had been else occupied and it simply hadn't occurred to her. Leaving her son watched over by the older serving woman, she quit the great hall.

The stairwell was dark and cold as she mounted it to the upper level. As she cleared the second floor landing, a hand shot out and grabbed her by the wrist. Startled, she almost screamed until she looked up and saw Tevin's dark eyes. He pulled her into a crushing embrace, his mouth descending on hers with powerful passion before she could utter a sound. It was a swift action, brutal and overwhelming, and meant to conquer.

But she was a willing captive. Her arms went around his neck and she was vaguely aware of being picked up and carried into her chamber. The door closed behind them and Tevin had enough presence of mind to bolt it. Alone, in private, now he did not have to worry over prying eyes or impressionable young boys. They were free to feel and taste only each other.

As he had done in the cathedral, his lips ravaged her, his tongue gentle, firm, experienced in her mouth. Cantia was his prisoner. His strength was too much for her to match so she surrendered to his onslaught, her small hands on his massive shoulders as he fiercely kissed her. When his mouth left her lips and he nibbled hungrily down her neck, it was all she could do to catch her breath.

He pulled the top of her shift out of the way, peeling it back to reveal a soft white shoulder. Cantia could hear him growl as his mouth worked her flesh, feeling the heat from his lips as hotly as if he were burning her. He pulled harder on the surcoat and ended up exacerbating the tear. The entire coat came apart in his hands and he tossed it to the floor. The woman in his arms was clad now in only her shift and he slowed his fevered pace, taking the time to actually feel her flesh underneath the thin material. It was slow, gentle, and erotic. He gazed into her eyes as his hands moved across her belly to hook around and cup her buttocks. His mouth descended on her again as he listened to the soft sounds of her gasping.

He was in pieces of armor which seemed to come off in steady rhythm. Cantia was adept at such things, having helped Brac on many occasions. She knew which fasten needed to be undone before the next piece could be removed and soon she had strewn sections of armor about the floor. The amazing part was that she had done it while Tevin ravaged her. When he was in his heavy breeches and tunic, he paused long enough to rip off his tunic and throw her back on the bed.

Cantia bolted up from the mattress before he could descend on her. Puzzled, he took her in his arms again to repeat the process but she balked.

"What is wrong?" he questioned, his lips against her face.

She shook her head. Then tears sprang to her eyes and Tevin forced himself to bank his fires. He looked at her with true concern. "What is the matter?"

She looked up at him, the lavender eyes brimming. "I cannot… the bed…"

He didn't understand. "I'm sorry, sweet, I don't…"

She jabbed a finger at the mattress. "We cannot use the bed."

His brows flickered with confusion. "Why not?"

She still had hold of him, silently pulling him around the end of the bed to the other side. As soon as Tevin rounded the frame, he could see bedclothes strewn about the floor in the four foot section between the bed and the wall.

"What is that?" he asked.

Her expression was one of shame and anguish. "I… I sleep there."

His dark eyes were soft on her. "Why?"

She gestured weakly at the bed. "Because it smells of Brac," she said softly. "I cannot bear it."

He understood, feeling guilt sweep him yet again. "Cantia," he murmured. "I am so sorry. You are still grieving and I've been nothing but overbearing and forceful with you. Forgive me, sweet."

She looked at him, her eyes wide. "You've not been overbearing or forceful at all. Moreover, at any time I could have refused you. I've not refused because I've not wanted to. I explained this to you, Tevin… what I feel for you is completely separate from what I have felt, or continue to feel, for Brac. I cannot sleep on a bed that smells of him because it is a fresh reminder of his loss every time I breathe it in. I will never heal if I continue to do that. And for my sake, for Hunt's sake, I must heal."

Tevin sighed, pulling her head to his lips and kissing her forehead. "I shall have the bed removed if it pleases you."

"I think that is best."

"No more sleeping on the floor. You'll catch chill."

She smiled weakly. "As you say," the mood between them, so passionate only moments earlier, had cooled. She continued to study him. "So is this the end of your onslaught for the day?"

His brow furrowed, somewhere between amusement and puzzlement. "Considering the circumstances, it probably should be, don't you think?"

She put her hands on his face, pressing her thinly clad body against his bare chest. "Nay, I do not," she whispered. "I would resume where we left off."

He couldn't help it. His arms went around her and his want for her ignited full-strength once again. He was coming to realize his fire for her was very easily stoked. As she lifted her mouth to him for a kiss, he spoke softly.

"Are you sure?"

"More than sure."

"On the floor?"

Her lips met his. "On the floor."

Mouths locked in a passionate embrace, Tevin went to his knees and Cantia with him. He laid her back on the mound of jumbled bedclothes, one hand behind her head and the other moving up her slender torso. Her breasts were full and luscious in his hand and he was suddenly very intolerant of the shift that still lingered between them. He pulled it off, indelicately, leaving her completely nude. He gazed at her a moment in the weak light of the chamber, his breath literally catching in his throat. He'd never seen anything so beautiful. Quickly, his breeches came off and he smothered her with his massive form.

Instinct took hold. Tevin kissed her so passionately that Cantia's head swam. She couldn't breathe with the force of his lust. His big hands moved the length and breadth of her body, hot and gentle yet powerful. When he closed over a bare breast, she encouraged him. When his heated mouth finally descended on a taut nipple, she held his head fast against her. Her body was wracked with excitement as his lips moved over every inch of her sweet, round breasts.

Since she was not a maiden, there was no fear when he wedged his big body between her legs. They parted easily for him, inviting him into intimate places. Tevin accepted the invitation and plunged deeply into her, listening to her gasps of pleasure. Gathering her up in his arms to both hold her close and to support his enormous weight, he began his measured thrusts into her sweet body, overwhelmed by the smell and feel of her. She was slick and tight. Never in his life had he experienced anything so wonderful. Never in his life had he expected to. But the lady cradled in his arms was just this side of heaven. He savored every thrust, every withdrawal, feeling her body draw him in deeper and deeper.

His mouth reclaimed hers, kissing her deeply. He loved the taste of her. Cantia's hands were on his hard buttocks, her nails leaving crescent-shaped marks in his flesh. In the throes of her passion, she drew blood, causing Tevin to spill himself deep inside her. The frenzied pleasure-pain had been too much for him to take and it was a wicked enjoyment he experienced. Even after he savored his release, he continued to move in her. There was far too much fire and passion for him not to continue lingering over the deliciousness of their union. He continued to move in her, to kiss her, long into the evening. But at some point he did stop, and at some point, they fell asleep in each other's arms.

They slept soundly on the floor in a disarray of bed clothes that now smelled like Tevin.

ଓ

THE BOTTLE PRISON was black but for the glow of a distant torch that filtered in through the opening in the ceiling. Charles could barely see his hand before his face, which is why he had taken to sleeping a great deal. There was nothing more to do. Moreover, sleep brought dreams, visions of Brac and he found comfort with his son. But then he would awaken, realize it had been but a dream, and close his eyes to beg for sleep once again. He had no idea how long he had been in the pit. Long enough, however, for his madness to grow.

Since the prison was so silent, the sounds of footsteps immediately roused him from his stupor. It was like hammer sounds in the deep. He leapt to his feet, unsteadily, straining to see who it was that approached from above. After a moment, he could see a face looming in the darkness but could not make out any features. His heart began to race.

"Who is it?" he demanded. "Announce yourself."

"It is Dagan, my lord," the knight lowered his face so that Charles could see clear his features. "I came to see how you are faring."

Charles looked up at the knight in the hole, recognizing him as one of the knights who had imprisoned him.

"I am still in my own dungeon, fool. How would you be?"

Dagan lifted an eyebrow. "My lord, I suggested the last time I saw you that a display of good behavior could possibly see you released from your confinement."

Charles put his hands on his hips. "Are you in charge of my dungeons now?"

"Lord Tevin has given assignments to his men. I hold the dungeons and the gatehouse."

"Then let me out."

"I cannot, my lord. Not without orders."

A food basket came down to him, lowered by a rope. Charles ignored it for a few moments, thinking to make a statement, but reconsidered when he realized how hungry he was. He did not know when last he ate. He grabbed the bread and mutton and chewed noisily. The basket was reeled back up.

"Did you consider my offer?" he called up to Dagan.

The knight knelt beside the opening. "What offer is that, my lord?"

"My son's wife for my freedom."

Dagan's attention lingered on the old man below. He was half-hoping to hear the question, half-hoping he would not. Truth be told, he was struggling. Dagan was an honorable knight, but he was also growing old and fewer opportunities were presenting themselves. Though the offer came from a madman, still, he could not completely discount it. He had actually allowed himself to entertain it and felt like a devil for doing so.

"I have not, my lord," he lied.

"Why not?"

"Because it is not reasonable, nor is it possible."

"But it is. Rochester, and my son's widow, belongs to me. They are mine to do with as I please, and I would offer Lady Cantia to you in exchange for my freedom."

Dagan sighed heavily. "Though your offer is generous, I cannot seriously consider it. In the first place, to release you from this prison would be in direct violation of my liege's order. Secondly, the lady and I would have nowhere to go. I do not have property and I would surely have to take her from this place."

"But *she* has property," Charles stopped chewing when he realized he might actually be able to bargain himself from this hell. "Her father left her two manors. They would belong to you if you married her."

"And where are these magnificent homes?"

"Gillingham is a fortified home to the west and Darland is another home a few miles to the southwest. They are wealthy holdings with grain and sheep production."

It was odd how Charles did not sound so much like a madman at all when discussing his daughter-in-law's holdings. Still, Dagan was not convinced. He was filled with guilt for even listening to the offer, but there was selfishness in him. He was almost forty years old and had nothing to show for it. A beautiful widow and her lands would be a small price to pay for disobeying his liege. Moreover, he could declare himself an independent lord with such wealth through marriage to Penden's widow. These were desperate times. He had to take what he could.

"Even if I were to accept your offer, my lord, were I to release you, Lord Tevin would simply capture you again," he said. "You could not stay here."

"Rochester is my home," Charles rumbled. "I am the Steward."

"But du Reims is your liege."

Charles tossed aside the half-eaten mutton. "Surely you know that what he has done to me is not right," his voice was low and pleading. "The man has imprisoned me in my own dungeon so that he may steal my fortress. Do you not see this?"

"He imprisoned you because you were a danger. Your grief has made you mad."

Charles threw down the bread and lifted his hands, like claws, into the weak light that streamed down into his cell. "There is no madness in my observations. Tell me that he and my son's wife are not conspiring against me as we speak. Tell me that du Reims has not taken over every aspect of Rochester. He wanted to be rid of me to confiscate my holding and has used any excuse he could think of to do so. Can you not see that?"

Dagan inevitably thought of the past few days. Lord Tevin had indeed spent a good deal of time with Lady Cantia and her young son. In fact, his attention had gone beyond mere concern, some thought. There was talk. Though Dagan wanted nothing more than to refute Charles' assertions as the ravings on an old man, he could not entirely. Some thought there was truth to what he said.

Without another word, Dagan stood up and quit the vault. Surprisingly, Charles let him go without vehement protests. He continued to stand in the weak light, listening to the footfalls until they faded completely and wondered if he would, indeed, ever find freedom from this place.

※

FAINT SHOUTS COULD be heard in the bailey beyond the lancet window. Tevin was enjoying the best sleep he'd had in a long time with Cantia wrapped in his arms. There was warmth and peace there, a wondrous world of satisfaction he'd never before experienced. It was enough to make him forget everything else. But the shouts eventually woke him and he sat up, his massive shoulders silhouetted against the soft moonlight. Cantia, jostled by the movement and by the fact that he had moved his big warm body, stirred.

"What is it?" she asked sleepily.

He didn't say anything for a moment, putting his hand on her head to comfort her. "I am not sure." He bolted up from the floor and collected his breeches. Cantia sat up, clutching the coverlet to her nude chest. She watched Tevin pull on his breeches in the darkness. Silently, he pulled on his boots and marched to the door. As she sat there in confused silence, Tevin suddenly turned around, marched back to her, bent over and kissed her gently on the lips. He kissed her again because she tasted so good. Retracing his steps, he quit the room and shut the door softly behind him.

Legs hugged up against her chest, Cantia had a smile on her face. His kiss had brought back memories of a most passionate encounter. Then her eyes moved to the bed she was unable to sleep on and inevitable thoughts of Brac came back to her. She put a timid hand on the mattress, feeling the linen beneath her fingers. Her tender thoughts of Tevin began to turn to thoughts of Brac. Lying back down on the warm bedclothes, she gazed into the darkness, torn between thoughts of two very different men.

Was she betraying Brac? The man had been in his grave a month and already she was fornicating with someone else. She wondered what Brac would say to her, or if she had died, if he would have found comfort so soon after her passing. Though she would not have wanted him to mourn the rest of his life over her, surely there was an appropriate length of mourning for one so well loved.

Perhaps what she was doing was wrong. Perhaps she was being too selfish and not giving Brac the appropriate respect. Tevin was new, exciting, kind and intelligent. But he was also her liege and had been very kind to her in her time of need. No matter that she told him the feelings she held for him were different from those she held for Brac. The fact remained that the situation was one of convenience. He was here, he was kind to her, and in her weak state, she had responded. She was beginning to think she was a very weak and foolish woman.

More thoughts filled her head, those of longing and grief and what the future might hold. A lone tear trickled down her temple, tears for Brac, for herself, for Tevin. She should have never allowed herself the warmth of Tevin's comfort. But she had needed it. She realized that she did not regret her actions for one moment, and perhaps that was her greatest guilt. She had wanted Tevin to touch her, to explore her, and she in turn had wanted to explore him. She did not think of Brac at all when Tevin was around. All she could think of was him.

Cantia didn't know how long she lay there, staring at the ceiling and thinking of Tevin. She didn't even know what time it was, though the room was a soft shade of gray so she imagined it was somewhere close to dawn. Suddenly, the door to the chamber opened and closed and she sat up quickly in time to see Tevin rounding the side of the bed.

His gaze fell on her, the nearly-black eyes intense. He was naked from the waist up and for the first time, she got a very good look at just how enormous the man's chest and shoulders were. A soft matting of dark hair covered his chest, hair that had been fuzzy and wonderful against her skin. Gazing up at him, all of the passion and excitement from the night before washed over her and she shuddered.

"Did you discover what the herald was about?" she asked.

He nodded. "I did."

She waited expectantly for him to continue, but he lowered himself to sit on the edge of the bed and looked at her. His gaze lingered and she smiled.

"Why do you stare at me?"

He lifted a dark eyebrow, a smile on the corner of his mouth. "Because you are so beautiful," he reached out, taking a strand of her hair between his big fingers. "Honestly, Cantia, it seems that all I can do is stare at you."

Her smile turned modest. "What is happening in the bailey?"

His eyes took on a hard cast. "Trouble, I'm afraid."

"What trouble?"

He sighed, leaning forward and resting his elbows on his knees. "It would seem that my cousin has arrived early," he said. "Geoff and his entourage are filling the bailey as we speak."

Her eyes widened. "So soon?"

"I'm afraid so. Unfortunately, he's made very good time upon the road and arrived sooner than expected."

"But… what do we do? Do I still go to Darland?"

Tevin was silent a moment, his gaze lingering on her lovely face. "Not right now," he said quietly. "You and Hunt will stay put. I will have Val brought up to your room. She can stay with you until I can figure out what's to be done."

"You intend to hide us?"

"For the time being."

"I do not mean to cause problems, but I am not sure how long we can successfully hide Hunt," she said. "He is a very active little boy. He will want to run and play."

"Then we must explain to him that, for now, he cannot," Tevin replied. "I'll think of something to tell him. Perhaps if we make it into a game, he will willingly go along."

"What kind of game?"

He shook his head. "I do not know. But we shall have to think of something."

She nodded, her mind racing to encompass all of the possibilities that might coerce her son in to playing a restrictive game. But her thoughts also inevitably turned to Val, and in doing so, she spoke before she could stop herself.

"If Val stays with me, then you and I…." she trailed off, unable to finish.

He looked at her. She looked so entirely beautiful in the early morning light. He was secretly glad that Geoff had come early, secretly glad that he would not have to send her away. He could not bear the thought of sending her away, not after last night. With his big hands, he reached out to take her face in his hands.

"Then perhaps I had better steal a kiss when I can," he said softly, kissing her gently on the lips. When he pulled back, their eyes met and they grinned at each other. "And more."

She smiled broadly as his mouth came down on her again, gently at first, then more insistently. He left the bed and ended up lying beside her on the floor, holding her in his arms and kissing her as if to never let her go. She was still nude, warm and cozy in the bedclothes, and in little time he pulled off his breeches and boots and joined her in that cozy warmth. His mouth moved across her shoulder, her chest, familiarizing himself with the taste of her. She most definitely had a taste, something between honey and silk. It was delicious, like food to a starving man, and he suckled deeply of her flesh.

The second time around, he was more familiar with her and it only served to intoxicate him. Her nipples were succulent and tender, the flesh of her belly delicious. He could hear Cantia's moans of pleasure and it spurred him onward until he reached the soft mound of curls between her legs. Even then, he did not stop. He continued to taste her, to savor every movement, every flavor. She had him by the hair as he held her tender core to his mouth, her legs over his enormous shoulders and his tongue doing wicked things. When he felt her stiffen in his hands, her body convulsing, he abruptly lifted himself and drove into her, feeling her tender walls throb around his manhood, drawing him deeper and begging for his release. But he could not answer so swiftly. He thrust deeply into her, so deeply that in little time her body was convulsing again and this time, he joined her.

Tevin lay with Cantia in his arms, still embedded in her sweet body, hearing the sounds wafting up from the bailey and trying not to listen. He did not want anything to interrupt this moment because he knew, more than likely, their next chance at being together would be far in the future. With his cousin around, there was no telling what was to happen during the course of his visit. Geoff was, at best, unpredictable. He found himself wishing he could run away and take Cantia with him, someplace where no king nor queen nor cousin could find them.

Someplace peaceful. He sighed heavily. He wondered if such a place really did exist. It was the first time in his life he'd ever entertained such a thought.

"What's wrong?" Cantia's muffled voice came to him.

He shifted slightly, gazing down into her sleepy-eyed face. "Not a thing in the world, madam. Everything is wonderful."

"But you sighed."

The corners of his mouth twitched. "I suppose I am sighing with contentment. Or with discontentment at the thought of leaving you."

Her head came up, mussed and lovely. "Leaving me? Where are you going?"

He gently pinched her chin. "Downstairs, to my cousin. Remember?"

She looked sheepish. "I thought you meant… well, it doesn't matter anyway. Surely if your cousin is here, you must go and retrieve Val immediately."

He just looked at her. "Does the thought of me leaving distress you that much?"

"Of course it does."

His smile broadened and he kissed her again, realizing he wasn't finished with her, and rolled her onto her back. As the sounds of the bailey below grew louder and the room brightened, he took her again, savoring every stroke, every touch. When they were finished after particularly strong and multiple releases and lay sated in one another's arms, the sound of a young boy at the door quickly roused them.

"Mam!" Hunt was pounding on her locked door. "Mam, I'm hungry!"

Tevin sat up, pulling Cantia with him. She looked apprehensively at the door until Tevin silently encouraged her to respond.

"A moment, Hunt," she called out. "Be patient and wait a moment."

"You cannot go to the kitchen," he reminded her with a whisper. "I will go and bring some food to you both."

She nodded. "And do not forget to collect Val."

He sighed heavily. "Madam, would that I have enjoyed my time alone with you, for I fear I shall not be able to survive until our next encounter. The strain will be more than I can bear."

"You will have to unless you can think of a better sleeping arrangement. We do not want an audience."

With a grin, Tevin tossed back the bedding and Cantia stood up, a little unsteadily at first and they both laughed. Her legs were slightly sore from the strenuous morning. But in the soft glow of daylight, Tevin had a full view of her delicious body and he was not disappointed. She was soft, round, and perfect in every way. Watching her heart-shaped bottom cross the room to collect her shift had him licking his lips at the sight of her. His heart was thumping loudly against his ribs, his breathing doing strange things.

Shift in hand, Cantia wandered near the bed in preparation for dressing and he abruptly reached out, taking her by the waist with his enormous hands and shoving his face into her belly. Cantia giggled softly as he nipped at her and kissed her flesh, but her giggles soon turned to moans of pleasure when his hands moved to her buttocks and his mouth began to tease the soft mound of curls between her legs.

"Tevin," her legs were growing weaker and she struggled to stop him. "Not now. Hunt is waiting."

His response was to gently shove her backwards on the bed. Cantia tried to leap up again but his big hands were on her, holding her down as he wedged his head and shoulders between her legs. His tongue was exploring her intimate pink folds and she had not the strength to resist. With her shift shoved into her mouth to bite of her screams, she experienced release after release at his expert tongue.

Twice, Hunt yelled at her from the other side of the door and she breathlessly quieted him. In her lust, she remembered thinking that she was glad he was only five years old and would not wonder why his mother sounded so winded. When Tevin was done with her and she lay satisfied, boneless and limp, he ran his tongue up her belly, to her breasts, and pulled her up to sit by the arms.

"Get up now," he grinned as she fell back over on the bed and he pulled her up again. "Your starving son is waiting and I must go retrieve his meal."

She started to fall over again, laughing when he put his enormous hands on her shoulders to hold her steady. The lavender eyes lolled open, twinkling at him.

"I do not believe that I can stand."

He laughed softly. "You'll have to. I must dress and I cannot do that and hold you upright at the same time."

She wrinkled her nose at him, grinning, and it was his signal to let go and hunt down his clothes. He found his breeches, his boots, and finally his tunic, pulling them on in that order. The entire time, Cantia sat on the bed, nude, and watched him. As he pulled the tunic over his head, he caught her staring at him.

"Sweetheart, get dressed," he urged softly. "I must open the door and I should not like for your son to see you stark naked. He might spread vicious gossip and rumors."

She smiled dreamily, watching him push the copper curls from his eyes. "Why do men fear you so? Since I have known you, I have seen nothing to warrant that reputation. You are one of the sweetest, kindest and gentlest men I have ever met."

He lifted his big shoulders. "With you, I certainly would not want to display any behavior that suggestion destruction or death," he said. "On the field of battle, or with my men, my behavior is… different."

"*How* different?"

He glanced up at her. "Look at me. Do I not look brutal and big? Frightening, even? I assure you, the reputation is well earned and I am proud of it. It has served me well. In fact, my brother was the one who would tell war stories of my skill to any and all who would listen. He said there was no one in heaven or earth who could best me on the field of battle."

"What was your brother's name?"

"Torston."

"You said that he died. When did he die?"

Tevin thought back on his younger, taller, and more volatile brother. He had been a quick wit, a brilliant study, and far too rash. He missed him terribly. "In a skirmish four years ago," he said. "My father had been mortally wounded and when my brother went to aid him, he was cut down as well."

"Oh," Cantia was saddened at the thought. "I'm sorry for you. How old was he?"

"He had seen twenty-five years." He approached the bed, waving his big hands at her. "Cantia, hurry and dress."

She started, as if she had completely forgotten that she needed to put her clothes on, and quickly pulled her shift over her head. The emerald surcoat lay at her feet where Tevin had ripped it from her body and she picked it up, tossed it over a chair, and went to the massive wardrobe against the wall. Opening the doors, the smile suddenly disappeared from her face. Tevin, fussing with the tie of his breeches, noticed she had come to a halt. He glanced over at her, realizing there were tears in her eyes.

He went to her. "What's wrong, sweet?"

She shook her head, blinking away the tears. "'Tis… only that Brac's clothes are still here. I keep forgetting. I must remove them."

Tevin looked at the jumble of garments, tunics and leather breeches and pieces he did not recognize. "You do not have to remove them until you are ready."

She looked at him, the light of surprise in her eyes. "Do you think I am not ready? Do you think I would have carried on with you all night as we did if I was not ready?"

He put his hands on her in a calming gesture. "I did not mean to offend you. I simply meant that you will not be forced to do anything you are not ready to do."

She reached in and began pulling the cluster of clothes out, onto the floor. Hunt yelled at his mother, again, and she shifted from Brac's clothes to her own, pulling a durable broadcloth surcoat on and securing it with a leather girdle.

"Coming, Hunt. Be patient."

Tevin had already walked to the door, his hand on the lock as he watched Cantia cinch up the girdle. She had a deliciously narrow waist, making her breasts appear rounder and larger. His thoughts began to turn lustful again but he fought them. Now was not the time. They had been selfish enough. Still, after a night like the one they had just spent together, he knew his thoughts would be only of her. It would be difficult to deal with his cousin and the situation the man brought with him.

The girdle was finally fastened and she smiled at him, slipping on the small leather slippers that would cover her feet. He smiled in return, feeling weak and warm and giddy. Over the past day, their relationship had deepened and expanded into something he had never known to exist. He couldn't even remember his life before this woman was a part of it and the warmth he felt, the satisfaction, was more than he could describe. It blanketed him, like a warm, enveloping embrace that encompassed his entire being. He felt so very fortunate.

"I shall open the door," he said quietly. "Let the boy see only you and I shall slip out when his attention is on his mother."

She nodded, moving towards the door. He reached out, touching her cheek, as she came near. Then he unlocked the door and pulled it back.

Hunt sat in front of the door with a ball in his hand. George, the dog, lay beside him, gnawing on his paw. Hunt looked up sharply from his toy as the door opened, his face full of impatience at his mother.

"I'm *hungry*," he said firmly. "I want porridge and honey!"

She lifted an eyebrow. "I am not sure I approve of your tone," she reached down and pulled him into the room, making sure to keep his back to Tevin. "Come in here now. I must speak with you."

Tevin, seeing the boy was properly distracted, slipped from the chamber. George wagged his tail at him, doggy eyes the only witness to the viscount being in Lady Cantia's room. With her peripheral vision,

Cantia saw Tevin disappear as she lifted her son up and kissed his face repeatedly.

"Mam!" he shoved against her, wanting to be put down. "I'm *hungry!*"

"I know," she set him down on the floor. "But we have a serious matter to discuss and it cannot wait."

He wasn't particularly interested. "What?"

Cantia sat on the edge of the bed so that she would be closer to his eye level. "The Earl of East Anglia arrived earlier. Did you know that?"

He shrugged, shook his head, and tossed the ball at George. Cantia grasped his arm gently to force him to focus on her.

"The earl is a very important and very busy man," she continued. "Although Rochester is your home, I must ask you to stay in my chamber with me until Lord Tevin tells us that we may leave to go about our business. That means that, for now, you cannot go outside and play. You must stay in here with me. We must…hide. Like when you play a hiding game. We are going to play a game."

He looked at her with his big blue eyes. "Why are we hiding?"

"Because we must not bother the earl. We must be silent and obedient and invisible. Do you know what invisible means?" When he shook his head, she continued. "It means that he must not see us. We must be like a ghost."

Hunt's face lit up. "I want to be a ghost!"

She smiled at him. "Of course you do. He must not see you at all. If you are very good and the earl never sees you, then there shall be a reward waiting for you when he leaves."

His happy face grew happier. "What reward?"

"What would you like?"

"Armor!" he shouted. "I want armor like my da!"

Her smiled faded. His innocent words depressed her so, whether because it once again reminded her of her now-fatherless son or because she imagined him as a grown warrior, she did not know. All she knew was that her son wanted to grow up so fast, to leave her and become a man. She wasn't ready to let him go yet.

"We will discuss it further when the earl leaves," she told him. "But if he sees you at all, no reward. No armor, no anything. Do you understand? This is important, Hunt."

He nodded emphatically. "Good," his mother said. "Now, I believe Lord Tevin is bringing us food. We will wait here for him."

"Do we have to be a ghost for him, too?" Hunt wanted to know.

She shook her head, her gaze drifting to the mussed bedclothes on the floor beside the bed. Just to look at them gave her a shudder of pleasure.

"Nay," she said, hoping she didn't sound as breathless as she felt. "We will not hide from him."

CHAPTER EIGHT

GEOFFREY DE GAEL, by all appearances, was a sane, well-behaved individual. He was the result of hundreds of years of careful breeding, fine bloodlines enhanced by a royal insertion here and there. Blond, with the same obsidian-dark eyes that Tevin possessed, he was three years younger than his stronger, larger cousin and a world of difference apart in character.

Women gravitated towards Geoffrey with frightening ease. It made his lustful games so easy to come by. Somewhere in his normal-looking head, something was terribly wrong and he literally knew no difference between right and wrong. He only knew what he wanted, what he lusted for, and he took it. The object could be land, a holding, a woman, a horse... anything that caught his eye. Not only was he unpredictable, he was also dangerous. He would draw a sword in the blink of an eye, kill, and hold no regrets. And there was never anyone to stop him.

That was why Tevin was so on edge. His cousin had always held a great liking for him, which made him somewhat immune to his cousin's madness, but everyone else did not possess the luxury of that immunity. Even now, he had paused in his quest to the kitchen long enough to make sure his sister was prepared to move up to Cantia's bower. On the third floor of the keep directly below Cantia's chamber, Val was ready and waiting. An alert from her brother almost an hour before saw her preparations complete. When Tevin finally stuck his head into the room and told her to move upstairs, she did so quickly. She, almost more than her brother, was aware of her what her cousin was capable of. She'd been avoiding it most of her life, so these moments were particularly tense.

The entire keep was in an uproar over the earl's visit. He had brought a huge retinue with him; knights, soldiers, servants and a couple of well-dressed women that served as both mistress and whipping post. They traveled with him wherever he went. He entered Rochester with the air of a conquering hero, his haughty gaze surveying all before him. The man knew his power and he made sure all around him knew, too.

But the earl's interest in the bailey soon wore thin and he made way to the massive stone structure that was the heart of the castle. Just as Geoff set foot in the keep, Tevin descended the last step from the upper floors and met him nearly at the door. The young earl smiled amiably at his cousin, clapping him on his massive shoulder.

"Well, cousin," he said, glancing about. "I can see you have this place well in hand. And a massive place it is."

Tevin nodded faintly. "I wish you'd sent word that you were arriving early," he said, trying to steer Geoff into the hall. "I would have been more aptly prepared for your visit. As it is, we're scrambling to show preparations worthy of your presence."

Geoff waved him off. "It is suitable," he said, still looking around. "Where is the steward?"

"Penden?" Tevin snorted. "With the son dead, the father has tumbled into madness. We had to lock him in the vault for his own safety. He was trying to kill himself."

Geoff lifted a dark-blond eyebrow. "Is that so?" he peered more closely at his surroundings. "Perhaps I should confiscate the property if the steward has lost his capacity to govern. Rochester is too strategic to leave in the hands of a madman."

A warning bell went off in Tevin's mind. "Rochester will not weaken any time soon as long as I am here," he put a hand on his cousin's shoulder and directed the man into the hall. "And I believe Penden's madness is temporary. His son was everything to him. He'll recover."

Geoff eyed his cousin. "Mayhap. It couldn't be that you want this place for your own, could it?"

Tevin lifted an eyebrow, an amused expression on his face. "It would not do me any good even if I did. You would simply take it from me."

Geoff laughed and slapped him on the arm. Fresh rushes, a warm fire and a hastily-assembled meal await them in the great hall. Cheese, great loaves of bread, and the last of the winter store of fruit graced the larger of the tables that lined the enormous hall. There was even a huge tray of warmed-over mutton. Geoff sashayed in the direction of the table, his gaze missing nothing; a servant, the stone used to build the hearth, the quality of the food. He was if nothing else, observant, which would make concealing Cantia, Hunt and Val something of a challenge.

Tevin knew this. He watched the man like a hawk as he collected a chalice of mead and propped his buttocks on the edge of the table. Geoff had a strangely smug expression on his face and Tevin could not figure out why, but he knew he didn't like it. There was something odd in his manner, even more than the usually oddness, and something that would undoubtedly show itself when the time came. Tevin wasn't at all thrilled with that thought. He tried to prepare himself.

The rest of his entourage trickled in from the bailey; a couple of good knights that Tevin knew, a few soldiers that took station by the door, and the two well-dressed women. And then, at the very end, came a face that Tevin was very familiar with. The small figure was being pushed on a chair that was fashioned with two very large wheels. They could hear the big iron and wooden wheels creaking as they rolled across the entrance to the keep, being lifted up over the steps by two soldiers. Tevin hadn't paid much attention to Geoff's followers other than the usual gang, which was why the sight caught him completely off guard.

Geoff was up off the table, slapping his cousin yet again when he saw the expression on Tevin's face. "See what I brought you? A present!"

Tevin ignored the man. Everything around him ceased to exist as he practically ran to the entrance, falling on his knees beside the wheeled chair. He collected the tiny hands that were outstretched to him.

"Bella," he breathed. "You're here, sweetheart. How...?"

Arabel Berthilde Solveig du Reims threw her frail arms around her father's neck. She was a little thing, no larger than a child of perhaps ten or eleven years of age, but she had a most unique and remarkable beauty. With her father's nearly-black eyes and cascades of blond hair, she was a striking picture, like a delicate little bird that needed love and protection. And her father, the powerful viscount, was extremely, if not obsessively, protective of her.

That was why his momentary surprise at her arrival suddenly transformed into something very angry and murderous. Oddly, he wasn't angry because he feared for his daughter's virtue against the lecherous earl. As immoral as Geoff was, he wasn't stupid. He knew that any suggestive move against Arabel would result in his death. Tevin was angry because, quite simply, he feared for his daughter's safety against external forces. He feared the world around her. And a trip from Thunderbey Castle to Rochester was wrought with peril for his only child.

"Father," Arabel squeezed her father's neck as tightly as her weak arms would allow. "Cousin Geoff came to Thunderbey to seek counsel with you. But I told him you were still at Rochester so he offered to bring me along. It's been so long since I have seen you and I missed you terribly. Wasn't that kind of him?"

A very simple explanation in a matter of seconds. Leave it to Arabel to know what her father was feeling, the excessive protectiveness and concern. Tevin tried hard to control his anger in the wake of her lovely, smiling face. He put his massive hands on her cheeks.

"Of course I am pleased to see you," he kissed her fair face. "But transporting you over miles of open road does not, in fact, please me. I left you at Thunderbey for a reason. You were safe there."

Arabel's features softened. "But I was alone. I wanted to come and see you. Why have you not come home yet?"

Tevin gazed into the eyes of his beloved daughter, suddenly feeling like a horrible man. He had not come home because he had wanted to stay near Cantia, pure and simple. It was wrong of him and in that instant he saw just how wrong it was. It had only been him and Arabel for many years. He loved her more than a man should probably love his child. He had left her alone while he went off to fight Geoff's war and then stayed because he was more interested in something at Rochester.

Geoff came up behind him as Tevin thought of a plausible answer to his absence and slapped him on the shoulder. "Are you pleased, then? How could I leave your lovely young lady at home when she so desperately wanted to see her father?"

Tevin cocked an eyebrow, rising to his formidable height as he faced his cousin. His stiff body language was evident. "You should not have risked her on the journey here," he said in a low voice. "She is very delicate. Traveling does not agree with her."

Geoff waved him off. "We brought her maid servants and she was protected by ten men. She was well taken care of in either case. What are you worried about?"

"I left her at Thunderbey to protect her, Geoff. You had no right to bring her to Rochester and put her in peril as you have. This entire area is under threat. You know this. God only knows what could have happened to your party on the open road."

Geoff simply shook his head, a smirk on his face. "You worry like an old woman. Arabel needs the adventure of travel. You keep her caged like an animal."

Tevin nearly took his head off for that remark. He was rather pleased that he had held himself in check. In lieu of saying something that could very well anger his cousin, he simply turned his back on him and scooped his daughter up into his arms. She beamed at him brightly.

"It's so good to see you, Father," she laid her head on his massive shoulder. "I have missed you very much."

"And I have missed you, sweetheart. What an unexpected treat this day has brought."

"Will you show me Rochester now?"

He gave her a little toss, listening to her squeals of delight. "Of course I'll show you this behemoth of a fortress if it pleases you. You've come all this way and I'll not disappoint."

"Are you angry with me?"

"Of course not."

Behind them, Geoff snorted. "What about me? What thanks do I get for reuniting father and daughter?"

Tevin cast him a long glance, letting him know that he was still mightily displeased. But he was, in fact, very glad to see his daughter. He could feel himself relenting. "My thanks for bringing my daughter safely to Rochester, Geoff."

Geoff grinned and winked boldly at Arabel. She just smiled, her spindly arms wound around her father's neck as if to never let him go. The two older maids that had tended Arabel since birth brought along the chair and followed close behind as Tevin took her on a brief tour around the hall.

"So now you see the great hall of Rochester," he looked up to the soaring ceilings and the two massive tapestries that hung near the gallery of lancet windows above. "This place is like a damn cathedral."

"Father!"

"Sorry." He pursed his lips contritely. Arabel was quite correct in reprimanding him for his harsh language. "Outside to the left are the kitchens and a massive kitchen yard. And above us are two more levels with chambers."

"Where is Val, Father?"

Tevin's brightened mood dimmed. He knew Geoff was somewhere near them, wondering if he had heard the question. Although his cousin knew that Val fought as a knight, he'd not said anything about her since his arrival and Tevin did not want to bring up the subject. He squeezed his daughter gently.

"She is not here at the moment." He continued back around the hall and headed for the entrance with the intention of going outside, but Arabel stopped him.

"Nay, Father. I want to see the chambers."

"Upstairs?"

"Upstairs."

Tevin dared to look around, then, to see if Geoff was still around. His cousin was seated on the table near the hearth, tearing apart of piece of bread and chatting with one of his knights. He was far enough out of earshot that Tevin felt he could speak with confidence.

"Do you remember what I told you about Cousin Geoff and Val?" he asked quietly.

Arabel wasn't stupid. She nodded after a moment's contemplation. "Aye," she said hesitantly.

"Then I would ask you not to mention Val when he is about. He likes her, too much, and we do not want to be put in a bad position because Cousin Geoff cannot control himself. Do you understand?"

Again, she nodded. "I am sorry, Father. I did not mean to say anything wrong."

He kissed the tip of her nose. "You did not, sweetheart. But we must keep Cousin Geoff away from Val."

"I know, Father. Where is she?"

"Upstairs. You must keep this secret. Can you do this?"

She nodded eagerly. "I would see her, please!"

He could not refuse her. Val and Arabel shared a very special bond. Val had been practically the only mother Arabel had ever known. Moreover, he would have the privilege of introducing his daughter to Cantia, something he realized that he was very excited to do. He had never faced a moment like this before, introducing his daughter to someone who was very quickly coming to mean a great deal to him. But along with the excitement came uncertainty. He hoped they would like one another. His nerves suddenly began to get the better of him, excitement and anxiety doing strange things to his stomach.

Instructing the old serving women to retreat to the solar to wait for them, Tevin took his daughter up the very narrow, winding staircase. The third floor was quiet and empty as he mounted the even smaller flight of steps for the fourth floor. By the time he had reached the landing, he had already bumped his head trying to keep Arabel from scraping the walls. Softly, he rapped on the first door to his right.

"'Tis me," he called softly.

The door thumped, jerked, and flew open. The first face he saw was Hunt's. The little boy growled at him like a bear. "Where's my *food*?"

Tevin's face fell. In the surprise of Arabel's appearance, he realized that he had completely forgotten about procuring a morning meal. Cantia came up behind Hunt, putting her hand over his mouth.

"Forgive him, my lord," she said, her inquisitive gaze moving between Tevin and the young lady in his arms. "His mood is foul when he's not eaten."

Val, who had been gazing from the window, turned to her brother and realized with shock that Arabel was in his arms. She gasped and flew across the room.

"Bella!" she cried softly, throwing her arms around both the girl and Tevin. "What are you doing here, sweetling? How did you get here?"

Arabel transferred her weak arms from her father to her aunt. Val took her from Tevin, cradling her sweetly and hugging her.

"I came with Cousin Geoff," Arabel said. "We had an adventure of travel!"

Val had nearly the same reaction as her brother. When her bliss at Arabel's sudden appearance faded, she was very concerned for the young woman's safety. She looked at her brother with accusing eyes.

"He brought her here with the entire region under threat of battle?" she said. "Is he mad?"

Tevin put up a quelling hand. "I have already had words with him, Val. What's done is done. Suffice it to say that Arabel is here, safely, and we are very grateful."

Off to his left stood Cantia and Hunt. Cantia's hands were on her son's shoulders as she watched the tender reunion. It had only taken her a matter of seconds to realize who the young lady was once the conversation began and she smiled gently as she watched Val waltz across the room with the tiny young woman in her arms. She looked over at Tevin.

"She has her father's comely looks, my lord," she said softly.

Tevin gazed over at her, his expression softening. Memories from the previous night flooded his mind, making him feel weak and giddy. He wanted very badly to reach out and touch her but dare not attempt it. In time, it would be acceptable for him to do so, but for the moment, there was still propriety to be observed. Especially in front of Arabel and Hunt.

"My thanks, my lady," he replied quietly. Then he winked at her. "If you do not mind a visitor, I shall retreat to the kitchens and bring Hunt his meal before he tears me limb from limb. I do not like the look in his eye."

Cantia nodded graciously. As she and Tevin gazed sweetly at each other, Hunt wriggled from his mother's grasp and made his way over to Val and Arabel. They were gazing out of the lancet window as Val pointed out the cathedral of Rochester in the distance. They were also speaking of Arabel's exciting trip from Thunderbey. The little boy stood next to them, eyeing the newcomer.

"What isth your name?" he tugged on Arabel's sleeve.

Arabel arched her neck back to look at him, made more comfortable when Val turned around. They both smiled down at the wide-eyed young lad.

"Arabel," she said in her very soft, very sweet voice. "What is your name?"

"Hunt." The boy sized her up and down. When he apparently decided she was worth talking to, he held out a hand containing a ball. "Do you want to play with me?"

Arabel's face positively lit up. "I do!" she pointed to the bed, indicating for her aunt to set her down. "Will you throw it to me?"

Hunt hadn't noticed anything wrong with the girl yet. He tossed her the ball before Val had set her down completely and it hit her in the forehead. While Cantia gasped, Arabel laughed and rubbed her head. Then she picked up the ball, tried to toss it, and it ended up on the floor. Hunt picked it up, threw it again, and hit her in the chest.

Tevin and Val watched the exchange carefully. Arabel could barely use her arms but she was trying with all her heart. And she was loving it. Hunt, surprisingly, didn't seem to mind that she couldn't toss the ball. He continued to pick it up off the floor, off the end of the bed, and toss it back to her. She couldn't catch it so it would end up in her lap. Cantia, fingers folded and at her mouth as if she were praying, watched the activity with some concern.

"Hunt," she admonished softly. "Young ladies do not catch balls. Perhaps you should play something that is more suited to the lady's tastes."

Tevin smiled faintly, approaching the bed. "I think that ball catching does run to her taste, does it not?" He put his hand on his daughter's blond head, smiling down at her as she beamed. "Arabel, I would like you to meet Master Hunt Penden and his mother, the Lady Cantia. They live at Rochester."

Arabel's big dark eyes focused on Cantia. They were wide and intelligent and Cantia smiled timidly. "It is a pleasure to know you, my lady," she said. "Welcome to Rochester."

Arabel smiled prettily, her gaze appraising and curious. "Thank you," she said. "Are you the lady of the house?"

"I am."

She looked at her father. "She is beautiful," she said. "Is she hiding here with Val, too?"

Tevin nodded, trying not to appear too grim. "Another secret you must keep."

Arabel looked back at Cantia. "But where is your husband? Surely he will protect you from Cousin Geoff."

Cantia's smile faded. It was the first time since Brac's death that she had come into contact with someone who hadn't known what had happened. She had to explain his absence, which strangely didn't upset her as she thought it might. "He was killed in a skirmish several weeks ago," she told her.

"Oh," Arabel looked rather regretful that she had asked. "I am sorry, my lady."

Cantia forced a smile, wanting off the subject of Brac. Though there was no longer any horrendous pain associated with the memory, it was still an uncomfortable one. She had done a great deal of healing and was unwilling to pick at the scabs that were healing over the wounds.

"If you would like to play something else with Hunt, he has a good many toys we can put to use," she suggested. "Perhaps your father will go into his chamber and collect some things."

Tevin had been watching the exchange between his daughter and Cantia with great interest. He was pleased to see that the initial meeting had gone well and he was more than pleased to see how Cantia had handled the question of Brac. In a strange, selfish reaction, it gave him hope that everything they had been feeling for each other, everything that had happened over the past day or so, was not simply a convenience or a mistake. It was real. He wanted it very much to be real. He took a step in Cantia's direction.

"After I play the part of the serving wench and bring Master Hunt his meal," he mussed the boy's blond hair, "then perhaps I shall have time to collect some things for you both to play with."

Hunt started to growl again but Cantia slapped her hand over his mouth. Tevin's gaze moved from Val to his daughter and finally Cantia before quitting the room. When the door closed softly, Cantia went to lock it as Hunt picked up the ball again.

"Catch!" he cried.

The ball hit Arabel squarely in the nose and drew blood.

03

IT HAD BEEN as he feared. Though Tevin had spent the remainder of the day with Geoff, his mind was not on his cousin's aimless chatter. As they had toured the stores, the stables, the yards, and some of the surrounding countryside, Tevin discussed the strategic importance of Rochester when what he really wanted to do was talk about Cantia's unearthly beauty. The sun began to wane in the west and they found themselves back in the solar with a hearty blaze and a bottle of Port between them, but still, all Tevin could think of was Cantia. Geoff was running on about the weak market for the wheat his serfs had harvested while Tevin struggled to focus on something other than lavender eyes. Finally, he'd had enough of the constant chatter and his own lack of focus. He wanted to get back to Cantia and the only way to do that was to shut his cousin up.

"Geoff," Tevin finally broke into the prattle. "Wheat and weather are not the true reason you have come. I received your missive a few days ago. Can we delve into the meat of this?"

Geoff took a long drink of the ruby Port. Behind him, the fire crackled softly as the room darkened with sunset. He savored the flavor, smacking his lips and studying the pewter chalice. "What is it you wish to know?"

Tevin raised an impatient eyebrow. "I suppose I wish to know what plans you have. This land is in turmoil. We have held hope for months that Matilda's invasion from Normandy was imminent, a hope fed by both you and her brother, the Earl of Gloucester. We have prepared for this moment. What has happened that we are now in support Stephen of Blois?"

Geoff was casual, even cavalier. "I do not need to explain my reason to you. You must have faith that I know best."

"Perhaps you do not need to explain it to me, but I am asking just the same. I have fifteen hundred men committed to your cause and I would like to know why I will now ask my men to fight for someone we have sworn to destroy."

"Do you not trust my decisions?"

"I have been ever supportive of your causes, Geoff. But I still wish to know why the change of heart. Please."

It was the softly spoken supplication that got him. Geoff went from nonchalant to animated in the blink of an eye. He slammed his chalice to the table and stood up, running his fingers through his blond hair.

Tevin watched him closely, with his usual unruffled attitude. He was genuinely curious to know the man's reasons and he was equally eager to be done with this conversation.

"Damnable Gloucester," he finally muttered. "It is his fault."

"Why?"

Geoff whirled on him, his expression taut. "Because we agreed to split Oxfordshire when Matilda returned to assume her right, but I have been told by others that Gloucester has already been in discussions with Lord Wallingford for the same purpose. Imagine, Wallingford instead of me! He is not even an earl, but a lesser noble of an old Saxon line, long bereft of money or dignity. The very idea is an insult. Therefore, I decided not to support Matilda and her treacherous brother, Earl Gloucester, if that is all of the loyalty they can show me."

Tevin watched him rave like a child. Petulant as it was, it explained a lot. No strong sense of country or unity destroyed Geoff. It was simply the deeds of a nobleman playing a political game. Tevin didn't know whether to slap him or laugh at him.

"It could not be because Wallingford and Gloucester are cousins, could it?" he said with more control than he felt. "Gloucester had no familial loyalty to you."

Geoff's dark eyes widened. "Nor I to him. Therefore, we fight for the true king. We fight for Stephen."

"Matilda has more of a claim to the throne than Stephen."

"Say that again and I shall throw you in the vault!"

Tevin did laugh, then. He couldn't help it. He shook his head and stood up, weary of the temper tantrum and eager to see Cantia. "The evening meal should be coming shortly," he said. "Why do you not retreat to your chamber and rest? Bathe if it pleases you. We'll speak more of this at sup."

As quickly as Geoff flamed, that was as quickly as he doused. The rigidity went out of his posture and he returned his attention to the fine wine. With long movements, he poured himself another measure. "I am not hungry," he grumbled, mouth to the rim of the cup.

Tevin was already moving for the door. "Then do not eat. But at least come and sit and enjoy the conversation."

Geoff took a long drink. "Where is Val?" he asked casually. "I've not seen her all day."

Tevin paused. By Geoff's tone, he knew the man had been waiting for the right moment to ask that question. And by his expression, Tevin was further convinced that he knew exactly what Tevin was up to. He was hiding her. Geoff was, if nothing else, intelligent. But Tevin stood his ground.

"She is occupied," he said evenly. "She likes to ride patrol, you know."

"Where is Arabel?"

"With her women, upstairs. She is exhausted from being dragged halfway across England."

"Will she join us for sup?"

"If that is your wish."

Geoff simply lifted an eyebrow and Tevin left the solar without another word. He didn't dare mount the stairs to the chambers upstairs, suspecting that Geoff would be following his movements. So he went into the great hall and exited out into the kitchens, thinking to throw his mistrustful cousin off the trail. He quit the kitchen yards and found himself marching through the stables on his way to the knight's quarters.

All the while, he knew his cousin's eyes were upon him, mentally if not physically. Geoff was suspicious of everyone and everything. By the time Tevin reached the knight's quarters, he was ready for a stiff drink himself. Something about Geoff's presence always put him on edge. He would take a measure of ale with his men before retreating upstairs, giving enough time for Geoff to forget about their conversation and, hopefully, Val.

He could not have known how wrong he was. Geoff did not follow Tevin any further than the solar entry. He had wandered to the door, watching his powerful cousin walk across the great hall and out of the door leading to the kitchens. But that was the extent of it. He knew the man was going to see to his men to repeat his conversation with the earl for their benefit. It was normal enough. The men had to know why they now supported the usurper and Geoff wasn't suspicious of Tevin in that aspect. But Tevin had been right in one way. Geoff's attention was indeed on Val and her whereabouts.

To his left was the staircase leading to the upper chambers. His dark eyes glittered, an inkling of an idea taking hold. Tevin was clever, but not too terribly. With his brutish cousin outside, Geoff was free to explore the keep and perhaps find Val. Aye, he knew that Tevin hid her from him. He'd always known.

He took the steps.

CHAPTER NINE

WHEN HUNT TIRED of the board game that Tevin had brought them to play with, Val took over and played against her niece. As the afternoon moved into night, Cantia sat with some needlework that had been a project for quite some time, alternately watching her delicate work and watching Val play against Arabel. As dusk darkened, she gave up on the needlework completely and watched the game instead.

Arabel was a brilliant girl. She was quite adept at game strategies, winning the last two games from her aunt. She was also quite humorous and Val laughed freely with her. Cantia could see a great deal of Tevin in the girl, but she could also see features and mannerisms that did not remind her of the girl's powerful father. Arabel had an upturned nose and a big dimple in her chin, something that did not ring of Tevin. Thoughts then turned to the girl's mother, a Germanic noblewoman who had abandoned her at birth.

Tevin said he would find the woman no matter what. He would discover if she was alive or dead. Were she dead, there would be no troubles and Cantia knew she would gladly marry Tevin. But if the woman lived, then the future for them would not be entirely honorable for Cantia knew, without a doubt, that she would stay with Tevin forever. She did not relish being branded a mistress. But she considered the reward well worth the risk.

The sun was nearly set when a soft knock came at the door. Hunt, nearest to the panel, thought it was Tevin bringing the evening meal and, being the starving child that he was, threw open the door before his mother could stop him. Cantia saw a strange man standing in the doorway and heard Val gasp. With that startled sound, she knew it could not be good.

The man had Tevin's black eyes. His gaze found Hunt first and then Val as she quickly stood up. He smiled broadly at his strawberry-haired cousin and was about to speak to her when Cantia also stood up and his focus was abruptly diverted. The moment he laid eyes on her, the mood of the room exploded. They could all feel it.

"Val," he stepped into the room, speaking to his cousin though his eyes were on Cantia. "Your brother said you were occupied. I had no idea he meant in ladylike pursuits. And who is your glorious companion?"

Cantia looked at Val, who had a rather sickened look on her face. "Greetings, Geoff," she said with more courage than she felt. "This is the Lady Cantia Penden. My lady, this is the Earl of East Anglia, my cousin."

Geoff was on Cantia in three strides. Reaching out, he took her reluctant hand and pulled it to his lips for a gentle kiss. "My lady," he said in a sultry voice. "'Tis a pleasure. I had no idea the Steward had such a lovely daughter."

Cantia wanted to shrink away from the man. She didn't like anything about him from the instant their eyes met. "I am not his daughter, my lord," she said. "I am Brac Penden's wife and this is my son, Hunt."

Geoff didn't even look at the sandy-haired boy, now standing beside him and watching him closely. His gaze was fixated on Cantia. "I heard of your husband's death, my lady," he said, still holding her hand to his mouth. "Please accept my sympathies. It was a terrible tragedy to lose him."

Cantia struggled not to yank her hand away. "Aye, it was."

Geoff's eyes were invading her, probing every inch of her face. "Surely so young and lovely a lady will not be widowed for long. That should bring you comfort."

It was a horrible thing to say. Cantia pulled her hand from his grasp, taking a discreet step away from him with Hunt still in her grip. She was having difficulty forming a reply to his crass statement when

Val was suddenly beside her, making an obvious attempt to distract her cousin.

"I was injured in a skirmish a few weeks ago," she said, hoping to capture his lustful attention away from Cantia. "Since then, I've spent most of my time in ladylike pursuits. Tevin thinks it's wonderful but I've found it boring. I'd much rather have a sword in my hand."

Geoff's attention was diverted from Cantia and his licentious expression morphed into one of displeasure as he focused on his cousin. His emotions were easy to read. "He told me you were out on patrol."

Val kept her steady expression. "I was."

Geoff just stared at her, knowing that wasn't the truth. But no matter, he'd found what he had sought and then some. After a moment, he snorted as if he found something humorous. His gaze moved from Val to Arabel, down to Hunt and finally back to Cantia. There it remained as if nailed into place.

"My lady," he held out his hand to her. "I have so wanted a tour of this magnificent place. Who better to grant my wish but you?"

Cantia looked at the outstretched hand with something of dread. After everything she had heard about the earl, she did not want to go with him in the least. In fact, it was an effort not to refuse and run for her life. She glanced at Val, who gazed back at her with a mixture of fear and sympathy. There was nothing she could do. There was nothing anyone could do. Geoff would not be refused.

"As you wish, my lord."

Cantia moved towards the door but did not take the earl's outstretched hand. She turned fully to Val as she progressed across the floor.

"You will accompany us, my lady," she said firmly, hoping her tone would infer to the earl that she would accept nothing less. "Lady Arabel, would you please mind Hunt while we are away? He will be no trouble."

Arabel's dark eyes were wide. "Mind... mind him?"

Cantia forced a smile at the girl. "He is a good boy. I believe you will do a fine job."

Arabel had never been trusted with any such task in her life. The situation in her life was always reversed. Everyone was charged with minding *her*. Cantia could read her naked fear, but in the next moment, there was a good deal of pleasure that someone would trust her with such a task. It was a responsibility she had never been given and she was shocked, and also grateful, for the opportunity. It made her feel grown-up.

"Aye, Lady Penden," she looked at Hunt. "I will mind him."

Cantia nodded confidently, holding out her hand to Val in the meanwhile. "Come along, my lady," she decided the best way to deal with Geoff was to show that she was not afraid of him. Truthfully, she hadn't a better plan at the moment. "I will give you a great tour also. You have been caged up inside the keep for so long that perhaps you've not imagined what more there is to this place."

Val took Cantia's hand and the women quit the room in a protective huddle. Geoff stood there a moment, not at all happy that his private little tour with Lady Penden was growing into something of a group activity. He did not give the children in the room a second glance as he followed behind the ladies and slammed the door. Hunt raced to the door and bolted it, turning to look at Arabel, sitting on the larger of the two beds in the room. The young lady's eyes were wide as the children stared at one another.

"Hunt," she said. "You know every inch of this place, do you not?"

Hunt nodded. "Where isth that man taking my mother?"

Arabel didn't know. She was too young to truly fathom what the man was capable of. All she knew was what her father had told her and that was only in the simplest of terms. But they were not good terms.

"You must go and find my father," Arabel insisted quietly. "Tell him that Cousin Geoff has taken your mother and Val. He will want to know."

"Why?"

"Because he will!" she snapped irritably, then cooled. "Please, Hunt. This is important."

Hunt pursed his little lips in thought. After a moment, he unbolted the door and peered into the dark landing beyond as if to make sure no one stood between him and his mission. Quietly, he slipped from the door and the big blond dog rose from his place in the corner, stretched, and followed. The door shut softly, leaving Arabel alone in the strange room.

As young as she was, her apprehension was quite adult.

○○

UNDER THE PRETENSE of introducing Geoff to Rochester, Cantia was really on the hunt for Tevin.

Her plan was to take Geoff to the living levels, not the private chambers. She thought that any introduction to a bedchamber, even for show, would put wicked ideas in his head and that was the last thing she wanted to do. Furthermore, she wanted to stay in public areas where servants and soldiers were about. And, she hoped, Tevin.

Cantia and Val still held on to one another as they descended the steps into the entry hall. Cantia chatted non-stop about the history of Rochester Castle, how there had been a castle since ancient times on the site, and how the current stone fortress was built by the Bishop of Rochester almost sixty years prior. Then the castle was lost to the House of de Gael twenty years later in a change of political winds and had been established with a military steward to protect both the town and the river crossing. Brac Penden's grandfather had been that steward those years ago, which had then passed on to Charles. It would have gone to Brac had the man survived the skirmish. Now, Hunt was the next in line.

Geoff listened with veiled patience to the history lesson. He knew all of it, better than Cantia did. He walked slightly behind the women, observing Cantia with glittering eyes. He noted the delicious sway of her backside, the way her lustrous hair caught the light. And he was particularly entranced by the lavender eyes and the soft, sensual way in which she spoke. He could have listened to her all day. In fact, he suspected he wasn't the only one interested in the woman's charms and began to speculate that his cousin had the woman shut up simply to keep her to himself. Tevin didn't keep mistresses, nor was he known to show particular interest in women, but Lady Penden's aura would be enough to seduce any man.

"And you, my lady," he broke into her prattle by gently grabbing her by the arm. "I would like to hear about you now. Tell me of your family."

Cantia struggled not to recoil from his grip on her arm. She had been so involved in her conversation, and in Val's presence, that his gesture startled her.

"But we were speaking of Rochester, my lord," she said. "I am of no consequence. The Penden line is far more interesting."

He ignored her statement. "Where were you born?"

She didn't like the look in his black eyes and a sigh of reluctance escaped her lips. But she answered. "Darland. 'Tis south of Rochester a few miles."

"And your family name?"

"Du Bexley. My father was descended from an old Saxon line, nobility that dates back hundreds of years."

"Is your father still alive?"

"Nay, my lord."

"Any brothers? Sisters?"

"Nay, my lord. Just me."

Geoff's dark eyes glittered. He seemed to be enjoying the interrogation. "Val," he said to his cousin, not taking his eyes off Cantia. "Go and procure us some refreshment. Lady Cantia and I will be in the solar."

Val's eyes widened. "But...."

"Go, now. I command it."

Val watched Cantia as her cousin held out his elbow to her. Her last glimpse of the pair was as they disappeared into the solar with Cantia's reluctant hand on Geoff's arm.

Val knew from experience that the only person who could help

Cantia was Tevin. He was the only man who had ever been remotely able to control their erratic cousin. In fact, she shuddered to think how her brother was going to react when he found out Geoff had gone on the hunt and discovered the trove of ladies. More than that, Tevin's feelings for Cantia were bound to unbalance the normally balanced man. Where Tevin had always dealt patiently with Geoff in the past, the event of emotion could see that drastically changed.

But he had to know. She was almost panicked to tell him. Just as she turned for the great hall with the intention of crossing through the kitchens and into the bailey, the entry door suddenly flew open and smashed back on its hinges. Val started as splinters of wood from the damaged door rained into the air. But even before she looked, she knew that Tevin had arrived.

Val barely had time to turn around as Tevin stormed into the entry and straight at her. The expression on his face was nothing short of murderous.

"Where did he take her?" he growled.

Val pointed towards the solar, grabbing her brother's arm as he shoved past her. Somewhere behind Tevin, she saw Hunt and the big yellow dog. The child's eyes were wide with fear and Val correctly surmised that somehow, Hunt must have gone running for Tevin the moment his mother had left the room.

"Tevin, wait," she hissed. "You must calm yourself. No harm has been done yet. Cantia is fine. There is no need for violence."

Tevin glared at her, his nostrils flaring. Val stared back at him. Having known the man her entire life, she knew what he was capable of. He had two distinct personalities; the calm façade that most saw, and the battle-mode warrior who was sometimes more animal than man. What she saw before her was the animal and she knew she had to soothe the beast or there would be blood at Rochester this night.

"Tevin," she shook him, attempting to snap him out of his rage. "Cantia is fine, do you hear me? He has not harmed her. And you must maintain your calm above all else. If Geoff suspects you have interest in

Cantia, it will create more of a situation. He'll see it as a competition. You *know* this."

His nostrils flared again, his obsidian eyes as black as night. "There will be no competition. I will kill him first."

He started to move past her again but she dug her heels in. It was like trying to stop a raging bull. "Tevin," she snapped softly. "Of course there is no competition. But listen to me, please. You must attend to this with calm and stay rational. Get through this situation with tact and then send Cantia away immediately. You cannot allow your relationship with Geoff to sour over her, for there is too much at stake."

"Aye, there is too much at stake. *She* is at stake."

Val grabbed his face, something she would have never normally done. But it was imperative that he focus on her and understand. "Nay, brother," she shook her head slowly. "Everything is at stake. Geoff controls everything. And you must be calm, for this situation is far bigger than Geoff having discovered your lady."

He was looking at her, though not entirely calm. "What do you mean?"

She smiled weakly. "Think about it for a moment. He has always been competitive with you. He has also always been threatened by you. He loves you and envies you at the same time. What do you think he will do if he suspects you are interested in Cantia and hid her away for your own purposes?"

He glared at her unsteadily. "I've no time for games, Val. Tell me what you mean."

She lifted an eyebrow. "He is unmarried, Tevin. If he thinks you are intent to claim her, he can take the competition further than you can. He can marry her and do not believe for one moment that he will not simply to emerge the victor against you."

Some of the color left Tevin's face then. He stared at his sister a long moment before finally wiping a massive hand over his face, struggling for composure. "Dear God," he breathed. "You are correct. You are absolutely correct. And he would do it, just to spite me."

Val nodded, relieved he was coming to understand. "He loves you, but he loves himself more. He would marry the widow and see nothing but good-natured victory in it. He would laugh at you the rest of his life for it."

Thankfully, Tevin was calming. But Val could see that his big hands were shaking with the internal struggle he was feeling. She gripped his hands tightly.

"Listen to me," she whispered. "You distract Geoff and I will remove Cantia. Tell him… tell him she is still in mourning and that it is improper for her to socialize. Then I will excuse the two of us and take her someplace where he cannot find her. I'll take her out of Rochester this night."

He looked at her, considering her words, knowing she was thinking more clearly than he was. In fact, he was so shaken he could hardly think. "That is more than likely the necessary answer."

"Of course it is."

He took a deep breath, laboring to relax. "Cantia mentioned the manor house in Darland as somewhere she and Hunt could stay until this was over. Perhaps you should take her there."

"We shall leave tonight."

As much as Tevin did not want Cantia away from him, he knew it was for the best. With Geoff's discovery of her, the situation was morbidly dangerous on many levels.

"Take Simon with you," he said quietly. "Get away from here as quickly and as quietly as you can. I shall come when I am able."

"You'd better not. He'll follow you if he thinks a game is afoot."

A flicker of pain ripped across his expression, just as quickly gone. But Val saw it.

"What is the matter?"

He averted his gaze, wiping the sweat from his brow as he looked anywhere other than his sister's probing eyes. "Nothing."

"I know you, brother. Why did you look so when I told you not to come?"

He sighed, his black eyes moving in the direction of the warm light emitting from the solar. He could hear soft voices inside, Cantia's voice, and he took another deep breath, struggling for calm.

"Cantia," he began, then shut his mouth. When he opened it to speak again, his tone was barely a whisper. "When I told you earlier that I did not know what I was feeling for her, I know now."

Val suspected she knew the answer before she even asked. "And what is that?"

"I fear… I fear that she has my heart, Val. More than that, she has all of me."

"You love her, then?"

"I must. I cannot explain what else I am feeling."

"Does she know?"

He shrugged those massive shoulders. "I've not told her if that's what you mean. But I… I have demonstrated my feelings."

"What do you mean?"

"I have bedded her."

Val tried not to appear shocked. But it was too much. "She just lost her husband, Tevin," she hissed. "How could you…?"

He could hear the concern, the pain, in his sister's tone and he put up a hand to silence her. "I did not force her. It was the most natural of things, as if we were always meant to be. It was the most amazing experience of my life, Val. Do not diminish it with your judgment."

She eyed him, swallowing what was left of her admonishment. She had never heard such emotion from his lips and a hand came up to gently slap him on the side of the head. "I do not judge, brother," she said quietly. "But I am concerned for the both of you. This is a delicate situation."

He gave her a wry expression. "You are telling me something I already know, all too well."

They could hear more voices in the solar. They even caught a glimpse of Cantia as she walked past the doorway, apparently showing Geoff something on the wall above her head. Tevin's eyes never left her and Val found herself watching her brother, envying him his feelings for the woman. She wished for such happiness, too.

"Well then," she took her brother's elbow. "Are you calm enough so that we may enter the solar?"

His gaze still lingered in the doorway. "I am. But I must make a slight alteration to our plans. You must go and find Simon and John. Tell them of our plans and tell them to prepare an escort immediately."

"Of course. Anything else?"

"Send Hunt back up to Arabel and tell him to bolt the door. Have Simon come for the children when he is finished preparing the escort."

Val nodded. With a deep breath, Tevin moved at a much slower pace towards the solar entry. He looked calm even if he did not feel it.

Val watched her brother disappear into the warm room beyond. Slipping in the direction of the shadows, she held her hand out to Hunt, who was sitting in the darkened stairwell with the big yellow dog. With a few whispered words to the lad, he disappeared up the stairs as Val disappeared into the bailey beyond.

CB

"I CAME AS quickly as I could," John addressed Simon before he even entered the dimly lit stables. "What's amiss?"

Simon already had three horses saddled. He was working on a fourth and swung the saddle in John's direction. The slender blond knight caught it with a grunt.

"We need to get the women and children away from de Gael," Simon rumbled as he tossed a saddle blanket over the leggy warmblood. "Val says he's already cornered Lady Penden. No telling what the man will do to her."

John swung the saddle onto the blanket Simon had just placed. "Then there's no telling what Tevin will do to de Gael," he commented quietly.

Simon looked up at him from beneath bushy eyebrows. "What do you mean by that?"

Swantey met his gaze. "Do not play stupid, Simon. You see how he looks at her. The man is enamored with her."

Simon scratched beneath his fuzzy beard. "And if he is? What about it?"

John moved to cinch up the saddle. "Nothing, I suppose. But if de Gael is stupid enough to make a move for her, we could have a damn bloody situation on our hands."

Simon simply wriggled his eyebrows and went for the bridle slung from one of the posts. "We already have a damn bloody situation on our hands," he muttered. "First Matilda, now Stephen. I do not even know whose side I am on anymore. I could be fighting for the bloody King of Joppa tomorrow for all I know."

John grinned as he finished securing the saddle. "All I am saying is that Tevin is three times the man de Gael is. Everyone knows how jealous Geoff is of his cousin. If they both start tussling over the same woman, there could be trouble."

Simon shoved the bit into the horse's mouth. "So we're removing the woman and her son to avoid any trouble. Val and Arabel are going, too. We've been ordered to take them to some manor house to the south and wait out de Gael's visit."

John watched his colleague finish with the bridle. "If we're expected to ride to war, won't de Gael notice our absence and wonder where we are? We've ridden to battle with Tevin for almost eighteen years. He'll be expecting to see us leading du Reims' men."

Simon finished with the last strap. "That's not my concern. I'll do as I'm told and so will you."

John merely shrugged. "It would be better to send Dagan and Gavril. I'd rather go to battle than sit idle with a woman and her son."

"But we were ordered to do it."

"We're senior knights. We belong in battle, not minding women and children. Besides, let Sutton and de Reigate put their time in with escort duties. Why should we miss out on glory against Matilda while those two ride to victory in our stead?"

Simon scratched his beard again. There was something nesting in it that itched. "I suppose you have a point," he sighed. "Perhaps we should go and find Dagan and Gavril and give them the duty. I'm sure Tevin doesn't care who escorts them, so long as they're properly protected."

"My thoughts exactly."

They found Gavril in the knight's quarters sharpening his broadsword. Dagan was found in the dungeons listening to Charles' madness. Within a half hour, both men were suited up and ready to ride.

CHAPTER TEN

C ANTIA LOOKED VERY calm, Tevin thought. Much calmer than he felt. As he entered the solar where Val had convalesced, his gaze was entirely on his cousin. He was afraid to linger on Cantia, afraid that Geoff would read emotion in his face. He was terrified he would give something away.

Geoff had a smirking grin on his face as he caught sight of his massive cousin. Leaning casually against Charles' enormous desk, he waved a hand at Tevin.

"Come in, cousin," he sounded suspiciously as if he was gloating. "See who I have found? Why, it's the lovely Lady Penden. Shame on you for keeping her locked up in her room. Why on earth would you be so cruel?"

Tevin cocked an eyebrow. "Because she is in mourning for her husband. It is not proper for her to be socializing and well you know it."

Some of the grin left Geoff's face. He wasn't expecting that answer. His gaze moved to Cantia, raking over her in a manner that made Tevin's blood boil. "Mourning?" he repeated. "Why should she do that? Penden has been dead over a month. She's far too young and lovely to waste her life in mourning."

Cantia had been watching the exchange on pins and needles. The moment Tevin walked into the room, she felt a sense of relief and joy that she could not begin to describe. It was as if her savior had walked into the room and it was all she could do not to run to him for protection. But in the few short sentences exchanged, she immediately understood where Tevin was leading the conversation. He was trying to help her in a way that no one could dispute, not even Geoff. Being the sharp woman that she was, she would help her own cause. She knew what she had to do, and she had to do it quickly.

With a muffled sob, she suddenly put her hand over her face and turned away from them. The soft sob turned into a flood of larger ones, pitiful and deep. It was drama at its very best. Geoff stood up from the desk, his dark eyes wide with surprise.

"What's this?" he demanded. "Why is she weeping?"

Tevin couldn't tell if the tears were real or not, but he was thankful either way. It made his reasoning much more stable. He sighed heavily as he looked at his cousin.

"Geoff," his voice was low with admonishment. "The woman is distraught. You really should have been more considerate. She is in no condition to entertain you."

Geoff lost all of his smugness. "I did not ask her to entertain me. I simply asked to be shown Rochester. It is my holding, after all."

"And I could have shown it to you." Tevin moved towards Cantia and gently took her by the arm. "She was in her chamber for a reason and you really should not have taxed her so. I am taking her back to her room and you will leave her there to properly deal with her grief."

Cantia was sobbing as if her heart were broken. Tevin had a good grip on her as he led her towards the door. Geoff just stood there like a dolt, watching the scene with a mixture of outrage and astonishment.

"She was fine until you came into the room," he told his cousin. "Why did she suddenly burst into tears when you appeared?"

Tevin cast him a long look. "She more than likely kept her composure simply not to upset you. But she can control it no longer."

Geoff's brow furrowed. "I do not want her to mourn any longer. It has been long enough. She must sup with me tonight and I will have no more weeping. I do not like it."

The problem was that Geoff meant every word. He was childish and demanding in such ways. Tevin continued with Cantia towards the door.

"Have pity, cousin," he said steadily. "The woman has lost her husband and her grief has not spent itself. Allow Brac Penden that mercy before you seek to erase him from her mind."

Geoff pursed his lips and put his hands on his hips. "I am not attempting to erase him, for God's Sake. I just want to talk to the woman."

"There will be other time for that," Tevin was through the door. "Go entertain yourself elsewhere. Leave Lady Penden to her sorrow."

Geoff would not be quashed so easily. He went to the door, hovering in the archway with an imperious stance as he watched Tevin gently help Cantia up the steps. "And don't think that I am not aware that you hid Val from me, either," he yelled after him. "Do you hear me? Do not hide her from me again!"

Tevin didn't say a word. He didn't have to. When he was out of sight, Geoff went back into the solar and, in a fit of rage, smashed Charles' big oak desk with the hearth shovel.

Tevin heard the sounds of crashing furniture as Geoff's temper tantrum gained speed. But he maintained a steady grip on Cantia as they reached the third floor landing.

"Are you all right, sweetheart?" he asked quietly.

She stopped weeping in an instant, the violet eyes turning to him without a hint of redness. "Of course," she replied, her gaze moving back down the stairwell towards the sounds of anger below. "But thank God you came when you did."

Tevin didn't like the sound of her voice. "Why do you say that? Did he move against you somehow? Did he try...?"

She shook her head, winding her hands around his forearm and laying her cheek against his enormous bicep. "He did nothing. In fact, he was quite friendly and curious. But the way he looks at me... I feel as if he is undressing me with his eyes and I want no part of the man. He makes my skin crawl."

Tevin's recently abated anger threatened but he fought it. Silently, he took her to the fourth floor, knocking softly on the bolted door. A demanding little voice shouted at him from the other side.

"Go away!" Hunt roared. "I won't open this door!"

Tevin looked at Cantia, who couldn't help but grin at her son's bravery. He fought off a smile as well.

"'Tis me, Hunt," he said quietly. "You may open the door."

It was several long seconds before the bolt was thrown, with some effort, and the door creaked open. Hunt's big eyes peered at his mother and Tevin before he allowed them inside. Tevin lifted an eyebrow when the boy slammed the door behind them and shoved the bolt into its socket.

"You make a fine sentry," he told the lad. "A man would think twice before crossing you."

Hunt gazed up at him, his face suddenly slack with surprise. "Really?" he asked, awed. "Did I thound fearsome?"

"Terribly."

He grinned proudly, looking over at Arabel to see if she heard. But the young girl with big black eyes was looking at her father.

"Where is Cousin Geoff?" she asked.

Tevin went to sit on the bed next to her. "He is down in the solar," he replied, taking Arabel's hand and kissing it sweetly. "I have decided to send you and your Aunt Val and Lady Penden on an adventure. Would you like that?"

She took the bait of the swift change in subject. "An adventure? Where?"

He smiled at her enthusiasm, his dark eyes twinkling at her. "To a faraway castle. You can pretend you are the Princess Fair and hide away from the evil dark knight who wishes to abduct you."

She grinned at her father. "Can I give this castle a name?"

"I suppose so. What would you name it?"

Arabel's eyes were alight. "Castle Mandragora!"

Tevin's eyebrows lifted. "Mandragora? Where did you hear that?"

The girl giggled nervously, looking between her father and Cantia. "I heard someone speak of it once," she said. "'Tis another name for mandrake. I just like the name. It sounds mysterious."

Tevin cast her a reproachful look. "Mandrake is used by witches and half-wits. What would you know of it?"

Arabel shrugged, glancing down at the big yellow dog when it brushed against her. "Some of the servants at Thunderbey were speaking of it, once. One of the women wanted it for her husband. She said it was an apro… aprodisiac. I did not ask what it was. Do you know?"

Tevin cleared his throat and averted his gaze, glancing up at Cantia with a pleading expression. Cantia could see the panic in his eyes at the young girl's question and she fought off a grin.

"I believe it has something to do with medicinal purpose," she said evenly, answering for the stricken father. "But I like the name, too. It sounds very powerful."

Arabel was successfully diverted from any more questions about aphrodisiacs. "Are we going soon?"

Cantia nodded. "As soon as I can pack a few things."

Arabel's expression was aglow with the possibility of another adventure. She'd spent most of her life safely locked away at Thunderbey and now she was about to have two great adventures all in the span of a couple of weeks. It was the stuff that young girls' dreams were made of.

"The sooner the better," Tevin grasped Cantia's arm gently and their eyes met. "Hurry and pack. I would have you gone within the hour."

Cantia gazed steadily at Tevin, not voicing what she was thinking. *When will I see you again?* But she smiled after a moment, nodding obediently as she moved for the wardrobe and pulled out two large traveling satchels. Tevin watched her, thinking the same thing she was, his heart squeezed with sorrow. She began shoving garments into the bags and he tore his eyes away only to see that Arabel was watching him intently. He felt a jolt, as if she could read his expression and know what was in his heart. He smiled warmly to cover his thoughts.

"We do not have to pack for you, I would wager," he went to her, laying an enormous hand on her blond head. "You've hardly been here long enough to unpack. Where is your baggage?"

"On the wagons that Cousin Geoff brought with him," she told him. "But what about Gerta and Mary? Will they come, too?"

She was referring to the two maid servants who had tended her since birth. Tevin thought a moment before shaking his head. "I think not," he stroked her head gently. "I must get you away quickly and those two will only slow you down. They will be safe here."

"But who will take care of me?" Arabel asked.

"I will," Cantia said before anyone else could respond. She looked up from packing and noticed that a few pairs of astonished eyes were on her. She smiled at Tevin and then Arabel. "I have only had a son all these years, my lady. I have always wanted a girl. It would be my pleasure and joy to tend you until such time as I am no longer needed. Would that be all right?"

Arabel nodded timidly, looking to her father to see what his reaction was. Tevin, however, wasn't quite sure what to say. "That is very generous of you, my lady," he said hesitantly. "But Arabel requires more than usual tending. She cannot… well, she cannot…."

"She is a strong, lovely young lady and I look forward to helping her," Cantia interrupted him, winking at Arabel. "It will give us a chance to become better acquainted."

Arabel smiled brightly while Tevin's eyes were riveted to Cantia. He wasn't sure what more he could say. She seemed so determined. As his dark eyes stared at her with some uncertainty, Cantia simply smiled at him and went back to her packing. He continued to watch her, every graceful move she made, until she was finished with one satchel and almost finished with the second. Then she stood up.

"I must get some of Hunt's things," she told Tevin. "May I go to his room next door?"

Tevin nodded silently, moving to open the door of the chamber and peering outside to make sure Geoff wasn't lingering close. Quietly, he extended a hand to her and she slipped her delicate hand into his as he took her out of the room.

"Hunt," he addressed the young boy, now lying on the floor with his big yellow dog. "Bolt the door after we leave. Do not open it until I return."

Hunt leapt up and slammed the door when Tevin and his mother quit the room. He hit Tevin in the rear as he shut it. In the dark hall landing, they could hear the lad throw the bolt loudly. Cantia giggled softly as Tevin merely shook his head.

"He is going to make a fine sentry," he whispered, reiterating his previous opinion.

Hunt's small chamber was cluttered with toys and old rushes. A bone for the dog lay near the sooty hearth. Cantia tripped over a cart fashioned with twigs as she made her way to a big chest near the wall. Tevin shut the door quietly and bolted it as she opened the chest and began removing garments.

"Good lord," she held up a pair of breeches with a big hole in the seat. She stuck her hand through it. "How on earth did this happen? That boy destroys more clothing than I can keep track of."

As she tossed the ruined breeches aside, Tevin walked up behind her silently. She was muttering to herself about a warm sweater that had a huge rip on the sleeve when he suddenly grabbed her from behind. Cantia gasped as his mouth slanted over her tender neck.

"I do not know when next I will see you," he murmured against her flesh. "The mere thought is driving me mad with sorrow and loneliness."

She moaned softly as he suckled on her shoulder. It sounded like a kitten's purr. "You know where I will be," she tried to sound confident, not sorrowful and lonely herself. "Darland is not too far. We will be quite safe."

"I will send a contingent of men along for protection," his hands were moving over her torso, feeling her softness, memorizing it for the lonely days to come. "I promise this separation will not be long. I can hardly stand the thought of it now."

She turned in his arms, winding her arms around his thick neck. Their gazes met and she smiled as he kissed her nose. "I am looking forward to coming to know Arabel better. She seems like a very sweet girl."

He kissed her forehead, her temple. "She is," he muttered. "But you should know that she has no control of her bodily functions and must wear a type of garment usually reserved for infants. More than that, she has started her womanly cycle and...."

Cantia cut him off before he embarrassed himself too much. She could see that he was uncomfortable speaking of such things. "Not to worry, Father," she smiled at him. "It will be no trouble at all."

He gazed down at her, the warmth in her expression, and felt himself softening towards her even more. He had always known her to be inordinately strong but to take on the care of his disadvantaged daughter deepened his respect for her more than he could express.

"To know that the people I love best in this world are going to be away from me for an undetermined amount of time is testing my control," he stroked her face. "I know this is the best course of action but my emotions have the better of me. Up until the day I met you, the only human beings that mattered to me were Arabel and Val. They are my family. And now, with you...."

He trailed off when he saw the look on her face. Cantia was staring at him with wide eyes. Tevin's ardor cooled at the look on her face.

"What is wrong?" he demanded softly. "Why do you look at me so?"

She opened her mouth to speak, seemingly unable to for a moment. She just stood there and shook her head. "What you said... you said that the people you love best will be away from you."

He nodded, pulling her against his broad chest. "Aye, I did. What about it?"

"I will be away from you also."

"I meant you."

She inhaled unsteadily, almost like a sob. "How can you say that?"

He smiled, amused. "Because it is the truth." His grip on her tightened. "Did you truly believe that my attentions towards you are anything less than blind, crazed adoration? Of course I love you, Cantia. Did you not realize that?"

Her eyes welled with tears as he watched. The hands around his thick neck flew to her mouth as if trying to stifle the tide of emotion. "It's not possible," she looked truly upset. "It cannot be possible."

He smiled gently at her even though his brow was furrowed. "Why not?" he asked, wiping away tears with his thumbs as they fell. "I did not intend to cause you tears. I simply meant to tell you what is in my heart."

She nodded quickly even as he spoke, as if knowing his reasons for expressing himself even before he said them. She threw her arms around his neck again, hitting him in the throat as she did so. He coughed, laughing softly as his big arms enveloped her.

"Your reaction is most confusing, madam," he whispered into her hair. "Are you horrified by my declaration or pleased by it?"

She sobbed softly into his neck. "I'm simply overwhelmed," she wept softly. "Brac has hardly been gone these few weeks and already I find love again? It doesn't seem possible. It does not seem right."

His smile faded and he pulled her out of the crook of his neck, his nearly-black eyes fixed seriously on her. "Why not?" he demanded softly.

She wiped at her eyes, struggling with her composure. "'Tis too soon."

He cocked his head, watching her lovely hands as they wiped away the tears. "Do you believe that there should be a proper schedule for love or do you believe it simply happens when it happens?"

She sniffled delicately, taking his question seriously. "It happens when it happens," her lavender eyes came up to capture him. "I think I knew I loved you the moment you lit yourself on fire at Rochester Cathedral. From that moment on, I just knew. It terrified and thrilled me beyond comprehension."

His smile was back and he pulled her gently into his arms once more. "Oh, Cantia," he whispered. "I cannot tell you how happy you have made me. I've never been this happy in my entire life."

She clung to him, holding him tightly. He hugged her to him for a long moment, savoring the feel of her warmth against him, her body against his, before his kisses resumed with intensity. Before long, he had her backed against Hunt's messy bed, laying her gently upon the straw and feather mattress and snaking his hands beneath her skirts. Cantia encouraged him to explore her, feeling his hands on her buttocks and thighs, helping him lower his breeches for his swift and heated entry.

He thrust firmly into her, his hands on her hips as he kissed her with a deep and abiding passion. It didn't seem to matter that they were still nearly dressed. All that mattered was that they demonstrate their feelings to one another and feel each other, one inside the other.

Cantia panted softly as he thrust into her, feeling her climax build and biting off her cry of passion against his shoulder as she peaked. Tevin answered shortly and she could feel his member throbbing deep inside her as he spilled his seed. Now there was a new element to their lovemaking, with true love involved that magnified the intensity of the act. The emotions involved were overwhelming and Cantia's eyes swam with tears at the tenderness of Tevin's touch, the feel of his flesh against her. When it was over, all they could do was lay there and hold each other tightly.

"I love you, Cantia," he confessed, feeling liberated and free that the truth had been spoken. "Never forget that. No matter how long we are apart, know that my love for you will grow by the day and I will come for you as soon as I am able."

She gazed up at him as he lifted his head, her lavender eyes glimmering. "Know that I shall be waiting every second of every day for that moment when we are together again," she whispered.

He smiled faintly, kissing her once more in a painfully sweet gesture before rising from the bed and pulling her up with him. As he secured his breeches, she smoothed her surcoat and returned to gathering Hunt's things. It was difficult for them to focus on the tasks at hand because they very much wanted to fall back into each other's arms. Cantia seemed to be the strong one and more than once gently pushed

Tevin aside or avoided his seeking mouth as she finished gathering her son's possessions. Finally, Tevin simply stood aside and watched her as she finished. She was mesmerizing to watch.

"When this madness is over and Geoff has returned home, I shall take you and Hunt to Thunderbey Castle," he told her. "I have a white and brown pony that Hunt might like. Someone gave it to Arabel as a gift but she cannot ride it."

Cantia went over to him and indicated for him to hold out his arms, which he did. She deposited a bundle of clothing in them.

"Do you not think to ask Arabel first if she would mind giving her pony to Hunt?" she asked, collecting the rest of her son's things. "Perhaps she does not want to give it to another."

"She would rather know the pony was being ridden and loved," he told her, moving for the door to open it. "She is a generous, reasonable girl."

"As her father is also generous and reasonable."

She winked at him as he opened the door, passing by him with her arms full. Tevin was in danger of pulling her back into his arms, knowing it might be the last time before their separation that he would be able to do so. Gently, he grasped her arm and kissed her forehead, his lips lingering on her flesh. Cantia closed her eyes with bliss, memorizing the feel of his lips against her. It was a swift, stolen moment of the sweetest measure.

Tevin released her and crossed the hall, knocking softly on the panel. He knocked again a few seconds later when there was no answer.

"Hunt?" he whispered loudly. "Open the door."

After a moment, the bolt was thrown and the door jerked open. A little blond head and big eyes gazed back at him expectantly. As Cantia pushed past Tevin and her son and on into the room, Tevin put his fists on his hips and gazed down at Brac Penden's son.

"Well, lad," he said, a twinkle in his nearly-black eyes. "Are you ready for an adventure?"

He couldn't recall ever seeing a bigger smile.

CHAPTER ELEVEN

IT WAS FORTUNATE that Cantia knew all of the minute details of Rochester, for when it came to sneaking the group of women and children out of the castle under Geoff's nose, her knowledge was invaluable.

Within the hour, they were able to pack one satchel per person, including Arabel, so that they could travel swiftly and lightly. Cantia changed Hunt into durable clothing, layers of it, including a little wool cap all the way from Monmouth. She was dressed in durable travel clothing as well, as was Val, who took charge of Arabel and made sure she was ready to leave. The older women moved swiftly and silently, knowing it was essential that timing was everything in this case. Tevin wanted to get them free of the castle when Geoff was the most distracted.

So they chose the evening meal to make their escape even though it would be dark and more difficult to travel. But it would also make their escape more difficult to detect. Tevin had been with Geoff for the remainder of the afternoon, keeping him occupied, until the evening meal was served and then he accompanied the man into the hall. Excusing himself on a pretext, he appeared at the chamber door to find four occupants, ready for travel.

There was palpable fear in the air, apprehension with the certainty of being able to execute their plan without being caught. Taking Arabel in his arms, Tevin led the way down the spiral stairs as Cantia took Hunt in hand plus their two bags, and Val took her possessions plus Arabel's. They moved quickly, carefully, like hunted animals. Hunt kept trying to get ahead of Tevin on the stairs and more than once, his mother had to yank him back. As they neared the bottom of the steps and into the range of the great hall where Geoff was in the process of getting drunk, the big yellow dog appeared.

"George, go back," Cantia hissed. "George, go!"

"Mam," Hunt grabbed the dog. "I want him to come. He isth my friend. Pleasth?"

Tevin shushed them both. He didn't want them to be overheard. "Quiet," he whispered. "Hunt, take the dog. Move along."

Hunt grabbed the dog by the rope collar around its neck and, with his mother urgently herding him, followed Tevin to the base of the stairs. Sounds and smells from the banqueting assaulted their senses. They could hear the low hum of conversation and the clanking of utensils. Tevin peered out of the stairwell, his dark eyes on the entry to the banqueting hall and the movement beyond. He felt like a fugitive, waiting to be discovered at any moment.

The placement of the table inside the room gave it a view of the doorway but not the entry hall beyond, so Tevin silently slipped from the stairwell and to the keep entry about twenty feet to his right, which led into an enclosed stairwell that sloped down to the bailey. He made sure Hunt, Cantia and Val were into the enclosed stairwell before following. The evacuation of the keep had been successful.

But his heart was still pounding with apprehension as they reached the bailey. It was dark outside as the full moon started to rise. In the shadow of the great keep, Tevin turned to Cantia.

"Get us to the postern gate," he commanded softly.

She nodded swiftly, grabbing Hunt, who had the dog, and pulled them along as they stayed close to the mighty keep, making their way to the west side where the interior bailey wall was very close to the keep. There was a gate that led to yards and the massive exterior wall beyond, so she slipped them all through the thick iron and wood gate.

Once they were through the gate, however, she came to a halt and faced Tevin. "From here, the only way out is through the front gate," she told him.

He nodded, heading back to the north and the gatehouse. "There are no worries at that point," he said. "My men are waiting there to take you out of this place."

Cantia pulled Hunt and the dog along as they scurried after Tevin, crossing the muddy outer bailey beneath the ghostly moon glow until they reached the main gate of Rochester, which was eerily lit with torches and guarded by men.

Rather than a large escort, Tevin thought it best to have a very small but well-armed party so it would not attract the wrong kind of attention. Therefore, he only had two knights riding escort, men of the highest caliber. Next to the gate astride their big chargers await Dagan and Gavril, not John and Simon as Tevin had ordered. He peered curiously at the pair.

"Where are John and Simon?" he asked.

Dagan answered. "They have commanded us to ride in their stead, my lord."

Tevin's brow furrowed with annoyance. "They did not say why?"

"Nay, my lord."

Tevin's frustration grew but there was no time to track down the two knights who had disobeyed his direct orders. The time to leave was now. He directed Cantia to a gray palfrey as Val went to her charger and prepared to mount. Tevin went to his sister.

"Are you well enough that you can ride with Arabel?" he asked. "I would rather that she ride with you, leaving Dagan and Gavril free to fend off any assaults should it be necessary."

Val nodded, holding out her arms for her niece. "I can ride with her and fight, too, if it is required."

Tevin shook his head even as he handed Arabel up to her aunt. "You will not fight with Arabel in your custody," he instructed in a low, firm voice. "Your duty will be to protect her at all costs. If there is any fighting, you will ride clear of it and get to safety. Is that understood?"

Val gazed down at her brother, for the first time hearing fear in his voice. She knew how hard this was for him, being separated from Arabel, and Cantia, but more than that, he was frightened for them because he could not go and personally protect them. Her emotionless brother was becoming emotional and she hastened to reassure him.

"I will protect her with my life," she assured him softly. "I hope you would already know that without me having to say it."

Tevin's features were tight beneath the moonlight. "I do," he replied quietly. "But for my own sake, I had to say it."

Before Val could reply, Arabel put her small hand on her father's big fingers. "We will be fine," she told him. "We are going to have a great adventure, remember? I am looking forward to visiting Castle Mandragora. My very own castle!"

She said it so happily that he couldn't help but smile. She really had no true concept of danger, having been protected by her powerful father all of her life. She had lived a rather sheltered existence, so all of this was, indeed, a big adventure.

"Listen to what Val tells you and be safe," he touched her cheek. "My love goes with you. I will see you very soon."

Arabel grinned and he turned away, savoring that as the last vision of his child before he would see her again. He tried not to let apprehension overwhelm him. Then he focused on Cantia.

She was astride the palfrey with Hunt behind her and the dog sitting next to the horse. She was facing away from him as he came upon her and he reached out, a massive hand touching the boy's back before moving on to rest casually on Cantia's arm.

When she felt him, she turned to look at him and he could feel his composure slip. There was sadness and longing in her gaze, and he forced a smile. They had already said their farewells, but it didn't make this moment of separation any easier. But already, it was killing him.

"I have studied my map and Darland is not too far to the south," he sounded comforting and business-like. "The knights will have instructions to take you south without stopping until they reach the manse. On a clear night with good weather, it should take two hours at the most. You will get inside the manse, make sure it is bottled up, and go about your daily lives until I come for you. Is that clear?"

Cantia nodded. "When will you come?"

His composure slipped another notch. "I do not know," he said, his voice considerably softer. "It could be in two days or two weeks. I have no way of knowing. But know that I will come as soon as I can. And I will miss you more with each breath I take."

The last sentence was whispered. Cantia smiled sadly, careful with her body language with Hunt so close. She wanted very much to throw her arms around Tevin and hug him tightly, but dare not make any attempt. The pain of not being able to touch him was almost too much to bear.

"Then we shall look for you every day," she said softly. "Please... please take great care, my lord."

All he could do was nod, his eyes conveying a thousand words his mouth and body could not. The moment of separation was here but he realized he wasn't ready for it. He knew he had to get away from her or risk breaking down in some manner, so he quickly turned for Dagan and Gavril, swallowing the lump in his throat. He was struggling.

By the time he reached his knights, his manner had turned snappish. "Have no doubt I will find John and Simon and they shall feel my wrath for having disobeyed my orders," his rumbled. "But for you, know this. You will follow the road south until you come to a fork in the road. It will be the first fork, a big one, and you will bear left. Follow this and you will pass through two small bergs. When you come to the third berg, that is Darland, and you will ask the lady where the manse is. She will direct you to it. You will remain with the lady and with Val until I come for you. Defend them with your life, for there is nothing in this world more important than those three women and that small boy. Do you understand?"

Gavril and Dagan nodded firmly. "Aye, my lord," they answered in unison.

Satisfied, Tevin motioned towards the gate. "Then make all haste."

The knights swung into action, snapping orders to the soldiers manning the gate. As the portcullis shrieked and began to lift, Tevin stood back and watched the party move out. He felt like his whole life was leaving him, watching Cantia in the moonlight as she spurred the little horse forward. The hardest thing he ever had to do was not issue a recall order. He knew they had to go. It was for the best. He blew a kiss at Cantia when he was sure no one could see him.

With a heavy heart, he turned back for the great stone keep of Rochester.

󠀠󠀠
❦

CANTIA REALIZED SHE was very close to weeping as they left the castle swiftly, silently, moving forth into the moonlit night like wraiths upon the land. Because the moon was so bright, there was no need for torches, a fortunate event considering they did not want to attract attention. Onward into the cold darkness, the party from Rochester traveled south and Cantia missed Tevin more with each successive step.

The road was not in the best of condition and more than once, the horses tripped in the ruts. Even though it was bright and their path well-lit, they ended up slowing their frantic pace because to go any faster, with the conditions, was dangerous. They were surrounded by open fields so their field of visibility was wide, adding to the decision to slow their pace. There were no places to hide for bandits or others who preyed upon open travelers these days, so as long as the knights had a clear field of vision, they were comfortable with the lesser pace.

Hunt had fallen asleep against his mother at some point and Cantia held the boy's hands at her waist, his little arms wrapped around her so he wouldn't slide off. In spite of her separation anxiety from Tevin, she was beginning to enjoy the travel with the ghostly moon and fairly mild weather. There wasn't a cloud in the sky and occasionally, a night bird would sail across the darkness. The more distance they put between them and Rochester, the more they all began to calm and settle in for the trip. With any luck, the hard part was over.

Dagan and Gavril eventually came to the fork in the road that Tevin had described and took the road to the left as instructed. They then continued on along a smaller section of road, now being intermittently dotted by clusters of dense, black trees. The trees made the knights nervous so they slung their shields, weapons at the ready, and that made Cantia nervous as well. Men prepared for battle invited apprehension and she found herself looking around, seeing if she could spy robbers hiding out in the growth. Her somewhat pleasant trip was turning apprehensive again.

Somewhere, an owl hooted as they passed through a particularly dark section of trees. It smelled heavily of leaves and wet, eerie phantoms lurking in the blackness. With Cantia caught up in watching the surrounding area for an army of murders to come flying out at them, Dagan, covering their rear, was watching Cantia.

When he had been summoned to escort the lady and her son out of Rochester, he had been in the vault in discussion with Charles again. Their conversation had been quiet and not overheard. During the course of that conversation, he'd come to a great many conclusions, not the least of which was the fact that he had decided to accept Charles' offer.

It hadn't been a simple choice, but one he felt was best for him. The difficultly had been in figuring out how to separate the lady from du Reims because the man was rabidly protective of her, and when he had been summoned to escort the lady and her son from Rochester, he considered it an omen. Perhaps God was telling him his decision had been correct, that it was indeed time to take charge of his destiny. It was an unbelievably fortuitous occurrence, one he accepted eagerly.

Now, there were only a couple of things that stood in his way. As the party from Rochester made their way south, Dagan made plans for Gavril and Val. True, his plans for the knights were not honorable and for that, he was sincerely sorry. But his mind was made up. It was the time in his life to take opportunities when presented or remain a lesser knight in du Reims' stable for the rest of his life. No wealth, no glory, no opportunities for him. This was his last chance.

Dagan knew that Gavril would not go along with his decision, which at this point, signed the man's death warrant. Val would be a problem also, but she was encumbered with the viscount's daughter, making her an easy target. The children would be spared and he would take them, plus Cantia, to the nearest church where he would marry the lady without delay. His plan was in place and he was prepared. As they neared a particularly thick cluster of trees and the moon was blotted out by the heavy canopy, Dagan began to move.

At the rear of the column, he spurred his charger forward and unsheathed a large dirk with a heavy steel hilt, one he used for close-quarters combat. He passed close to Val on his right, slugging her on the back of the head as hard as he could and sending her toppling over onto the ground.

As Arabel, who fell off of the horse along with her aunt, screamed in shock and fear, Gavril turned around towards the source of the scream only to see his cousin bearing down on him. Startled, the man didn't have a chance to unsheathe his sword before Dagan threw the dirk at him, catching him in the neck.

Gavril plummeted to the ground, the enormous dirk in his neck that had not only cut off his air supply, but had severed a major artery. He lifted his hand to remove the weapon, but before he could even get a grip on it, he bled out all over the rocky, uneven road. Gavril de Reigate's life ended with a view of the heavens above on a lovely night, wondering what in the world had happened to make it all end this way.

With all of the screaming and chaos, Cantia's palfrey had bolted off the road, dumping both her and Hunt onto the ground. As she picked herself up and grabbed her son, having no idea what was going on, Dagan came thundering in her direction.

"Halt!" Dagan bellowed, seeing that she was preparing to run. "Stay where you are."

Frightened, Cantia froze. "What has happened?" She could hear Arabel crying. "Arabel! Is she injured? And where is Val?"

Dagan pulled his foaming charger to a halt, gazing down at the lovely Lady Penden and her tow-headed son. He tried not to feel guilty for what he had just done.

"Stay here and do not move," he instructed.

Uncertain, Cantia did as she was told, holding tight to Hunt as Dagan reined his charger over to where Val was lying unconscious in the grass by the side of the road. Arabel was sitting beside her aunt, weeping, as Dagan dismounted his charger and picked the girl up. Arabel wept harder, trying to resist him, as he carried the girl over to where Cantia and Hunt were huddled. Cantia instinctively held out her arms to the girl and Dagan deposited her into the waiting embrace.

Cantia wasn't a particularly large woman so holding Arabel was somewhat cumbersome, but she held her as tightly and as securely as she could manage. Arabel wrapped her thin arms around Cantia's neck, sobbing, as Cantia shushed her softly. Dagan stood in front of the pair, fists resting on his hips.

"Now," he began softly, with a firm yet sinister cast to his tone. "You and I have something to discuss, lady."

Cantia looked up from Arabel's lowered head. "What...?" she shook her head, her fear and confusion growing. "What are you talking about? Have we been attacked?"

Dagan shook his head. "We have not," he said. "What I did was necessary."

Cantia stared at him, his angular features beneath the muted moonlight, and her heart began to pound. "What *you* did?" she repeated. "What do you mean?"

Dagan wouldn't look over his shoulder at the carnage he had created. It was easier to pretend he was still an honorable knight if he didn't see it.

"Charles Penden has presented me with a proposal that I have decided to accept," he said. "You are to be my wife and, along with that, your property shall become mine. It is my intention to ransom the viscount's daughter for Charles Penden's release and your dowry, whereupon you, me, Charles and your son will be able to live quite comfortably anywhere we choose."

Cantia stared at him. It began to occur to her that what happened was not a random attack from unseen bandits, but an enemy that had come from within. Dagan, the big, quiet knight she'd barely said two words to since she had met him, had turned and Charles Penden was at the heart of it. By hook, crook or magic, Charles had somehow bewitched the man to turn against her. *Damn him!* Furious, terrified, she snapped.

"I am not Charles Penden's chattel to be brokered," she backed away from Dagan with Arabel in her arms. "And I am certainly not to be brokered to a lowly knight in exchange for a madman's freedom. Have you lost your senses?"

Dagan remained cool. "Fortunately, no," he said, rather drolly. "I realize this is something of a shock, Lady Penden, but perhaps you will come to understand my reasoning if would allow me to explain."

Cantia was still backing away from him, nearly in a panic. "I will not listen to anything," she snarled, trying to get a glimpse of Val still lying in a heap near the road. "Let me see to Val immediately and you had better pray that she is not severely injured, do you hear me? You will go back to your horse and wait until we are ready to continue."

She was giving orders, trying to gain control of the situation, but Dagan would not relent. "You may not see to Val," he was standing between Cantia and Tevin's downed sister. Then he looked at Hunt, huddled apprehensively behind his mother. "Master Penden, you will go and retrieve your mother's palfrey. She is over by the tree line."

He was pointing but Hunt shook his head fearfully and burrowed his face into the back of his mother. Cantia was trying to edge her way in Val's direction.

"I am not going anywhere with you," she snarled. "You are mad, do you hear? I am going to help Val and I will kill you if you stand in my way."

Dagan's movements were slow, deliberate, as he kept himself between Cantia and Val. Cantia was trying very hard to reach the woman but it was difficult considering she had the burden of a small boy and a crippled girl. Dagan admired the woman's pluck.

"I understand and appreciate your loyalty, but you will forgive me when I deny you again," he said evenly. "Send your son to get your palfrey. I've already killed two this night and a third would not be such an effort if I feel my wants are not being met."

Cantia's rage took a dousing. She stared at the man. "Why are you doing this?" she finally asked, hoarsely. "What have we done that would make you do this to us?"

Dagan struggled against his innate sense of regret, of uncertainty. It was difficult to stay on course. "Nothing, my lady," he said after a moment. "But you must understand that you do not have any choice in the matter. The decision has been made. It would be best if you do not resist."

"Please… do not do this."

"Tell your son to retrieve your horse. Do it now."

Sickened, terrified, she swallowed her resistance and sent Hunt to gather the mare. In her arms, Arabel was sniffling and trembling, and she squeezed the girl reassuringly. The truth was that her arms were beginning to hurt, carrying the girl around, but she would not let on. The only other alternative was for Dagan to carry her and Cantia wasn't about to let the man touch her.

Frightened and edgy, Cantia found herself wondering how she could get herself and the children out of this. As it turned out, Geoff wasn't the one to worry about at all. It had been Charles and a rogue knight. The irony of the situation was unfathomable. She wondered if she would live long enough to tell Tevin.

As she stood several feet away from Dagan, inspecting the man, trying to determine her next course of action, a shrieking sound pierced the air a split second before something hit Dagan in the chest and the man grunted, hurling to the ground. Startled, Cantia screamed, realizing there was a big arrow protruding from Dagan's torso. Behind her, she could hear Hunt yelling, the yellow dog barking, and the palfrey nickering fearfully.

As she turned around, she could see men rushing from the trees. They were shrouded by shadows and it was difficult to get a good look at them, but she could hear Hunt hollering and panic swamped her.

"Hunt!" she screamed. "Hunt, come to me! Run!"

It was a futile call because Hunt was already being swallowed up by the phantom men. They were everywhere, like a swarm of locusts, and she could hear their frightening chatter. They only used the light of the moon to guide them as they overcame their victims. The next thing Cantia realized, someone put a blanket over her head as she tried to get away with Arabel in her arms. Struggling, fighting, Arabel was taken from her and she could hear the young girl screaming.

Terrified, Cantia fought like a wildcat as someone picked her up and hauled her off, wrapped up in a hot, smelly blanket so she couldn't see or get her arms free. She began screaming for the children, calling their name, before finally resorting to begging for their lives. But her abductors never said a word to her. They just kept running.

As quickly as they had emerged, they disappeared back into the darkness, leaving two dead knights in their wake.

CHAPTER TWELVE

IT WAS NEARING NOON on a day that was showing the promise of warmer weather. A cloudless sky glistened overhead and Tevin found himself gazing from the lancet window, looking up to the sky and wondering how Cantia was faring. The solar of Rochester had a west-facing window and he leaned against the sill, watching the birds flock over the river, hearing the distant bells of the boats. It was lovely and serene, but it meant absolutely nothing to him without Cantia by his side.

He hadn't been away from her for more than twelve hours but, as he had predicted, he missed her more with each breath he took. It was a physical pain, manifesting itself in his chest until he could scarcely breathe. He turned away from the window, his thoughts moving from Cantia to Geoff and thankful for the fact that his cousin had drank himself into a stupor the night before and was still sleeping off the excess. The man hadn't given the effort of thought to the missing Lady Penden or to Val, and Tevin was grateful. The delay had given him time to think up a plausible reason for the missing. He was prepared.

So he went back to his map table, studying the area north of the Dartford crossing where two of Geoff's men, who had been in the area only yesterday, had come to Rochester with tales of an armed buildup. An army was gathering and Tevin was preparing to send more of his trusted men into the area as spies to see what more information they could gather.

He immediately thought of Simon and John for the duty, those two disobedient knights who had shrugged the escort duty to Dagan and Gavril. He hadn't seen the men since yesterday but he knew they were around, more than likely attempting to wait out their liege's displeasure. He smirked when he thought of sending the pair on a scout mission into dangerous territory. Perhaps running into an ambush or having arrows shot at their head would make them sorry they had disobeyed their liege on the relatively easy escort mission.

As he settled down to figure out a covert route for his men to take where they could make a quick escape, Myles appeared in the doorway.

"Tevin," his voice was low, swift. "You must come immediately."

Tevin didn't give thought to the fact that the man did not address him formally. He was more concerned with the tone of his voice.

"What is the matter?" he asked.

Myles' expression tightened. "No questions," he hissed. "You must come. *Now*."

He ducked out of the doorway, heading for the keep entry. Tevin follow, more curious than concerned, as they made their way out of the keep and headed towards the knight's quarters. Myles was walking quickly, stiffly, all coiled up like a spring ready to pop as they crossed the ward and approached the thick stone building that housed the knights. Built against the perimeter wall of Rochester, it was a squat, imposing structure.

It was moderately dark inside due to the fact that the building had no windows except for big ventilation holes up by the roof line. The floor plan consisted of a large common room and six smaller sleeping chambers. It was dusty and dark at any given time. There were a few senior men-at-arms crowded into the common room, eyeing Tevin with some concern as he entered. Tevin didn't particularly notice the expressions, as he was more focused on Myles as the man led him into a tiny corridor and indicated the first room to the right.

Tevin stuck his head into the chamber, his gaze first envisioning a darkened room and nothing more. Then, he saw a big yellow dog lying next to the small bed and it took him a moment to realize it was George. George lifted his head when he saw Tevin, big sad doggy eyes gazing up at him as the tail thumped wearily against the floor. The last Tevin had seen of the dog, he had left with Cantia and the rest of the group. Startled to realize the dog had returned, his gaze moved to the bed.

Val lay upon the mattress, bruised and beaten. Lying on her right side, she had a massive compress of some kind against her head and neck. Tevin must have made some kind of noise because her eyes opened and she turned stiffly to look at him as he collapsed to his knees beside the bed. Tevin's face was white with terror.

"Val," he hissed. "What are you doing here?"

Val's eyes filled with tears and she grasped her brother's hand. Her lovely face was scraped from where she had fallen on it and the lump on the back of her head was causing her horrific pain. She clutched at Tevin.

"Oh, Tevin," she wept. "We... we were ambushed. They killed Dagan and Gavril, and took Cantia and the children."

Tevin felt as if he had been hit in the gut. He couldn't breathe and he could feel his face flushing hot, then cold again. He began to shake uncontrollably, holding on to Val's hand with a death grip.

"What happened?" he struggled with everything he possessed to remain calm. "Did you see who it was? Did they bear colors or anything else of note?"

Val was weeping in pain and sorrow. "Nay," she breathed. "I was knocked unconscious and when I woke up, Dagan and Gavril were dead and Cantia missing. I... my head... it was difficult to move so I do not know how long I lay in the grass before rising to my feet. It was nighttime when the attack happened and at least dawn when I awoke. I started to walk back to Rochester and found Dagan's charger a little way up the road. I was able to ride him back here so I could tell you what happened."

Tevin could see how badly she was injured. He stroked her head, gently, though his hand was trembling. "I can only imagine how much pain you are in," he murmured. "You were very brave, Val."

Val's eyes spilled over. "I am so sorry, Tevin," she whispered. "I never saw what hit me. I had no chance to defend Arabel or Cantia."

He shook his head, soothing her. "It is not your fault," he said, but his voice was tremulous. He tried to keep his head, asking questions that might help them make sense of it all. "You heard or saw nothing before you lost consciousness?"

"Nothing. All was peaceful."

Tevin could feel men next to him and behind him, listening to Val's story. He could feel their concern, their rage, waiting orders from Viscount Winterton on how to proceed. From the corner of his eye, Tevin caught sight of heavy, dirty boots. He knew those boots and fury surged through him as he turned in the direction of Simon. John was standing slightly behind him, both knights distressed with what they were hearing.

But their distress wasn't nearly what Tevin's was. Veins stood out on his forehead as he faced his insubordinate knights and struggled not to explode in all directions.

"*You* were supposed to escort them," he jabbed a big finger at the men. "By what right did you disobey my order and give the duty to Sutton and de Reigate?"

John took a step back from his furious liege but Simon stood his ground. "We reasoned that, as new knights, they were in need of earning your trust and escorting the ladies was an opportunity to do that," he said steadily. "Moreover, de Gael was expecting to gather a force against Matilda and we would serve you better in battle than as an escort."

Tevin was quickly veering out of control, looking for something, or someone, to focus his grief on. His body tensed as he took a menacing step in their direction.

"I will decide how you will better serve me," he snarled. "You were expected to ride escort and now see what has happened? Dagan and Gavril have been killed and Lady Cantia and my daughter are missing."

Tevin was as furious as anyone had ever seen him, Simon and John included. They had both served Tevin long enough to know that the only thing they could do was beg forgiveness. Otherwise, the situation would get violent. Du Reims was known to have a vicious temper when roused.

"Forgive, my lord," Simon dropped his head submissively. "Certainly we would have done all in our power to have prevented such a thing. We beg your forgiveness."

Tevin wasn't satisfied. If anything, the submissive gesture only infuriated him more and as he lifted a hand to grab Simon by the hair, Myles intervened.

"Nay, Tevin," he said calmly, turning the coiled man back towards his sister. "It was not their fault. Had they been there, they would more than likely have been killed as well. At the moment, we have more important things to deal with."

Tevin allowed Myles to refocus him on Val, mostly because he knew, at some level, the man was correct. Simon and John, disobedient as they had been, were not responsible. So he returned his attention to his sister, feeling the cracks in his composure grow deeper and more pronounced. He was shattering and there was nothing he could do to stop it. Somehow, he ended up back on his knees beside Val with Myles kneeling beside him.

"Val," Myles put his big hand on Val's head, tenderly. "How long were you riding before this happened?"

Val thought a moment. "About… about an hour. Not long."

Myles looked at Tevin. "That cannot be too far away," he said. "I will assemble a strike force immediately."

Tevin could only nod. He wasn't sure he was capable of much more, fighting against emotions on a level he had never before experienced. All he knew was that he wanted to collapse in sorrow, yet in the same breath, he wanted to kill like he'd never wanted to kill in his life. It was an odd combination.

As he was laboring against intense grief, he noticed Myles as the man kissed Val on the forehead and quit the room, but he didn't give the gesture a second thought. He could hear Myles snapping orders to the others as he went, clearing out the rooms and getting the men moving. Somewhere in the chaos, the voices of Simon and John could be heard, and a whole host of men-at-arms were being roused. The viscount's trusted men were in action once again, doing what they did best, but the viscount himself was unmoving. Tevin remained on his knees beside his sister, becoming more despondent by the moment.

Val watched her brother, seeing the turmoil in his eyes. "There was no blood that I could see," she told him. "Our baggage was missing as well. It was a robbery, I am sure, taking Cantia and the children simply because...."

"Because she is the most beautiful woman they have ever seen," his lower lip began to tremble as he closed his eyes tightly against the horrific mental images that were swamping him. The tears came and Val watched as her brother, the most powerful man she'd ever known, succumbed to bone-numbing grief. When his dark eyes opened, they were intense against his pale face.

"It is my fault," he hissed. "Had I not... I sent her away, I sent you all away, to escape Geoff and see how my plan has come to ruin. Had I only kept everyone here...."

Val grasped his wrist, squeezing. "You did what you had to do," she insisted softly. "You had no choice. You believed you were doing what was best for all of us."

He wasn't soothed. He wiped at his eyes, fighting off a sob. "And Arabel," he whispered miserably. "My Dear God, my daughter... what has happened to her?"

Val could see her brother was verging on a collapse and she struggled to sit up, to comfort him.

"Tevin, listen to me," she held on to his big hand. "You are impeccable in your judgment, always. We all trust you with our lives. What happened... it was not your fault and you must not blame yourself."

He dropped his chin to his chest, lowering his head until he fell face-first onto the mattress beside his sister. "I made the decision," he wept. "There is no one to blame but me. If Cantia and Arabel have come to ruin, I... I cannot live with the guilt. I will not live without them."

Seized with horror, Val grasped his face, forcing him to look at her. She was angry, exhausted, weak, tears brimming in her dark eyes.

"Listen to me," she hissed. "I have lost my mother and father and one brother. You are all I have left and I will not hear this, do you understand? I hate you for saying such things, Tevin. It was not your fault. None of this was. Take a stand and be the strong man that I know you are, for weakness and self-pity do not suit you. If Cantia and Arabel are still alive, you shame them with this behavior. They need your help and all you can think of is yourself."

Tevin looked at his sister, so pale and angry, hearing every word like a hammer in his brain. But as he gazed at her, her meaning began to set in and he realized she was right. If Cantia and Arabel were indeed alive, they were waiting for him to save them.

Tevin was a smart man. He knew his power and he knew what he was capable of. No matter who had taken Cantia and his daughter, he had the resources and the resolve to find them. And when he did, no matter if it was Lucifer himself, he could and would defeat them. No battle in his life would ever be more important than the one to come. Perhaps all other battles he had been involved in were simply practice for this one. It was the only one that mattered.

"I am sorry," he said after a moment, swallowing his tears and laboring to regain his composure. "You are right, you are entirely right. Forgive me my moment of weakness."

Val could see he meant it. She could see the light of sanity returning to his dark eyes and she sighed heavily, with great relief, lying back against the pillow.

"There is nothing to forgive, brother," she murmured. "We are all entitled to moments of temporary insanity. What matters now is what you intend to do. Myles is assembling your men in the bailey."

Tevin drew in a deep breath, wiping his face of any remaining moisture and squaring his enormous shoulders. He stood up, rather unsteadily at first, as he shook himself and regained his composure. As he calmed, his mind began to work in only the way Tevin's was capable. It was steely, deep, and far-reaching. He drew on those characteristics to pull him through the crisis.

"Geoff will see the men assembling in the bailey and he will want to know why," he said, hearing the muted sounds of men and horses. "I have no choice but to tell him the truth. There is no point in lying to the man. He will know that Cantia and Arabel have been taken and we must retrieve them."

Val watched him pace in the tiny room. "He may want to ride with you."

"Let him. But he will take orders from me."

She didn't say anything for a moment, watching as the great warlord made a strong return. This was the brother she knew, the deadly and cunning warrior that no man could best. She sought to help him as much as she could.

"As I told you, it took me about an hour to return to Rochester, and I am supposing Dagan and Gavril's corpses are still where I last saw them," she said quietly. "That will be your starting point. As I recall, it was a rather wooded area, so they could have traveled in any number of directions but it should not be difficult to find trampled paths through the foliage. The trees worked both for and against them. It shielded them from our party, but it will also leave a trail for you to follow."

Tevin nodded, his mind already moving to the ride south. He looked at his sister, seeing her wounded body as the result of the attack, and his focus shifted to her for the moment. "Has the surgeon already examined you?"

She nodded faintly. "Right before you came."

"What did he say?"

"That I have a crack on my skull and I am bruised, but that I should heal."

"Then I am grateful for small mercies this day." His dark eyes bore into her. "Have no doubt that I will return, and when I do, it will be with Cantia and Arabel."

Val smiled faintly. "Do not forget Hunt."

"Never."

Forcing a smile at his sister, Tevin moved to the doorway but paused before he left the room completely. "Val?"

"Aye?"

He gave her a rather reproachful look, as much as he could muster. "Do not believe for one minute that I did not see de Lohr kiss you," he said. "Take heed that I will deal with his bold actions upon my return."

Val started giggling. "You will not."

"I will."

"Leave him alone or you will face my wrath."

He scowled. "Are you saying that you… you *approve* of his actions? His forwardness? His slobbering lips against your flesh?"

"All that and more."

His scowl turned into an expression of outrage. "What *more* is there?"

Val's giggles turned into full-blown laughter, wincing because it hurt her head to laugh so much. She waved her brother on. "I will not tell you. Go now and find Cantia and Arabel."

He broke down into a smile. "I will."

"Do not come back without them."

His smile faded and a deadly gleam came to his eye. "I swear I will not. With God as my witness, I will not."

Val believed him implicitly.

○3

IT WAS MORNING. Lying on the same blanket that had covered her head for most of the night, Cantia could see the soft strains of early morning light infiltrating the shelter. It was cold but she had her arms around Arabel and Hunt, both children sleeping soundly in the early morning. But Cantia had never felt less like sleeping in her life.

She really wasn't sure where she was, and she had no idea how long they had traveled to get here. It felt like days. The men who had abducted her had hardly said a word between them, and they didn't speak to her at all until they reached their encampment. Then, their only words were directions to enter the shelter and stay there with the children. She did, mostly because Arabel was weeping hysterically and she wanted to soothe the young girl. She didn't even bother to speak to them or ask any questions, at least for the moment. All she wanted to do was make sure the children were well. She would deal with the rest later.

Now it was morning and she could hear the birds chirping, awaking to the new day. She lifted her head, looking around the tent, hearing sounds all around them. People were talking and there was the soft crunch of leaves as they moved through the forest. She smelled smoke. Feeling some bravery, as well as outrage and confusion, she got up and dared to step outside.

It was brisk and clear. Cantia glanced back at the shelter that had housed them through the night. It was made from leaves, rocks, pieces of wood, basically anything that would fit together and hold a shape. They were in an area that had some rolling hills to it and this particular shelter was backed up into the base of a rise so that the back end of it was pushed into the dirt. She stood by the door, looking around the area now that daylight had come, and she could see an entire camp spread out before her.

There was a surprising number of people milling about, collecting wood for the fire and water for cooking. A small stream ran over to her left, about a dozen yards away, and she could see both men and women drawing water. There also seemed to be a massive cooking fire off to the right, just outside of a hedge of trees, and she could see a few people gathering around it.

Increasingly puzzled, she stepped away from the door, growing more interested in her surroundings, when someone abruptly grabbed her by the wrist.

Startled, she shrieked as he yanked her away from the stone and wood shelter, pulling her with him as he walked towards the massive cooking fire in the near distance. The man who had her in his grasp wasn't particularly large, but he had a strong grip as he pulled her along. He looked at her and Cantia could see that he was older, with stringy dark hair and flashing dark eyes, and his body was lithe and wiry. Then he smiled at her, a rather insane gesture, and she was stabbed by fear.

"See who I have!" he bellowed to anyone who would listen. "Our prize has awoken!"

Some of the people began cheering and Cantia tried to pull away from him as he dragged her over to the cooking fire. He yelled some more, drawing a crowd, and people began to come out of their lean-tos and shacks to see what all of the commotion was about. By the time they reached the cooking fire, Cantia was nearly in full-blown panic, trying desperately to pull away from the man. As they came to a halt in a crowd of dirty, smelly, loud people, he slapped her across the face when she tried to kick him.

"That will be enough from you, woman," he growled, his mad-like grin vanished. "Behave yourself."

Cantia's hand flew to her stinging cheek. It hadn't been a hard slap, but it had been enough to smart. "Behave *myself*?" she repeated, angry and afraid. "You abducted me and my son, and you have the gall to tell me to behave?"

The crowd snickered as the man just looked at her. Then, that crazy grin returned. "Ah," he said, almost sweetly. "Listen to her speak. She is a fine, fine lady with a noble background. Is that not correct, little chicken?"

Cantia glanced around at the crowd nervously. "Who are you? Tell me your name."

The man snorted. "Still, she makes demands. This is a woman used to having her way."

The crowd cheered and jeered and Cantia was struggling not to become completely terrified. "I was not making demands," she clarified, hoping she didn't sound arrogant. She didn't want to appear demanding in front of this rather rough group. "I was simply asking a question. Who are you and why did you abduct us?"

Without letting go of her wrist, the man bowed deeply. "M'lady," he said mockingly. "I was under the impression we were saving you."

Cantia's fight came to a halt, stumped by his statement. She looked at him, shocked. "What... what do you mean?"

The man mimicked her expression. "Were you not in danger? Were you not about to be abducted by that knight, perhaps even worse?"

Cantia was at a loss, suddenly not feeling so completely frightened. "You saw what happened?"

The man nodded confidently. "We had been trailing your party for some time," he said. "We saw the knight kill his two colleagues and set upon you. So we saved you and your children."

He seemed very proud of himself. Cantia was completely baffled. "You *saved* us?" she repeated. "What in the world is going on here? Why were you following us?"

The man shrugged. "Because you were there," he said simply. "To tell you the truth, we were going to rob you but when we saw the knight turn against you, we decided to act. Perhaps it was because of the children or perhaps it was because we still seek your riches. I do not know. Perhaps we may kill you after all."

Cantia was back to fear again. "Please do not kill us," she begged softly. "If it is money you seek, then I can promise you a handsome reward if you return us to Rochester Castle."

The man's careless and rather humorous posturing fled and he peered at her, clearly interested.

"Rochester Castle?" he said, somewhat incredulous. "Is that your home?"

She nodded eagerly. "Aye," she replied. "My... my husband is Viscount Winterton. He will pay you a great deal of money if you return the children and me unharmed."

The crowd rumbled restlessly and the man seemed to lose some of his confidence. In truth, he looked rather uncertain.

"Winterton," he repeated. "Is he not part of East Anglia?"

By his tone, Cantia wasn't so certain that was a good thing. She didn't like the way he said it. But she didn't back out, not after she'd already divulged the information.

"Aye," she said, eyeing him, eyeing the crowd. "Please return us to Rochester. I will make sure you receive a goodly reward."

The man let go of her wrist. He seemed to be oddly subdued, unusual for a man who had been so animated moments before. He looked around the fire, at the faces of the dirty and destitute people, seemingly lost in thought. Cantia watched with mounting apprehension as he seemed to ponder her offer.

"He will kill us," he finally said.

Cantia shook her head. "Nay, he will not," she insisted. "You did indeed save us from a rogue knight. My husband will greatly reward you, I promise."

The man's gaze lingered on her. "Winterton is a man without mercy. I should know. His army burned my village and destroyed my home. My family and I had to take refuge in the forest because we have nowhere else to go. Now we live here, with these fine people, and we take what we want."

With that, he grabbed her wrist again and yanked her roughly in the direction they had come. The crowd yelled and cheered as the man spouted all of the terrible things he planned to do to the prisoner.

Terrified, Cantia was back to fighting him again, scratching and kicking, until he tried to slap her again but missed. Then she threw herself to her knees, trying to stop the momentum, but he simply pulled her along, dragging her through the grass and dirt, collecting leaves against her knees as he pulled. By the time they reached the shelter where Hunt and Arabel were sleeping, she was verging on panicked tears.

"Please," she begged. "Do not hurt me. *Please.*"

He didn't reply other than to yell victoriously at the crowd in the distance and throw open the shelter door, tossing Cantia inside.

Cantia fell to the ground, nearly landing on Hunt. The boy had been awakened by all of the commotion and was sitting up, rubbing his eyes and crying when he saw his mother sprawled on the ground. His weeping woke up Arabel, who lay next to him but was too weak to sit up as he was doing. She just lay there, crying, with her hands over her face.

On the ground, Cantia cowered as the man entered the shelter behind her and slammed the door. She was horrified at what she was sure was about to happen, in front of her son and Arabel no less, and the tears began to come. Still, she didn't give up. As the man came close, she put up a booted foot to kick him away. She was going to fight him or die trying.

But instead of descending on her, an odd thing happened. The man veered over to the wall where Cantia's satchels sat, fairly intact. Cantia watched him, terrorized, and saw he was going for the bags. As she watched, he unfastened the leather ties and opened up the satchel. Then he began to rummage around.

"You have some fine things," he said, pulling out a luscious topaz-colored silk surcoat and holding it up to the muted light. "This is beautiful. Where did you get it?"

Cantia was still on the ground, confusion mingling with her terror. She slowly began to push herself up.

"I... uh, that is to say, I bought the material in London," she said hesitantly.

"Did you sew it?"

"I did."

The man looked at her over his shoulder and she saw a glimpse of that insane smile once more. "You have great skill," he said, turning back to the contents of the bag and pulling out a blue cotton surcoat. "If you are the viscount's wife, do you not have women to sew for you?"

Cantia eyed Hunt as the boy wiped tears from his face. "I do," she said. "But I enjoy sewing."

The man simply nodded, throwing the topaz silk over his shoulder as he continued to rummage around in the bag. "My mother used to sew, and sew very well," he told her. "I developed an eye for fine work. Based on your wardrobe alone, I believe that you are Winterton's wife. It takes money to purchase what you have."

Cantia didn't know what to say to that. She pushed herself to her knees and crawled over to the pallet where Hunt was sitting. She sat beside him, wrapping her arms around the boy to comfort him.

"What are you going to do?" she asked.

The man finished with one satchel and began digging around in the other. Then he looked up at her, flashing that toothy grin. "Steal your clothing."

Cantia didn't say anything. She wasn't entirely sure what was happening, so she looked down at Hunt, kissed him on the forehead, and reached out a hand to hold on to Arabel, who was still lying there, weeping.

"Please," she said after a moment. "Can you not see that this child is very ill? We must return to Rochester."

The man glanced over his shoulder at the young girl still lying on the pallet. She was very tiny, very thin, and seemed to be unable to use her arms or legs very well. He shouldn't have cared about it but he was curious nonetheless. In that curiosity was a fraction of inherent pity.

"What is wrong with her?" he asked.

Cantia held Arabel's hand tightly. "She was born this way," she said softly. "She is crippled and I am sure the abduction last night has severely weakened her. She cannot take such excitement. Please… have mercy and return us."

The man's rummaging slowed to a halt. He looked at the trio on the pallet, seeing their scared and tired faces. For the first time that morning, he began to show signs of uncertainty and perhaps even remorse.

"My name is Gillywiss," he finally said. "These people, *my* people, live here because one way or another, we have been chased or scattered from our homes by men such as your husband. Why should I show mercy to you?"

Cantia wasn't without pity. She knew that those who did not live in castles were subject to terrible things. She knew that times were dark and desperate.

"Because the children and I have done nothing to harm you," she said softly. "We are innocent, just as you are innocent. Would you punish us for things beyond our control?"

"No one is innocent," he snapped softly. "Your husband is evil, lady."

"My husband is a good man," she replied, anger now joining the other emotions she was feeling. "He is kind and generous and sweet, and he cares very much for his family."

"He is a murderer!"

"He is commanded by those in power and does what he is told to do," she fired back. "He does not murder for the sake of murdering. He is part of this terrible war that is going on, brother against brother, where all men suffer. *I* have suffered. I have suffered great loss because of this foolish contention between Stephen and Matilda, so do not think to lecture me on the evils of battle, for I have lived them."

He was not convinced. "What have you possibly suffered?"

She looked away from him. "Death," she muttered. "The death of someone very close to me. Never imagine you are the only one who has suffered through death and loss."

"Who has died?"

Cantia looked at Hunt, her gaze soft and lingering. "His father," she replied. "He was killed in an ambush, more than likely by people such as yours. You think my husband a murderer? Perhaps you should see it from my perspective."

"Winterton is not his father?"

"Nay."

Gillywiss stared at her, surcoats in hand, preparing a sharp retort that simply died on his lips because she would not understand, anyway. But she had a point. He was an odd man, odder still because he stood up and pulled the surcoat over his head and tried to fit into it. Cantia watched, increasingly baffled, as the man tried to pull a substantially smaller garment onto his frame. When he caught Cantia and Hunt looking at him rather strangely, he flashed that crazy smile.

"Lady, you will scream now," he told her. "Scream until I tell you to stop."

Cantia still wasn't over their conversation, but he apparently was. Like someone had lit a flame, his demeanor change was instantaneous. When he waved his hands at her as if to encourage her to obey him, she took a deep breath and screamed, perhaps fearful of what would happen if she didn't.

"Again!" he commanded. "Scream as if I am violating you in every possible way. Do it!"

She let go of Hunt and moved away so she wouldn't be screaming in his ear. She howled and cried, on and on for several minutes as Gillywiss tried on her surcoats and fine things. Belts that wouldn't fit around his waist were put on his head, like a diadem, and he pulled the fine silk stockings onto his arms, smelling them. In fact, he smelled and touched everything, and when he came to a vial of expensive perfumed oil, he spread it liberally on his hands and inhaled the heady rose scent.

After many long minutes of screaming, Cantia was growing tired and her throat was beginning to hurt. When she thought perhaps Gillywiss had forgotten about her as he focused intently on her clothing, he finally waved a hand at her and she ceased.

"Well and good for you, my lady," he said. "You scream like a stuck pig."

Cantia rubbed her throat, eyeing the man who had at least two surcoats pulled over him, one belt around his head and another around his neck. He had found her small and precious glass hand mirror wrapped up in her satchel and was using it to look at himself. All the while, Cantia's eyes never left him. She had no idea what the man was doing or, furthermore, what he planned to do. She was on edge every single second, watching and waiting.

Finally, Gillywiss began to take everything off. He carefully rolled the surcoats, tucking them back where he found them. The belts were cautiously put back and the mirror was wrapped up in the heavy linen he had found it in. Everything went back as nicely and neatly as when he found it. When he was finished, he stood up and faced the three captives.

"You did not see me do this," he instructed.

Cantia understood he meant the entire episode with the clothes because he was pointing to her bags with a wagging finger.

"As… as you say, my lord," she said, somewhat confused.

Gillywiss put his hands on his hips and approached her, pensively. "And the screaming," he said. "If anyone asks, you will tell them I ravaged you thoroughly. Is that clear?"

Cantia nodded. "Aye, my lord."

Gillywiss' gaze lingered on her a moment before looking to Hunt and Arabel, both children gazing up at him with some puzzlement and fear. "You both," he pointed. "You will not tell what you saw here today. Do you understand? If you tell, very bad things will happen."

Hunt and Arabel nodded apprehensively but said nothing, and Gillywiss returned his attention to Cantia. It looked as if he wanted to say more but refrained. Suddenly appearing rather depressed, a far cry from the animated man of earlier, he turned for the door.

"I will send you food," he said.

He quit the hut, shutting the door behind him. Cantia stood there, staring at the panel, wondering what in the world had just happened. It was the strangest thing she had ever seen. Baffled, she sat down next to Hunt on the dirty pallet.

"Mam?" Hunt tugged on her arm. "What will we do?"

Cantia drew in a long breath as she looked at her son. "I do not know."

Hunt's little brow furrowed in thought. "We should esthcape," he said firmly. "We should run away."

Cantia had thought of that, too. She ran a hand over her son's blond head. "We cannot," she said softly, looking to Arabel, who was lying beside them. "We cannot leave Lady Arabel behind, and we cannot carry her with us, so we must stay here to protect her."

Arabel was gazing up at the pair. "Please," she said softly, "if you escape and run back to my father, you can bring help."

Cantia smiled faintly at the girl. "That is very brave, but I will not leave you," she said. "Until we can think of something else, we will all stay here together."

Arabel was coming to feel guilty, as if she were holding Cantia and Hunt back. "You cannot put yourself in such danger, my lady," she insisted. "They will not harm me, but I fear they will do terrible things to you. You must escape and you must take Hunt with you."

Cantia reached out and grasped the girl's hand, squeezing it. "I will not leave you," she said softly. "There is nothing more to discuss. Meanwhile, we must figure out how we can get word to your father."

Hunt had all manner of ideas on how to send word to Tevin, not the least of which was catching a bird and tying a note to its leg. Then he thought they could catch a fox and tell it to run to Rochester. As Cantia gently shot down every idea Hunt had, Arabel was making plans of her own. She may have been crippled, but she wasn't to be discounted in their quest for freedom.

She would get them out of there.

CHAPTER THIRTEEN

"AND I TOLD YOU that I forbid you to go search for them at this time," Geoff snarled at Tevin. "It is your fault they were abducted in the first place so I will not allow you to use my resources to hunt down a woman who is nothing more to you than a possession. I have had an entire patrol of men wiped out near the Dartford Crossing and have commanded you to drive back those who have now commandeered the bridge. I want it back."

Tevin was as close to striking Geoff as he had ever been in his life. Had de Lohr not been standing between him and Geoff, he more than likely would have ripped the man's head off. Instead, he took a step back when Myles gave him a gentle shove on the chest, pushing him back and away from the confrontation. In the solar of Rochester, tempers were running high as precious time was wasted with Geoff's delays.

If Geoff knows of your feelings for Cantia, he will see this as a game. Val's words were rolling over and over in Tevin's mind and he struggled to keep his mouth shut about anything with regard to Cantia. Geoff could not know she meant more to him than anything on earth. In fact, Tevin did not use Cantia as the focus at all. He used someone else.

"It is not Cantia I am after," he rumbled. "I have explained this to you. My daughter is missing, Geoff, and I will find her. I am going in search of my child and you cannot stop me."

"I can!"

"Then you shall have to kill me. Shall we retreat outside and face off against one another?"

Geoff backed down, but only slightly. He was still red about the face, twitching with fury. He had been pulled out of a dead sleep to face a problem he should not have to be facing, and he was very angry at his cousin for creating the situation. High and mighty Tevin always thought he knew best. Geoff was both thrilled and angry that his arrogant cousin had made a mistake.

"You should not have sent them away in the first place," he pointed an accusing finger, spittle flying from his lips. "Why would you do such a thing?"

Tevin cocked a dark eyebrow, fists resting on his hips. "You know why."

Geoff's lips curled in a sneer. "If I knew, I would not have asked."

Tevin's eyes narrowed. "Because you cannot be trusted," he said. "You have no self-control when it comes to a woman, *any* woman, so in order to protect the women residing at Rochester, I was forced to send them somewhere where you could not get to them."

Geoff's twitching grew worse. "You have no say in how I conduct my life, Tevin. I take what I want."

"You cannot take Lady Cantia, Val, or Arabel. In order to curb your temptation, I sought to move them out of your reach."

Geoff smacked the table in front of him. Then he threw the cups that were on it, followed by the pitcher half-filled with wine. Ruby red liquid sprayed on the stone walls as Geoff flirted with the boundaries of a temper tantrum.

"And you were punished for it," he seethed. "Val is injured and Lady Cantia and Arabel are missing. *You* were wrong, Tevin, not me. You cannot blame me for your failure."

Tevin's composure slipped a notch. "If you had any self-control, I would not have had to send them away, so do not turn this around as if I am the one with issues. If you would act like a man once in a while and not a spoiled child, we would not have this problem."

Geoff ripped off a barbaric yell and charged Tevin. He ran at him crazily, hands out like claws, and Tevin easily side-stepped the man, causing him to trip over a chair and crash into a wall. As Tevin faced him, waiting for his next move, Geoff pulled himself off of the wall and plunged a hand into his tunic, rooting around until he withdrew a wicked-looking dirk. He flashed it at Tevin, and the stakes of the game changed dramatically.

With another yell, he charged Tevin again, dirk held high. Tevin was prepared. As the man drew near, he reached out and grabbed his wrist, twisting it around until Geoff screamed with pain. Geoff ended up biting Tevin's bare hand and when Tevin let go before he could break the skin, Geoff brought the dirk to bear on Tevin's neck.

In a movement for self-preservation, Tevin lashed up a big arm, blocking the dirk as he grabbed Geoff around the throat with his other hand. He'd only meant to disarm him but by the way he grabbed Geoff, he ended up snapping his skull upward at an awkward angle. Bones snapped. The dirk dropped, and so did Geoff.

As quickly as the battle started, it was over. Tevin gazed down at his cousin as Myles, having been over by the door for the duration of the fight, rushed to Geoff's side and felt for a pulse. After a moment, he shook his head and looked up at Tevin.

"He is dead," he said quietly.

Tevin's brow furrowed with disbelief. "He cannot be."

"He is."

"Are you sure?"

"Verily."

Tevin's stunned gaze moved between Geoff and Myles. "But... but I was not trying to kill him," he said after a moment. "I was only trying to disarm him."

Myles' gaze lingered on Geoff. "I know," he said. "I saw what happened. He was trying to kill you, Tevin. You did what you had to do."

Tevin wasn't sure if he felt better or worse by that statement. Disbelief and shock overwhelmed him, so much so that he ended up stumbling back against the heavy table behind him as he attempted to wrap his mind around what he had just done.

"Oh...God," he hissed. "I did not mean to do it."

Myles could see how shocked he was. "Tevin," he said softly, firmly. "The man was trying to kill you. You defended yourself. What happened was an accident. Although I normally refrain from speaking ill of the dead, you know as well as I do that Geoff was a vile, corruptible man. His death is not an unwelcome one by any means. You did us all a service."

Tevin was still struggling although he wasn't sure why. Perhaps it was simply the swiftness of it and the fact that he truly hadn't been trying to kill him. He and Geoff had been given to tussles in the past, but nothing like this. He looked at Myles, his dark eyes intense as he came to terms with what he had done.

"The truth is that, at some point, Geoff would have tried to kill me or have me killed," he said, his voice hoarse. "He both loved and hated me, but mostly, he envied me. I know that as well as anyone. But all I can think of now is that the women in my family are finally safe. If that is a selfish thought, then I do not apologize. It is the truth."

Myles nodded in agreement, making his way over to him. "There is something else you must think of also."

"What?"

"You are now the Earl of East Anglia," he reminded him softly, a twinkle in his eye. "Long live the earl."

Tevin stared at him, realizing he was right. In the blink of an eye, the powerful Viscount Winterton had become the extremely powerful Earl of East Anglia. He reached out, grabbing Myles by the wrist as if to confirm the truth. His eyes were wide on Myles, who broke into a smile.

"Aye, Tevin," he affirmed quietly. "It is you. What is your first command, my lord?"

Tevin struggled to push through his shock. He now commanded thousands. "I... I am not sure," he hissed. "This is a day I never thought would truly come, at least not like this."

"The day has come. Give me a command."

Tevin maintained his grip on Myles' wrist. "It is strange that all I can think of at this moment is my father," he said softly. "He was

Winterton for so long. It was always my father who would succeed as the earl, never me, at least not until four years ago when I lost both my father and Torston."

"I remember."

"Now that the time has come, I feel…surprise. Unadulterated surprise."

Myles' expression tightened. "You must put that aside," he said. "I realize you are shocked, Tevin, but much requires your attention at the moment. Be shocked later if you must, give in to your astonishment at that time, but right now we require your level head. We need it. Much is going on and we require your wisdom in all things. What will your first command be, my lord?"

Tevin looked at the man, knowing he was correct in every facet. Too much depended on Tevin at the moment and he drew on that strength, that inner force of character, to settle himself. He had to. Forcing himself to think, he pushed himself off the table.

"Have Geoff's body taken out of here," he said as he moved towards the door. He couldn't bring himself to look at his cousin lying in a heap on the floor. "Have the servants prepare his body so we can move him to Rochester Cathedral."

"It will be done," Myles said smartly. "But what of you? What shall you do now?"

Tevin's mind was working. "I will be riding for Cantia and Arabel," he said. "There is nothing more important to me at this moment, not even Anglia. However, you will send word to all of our allies, including Matilda and Stephen, informing them that I have assumed the earldom at Geoff's passing. You will also call a meeting with all of my close allies to discuss the situation and how it will now affect them. My loyalties shall be made clear."

Myles paused by the door, bringing Tevin to a halt. "What would that be, my lord?"

Tevin's jaw ticked. He was gaining confidence and lucidity by the second. Now, he was doing what he was born to do. Finally, Anglia was in the hands of someone wise and intelligent. It was time to reclaim Anglia's good name and take a stand in this land of chaos and greed. When Tevin looked at Myles, it was with all seriousness.

"Brac Penden did *not* die in vain, regardless of who we support" he said pointedly, with emotion. "Discover who holds Dartford Crossing and tell them that I would meet with them when I return. I would suspect we are already allies. Stephen is the rightful king and I intend to support the man."

Myles nodded, warmth in his pale blue eyes, as he marched off to carry out the earl's orders. Tevin stood in the doorway a moment, still stunned, yet knowing what he had to do. Even though he'd never truly lusted after Geoff's title and power, he realized he was more than ready to assume the mantle. He'd been bred for this moment.

He was East Anglia.

☙

VAL WAS DEAD asleep when the door to her chamber opened, creaking and old. In fact, it was stuck, making noise that awakened her. Exhausted and drugged on something the surgeon gave her, she could barely open her eyes.

Myles came into the room, kneeling down next to the bed. His fair face was serious as he put a gentle hand on her shoulder.

"Val?" he said softly. "Are you awake?"

She inhaled, long and deep, before nodding her head. "I am," her eyes lolled open, looking at him. "What time is it?"

"Almost dawn," Myles caressed her shoulder gently. "I have come to tell you that something has happened."

Muddled though she may be, those words had meaning to her. Val blinked her eyes, struggling to focus. "What has happened?" she looked apprehensive. "Tevin? Is he well?"

Myles shushed her softly, cutting her off. "Geoff is dead," he informed her. "Your brother is now the Earl of East Anglia. I am summoning men at this moment to spread the word, and then I am riding to Dartford Crossing to find out who holds the bridge. Your brother needs to speak with them. I am telling you all of this in case Tevin comes to you. He is somewhat overwhelmed by everything at the moment so he make seek solace with you. I wanted you to be prepared."

Val understood most of what he said, but she was still focused on Geoff's death. Her pale face slackened. "Geoff is *dead*?" she repeated in a whisper. "What happened?"

Myles sighed as he moved from caressing her shoulder to stroking her hair. "He attacked Tevin in anger," he said quietly. "Your brother was trying to protect himself and accidentally killed him."

Val's eyes widened. "My God," she gasped. "Where is my brother?"

"Inside the keep, but I suspect he will make his way out here to you shortly."

"Is he not riding for Cantia and Arabel?"

"Aye, he is. He says there is nothing more important to him at this moment, not even Anglia."

Val thought on that a moment. Then she tried to sit up. "I must go to him," she grunted. "I must find my brother."

Myles threw an arm across her shoulders, preventing her from rising. She was fairly weak and didn't give him much of a fight. He was able to push her back to the bed without a significant struggle.

"He will come to you, I am sure," Myles insisted softly. "Be at ease, Val. I do not want to see you further injure yourself."

There was something in his tone that made Val take a closer look. For a man who, as long as she had known him, had only spoken of warring things and other trivial subjects, it was a tone of voice she had always wanted to hear from him. Perhaps his sympathy for her injury would cause him to say something sweet to her, something she had longed for. Perhaps he would say that he felt more for her than just knightly camaraderie.

"Why not?" she asked softly.

He appeared confused by the question. "What do you mean?"

"Why do you not want to see me injure myself further?"

Myles stared at her. But as he did so, something in his blue eyes changed. They seemed to soften, grow liquid and warm. A faint smile tugged at his lips.

"Because I do not," he whispered. "That is all you need to know."

She could sense humor and her dark eyes glittered. "That is not true," she murmured. "I need to know everything. Tell me, Myles."

His smile grew although he fought it, biting his lip as he averted his gaze. "I cannot tell you."

"Why not?"

"Because I am a coward."

She grinned. "Myles de Lohr, you are no such thing. Tell me why you do not wish for me to injure myself further or… or I swear I will never speak to you again."

He cast her a sidelong glance. "Never?"

"Never. Never, ever."

"That is a very long time."

"It is. Are you willing to take that chance?"

He sighed heavily, although he was still having difficulty looking at her. "Can you at least give me time to determine what it is I need to say before you cut me off completely? I do not want to say the wrong thing."

She did giggle, then. "How on earth can you say the wrong thing? Myles, you had better tell me what I wish to hear or there will be serious consequences."

His grin broke through. "I do not like consequences."

"Would it be easier if I spoke first?"

His grin faded and he looked at her, then. In fact, he looked both curious and hopeful. It was a strange combination.

"Aye, I believe it would," he confided.

Her smile faded as well, though it didn't vanish completely. She gazed at the man, his handsome face, someone she had known for many years. She had always been very fond of him, made stronger now with age and experience. She couldn't remember when she hadn't longed for him in a way that made her heart race and her palms sweat. Reaching out, she gently touched his wrist.

"Very well," she whispered. "Promise you will not laugh."

"I will not laugh, I swear."

She nodded her head, almost reluctantly, as she summoned her courage. "I know I am not a fine lady with elegant pursuits," she admitted. "But I am strong, brave, and of good character, and I swear I would love you forever if given the chance. I would do all in my power to make you happy and content, Myles. Perhaps you do not feel the same way about me but I would be honored if you would at least give me the chance."

His smile was completely vanished as he stared at her with big eyes. After a moment, he took the hand she had placed on his wrist and brought it to his lips, kissing it reverently. Val had no idea why tears sprang to her eyes, but they did. They streamed down her temples as she watched him gently kiss her hand, her wrist. It was the most wonderful moment she could have ever imagined. When he was finished kissing her hand, he moved to her head, very carefully cupping her face between his two big hands. He just stared at her.

"You are far braver than I am, my lady," he murmured. "You have spoken everything that is within my heart but I have been too afraid to speak the words. I never thought… I did not believe you would be receptive."

She grinned at him, thrilled beyond measure at his tender touch. She had dreamt of this moment and now that it was upon them, she could never have imagined it to be this wonderful.

"I am receptive," she whispered.

He lifted his eyebrows. "Enough to give up the sword to become my wife? I do not want to marry a woman who can out maneuver me in battle or best me in a fight."

She giggled. "I promise that I shall lay my sword down if I am your wife. Unless, of course, you ever have need of me."

His eyes glittered as his gaze drifted over her forehead, her eyes, the shape of her lovely face. "I will have need of you," he whispered as his face loomed closer. "But not in that fashion."

His lips claimed hers, a sweeter kiss neither of them had ever known. He suckled her lips, tasting her for the first time, thinking he'd been a fool not to have done it sooner. The gentle kiss turned passionate and, instinctively, he moved to put his arms around her and pull her close but she yelped in pain as he tried. Startled, horrified, he backed off.

"I am so sorry," he whispered. "I did not mean to hurt you."

She laughed it off, her lips red and moist from his attention. "Not to worry," she assured him. "It is of little consequence considering I have been waiting for weeks for you to kiss me as you just did."

His grin returned, as did his hands to her face. "Why did you not tell me this?"

It was her turn to look horrified. "And risk your rejection, or worse? You would have thought me to be a horribly forward creature."

"I would have thought you to have given me an invitation of a lifetime."

She giggled and he kissed her again, being very mindful of her injuries. But he had duties to attend to, much as he was reluctant to leave her. Only when Val swore she would not leave the bed and would wait impatiently for his return did he force himself away from her. Heart racing and limbs tingling, he quit the knight's quarters.

Tevin wondered why Myles had such a huge grin on his face when he saw him crossing the bailey a few minutes later. Realizing he had just come from the knight's quarters, he began to suspect why.

CHAPTER FOURTEEN

THE DAY HAD been long and tense, bouts of fear coming in waves as the sun traveled the sky. Sometimes, Cantia was quite calm, but other times, she was in tears of terror. Yet none of those feelings were particularly productive. As Cantia sat in her prison along with Hunt and Arabel, she truly wondered what was to become of them.

The camp had been active all day. At least, what she could hear from inside her dark and smelly prison made the place appear very active. Sounds of people were all around her, shouting, working, doing what they needed to do in order to survive. After Gillywiss had left them, no one had bothered them except for a woman who had come to bring them food. She brought them a rather large fare of small apples, pears, three roasted rabbits, and two large loaves of dark bread. Cantia and the children had eaten until they nearly burst.

With bellies full, they were able to think more clearly. Arabel still seemed to be feeling poorly, having slept all morning and into the afternoon, and Cantia was very concerned for the girl. There was a hole dug in the ground in one corner of the hut that they quickly discovered was the chamber pot because it smelled up the entire room. Cantia had helped the girl use it, once, as Hunt sat at the other end of the hut and faced the wall to afford Arabel some privacy.

Arabel had been embarrassed that she required such assistance but there wasn't much she could do about it, so she thanked Cantia profusely for her kindness and swore she'd be as little trouble as possible. Cantia had merely smiled and touched the girl's cheek affectionately. As a mother, it was in her nature to be helpful to a child and she truly didn't mind. Every time she looked into that beautiful face, she saw Tevin. She was happy to do what she could.

The dusk settled cool and dark, and as the moon began to rise, silver shadows were cast upon the land. Owls hooted and other creatures of the night rooted around for their supper as Cantia sat on the ground next to Hunt, her arms around the boy as the hut grew very cold and dark. As she rocked Hunt, attempting to lull him to sleep, the door to the hut jerked open.

Startled, Cantia stopped rocking her child as Gillywiss entered the chamber and pulled the door shut behind him. He had a fish oil lamp in his hand, a bowl of liquefied fat with a floating wick that gave off a significant amount of smoke and light. His dark eyes found her in the dim hut and, as she had seen earlier in the day, he flashed her a rather crazed expression complete with big toothy smile.

"My lady," he greeted. "And how are you faring on this beautiful night?"

Cantia was in no mood for his jovial attitude. "Cold," she said flatly. "It is cold and dark in here."

He looked around as if just noticing the darkness. "So it is," he said, finding more interest in her bags over by the wall. "Do you not have something warm to wear?"

Cantia watched him set the lamp down and pull open a satchel. "We need a fire," she said. "The children need warmth that cannot be provided by clothing."

Gillywiss was back to digging around in her bags, pulling forth the garments he had so carefully replaced earlier in the day. As Cantia watched, the man began pulling them on again, inspecting the fine fabric, running his fingers over the delicate stitching. It was the second time that day he had come to put on her clothes and rifle through her belongings, and Cantia was quite curious about his behavior. In moments like this, she could almost believe he was non-violent and rather sympathetic. In fact, she thought she might try to take advantage of his fascination for her wardrobe.

"My lord," she said softly, "if you like the coats so much, I would happily exchange them for our freedom."

Gillywiss looked up from the orange-colored surcoat he was presently inspecting. His dark eyes were curious on her, perhaps even interested, but before he could reply, Arabel spoke.

"My lord," she said in her sweet, child-like voice. "I am the Lady Arabel du Reims. My father is Viscount Winterton. As Lady Cantia said, he will reward you greatly for delivering us to him, but I would like to offer you all that I have so that you may let us go. I… I have fifty gold crowns, some jewelry, a white goat and a black and white pony that I would give you if you will only let us go home. I promise I will have these things brought to you if you will… please, I just want to go home."

The last words were spoken in tears. Cantia went to the girl to comfort her, pulling her up into her arms and rocking her gently. Arabel was so tiny that it was like holding Hunt on her lap, and Cantia soothed the girl softly.

Gillywiss was watching the exchange carefully. He wasn't very adept at hiding his feelings so he looked away, back to the satchel, and began to pull out more belongings. He could hear Arabel weeping and Cantia's soft words, and it fed both his guilt and his irritation. As his rummaging began to grow more agitated in motion, he began to realize there was someone beside him. He turned to see Hunt's big blue eyes gazing up at him.

"Do you have a boy?" the child asked.

Gillywiss seemed reluctant to answer but he did. "Nay," he replied. "No boy. Just girls."

"A wife?"

"She is dead."

He turned his attention back to the bag and Hunt joined him. The little boy reached into his mother's bag and pulled forth a beaded belt, handing it to Gillywiss. The man slowed his digging, meeting Hunt's gaze with some reluctance. It was clear that he was having some difficulty ignoring what was going on around him. Arabel's weeping was pathetic and sorrowful, and Gillywiss was feeling it.

"I am not a bad man," he finally said, looking over at Arabel and Cantia. "There are those in this village who would slit a man's throat as easily as speak to him, but I am not one of them. You have nothing to fear from me."

"Please take my offer," Arabel sobbed. "I want to go home. I want to see my father."

Gillywiss looked at the frail young girl, his sense of remorse growing. He wasn't any good at fighting off his feelings, torn between knowing he shouldn't care yet inherently caring. A sick child's tears were not to be ignored.

"You would do this?" he finally asked her, some disbelief in his tone. "You would give me everything you own just to go home?"

Arabel nodded vigorously. "Aye, I would. Will you not accept, sir?"

Gillywiss pondered her words before letting his gaze move to Cantia and then to Hunt. He knew about the nobility of this country. He knew they were all arrogant and greedy, men and women included. They sucked the peasants dry and still hungered for more. He'd spent his entire life knowing these facts, yet when he looked at Cantia and the children, he did not sense greed or arrogance.

In fact, he sensed a good deal of compassion, of intelligence, and of kindness, especially from Cantia. She was a strikingly beautiful woman, to be sure, and he knew he could sell her to the highest bidder for a great deal of money. But the truth was that he had no desire to sell her. She intrigued him greatly. The whole family did, and he wasn't exactly sure why.

"Tell me something," he sat back on his bum, Cantia's fine things still on his head or in his hand. "You have a desire only to see your father?"

Arabel nodded firmly. "Aye, sir."

"Why not your mother? I do not understand the relation of this woman to you. She says she is the viscount's wife, yet she is not your mother?"

He was pointing at Cantia, who looked at Arabel as she thought of an explanation. "Arabel's mother abandoned her when she was a baby," Cantia said softly, hoping that if she divulged personal details, the man might feel more of a connection to them and, therefore, more sympathy in his decision to let them go. "She knows no mother."

Gillywiss lifted an eyebrow. "But you are the viscount's wife?"

Cantia hesitated a moment before shaking her head. "Not in the eyes of the church," she whispered. "But we are married in our hearts. That will never change."

Arabel hadn't heard of the true relationship between her father and Lady Cantia when she had been at Rochester, but in truth she wasn't surprised. She had seen the way her father looked at Lady Cantia and, if she thought on it, she wasn't all that upset about it. She liked Lady Cantia and she wanted her father to be happy. He was, in fact, a very lonely man, and Lady Cantia was very kind. More than that, she understood why her father could not marry Cantia. She was young, but she wasn't ignorant in the least. Like her father, she was exceptionally bright.

"My mother left me when I was born," she said. "Although my father told me that she had to go away, I know it was because she did not love me. I was born sick and I must have chased her away and made her ashamed. My father cannot marry again because he is still married to my mother even though she ran away from us."

Gillywiss was listening seriously to a rather tragic, and very personal, story. His dark gaze found Cantia. "Is this true?"

Cantia couldn't look at him. These were thoughts and situations that she had only discussed with Tevin. Now a stranger was hearing them and she was uncomfortable.

"Aye," she murmured, looking at Arabel and stroking the blond head. "Arabel's mother ran away fifteen years ago and no one knows what has become of her. Tevin… Viscount Winterton… has every intention of hunting the woman down, or at least finding out what has become of her, so that we can be married."

"Do you know where the woman has gone?"

"Paris, he was told, but that was many years ago."

"Her name?"

"Louisa," Arabel said before Cantia could reply. "Louisa Berthilde Solveig Hesse. I am named for her. She is from the House of Hesse. Do you know where that is?"

Gillywiss smiled faintly. The young girl sounded as if Hesse was perhaps at the ends of the earth.

"Germanic," he said, looking to Cantia again. "Then you are the viscount's mistress."

Cantia had told Tevin once that she would be his mistress even if they could never be married simply because she loved him. It was usually a shameful title, but she was not ashamed, not in the least. She looked Gillywiss squarely in the eye.

"Aye," she answered without reserve. "I am very proud of it, and of him. He is a remarkable man."

Gillywiss, pondering the conversation, returned his attention to the satchels against the wall, now open with items scattered. He began to dig around in the bottom of the bag, searching for items he had missed the first time around, but as he groped around, he could hear voices in the forest that were growing louder.

Gillywiss stopped in his rummaging, ears poised and listening. The voices were drawing closer and without delay, he shoved Cantia's items back in the bag far more carelessly than he had the first time and cinched the bag up. Then he kicked it over against the wall and rushed to the door, opening it just as several people came upon the cabin.

Hunt heard the loud voices and ran to his mother, who gathered him upon her lap and held him tightly. Cantia also made sure to position herself between Arabel and the door, both hiding and protecting the girl. Gillywiss had the door wide open as the group approached.

"What is your trouble?" Gillywiss boomed.

Men were muttering and women seemed to be weeping. "Marna is having her child," a woman said fearfully. "It cannot be born without help. We must send for a physic."

Gillywiss was confused. "What do you mean it cannot be born without help?" he demanded, looking to the group. "And where do all of you think to go? It looks like a mob."

"We were collecting money to pay the physic," one man said.

Gillywiss waved at them irritably. "We cannot bring a physic here," he snapped. "If we bring someone from the outside into our lair, the authorities will know where we are. All of you know this. There are many wanted men here, men who will not be jeopardized. Do what can be done for Marna but there will be no physic."

"But...!" a woman's voice pleaded. "We cannot simply let her die. Marna and John have waited for this son and...!"

"And they have already lost three," Gillywiss sounded angry and impatient with them. "This child will be dead like the others. Go back to your homes and let God's will be done."

"She is your own sister, for the love of God!"

"And she understands that I cannot allow our people to be put in jeopardy for her sake. Two lives are not worth many."

"I will help her."

The soft voice came from behind Gillywiss, inside the hut. Startled, Gillywiss, as well as a few of the people milling outside, turned to see Cantia moving forward in the darkness. Her lovely face was serious and calm.

"I will see what I can do," she said evenly. "I have helped birth many a child. Perhaps I can do something."

The women seemed willing, the men hesitant. Cantia's gaze was unwavering upon Gillywiss as she hoped he would allow her to help the woman and perhaps thereby gain even more sympathy from the man in her quest to be released. When she should have felt guilty of her ulterior motives other than the milk of human kindness, she couldn't muster the will. She was determined to do anything she could in order to secure their release and this was a brilliant opportunity.

"No," Gillywiss said flatly.

"Aye!" a pair of women cried, moving for Cantia and reaching out to grasp her. "Let the lady help!" one of them wept.

The women had Cantia by the wrist, pulling her from the hut. Gillywiss started to protest but he was drowned out as more women took up the cry and began parading Cantia across the dark encampment, heading for a cluster of huts off to the northwest. Annoyed, he went in pursuit.

Cantia was most interested to realize that the group of women had been able to override Gillywiss' wants. She tucked that knowledge back in her memory, wondering if she would have need of it at some point, as the women took her to a hut wedged beneath a pair of big oaks. The structure was made from rocks and sod, just like the others in the clandestine village, and the door itself was very nice and looked as if it might have been stolen from a manse or even a church. It had saints and gargoyles carved into it. Cantia was looking at the door curiously when it abruptly opened.

More women were inside the cramped hut, the smell of smoke and some kind of herb very heavy in the air. It was dark and crowded inside, and Cantia suddenly felt a little uncertain as someone gently pushed her inside. Maybe this wasn't such a good idea after all. But she heard groaning and struggled to adjust her eyes to the dim light. On a pallet in one corner of the room, a heavy-set woman lay on her back and moaned. The sound was enough to drive the uncertainty out of Cantia.

Dropping to her knees next to the miserable woman, she went to work.

෬

"HUNT, YOU MUST," Arabel hissed. "No one is watching us right now. You must escape and tell my father where we are."

Hunt was looking at Arabel dubiously. "But I do not know where we are," he said. "And what about my mother?"

Arabel thought quickly. Her mind was very cunning, like her father's, as she tried to think of a way out of their predicament.

"I would go if I could," she whispered. "But I cannot. You are our only hope, Hunt. Your mother is in trouble and I fear what they will do to her. Can you not see that?"

Hunt nodded solemnly, fearfully. He was too young to fully grasp what kind of trouble his mother was in, or they were in generally, but he knew the situation was bad. And he was scared now that his mother had left them. Brow furrowed, he plopped next to Arabel as she lay on the makeshift pallet of rushes and musty skins.

"What do I do?" he asked. "How do I go home?"

Arabel put her slender hand on his wrist. "Do you remember the night we were captured that the moon was very bright?"

Hunt nodded. "It was big, like a big white wheel of cheesth."

Arabel smiled at his lispy tongue. "Aye, it was," she said. "When we left Rochester, the moon was on our left, to the east. Do you remember that too?" As Hunt nodded again, she continued. "If you go outside now, the moon should be in the same place. It is so bright that you will be able to see. If the moon was on our left when we headed away from Rochester, if you keep it on your right, you should be heading back towards Rochester. Do you understand?"

Hunt's face scrunched up a bit as he thought on her words. Arabel could see he didn't quite understand what she was saying so she rubbed her fingers in the dirt beneath them and proceeded to smear it across Hunt's left arm.

"That is your left side," she said. "You want the moon to be on the side that does not have dirt smears on it."

Hunt lifted both arms, looking curiously at the dirt, until his face eventually washed with an expression of understanding. He grinned and slapped at his right arm.

"The moon thould be over here," he said happily.

Arabel nodded. "Aye," she was thrilled he was coming to understand. But her excitement was damped by the fact that a very young boy would be running off into the wilds in an attempt to save them all, out into the wilderness where any number of things could happen to him. It was a terrible gamble. "I am afraid for you all alone in the woods, Hunt, but I fear we have no other choice. I think you are very brave. I think you can save us all."

Hunt wasn't particularly thinking about the danger. He was a little too young to completely grasp the concept because in truth, he'd spent his entire life safely protected at Rochester. Wandering the countryside had never been an option for him. But he did like that Arabel had called him brave.

"Knights are brave," he said.

Arabel grinned. "You are a very brave knight. Will you save us, Hunt?"

He nodded firmly. "I wish I had my sword."

Arabel looked around their hut. There wasn't anything she could see that remotely resembled a weapon.

"Perhaps a sword would only slow you down," she suggested, trying to discourage him from making a weapon the focus of his mission. "If you do not have anything heavy to carry, you can run swiftly, like the wind. If you see trouble, then you will hide. A sword would make it difficult to hide."

It made no sense, and it was somewhat a lie, but Hunt thought seriously on her statement. Arabel was growing increasingly anxious for him to be on his way, terrified with every moment that passed someone would appear and Hunt would be unable to slip away. Hunt didn't seem to have the same sense of urgency that she did. She grasped the young man by the hand and squeezed.

"You must go now," she insisted softly but firmly. "Leave this hut and run far away from this camp until you see the moon, then keep it on your right side. Keep running, Hunt, until you come to a town or a church. Ask the people there where Rochester Castle is and ask for their help. If you tell them my father will reward them for helping you, it should make asking for assistance a simple thing."

Hunt pondered her instructions, finally nodding his head and jumping to his feet. He brushed off his dirty knees. As Arabel watched with anticipation, Hunt went to the hut door and put his hand on the crude wooden latch. In fact, the entire door was crude and not very well made, as if someone had pieced it together with scraps of wood and branches. Dried grass or moss plugged up the holes. Hunt pulled at the moss, tossing it to the floor, until there was a big enough hole to look through. The child peered out into the darkness.

"It isth very dark," he turned to Arabel after a moment, his expression uncertain. "Where did my mother go?"

Arabel could see that he still didn't completely grasp the situation and struggled not to become short with him. It was as if they kept backtracking on what she had explained to him but then she had to remind herself that the child was only five years old.

"I do not know," she said with strained patience. "That is why you must run, Hunt. You must find help. I know you can do this. You are a very brave knight, are you not? Perhaps my father will reward you with a real sword for your courage."

Hunt was intrigued with the thought. "Can I kill someone with it?"

"If you must."

Hunt grinned. "Then we can have a grand funeral," he threw up his arms happily. Then the arms came down and he cocked his head. "Are you sure he will give me a real sword?"

"I promise."

Hunt believed her. He had no reason not to, mostly because Tevin had already given him a new sword so he knew the man was good for such a thing. Moreover, Arabel was sure he could be brave and save them all, and that meant a good deal to his little heart. He wanted to save them.

Scooting to the door, he peeked out of the hole he had made to see that the camp seemed to be very quiet for the most part. With a glance at Arabel, who nodded her head encouragingly, Hunt very carefully pulled open the door. It was dark outside, with trees and bushes of matted foliage around them, but there were no people at all. He could see bonfires in the distance as people moved about and cooked their evening meals, but there was no one in close proximity of their hut. It appeared they had all headed off with his mother and Gillywiss. The vacancy of the immediate area fed his bravery.

"I'm going," he hissed loudly at Arabel. "I will bring an army back."

Arabel nodded eagerly. "Remember to keep the moon on the side of your body that does not have the dirt smears. Run until you find someone who can take you to Rochester!"

Hunt just waved her off and quit the hut, pulling the door shut behind him. Arabel lay there, listening to his soft footfalls fade off as the crunching of the earth and grass grew faint. Once the sounds had faded completely, Arabel felt rather hollow and desolate. She wondered what she was going to tell Lady Penden when the woman returned. She wondered what would happen if they never saw Hunt again. He was a very little boy, now out in a very big and dangerous world.

Closing her eyes, she wept and prayed.

CHAPTER FIFTEEN

WHEN SIMON AND JOHN rode for the Dartford Crossing to carry the news of the new Earl of East Anglia and to assess who currently had charge of the bridge, Tevin took a rather large party towards Darland in search of Cantia, Hunt, and Arabel.

Myles rode with him as the three hundred man army traveled south. He was originally supposed to ride for the bridge but changed his mind. He thought he would be better served riding with Tevin if for no other reason than to keep the man calm. Moreover, Val had asked it of him and he would not disappoint her.

After making arrangements for Geoff to be prepared and delivered to Rochester Cathedral, and assembling the two separate armies, it was late afternoon by the time Tevin's party left Rochester and he was seriously edgy because of the delays. Fortunately, the day was clear with scattered clouds, making their travel easy enough on the rutted roads. Armed to the teeth, they were prepared for anything. Moreover, Tevin had murder on his mind and the entire troop was aware of it. This was more than a rescue. It was vengeance. Du Reims was out for blood.

As Val had told them, approximately an hour south of Rochester saw them come across the bodies of Dagan and Gavril. Gavril had a knife in his throat while Dagan had taken a big arrow to the body. Tevin stood over the man, gazing down at him, knowing the arrow hadn't killed him right away. There was a huge amount of dark, gooey blood underneath and around him, suggesting he had slowly bled to death.

Sickened, terrified for Cantia and his daughter, Tevin struggled to keep a level head as he had a few of his men take Dagan and Gavril back to Rochester. Meanwhile, he pushed himself to focus on finding whatever trail the attackers had left behind because he found it easier to cope with his feelings if he focused on finding any evidence of their departure. Somewhere in this expanse of grass, weeds, mud and trees had to be clues. He was determined to find them.

Eventually, he had about a hundred of his men carefully combing the area for any signs of Cantia, Arabel and Hunt. Tevin, Myles, and the remainder of the army remained on the road, studying it for hoof prints or any recognizable pattern, but eventually realized that it was a futile quest because the hard-packed road wasn't easily giving up its secrets. Whatever foot of hoof prints there had been had dissolved or blown away long ago.

After a half-hour of inspecting the countryside, a few of Tevin's men found what they thought was a trail leading off to the south. Spurred by the discovery, Tevin lead the entire brigade south until they came to what they believed was the trail's end. A small village with a rather large church sat along the banks of a gentle creek and Tevin showed no mercy as his men plowed into the quiet little berg.

Peasants were roused, bullied and terrified as Tevin's men did a house to house search. The weeping of women and children could be heard as the town's priest intervened, begging to know why the men were raiding the town. Tevin explained, as calmly as he could, that he was looking for his family and would burn the town to the ground if he did not find them. At the moment, he was not permitting his men to do anything more than roust people and search houses, but that would very quickly change if he did not get what he wanted.

The priest, sensing death for his flock if they did not comply with the enormous warlord who had yet to fully identify himself, began shouting to the people as to the reasons behind the raid. Trembling and uncertain, the word was passed until two young men eventually came forward and produced a pair of well-made weapons.

Myles, who was on foot as Tevin sat upon his charger to supervise the raid, inspected the dirks in the shaking young hands.

"Where did you get these?" he asked.

The priest, standing next to the young men, nudged the one closest to him. "From... from a dead knight, m'lord," a skinny youth choked out a reply. "He had a knife through his neck. We... we came across him early this morning when we were searching for a lost lamb. He was already dead when we found him, m'lord, I swear it. We didn't kill him."

Myles removed the dirk from the young man's grasp, inspecting it closely. Then he eyed the pair. "You say he was already dead?"

"Aye, m'lord."

"What time was this?"

"At dawn, m'lord."

"And you saw no one else?"

The two young men passed glances. "There was another knight," the youth said, hanging his head. "We took this other knife from him."

"And he was already dead, too?"

"Aye, m'lord."

"You saw no women or children?"

"No, m'lord. There was no one."

Myles believed him, for one very good reason. The young men would not have appeared with the simplicity of stolen dirks to save their village from destruction had they been guilty of more heinous crimes. At least, that was Myles' suspicion. Moreover, they didn't have the look of bandits, and Myles had seen plenty to know. They looked like farm boys. Still, he eyed them both critically, as if his piercing gaze would cause them to break down were they holding anything back.

"Then it must have been your trail we followed," Myles muttered.

The young men didn't know how to answer. They kept their heads down as the priest watched Myles very closely.

"Will you please stop what you are doing, my lord?" the pale old man asked. "These are good people. They do not have your women and children."

Myles looked at the man. "Even so, they are still missing and we will find them," he said. "If you know anything, priest, now would be the time to tell me."

The priest shook his head. "I do not, my lord, I swear on our Most High," he said earnestly. "But these lands abound with murderers, thieves and bandits. We have to fight them off ourselves quite frequently."

Myles knew that. It was a wild and lawless land these days and the people reflected that. Everyone lived with fear in their hearts and weapons in their hands. He was starting to feel some despondency as he tightened up his gloves, wondering how he was going to deter Tevin from ripping the rest of the village apart.

"You would not happen to know were any of those murderers are, would you?" he muttered drolly. "Perhaps they are living out in the open somewhere with great bonfires that will guide our way to them."

The priest cocked his head. "In fact," he said, "there is a rather large camp of outlaws not far from here. They raid our stores quite frequently and I even caught one of them trying to steal from the church. I told him he would burn in hell and he laughed at me."

Myles was somewhat interested in what he was saying. "Where is this camp?"

The priest pointed to the northeast. "That way, a few miles. If you take the small trail from the town that leads over the stream, follow it until it ends and keep going. You will run into the camp less than an hour later."

It was as good an option as anything else. At least it would be something to focus Tevin on other than the innocents of the scared little village. Nodding his thanks, Myles marched back towards his charger, and towards Tevin, whistling loudly between his teeth as he went. When the soldiers turned to him, he issued orders to cease their activities and mount their horses. Tevin, having heard the command, waited impatiently for Myles to come within earshot.

"These people did not take Cantia or Arabel," Myles said before Tevin could yell at him. "However, the priest has told me of an encampment of outlaws a few miles to the northeast. I suggest we focus our attentions there."

"How do you know Cantia isn't here?" Tevin demanded as Myles mounted his horse.

"Because the trail we found was from those two frightened young men over there," Myles said, pointing in the direction of the priest and a small, frightened crowd. "The men were hunting down a lost lamb and came across Gavril and Dagan. They stole a few weapons off of them. They said that when they found the knights that they were quite alone. No one else was around. The priest suggested we try the known outlaws in the area. More than likely, they would have what we are looking for."

Tevin wasn't happy but, truth be told, but it made some sense. Outlaws would more than likely be to blame, as villagers did not usually ambush travelers on the open road. So he allowed Myles to issue commands as the men gathered and sped off to the northeast section of the village where a small footpath led to the stream and then continued on the other side.

The sun was nearly gone as the army raced northeast, tearing up meadows and forests and foliage as they went. Horses thundered and snorted, and the destriers that Tevin and Myles rode, excited by the sense of urgency in the air, charged at the head of the pack and snapped at anything they drew close to. They believed they were heading into battle and for Tevin, too, it was his sense as well. His apprehension and fury were driving him.

Less than an hour into their ride, the group headed into a particularly dense cluster of trees and Tevin and Miles had to raise their visors to see in the weak light. They could see something up ahead. Tevin raised a hand, calling a halt to the brigade, as they sighted the faint flickers of fires in the distance.

As they slowed their pace to study the distant flames, an arrow zinged past Tevin's head. Startled, Myles snatched the crossbow tethered on the right flank of his horse and lifted the weapon, pointing it in the direction that the arrow had come from. As the men spread out to capture whoever had fired the arrow, Myles caught movement when the man, stationed in the trees and covered with soot to conceal himself, launched another arrow.

This arrow had flame to it, sailing in an arc towards the distant fires. Myles launched his own arrow at the man, hitting his mark and watching the man fall to the ground in a heap. Even though he'd taken out the lookout, the damage was done. The flaming arrow had been a warning signal to the camp and Tevin knew their cover was blown. In the darkness, in the trees, he slammed his visor down and unsheathed his broadsword.

"We have been announced," he said to Myles. "Make no delays. If Cantia and Arabel really are in that camp, they might try to kill them with our appearance."

Myles spurred his charger after Tevin, listening to the sounds as the distant settlement began to take up alarm cries. As they plowed through the trees and into the perimeter of what appeared to be a very large encampment, Myles headed in one direction to search and Tevin headed in the other.

He could only pray, for all their sakes, that they weren't too late.

○3

"YOUR SON, MY LADY."

Cantia was smiling as she handed over the swaddled, screaming bundle to the exhausted mother. Overjoyed, the red-faced woman accepted the child, weeping as she gazed upon the angry little face for the first time. Cantia watched the joy, remembering well when she had given birth to Hunt and the euphoria she and Brac had experienced. The joy of the successful childbirth was almost enough to ease the fear of her captivity and she took a few moments to forget her predicament.

As she watched the new mother, she began to wonder if she and Tevin would ever be blessed with a child. She had lost one pregnancy before Hunt was born and had not conceived again since his birth, so she wondered if she was even able to have any more children. Brac had never said a word about it although she knew he would have liked more children.

She wondered if Tevin would become disappointed in her if she wasn't able to bear him a son. It really wasn't something she'd thought about until now. Cantia was torn between wanting to provide Tevin with more children and knowing any children they had together would be bastards. But she pushed those thoughts aside to focus on the new mother and baby at her feet.

"See if he will suckle," she encouraged. "Put him on the breast and feed him."

The new mother moved her shift aside to expose a big, plump breast and put the infant to the nipple. The baby latched on and began to feed eagerly and, at that point, the other women in the hut crowded around and took over, and Cantia knew her job was finished.

She had done what she had been called to do. After initially examining the woman, she realized that the child had been turned about in the womb. She then proceeded to oil the mother's belly up with grease and massage the child until the baby rotated around so he was facing head-first. She'd seen the midwife at Rochester grease up bellies when babies were facing the wrong direction and, fortunately, her observations had paid off. She'd been able to help.

It was an action she hoped would sway Gillywiss. The man had been seated just inside the hut door during the entire event, his eyes on Cantia as if afraid she was going to disappear. As Cantia washed her hands in clean water, she stole a glance over her shoulder at the man still sitting there in the shadows. With a deep breath for courage, for calm, she made her way over to him.

"I have never known a man to remain in the same room as a woman giving birth," she said. "You are very brave."

Gillywiss was gazing up at her from his position on the stool. He was leaning back against the wall of the hut, his dark curly hair wild around his somewhat pensive face. He seemed quiet and introspective. He was just watching her as she dried her hands on her surcoat.

"Where did you learn to do that?" he asked.

She cocked her head curiously. "What?"

He gestured at the woman with the infant. "Deliver a child like that. Are you a physic?"

Cantia finished drying her hands off. "Nay," she said. "But as the lady of Rochester, people come to me for help. I have learned a few things in my time."

Gillywiss nodded faintly, still eyeing her. "Then you have my thanks," he said quietly. "My sister has already lost three children. You have given her new hope."

Cantia looked over her shoulder at the woman feeding the newborn, seeing the joy on her face. "Hope is what keeps us all alive," she said softly. "Peasant or nobleman, it is what drives us to rise in the morning and look forward to a new day. Hope is what keeps us bound to our loved ones and wish better things for them."

"Is that what keeps you bound to Winterton?"

Cantia turned to look at the man, some hesitance in her expression. "I am bound to him because I love him and for no other reason than that."

"But you can never be his wife."

"Perhaps that will change one day."

"Is that what you hope for?"

Cantia paused, her brow furrowing in thought. "Aye," she whispered after a moment. "I suppose I do."

"Then why does he not find his wife?" Gillywiss wanted to know. "If he wants you to be his bride, why does he not find the one who deserted him and his daughter? I do not understand."

Wearily, Cantia sank to the stool next to him, feeling very depressed and exhausted all of a sudden. She had no idea why she continued to share her darkest secrets with a man she didn't even know. Originally it had been to gain his sympathy. Perhaps now it was because he seemed rather wise as an outsider looking in.

"He does not know where, exactly, she is," she shrugged after a moment. "The woman's father thought perhaps she had run off to Paris, but it all happened so long ago. It is quite possible she is no longer alive."

"But it is equally possible that she is," he said. "If Winterton loves you, why does he not do all he can to find her?"

Cantia sighed gently, her gaze lingering on the woman and child near the fire. "He will," she insisted softly. "To be truthful, we have not... well, we have not been together very long. There has not been much time for him to search out his wife. Perhaps he will eventually, provided that... well, provided that I return to him."

Gillywiss watched the pain and fear ripple across her features. "Is that what you wish?" he asked.

She turned to look at him as if surprised by the question. "Of course it is."

Gillywiss studied her a moment before cocking his head thoughtfully. "If you had a choice, what would you wish for most? To be returned to your warlord or to discover the fate of his wife?"

"To be returned to him."

"You say that without hesitation."

"I say it because I love him. As long as we are together, all else is secondary."

Gillywiss could see she meant it. He found his gaze returning to his sister, who was cooing sweetly to her new son. One of the attending women opened the elaborate hut door and the woman's husband came in, bursting into tears when he saw the healthy boy. Gillywiss watched the scene, the strong emotions involved, and could not help but be moved by it.

Gillywiss was an odd man and a very strong leader. He'd lead his little group of outlaws for quite some time, earning their respect as well as their fear. He was unpredictable and perhaps a little mad at times, but he was cunning and intelligent. He was also a man with a secret, something that had become evident as he had pawed through Cantia's clothing.

In a world where men were defined by their behavior, demeanor and deeds, Gillywiss would spend hours alone and in hiding, dressing in women's clothing and wondering if he looked beautiful. He felt far more comfortable with women than with men, which is why he felt much pity for the lady of Rochester. She was in love with a man she could never marry, a fine woman with a compassionate heart, and he instinctively felt pity for her. Much like him, she was suffering in silence.

"Paris," he repeated, more to himself than to Cantia. "I have relatives in Paris. Perhaps I should send word to them to see if they have ever heard of this Louisa of Hesse."

Cantia looked at him with surprise. "Why would you do such a thing?"

Gillywiss was looking at his sister as he spoke. "In truth, I do not know," he suddenly grinned that wild toothy grin that Cantia had seen before. "Perhaps because you have saved my sister and my new nephew. Perhaps because you have shown me you are not the typical noble bitch we have all come to expect. You have paid us a good deed and perhaps I should show you one as well."

Cantia could hardly dare to hope. "If that is true, then all I would wish for is to go home. Please, Gillywiss. It is all I could want."

Gillywiss pulled his gaze off his sister and focused on Cantia, seeing the utter eagerness and faith in her eyes. He could feel himself relenting.

"We will discuss it in the morning," he finally said. "Nothing can be done tonight. Perhaps I will send you home and send word to Paris anyway. My family lives in the crevices and underground of that great and dirty city. They know everything. Perhaps they will know."

Cantia fought off tears of relief as she sighed heavily, a great release of fear and sorrow and anticipation. She wouldn't push Gillywiss anymore this night. He had promised to speak on the matter more in the morning and she looked forward to that moment.

She was murmuring quiet prayers that she would see Tevin again very soon when distant shouts caught their attention. Gillywiss bolted from the stool and threw the door open, his sharp gaze moving over the darkened encampment. Cantia went to stand behind him, puzzled, as the cries of alarm grew louder. She could hear the thunder of horses and the screams of men. Before Gillywiss ran off, he told Cantia to go back inside and bolt the door. As he ran away, Cantia didn't obey. She charged out into the darkness to see what was amiss.

After that, all dissolved into chaos.

CHAPTER SIXTEEN

Tevin tore into the east side of the settlement wielding his broadsword. His men were plowing into the clusters of huts under orders to search every room, hearth, socket, and corner. No stone was to be left unturned. They took their command and their mission seriously. Tevin could hear the screams of the inhabitants as he barreled into a small group of huts and used his broadsword to slice off a corner of the nearest sod roof.

Three women huddled inside the hut, screaming when they saw a very big man in well-used armor hovering over them astride a fire-breathing charger. Tevin yelled at them, demanding to know of a stolen woman, girl and young boy in their midst, but the women were either too stupid or too terrified to answer him, so he chopped away more of the roof to get a good look at the interior of the hut.

Chunks of sod and pieces of wood rained down on the screaming women, but it didn't take long for Tevin to see that no one else was inside the structure. Satisfied that Cantia or Arabel weren't inside, he moved on to the next hut and did the exact same thing.

Tevin had several soldiers behind him, conducting a more thorough search of the properties he was tearing apart. The men were also confiscating anything of value and storing it on their horses, of which Tevin didn't particularly care. If these people were outlaws, and it looked very much like they were all tucked away secretly in the forest, then whatever possessions they had were more than likely stolen anyway, so he took no issue with his men taking stolen goods from thieves.

As he finished with one group of shacks, he caught sight of another cluster of huts several dozen yards away and was intent to raid those next when he caught a glimpse of a very small hovel shoved back in a thick cluster of trees off to his right. The rear of the structure was backed up into a small rise or hill, in fact, nearly hidden from his view, so he took the time to spur his charger back into the darkened area. He wasn't going to miss anything.

The trees were thick enough as he approached that he was forced to dismount and he did so, marching upon the hut and kicking the door in. Sword wielded defensively, he noted that the hut was very dark and presumably empty. He really couldn't see anything at all and it was very still inside, seemingly unoccupied. He was about to turn away when something on the floor twitched.

He raised his sword as he moved into the hut, realizing that someone was lying on the ground all covered up. It was so dark that he couldn't make anything out until he was nearly on top of the pile of quivering furs. He was about to bark at them when soft crying met with his ears. It took Tevin a moment to realize that it was, in fact, very familiar crying. His breath caught in his throat.

"Arabel!" he gasped.

Arabel had been lying on the ground with the musty furs up over her head, terrified at the sounds going on all around her. When someone kicked the door to the shack open, she was certain she was about to be killed. Her father's voice was the last thing she expected to hear and the furs came away from her face, her eyes open wide in astonishment.

"Father!"

Tevin dropped his sword and swooped down on his daughter, picking her up and holding her tightly against him. Truth be told, there were tears in his eyes and a lump in his throat as he savored the feel of her. Even though he had hoped to find her, he could scarcely believe it.

"Sweetheart," he breathed. "Are you well?"

Arabel had her father around the neck so tightly that she was nearly strangling him. She nodded fervently.

"I am," she said. "I am fine. Oh, Father, how did you find us? Did

Hunt send you?"

Tevin's joy was tempered with confusion and apprehension. "He did not," he said, pulling back so he could look her in the face and see for himself that she was well and whole. "Where is Hunt? And where is Cantia?"

Arabel was breathless. "Hunt went to find help," she started to tear up as the situation overwhelmed her. "I told him to escape. I told him to go to Rochester to send you back to save us."

Tevin didn't like the sound of that at all, especially with his men raiding the settlement. A little boy could very well get swept up in the chaos, or worse.

"*When* did he leave, Arabel?" he asked, trepidation in his tone. "Which way did he go?"

Arabel was trying not to feel horrible and apprehensive, but she wasn't doing a very good job. Her tears broke through. "He left only a short time ago," she said, sniffling. "Father, I… I made him do it. I told him he had to find help for us and that we were all depending on him."

She was starting to cry and Tevin soothed her as much as he could, although he was feeling much anxiety and panic.

"We will find him," he assured her, collecting his sword and carrying her out of the hut just as several of his men rode up. He looked to the seasoned soldiers around him, men bearing weapons and torches. "Hunt Penden is around here somewhere, possibly hiding. Make all due haste to find the boy. I do not want him caught in the madness and injured."

A few of the men tore off to search while one man, one of Penden's men, dismounted his horse and began prowling the landscape on foot, calling Hunt's name. As the search for Hunt commenced, Tevin turned to his daughter once more.

"Arabel," he sounded as if he was begging. "Where is Cantia?"

Arabel shook her head, wiping tears off her cheeks. "She went away," she said. "Someone needed help and some of the people took her away. I do not know where she has gone."

Tevin fought down more panic, now for Cantia. "Is she gone from the camp?"

"I do not believe so. Someone was sick, I think. She went to help."

"So she is here, somewhere?"

"I think so."

"Is she well?"

"She is well, Father."

The knowledge helped Tevin's state of mind tremendously. *She is well, Father.* He found himself muttering a silent prayer but in the next breath, he was seized with the overwhelming desire to find her. She was here, somewhere, and he had to get to her. As he approached his charger, Myles came thundering up. His fair face slackened as he recognized Arabel.

"Lady Arabel," he sounded relieved and surprised. He looked at Tevin. "Where did you find her?"

Tevin jerked his head in the direction of the darkened shack. "She was in there," he said. "But Hunt is missing. Apparently, he ran off to find help. He is out here, somewhere, de Lohr. Find him."

Myles was even more panic-stricken than Tevin was at the thought of Hunt wandering around the dangerous settlement. He bolted off, calling Hunt's name, as Tevin mounted his daughter on his war horse and mounted behind her. He didn't particularly want to take her with him as he hunted for Cantia but he had little choice. He wasn't going to let her out of his sight.

The settlement was in complete bedlam by the time Tevin and Arabel rode into a clearing in the center of the encampment. There were two massive bonfires blazing with the remnants of supper cooking on them. Word had spread that Lady Arabel had been found, but Lady Cantia and her son were still missing. Three hundred armed men could do a lot of damage, and they certainly did as they ruthlessly searched for Lady Penden and her son.

Tevin stayed directly out of the search purely because of Arabel. He lingered near the bonfires as his men searched around him. He was joined periodically by his senior men, bringing him reports of sections searched that had turned up nothing. He tried not to let his apprehension get the better of him as time went along and still no Cantia or Hunt.

Eventually, he dismounted his charger and began to pace, watching his men rip the place apart in their quest. He wanted them to rip it apart even more. If Cantia and Hunt didn't show up soon, he was going to have them burn it for good measure. Fury and fear were fully entrenched in his chest, like great claws, threatening to tear him asunder.

But those emotions were doused when he heard someone call his name. It was a female voice, a familiar call, and his panic evaporated.

Tevin spun around in the direction of the voice, so swiftly that he nearly lost his balance. His gaze found Cantia walking towards him out of the darkness, her beautiful face full of disbelief. Here they were, in the middle of madness, and she was walking towards him as easily as if she were out for an afternoon stroll. She was looking at him as if she could hardly believe her eyes and Tevin found that he couldn't breathe. All he could do was run at her.

Cantia ran, too, and suddenly she was up in Tevin's arms, sobs of relief and joy bursting out all over the place. She had her arms around his helmed head and somehow, he ripped his helmet off and still managed to hold her tightly, now kissing her furiously as she sobbed. His lips were all over her face, tasting the salt from her tears.

"Sweetheart," he gasped in between kisses. "Are you well? Have they harmed you?"

Cantia shook her head, her hands in his long hair, returning his kisses. "Nay," she wept, finally pulling away from his furious mouth so she could breathe. "I have not been harmed. I am well."

Tevin couldn't seem to stop kissing her but when his movements slowed, he hugged her so tightly that he heard her spine pop. He eventually set her to her feet, his enormous hands cupping her face simply so he could look at her. Heart pounding as he tried to calm himself down, his dark eyes drank in every beautiful line.

"You are sure you are well?" he asked, his voice trembling.

"I am sure."

"Swear it?"

Cantia nodded, running her fingers across his lips and watching him eagerly kiss her flesh. "They did not harm us," she stressed, becoming increasingly aware of the screams and shouts going on around them. "Please call your men off, Tevin. These people have not been cruel in the least."

He was confused, suspicious. "But they abducted you and killed two of my knights," he said. "How can you say they have not been cruel?"

Cantia's features paled. He could see it even in the moonlight. "Dear God," she breathed. "Val...?"

He shook his head. "Val is alive," he assured her. "I was referring to Dagan and Gavril. Val made it back to Rochester to tell us what happened. She is injured but she will survive."

Cantia breathed a heavy sigh of relief. "Praise God," she said sincerely. "I was so worried about her. Dagan hit her very hard."

Tevin's brow furrowed. "*Dagan* hit her?" he repeated. "What do you mean?"

Cantia's features hardened with anger and disgust. "Exactly that," she said. "It was Dagan who betrayed us, Tevin. He hit Val on the head and then killed his own cousin so they could not interfere with his plans. It would seem that Charles promised the knight my hand in marriage. He was planning on taking me to the nearest church to be married and then he was going to ransom Arabel to you in exchange for Charles' freedom. He had all manner of grand and terrible plans to marry me and become a wealthy man, all thanks to Charles' scheming."

Tevin stared at her. "What madness is this?" he could hardly believe what he was hearing. "You are certain that is what Dagan told you?"

Cantia nodded. "He threatened to hurt Hunt if I did not comply," she said, thinking back on that horrible moment in time. "Just as he was preparing to take us away, Gillywiss and his people came out of the woods and put an arrow in him. Then they spirited us away so, in a sense, they really saved us. You owe them much."

Tevin was furious, confused and overwhelmed by the entire story. After a moment's hesitation, he turned to a couple of soldiers standing nearby and barked orders for them to cease the raid. Those two men disbursed, calling out commands to the group as a whole, and the entire force began to wind down their assault.

Tevin watched his men for a moment to make sure they were obeying before returning his attention to Cantia.

"Who is Gillywiss?" he asked. "Is he the leader?"

Cantia nodded. "These people are all homeless, as you can see," she gestured to the upended camp. "Some are outlaws, but some have simply been displaced. They live here because they have nowhere else to go and they were indeed following us with the intention of robbing us as we rode south to Darland. When Dagan attacked, they killed him and took Hunt, Arabel and I back to their settlement. Even if they are thieves, they saved us that day. They truly did."

Tevin was astonished. He stared at Cantia for several long moments, digesting her story, before feeling the familiar fury again. Only this time, it was at Charles.

"Penden," he growled. "Damn him… I can only imagine what tales he fed Sutton. But I simply cannot believe the man was fool enough to believe him."

Cantia sighed faintly, squeezing his hand. "He can be rather persuasive," she said quietly. "Who knows why men do what they do? Perhaps Dagan saw an easy way to riches. Charles has a great deal of personal wealth as the Steward of Rochester. He must have promised Dagan a great deal."

Tevin shook his head, frustrated. "Sutton and de Reigate were bachelor knights when they came to me, but they had served the Earl of Essex for some time prior and the man gave them a strong recommendation." His thoughts lingered on the rogue knight a moment. "It would seem that Charles Penden and I have much to discuss upon my return to Rochester. In fact, it makes me wonder who else the man has poisoned with his lies. I do not want to spend my time at Rochester looking over my shoulder or worrying over your safety."

Cantia watched him carefully. "What do you intend to do?"

Tevin merely lifted an eyebrow but he would not look at her. His gaze moved out over the compound, now settling into a brittle and harsh state of existence now that his men had backed off from their raid.

"I would speak with de Lohr and see what his thoughts are on the matter," he replied. "He knows Penden as well as anyone. I will speak with Myles and make my decision."

Cantia wasn't sure what more she could say. She was afraid of what Charles was capable of, too, so she wrapped her arms around Tevin's waist and hugged him tightly. Tevin swallowed her up in his big arms, his face buried in the top of her head as he relished the feel of her. She was safe, and alive, and he was deeply thankful, but the information regarding Charles and Dagan had him gravely concerned.

His thoughts were still lingering on Penden when Cantia lifted her head and caught sight of Arabel upon her father's charger. She smiled thankfully at the young woman, who smiled timidly in return, and then glanced around as if looking for something more. It didn't take a great intellect to figure out what she was searching for.

"Where is Hunt?" she asked.

Tevin passed a glance at his daughter before replying. "My men are looking for him," he said evenly. "In fact, Myles is searching for him personally. We will find him."

Cantia's brow furrowed. "But I left him with Arabel," she said, looking to the young woman. "He was with you, was he not?"

Arabel's features fell, feeling some panic and sorrow, but Tevin spoke before she could spill her fears and terrify Cantia with tales of her missing son.

"Hunt apparently decided to leave and go find help," he told her as carefully as he could. "He cannot have gone far. I have dozens of men searching for him right now, so do not worry overly. We will find him."

Cantia was confused, now with a creeping sense of fear. "*Leave* to find help?" she repeated. "But why would he do that? He would not even know where to go."

Tevin could feel her panic. He sought to soothe her before she could veer out of control.

"Sweetheart, perhaps he got scared and ran off," he said, not wanting to incriminate his daughter as having a hand in Hunt's departure. "He is a young boy and young boys often do unpredictable things. What matters now is that I have many men searching for him and we will find him. I do not want you to worry."

Cantia would not be soothed. She looked up at Arabel. "Where did he go?" she wanted to know. "Did he say anything to you?"

Arabel was tongue-tied, looking to her father for help. Tevin opened his mouth to answer for her when the thunder of chargers caught their attention. De Lohr was riding towards them at breakneck speed, pulling his excited charger to a halt several feet from Tevin's horse, which began to get excited as well. Arabel shrieked as the horse danced and Tevin ably calmed the excitable beast.

"What goes on, Myles?" Tevin demanded. "Where is Hunt?"

Myles was edgy. He yanked off his helm in a frustrated gesture, propping it on the saddle in front of him.

"We are expanding the search," he said, seeing Cantia and nodding his head in her direction. "My lady, it is good to see you safe and whole"

Cantia ignored the greeting. "Where is my son?"

Myles sighed heavily, hesitance in his manner. "I do not know… yet," he said, trying not to sound too discouraged. "But rest assured, Lady Penden, that I will find him."

Cantia had tears pooling in her eyes by the time he was finished, realizing that her son was still missing and no one seemed to know where he was. Tevin could see how frightened she was and he rubbed her back soothingly, trying to ease her as the search went on for her son. Upon the saddle, Arabel watched Cantia and tried not to feel too guilty. She was verging on tears as well.

Myles wiped the sweat off his brow and plopped his helm on again, turning his charger towards the south with the intention of resuming his search when a shout filled the air. It was very loud, causing them all to look towards the source. Out of the darkness of the trees to the east came several figures, one of them carrying a squirming little boy. Cantia gasped when she realized it was Hunt in the arms of Gillywiss.

With a cry of joy, she broke free from Tevin and started to run towards her son, but that joy turned to horror when she realized that Gillywiss had a dirk pressed up against Hunt's pale little neck. She came to a halt, her eyes wide.

"What are you doing?" she asked as calmly as she could. "Why do you hold my son?"

Cantia could hear broadswords unsheathing around her and she held out a quelling hand to Tevin and Myles, silently asking them to be still. She kept her focus on Gillywiss, whose eyes had that familiar wild look about them. She didn't like it in the least.

"I was rushing to see what the trouble was and what do you think I found?" Gillywiss was being rather grandiose, like he had been the night they had been brought into the camp and he had made a big show for his people. "Someone had caught this little boy trying to escape from camp. But, it seems that an escaping prisoner was the least of my worries."

Cantia sighed heavily, trying not to look at her son as he struggled against Gillywiss' grip. She knew what the man meant without even asking.

"Please," she begged softly. "You must understand they did not know what they would find when they came here. For all they knew, we were being held in horrible conditions, or worse. They did not know that you have not been cruel to us, but I have explained the situation and they will withdraw, I swear."

Gillywiss' wild-eyed expression faded into a countenance that Cantia had never seen before. It was hard and deadly. His gaze moved to the men behind Cantia, hardened warriors in expensive armor and with expensive weapons. He fixed on Tevin, standing slightly behind Cantia, and assumed it was the viscount because he was standing so close to her. His attention drifted over the enormous warrior with the long hair.

"You are Winterton," he said, a statement and not a question.

Tevin was fixed on the man. "I am the Earl of East Anglia," he said in his deep, authoritative voice. "If what the lady has told me is true, I owe you my thanks. But that mercy shall be at an end if you do not let the boy go immediately. Release him to his mother and I shall have no quarrel with you."

Cantia was watching her son squirm when Tevin's words registered with her. *I am the Earl of East Anglia*. Confused, she turned to the man questioningly, but his dark eyes were riveted to Gillywiss.

"The earl?" he repeated. "You are not Winterton?"

"I was. That status has changed."

Gillywiss thought on that a moment, as did Cantia. Gillywiss seemed to be considering it while Cantia's sense of confusion only grew.

"So you are authority personified," Gillywiss said.

"I am."

"I have never met an earl before."

"Now you have."

"Then if that is the truth and you want this boy returned, you will have to make some concessions, Lord Earl."

Tevin's hard expression didn't waiver. "I do not negotiate with outlaws," he said. "Return the boy or we'll burn this place to the ground."

"If you do, the boy will not survive."

"If you kill him, you will not survive, either."

"Wait!" Cantia threw up her arms, putting herself between Tevin and Gillywiss so they would stop threatening each other. She turned to Gillywiss with pain in her expression.

"Please give me my son," she begged softly. "Nothing more will happen to you or your people, I swear. But if you must have a hostage, then I would rather you take me and let my son go."

Gillywiss wasn't finished posturing with Tevin yet but he forced himself to look at Cantia's frightened face. The inherent compassion that the man kept so closely guarded began to flicker, seeping through the cracks of his composure. Cantia somehow had that ability over him, as she'd already proven.

"You are a lady of great sacrifices," he said after a moment. "What has he ever done for you?"

Cantia knew he meant Tevin. She sighed again, averting her gaze after a moment. "He gave me the will to live again," she confessed, daring to look at the dark-eyed outlaw. "I tried to kill myself after the death of my husband. No matter what you may think of him, know he has given me my life back and for that, I am grateful. I am sorry that he raided your settlement, but you know why he did it. He was looking for me. Now, please give me my son so we can return home. I would consider it a personal favor."

Gillywiss' eyes glittered at her. Then, without another word, he released Hunt, who went running to his mother. Cantia threw her arms around the boy and picked him up, cradling him. She couldn't help the tears in her eyes as she focused on Gillywiss.

"Thank you," she whispered. "Your mercy is appreciated."

Gillywiss watched the mother and son cuddle, acutely aware of what else was going on around him as Myles silently ordered the men to mount and retreat. The earl's soldiers were clearing out. Tevin went over to Cantia and Hunt, putting an enormous hand on Hunt's back and peering at the child to make sure he was well. Seeing that the boy was unharmed, merely shaken, he looked at Gillywiss.

"I will again thank you for your service in saving the lady, her son, and my daughter," he said. "If ever you have need of something in the future, do not hesitate to send word to me. I consider myself indebted to you."

Gillywiss eyed the very big earl. He was a handsome devil with his piercing eyes and long hair, and even though he'd only been confronted with the man for a few minutes, he could already see the genuine emotion between him and the lady. It was hard to miss. He scratched his head, his focus moving between Cantia and her son, and Tevin.

"You and your men came to my village, once," he said. "You burned it to the ground."

Tevin was not remorseful. "In the course of my duties, I have burned many villages. It was nothing personal against you."

Gillywiss couldn't argue that point. It was the truth. But he wasn't finished yet. "Because of you, my family and I had to flee. Now we live here and you have torn this up as well."

Tevin's eyes drifted over the settlement, now quieting that his men had ceased their raid. People were walking around, picking up the pieces.

"I was looking for Cantia," he said, his dark gaze fixing on Gillywiss. "I would stop at nothing to find her. Surely you can understand that."

"Will you not apologize?"

"No."

Gillywiss contemplated his reply. "Then we will require restitution, Lord Earl."

"You shall have it. Consider it a reward."

Gillywiss was rather surprised by the answer. There had been no hesitation. It wasn't an apology, but he really didn't care. More and more, he was coming to see that the warrior felt the same for the lady as she did for him because a lesser man would not have agreed so readily. The man had the only thing he cared about and was showing his thanks.

"If she means so much to you, why do you not marry her?" he wanted to know. He was, in truth, a nosy man. "Why have you not searched for the wife that ran off on you years ago? Is this lady, this lady who was the very reason you tore up my camp, not worth it?"

Tevin was rather taken aback by the fact that this stranger, this outlaw, knew intimate details about his personal life. He looked at Cantia who was, by this time, looking at Gillywiss. She still had Hunt in her arms, all wrapped up around her torso.

"I told you why," she said before Tevin could reply. "You will not question him. It is none of your affair."

Gillywiss' brow furrowed, like a scolded child. He finally made a face at her and kicked at the dirt, having a hard time looking her in the eye.

"I do not suppose he would let his daughter take up with a married man, no matter how much they loved each other," he muttered. "Yet he sees nothing wrong with taking up with you."

Cantia looked at Tevin, somewhat apologetically, and was surprised to see that Tevin was actually listening to the man. Finally, he just shook his head.

"I am not entirely sure what you have been told, or why you have been told." He was scolding Cantia and she knew it. "However, I will tell you this since you seem so concerned, I have every intention of seeking out the woman who abandoned me and my daughter those years ago, but the days have been rather busy for me lately. Times are dark and difficult, especially with those in a position of power. There has been much sacrifice all the way around."

Gillywiss shook his head faintly. "'Tis not only with those in power," he gestured to his encampment. "Those who have nothing suffer worst of all. It is as if the land itself is undone and darkened with such evil, as if Christ and his angels are sleeping and demons are let loose upon us all."

Tevin lingered on his words. "For an outlaw, you are particularly insightful," he said. "You understand the wickedness and lawlessness of this time."

Gillywiss seemed rather pensive, glancing at Cantia. "And happiness in and of itself is rare," he said quietly. "Perhaps… perhaps that is why I asked of your intentions towards the lady. Happiness these days is difficult to come by and should not be treated casually."

Tevin wasn't going to get into an in-depth discussion about his feelings for Cantia with the man so he turned to see who was still lingering nearby. Spying Myles astride his big charger, he motioned the man forward.

"Round up those who have stolen from these people and have them deposit whatever they have taken here in this clearing," he said, his voice low. "We shall return what hasn't already been eaten or otherwise disposed of. Are you carrying any coinage?"

Myles dug around in his saddle, into a hidden compartment where he usually stored coin or valuables. He pulled out a small leather pouch and tossed it to Tevin, who opened it up and counted what was inside. Then he closed it back up and made his way back over to Gillywiss.

"Here," he said, tossing the man the pouch. "This should be sufficient for the moment, but I will send more at a later time."

Gillywiss deftly caught the sack, opening it and peering inside. When he saw all of the coins, his eyes widened and he looked at Tevin with that crazed, wild-eyed look that Cantia was familiar with.

"This is better than robbery," he announced, turning to those people hovering behind him. "It seems to be more lucrative to save the nobility than steal from it."

His followers laughed and he tossed the purse to one of the women, watching her and a few others excitedly count the coins. Then he returned his attention to Tevin.

"The lady said you were generous, Lord Earl," he announced. "It would seem she was correct."

Tevin gave him a faint grin in reply, thinking it was time to return to Rochester as the hour grew late and the darkness grew damp. He was particularly concerned for Arabel's health, so he turned to Myles.

"If you will take Cantia and Hunt with you, I will take Arabel with me," he said, motioning towards the general direction of the main road that lead to Rochester. "Gather the men. We return."

Cantia heard his order, disappointed that she would not be riding with Tevin but understanding. Arabel didn't really know Myles and would be much more comfortable with her father. Tevin must have been reading her mind because when he was done peeling Hunt off of her and handing him up to Myles, he took her sweetly in his arms and hugged her. Then he kissed her forehead and both hands, preparing to lift her up to Myles when Gillywiss stopped him.

"My lady," he said, his focus on Cantia. "Do you remember what I told you earlier about my relatives in Paris?"

Cantia cocked her head thoughtfully. "I am not sure," she said. "What do you mean?"

Gillywiss grinned that toothy grin. "I will find this woman," he said confidently, "so you can marry your great Lord Earl. I will find this woman who stands between you and your happiness."

Cantia could help but grin because he was. He was being boastful and, in truth, she didn't particularly believe him, but she humored him.

"If it is God's will," she said softly.

"For my sister's life and my nephew's life, I vow to repay you," he said, back to his grandiose style. "I will find this woman and bring her back to you."

Cantia simply smiled, graciously acknowledging him as Tevin lifted her up to Myles. She settled in behind him as Tevin mounted his own charger, collecting his daughter carefully into his arms.

The last Cantia saw of Gillywiss, the man was waving at her as if she were departing on a great and dangerous journey, not as the man who had once been both captor and savior. It was rather strange. The further away she got, the more vivid his waving became until he was literally jumping up and down.

As she watched him, it occurred to her that she had not collected her bags but in the same breath, she realized she didn't particularly care. She would leave them for Gillywiss, since he was obviously so enamored with her things. Perhaps it would give the man, that complex, puzzling and intelligent man, a little of the happiness he had spoken of. He didn't seem like a very happy man. Besides, from what she had seen, he liked her things far more than she did.

The thought made her smile.

CHAPTER SEVENTEEN

THEY REACHED ROCHESTER in the middle of the night, a castle and keep lit by dozens of flaming torches casting soot and smoke into the darkened sky. It was a massive bastion against the night, a sight that Cantia found extremely comforting. Finally, after a wild, dangerous and unpredictable few days past, she was home. The outcome could have been so much different and she did not take her safety, or anyone's safety, for granted.

The women who tended Arabel, having been summoned by a soldier who had run all the way from the gatehouse, were waiting as Tevin entered the fire-lit inner bailey. Tevin handed his sleepy daughter into their waiting arms. As the returning army around him disbanded, he dismounted with the intention of helping Cantia and Hunt. Before he could reach them, however, he called out to the senior soldier who had charge of Rochester in his absence. The big, war-worn soldier was lingering nearby.

"Have Simon and John returned from Dartford yet?" he asked.

The soldier shook his head. "Not yet, my lord," he replied. "I will send word as soon as they are sighted."

"Any word of trouble from the bridge?"

"None, my lord."

Nodding, Tevin continued to de Lohr's charger where the man was still astride along with Cantia and Hunt. Hunt was sleepy, grumpy, and practically fell into Tevin's arms as the man reached up for him. But that grumpiness was forgotten when the big yellow dog came charging out of the darkness and Hunt was reunited with his very best friend. Cantia watched the reunion as Tevin helped her down from the horse and set her on her feet.

"Hunt," she instructed softly. "Take George up to your chamber, please. I will be up shortly."

Hunt yawned, hugging the big dog around the neck. "But I am hungry," he said. "I want thomething to eat."

Cantia shooed him in the direction of the keep. "I will bring you something," she said. "Take George and go now. Get out of those dirty clothes and put a sleeping tunic on."

Hunt yawned, and grumbled, but did as he was told. Cantia watched him head towards the keep, alternately petting the dog and dragging him by his rope collar. When the child mounted the steps to the keep, she turned to Tevin.

He looked particularly drawn for some reason. Weary, yet edgy. She couldn't quite put her finger on it and she smiled at him when their eyes met.

"It is very late," she said softly.

He grunted in agreement. "Indeed." His dark eyes were intense on her. "Tell me the truth, Cantia. Are you sure you are well after all of this?"

Cantia nodded reassuringly. "I am, I promise. I told you that Gillywiss and his people did not harm me."

"I was not speaking of Gillywiss. I was speaking of Dagan."

Her smile faded. "He did not touch me," she said. "He never came close. But the things he said… Tevin, I have not wanted you to make any move against Charles more than you already have, but I will be honest and say that the man is coming to frighten me. If he offered Dagan my hand in exchange for his release and other promises, who else has he spoken to? What more poison has he spread?"

Tevin nodded, eyeing Myles as the man dismounted his charger. "I intend to have that conversation with de Lohr right now."

"What do you think you will do?"

Tevin shook his head. "I am not entirely sure, but I will not keep Penden at Rochester to wreak havoc. I will more than likely send him to one of my other holdings and keep him locked up for good. In any case, the man will be removed from Rochester and punished for what he has done. I do not want you to worry over it."

Cantia's lavender eyes were sorrowful yet relieved. "I will not," she said quietly. "But we will have to think of something to tell Hunt. He loves his grandfather, you know. He has lost his father and now will lose his grandfather. That is much loss for a child."

"I know it is, but we will explain the situation to him the best way we can and he will accept it. He is young and resilient, and this is where this conversation shall end for now. It is late and I want you to go inside and go to bed. I will join you in a while."

Cantia resisted. "I would like to see to Val first, if I may."

Tevin knew that neither his sister nor Cantia would sleep well without having seen each other and gaining reassurance that everyone was well and whole. He gestured towards the knight's quarters.

"She was in there the last I saw," he said. "I do not know if they have moved her."

Cantia cocked a disapproving eyebrow. "You put her in that musty place?" she scolded him. "Shame on you, Tevin. I will see her removed immediately and put in the keep where she belongs."

Tevin put up his hands as if to defend himself. "It was not my doing, but de Lohr's," he said. "And before you become too angry with me, know that Val seemed to want it, too."

She looked at him curiously. "What do you mean?"

He puckered his lips wryly. "I mean that you were right," he said, lowering his voice as he moved towards her and captured a soft hand. "There is something between them, although Val would not admit much to me. Perhaps she will tell you all of it."

Cantia grinned as she watched him kiss her fingers. "She will tell me everything," she said confidently. "But I will not tell *you*."

He lifted a dark eyebrow. "You had better tell me everything if you know what is good for you." He winked at her when she giggled. "But move her into the keep if it pleases you."

"I will."

Cantia removed her hand from his grip and headed towards the knight's quarters but Tevin called out to her.

"One more thing," he said.

She paused and turned to him. "What would that be?"

His eyebrow was still lifted, almost in disapproval. "Putting aside the question of how the subject was even broached with that outlaw, you and I will have a conversation about what, exactly, you told him about my reasons behind not being able to marry you."

She knew the subject would come up. She was frankly surprised it had taken this long, and her good humor fled. "And you and I will have a discussion about why you told him you are the Earl of East Anglia."

"Because I am."

She was serious. "I was thinking all the way back to Rochester that you would not have returned us if Geoff was still in residence," she said quietly. "What happened to him?"

"He is dead."

"How?"

"He attacked me and I killed him in self-defense."

Cantia sighed, thinking of the greater implications of that softly-uttered statement. "I suppose I should be happy about this but I can see by the look on your face that you are torn," she said softly, perhaps with sympathy. "What are you feeling, sweetheart?"

He hadn't really thought about it since it happened. There had been so much else on his mind. After a moment, he made his way over to her and put his arms around her, pulling her close. In the shadow of Rochester's mighty keep, he hugged her tightly.

"I am not sure," he replied. "It all happened so fast… Geoff was furious because I had sent you and Val away, and you were abducted, and he refused to let me send out men to search for you. We argued and he attacked me with a dagger. As I was deflecting his blow, I snapped his neck. I did not mean to do it but it happened. I cannot understand why I am not deliriously happy about it, but I am not. Geoff was a vile creature and we are better off without him. I know that better than anyone."

"But he was your cousin, your blood, and for that reason alone you are torn."

"Perhaps. But it is done. I will not linger on it."

Cantia hugged him close. "This means a great many things will change for you."

"That is true," he whispered. "But it all means nothing without you by my side. You are my all for living, Cantia. Always remember that."

She pulled her face from the crook of his neck, smiling up at him. "As you are mine," she whispered. "We will speak more of all of this later, but for now, I wish to see Val and then I wish to sleep for the next hundred years. I am exhausted."

He nodded. "I know, sweetheart," he said, gesturing towards the knight's quarters once again. "Go and see Val, but do not be too long. I will join you upstairs shortly."

Blowing him a kiss, Cantia headed off to see to Val, her thoughts lingering on Tevin and his newly acquired earldom. It was an enormous event and she was very proud of the man. It would seem that much had happened in the past two days, life changing events that she was trying to come to grips with. Her mind was a little muddled by it all.

Val was ecstatic to see Cantia, and the two women chatted until Tevin finally came looking for Cantia and had to separate them so he could get Cantia up to bed. But Val wasn't to be alone for long. Soon after Cantia and Tevin left, Myles joined Val in her dark little room.

When dawn came, he was still there.

CB

"I AM GOING to do all of the speaking and you are going to do all of the listening," Tevin's tone was a growl. "Is this in any way unclear, Penden?"

In his bottle prison, Charles looked filthy and haggard. The time spent in captivity had not been kind to him. His body had aged tremendously and his mind had entered that dark and shadowed realm of madness, now waiting anxiously for word from Sutton on the success of their plan. Du Reims' appearance was not a good sign, and he eyed the man with animosity.

"What time is it?" he barked.

"Dawn."

Charles waved listlessly at him. "Speak then," he said. "But know there is nothing you can say that will interest me in the least."

Tevin's expression was like stone. "I beg to differ," he said. "Let me be the first to inform you that your plans with Dagan Sutton have been foiled. Dagan is dead and your schemes along with him."

Charles' eyes took on a strange glimmer. "Be plain."

"I am. Dagan was killed while attempting to abduct Lady Cantia for the purpose of marriage, I am told, at your prompting. You were to provide the man a dowry for the lady if he married her."

Charles' gaze remained steady. He could see de Lohr and two of du Reims' other knights standing behind him, big sentinels lurking in the shadows. Charles looked at Myles.

"You serve *me,* de Lohr," he rumbled. "You will defend me against this… this usurper. He accuses me of something he cannot prove and I will have my satisfaction."

Myles could see the madness in Charles' eyes and it both saddened and enraged him. He had been particularly close to Brac and knew the man would have been devastated by his father's actions. He found that he was furious on Brac's behalf more than anything. So many of Charles' actions were disgusting in so many ways.

"Dagan confessed everything to Lady Cantia," he replied, deliberately leaving out "my lord". "She has informed us of your scheme with Sutton. I will not defend a guilty man."

Charles flared. "You would believe that bitch over me?" he snarled. "I will have your hide for this."

Before Myles could reply, Tevin stepped forward. "That woman is the only thing standing between you and certain death," he rumbled.

"She has asked me not to kill you and as of this very moment, I will not. But if I ever hear you call her a disparaging name again, I will slit your throat and take great pleasure in your lingering and bloody death. Is this clear?"

Charles gazed at Tevin, a wicked flash in the dark eyes. Either he was too crazy or too arrogant to be intimidated. After a moment, a hint of a mocking smile creased his lips.

"You have wiped everything of Brac off of her, have you not?" he snorted. "My son was barely cold in his grave before you were bedding his wife. Have you flushed her veins with your scent and wiped all taste of Brac from her lips? You are a vile bastard to take advantage of a woman in mourning."

"And you are a vile bastard to shame your son with your behavior towards his widow."

The smile on Charles' mouth faded and he turned away, the insanity in his veins building. Tevin could see the tremor in his movements, the twitch in his eye. He knew there was no reasoning with a madman, and Charles Penden was far gone with madness. It started the moment those arrows struck Brac.

"She is mine to do with as I please," he muttered. "As the Steward of Rochester, she belongs to me."

Tevin could feel his body tense, his fierce sense of protectiveness for Cantia overwhelming him. He pressed up against the rusted iron grate that separated him from Charles.

"And I *am* East Anglia," he rumbled. "De Gael is dead and the title now belongs to me, which means Rochester belongs to me and everything about it. You take orders from me now, Penden, and I will have the truth. Did you offer Cantia in marriage to Dagan Sutton for a price?"

Charles was looking at Tevin without turning his head, a sort of ghoulish slant of the eye that was unnerving and piercing. "You boast like a fool," he hissed. "How do I know you are truly East Anglia?"

"Because he is," Myles confirmed before Tevin could. "Geoff de

Gael is dead and Tevin du Reims now controls East Anglia. He is now your liege."

Charles turned his head now, looking between Myles and Tevin with his sick-eyed expression.

"You have become his dog, de Lohr. I do not believe you. And given the chance, I will do all I can to destroy the chain of command until I am in control of Rochester once again." He was focused mostly on Tevin now. "I promised Cantia to Sutton because I wanted to be free of this unrighteous prison, but the idiot evidently perished before he could carry out my wants. I do not know how he died but I do not care. All I am sure of is that Cantia is the cause of everything and I swear, given the chance, that I will kill her. She deserves nothing less for everything she has caused."

Myles stared at the man. He didn't dare look at Tevin. After a moment, his handsome features twisted with confusion, for he was genuinely and truly baffled.

"What in the world has that woman done to you to make you hate her so?" he asked.

Charles' expression didn't waver. "She took my son from me," he grumbled. "She took him from me and then turned him against me."

"You mean she married him?"

Charles looked away. Myles simply shook his head. "She was your son's wife," he said. "Brac loved her. She was very good to him. She gave birth to your only grandson. Why should you hate her for such things?"

Charles wouldn't answer. When the wait became excessive and Myles finally dared to look at Tevin to see what the man's reaction to all of this was, Charles spouted off one last time.

"I am in this prison because of her," he mumbled. "If it takes me to the end of my life, I will ensure that the woman pays for what she has done to me."

"Then the end will come sooner than you think." Tevin didn't hesitate. He turned to Myles. "Brick up this doorway. The man is a poison that must be stopped because I believe every damn word he says. He will never stop unless I stop him first."

Myles wasn't shocked by the order. It was a cruel world and one did what one must do in order to survive. To protect Cantia, Hunt, and the rest of them, the harsh deed had to be done. They all knew that Charles would not be stopped and, short of running the man through with a blade, there was only one way to put an end to the madness-bottle him up in the prison that was to become his tomb. Charles screamed until the last brick was seated.

When Cantia heard the news, for Brac's sake, she wept.

CHAPTER EIGHTEEN

SEATED IN THE SOLAR with Val, Cantia was working on a piece of embroidery she had been toying with for several months. It was an ambitious piece with butterflies and flowers and as she sat in the mid-morning sun, she began to realize she'd hardly seen Tevin since their return two days before.

Certainly, she had seen him during meal time and they'd spent the nights wrapped in each other's arms but for the most part, he was extremely busy as the new Earl of East Anglia and she only caught fleeting glimpses of him now and again, usually in passing. She missed him terribly but she was deeply grateful to be home, resuming a normal life.

And she was deeply grateful for Val's company. The woman had recovered fairly swiftly from her injuries and this was the first time Cantia had allowed her to sit up for any length of time.

Dressed in a soft, mustard-colored surcoat and struggling to learn the finer points of needlework, Val sat across from Cantia on this bright morning, tackling the somewhat simple scene of the sun rising over mountains. Cantia had helped her sketch out the scene with charcoal and stretch it out over the oak frame, and now Val was attempting to embroider her design. She wasn't having much luck but she was trying very hard.

A dog barking caught their attention and Hunt suddenly raced through the keep entry with George on his heels. Cantia called to her son to slow down but the boy yelled something back about fresh currant bread and that was the reason for his rushed pace. Cantia shook her head in resignation, grinning when she caught Val laughing at her.

"Trying to slow that child down is like trying to stop a raging river,"

Cantia sighed. "When he first learned to walk as a baby, he went straight to running."

Val giggled as she took another stab at the linen. "Perhaps the next child will not be in so much of a rush."

Cantia shrugged, focused on her embroidery. "Perhaps," she said. Then she eyed Val. "Speaking of children, when were you planning on telling me about Myles? I have given you almost two whole days to tell me and still you say nothing."

Val's cheeks immediately flushed a deep shade of red. She kept her eyes on her embroidery for a few moments until she could stand it no longer and looked up, almost sheepishly, at Cantia. She was met by a knowing smile.

"He…." she broke out in a toothy grin and tried again. "I was going to tell you, truly. He has finally stopped seeing me as a fellow knight and views me as a woman."

Cantia's smile broadened. "And why not?" she said. "You are a very beautiful and accomplished woman, and it is time he realized it. When can we expect the wedding?"

Val giggled a silly, giddy laugh. "I am not entirely sure," she said. "Myles has said he will speak with Tevin but I suspect he fears my brother in that regard, so I may have to ask Tevin's permission myself."

Cantia was giggling with the woman. "Nonsense," she said firmly. "Myles will ask Tevin and your brother will be very happy to give his blessing. I know he is very happy for you."

Val's giggling faded and her expression turned serious and nearly wistful. "I never thought this would happen to me," she said softly. "Men do not usually find affection with women who can fight as well as they can, so to have Myles' attention has me thrilled as well as surprised."

Cantia's features were warm. "I have known Myles for many years," she replied. "Brac thought a great deal of him, as do I. He is a wonderful man and I am truly thrilled for you."

Val's expression shifted into one of uncertainty and the grin returned. "Perhaps... perhaps you will help me with my wedding preparations."

Cantia was excited. "You can wear the dress I married Brac in," she said. "It should fit you very well. In fact, I do believe I shall tell Tevin to seek out Myles and give his blessing today. I do not want to wait for your happiness."

Val blushed furiously, grinning, as she turned back to her embroidery. Cantia's gaze lingered warmly on the woman before Hunt rushed into the solar and interrupted her thoughts.

The boy had a huge slab of bread in his hand, slathered in butter, and he rushed at his mother and directed her to take a bite. The bread, although smelling wonderful, didn't seem particularly appealing to her, so Cantia chased Hunt away and told the boy to play in the yards. But Hunt didn't want to go outside. He wanted to go upstairs and visit Arabel, so Cantia waved him onward.

As Hunt charged from the solar with the yellow dog trailing after him, hoping for some crumbs, Tevin and Myles entered the keep. Hunt smacked into Tevin's leg, leaving a smear of butter on the leather breeches, but barely stopped to apologize as he raced up the steep spiral stairs. Lips twisted wryly at the butter splotched on his leg, Tevin entered the solar and pointed at his leg.

"I would ask for some bread to put this on," he said to Cantia.

It took Cantia a moment to realize what he meant. She fought off a grin as she stood from her chair and grabbed the hem of her surcoat, bringing it up to wipe off the white paste.

"He was in a hurry," she said apologetically. "I am sorry."

Tevin watched her clean him up, his twisted lips turning into a smile. "'Tis of no matter," he said, kissing her on the cheek when she finished. His dark eyes glimmered warmly at her. "In fact, I have a lull in my duties and thought I would come to keep you company but I see you already have companionship."

Cantia grinned at him and wound her hands around his big forearm affectionately. "You may take me for a walk around the grounds. I am sure Val does not need us or want us here at the moment."

Tevin lifted his eyebrows questioningly when he realized Myles was in the room as well. Clearing his throat as he became aware that perhaps Val and Myles should like to be alone, he turned to leave the room.

"Behave yourself, de Lohr," he said as he passed through the doorway. "I have eyes and ears everywhere."

As Val giggled, Myles simply shook his head. "As you say, my lord."

In the entry, Cantia called back to them. "Pay no heed, Myles," she said. "I will keep our lord occupied. He will not have time to worry over you."

Cantia grinned as she listened to Val's laughter. As Tevin, somewhat disapproving that she had circumvented his authority with Myles and his sister, opened the entry door for her, Cantia sweetly patted his cheek and led him down into the bailey.

It was a mild afternoon of lazy clouds and bright sun as they began their walk across the grounds. Cantia had her left hand lodged in the crook of his right elbow and Tevin had a firm hold of her as they headed towards the gatehouse. He forgot all about Val and Myles, consumed with the feel of Cantia by his side. He had missed it.

"When were you planning on burying Geoff?" Cantia asked, shielding her eyes from the glare of the sun as she gazed off towards Rochester's soaring cathedral. "You've not said a word about it."

Tevin glanced off towards the cathedral as well. "That very subject has been one of the things that have occupied my attention," he replied. "I have had to send word to Saxlingham Castle to see what Geoff's mother, my aunt, would do. She may want him returned to her. I have not yet heard from her so Geoff's body remains at the cathedral stored in an unused vault."

Cantia glanced up at him. "I did not know his mother was still alive."

Tevin nodded. "She is very old, but still alive. I have not seen her in years."

Cantia nodded in understanding. "I see," she said, glancing at the gatehouse as they drew close. That inevitably brought about thoughts of Charles, bricked up in the depths, and she couldn't help but shudder. Her thoughts shifted quickly from one to the other. "I cannot help but wonder what Brac would say to all of this."

He glanced down at her. "All of what?"

She tilted her head in the direction of the gatehouse. "His father," she said quietly. "I know you did what you had to do to protect us, but somehow I still feel such sorrow for Brac's sake."

Tevin knew that. He'd seen it from her for the past few days, and his manner grew subdued. "Let me ask you a question."

"Of course."

"If Brac was still alive and his father behaved threateningly towards you, what would the man have done?"

"I told you before. To spare me, he would have killed him."

"So why do you feel sorrow?"

Cantia sighed heavily. "I am not sure," she admitted. "Perhaps because Charles' madness would have hurt him so. Brac and his father had a good relationship. Charles thought the sun rose and set on the man. It saddens me to see it all deteriorate so badly, not only for Brac but for Hunt's sake as well."

"Has he asked about his grandfather?"

"He has, a few times, but I simply changed the subject. I cannot keep avoiding it forever, however."

Tevin sighed knowingly. "Then I will explain the situation to him. Perhaps I will tell him that his grandfather has simply gone away and leave it at that."

"You would lie to him?"

"How do you think he will react if he knows the truth? He is a young boy and impressionable. He will not understand why I have done what I did, so in order to spare him for the time being, I will omit certain truths. When he is older, I will tell him everything and pray that he understands my reasoning."

Cantia gazed up at him, forcing a smile. "He will understand," she murmured, then lay her head against his bicep affectionately. "But I do not want to linger on such things today. It has been ages since we have spent time such as this and I would have that time spent on happier things."

He grinned. "What, for instance?"

"Your sister," she said firmly. "Let us speak of the permission you are going to give Myles to wed her."

His smile vanished. "Permission to marry?"

Cantia didn't back down at his nearly threatening tone. "Aye, you are going to give it, and give it today. I will not wait to see Val happy. She loves him, you know. At least… at least one of us should be allowed to marry the man we love."

Tevin's good humor faded completely. Her words were like a punch in the gut, something they hadn't discussed since the day Tevin had confessed everything to her. It seemed like ages ago. He didn't want to think about it but knew that ignoring it wouldn't make it go away. He sighed heavily.

"Cantia…."

She cut him off. "Please, Tevin. Do this for me."

He came to a halt and faced her, his hands on her arms. "Everything I do is for you," he acknowledged. "But Val is…."

Cantia cut him off a second time. "Val is in love with Myles and he with her," she said, her eyes filling with tears. "You must understand what it is for a woman to love a man so much that he is all she can taste or feel. To be kept from completing that circle of love and devotion, to be kept from marrying him and becoming his wife, is nothing short of torture. I live that torture more and more every day. Therefore, please tell Myles that he may have permission to marry Val. I ask this of you."

Tevin could see the emotions in her expression and it raked at his heart like great clawed talons. "Do you not think it tears at me also?" he whispered gently. "Do you not think it eats at me every day, more and more, until I can hardly breathe? I love you more than life itself, Cantia.

You are my all for living. Surely you know that."

"I know that."

Tevin regarded her a moment, her expression, reading the flicker in her eyes and the expression on her features. He could see something in the depths.

"But you need proof." He thought he understood what she was thinking. "I told you I would find out what had become of Louisa but I have made no effort to do so yet."

Cantia shook her head, wiping at her eyes. "That is not true. I know that…."

This time, Tevin cut her off. "Aye, it is," he insisted. "So much has happened over the past few weeks that I have been swamped with what I thought were more important things. I should have sent out messengers long ago to find out what I could of Louisa but I have not. I beg your forgiveness, sweetheart, truly."

Cantia shook her head firmly, putting her fingers over his lips to silence him. "I know you have been occupied," she said. "You have had very important things to attend to, I do understand that. But finding Louisa… it is a risk, after all. We could search for years and never know, I suppose."

Tevin put a big hand on her head, stroking her hair with tenderness. "I was thinking," he ventured, "that if we could perhaps get a signed statement from her father saying that she abandoned her marriage and her child, that the church would perhaps annul the marriage on that basis. It is worth a try."

Cantia looked hopeful. "Where is her father?"

"Saxony."

Her face fell somewhat. "That is a long way away. Would you go yourself?"

He nodded. "I would."

"You would not leave me here, would you?"

His dark eyes flickered. "I could not stand to be separated from you for so long," he said. "We could take Hunt and Val and Myles also. It would be a grand adventure for us all and perhaps we could be married in Saxony. I am sure I could convince her father to help us."

Cantia was back to being hopeful. "Oh, Tevin," she gasped, throwing her arms around his neck. "It would be the most wonderful thing."

He hugged her tightly. "It is settled, then."

"It is," she said, releasing him. "But do not forget that Gillywiss swore he would look for Louisa as well. Perhaps if the annulment fails, we can look to him for his assistance."

Tevin cocked a dark eyebrow. "Which reminds me," he said. "I have not yet asked you why you told the man so much personal information about us."

Cantia shrugged as she tried not to look too contrite. "The truth was that he *was* holding us prisoner for a time," she admitted. "He threatened us. I thought that if I told him something about me, it might make him more sympathetic towards us and let us go. He discovered I was not your wife but your mistress and… well, the conversation took a turn as to why you could not marry me."

Tevin could see it was a logical progression but he was still uneasy about it. "How much does he know?"

"Most of it. What I did not tell him, Arabel did. She was afraid and her mouth simply ran amuck. Please do not be angry with us."

He shook his head. "I am not," he said. "But I will admit I am uncomfortable with an outlaw knowing so much about me and my life."

Cantia thought on the very strange man she had come to know. "I do not think he is truly a bad man," she said. "He was rather odd and pitiful, actually. He seemed to like my clothes a great deal. He tried them on more than once."

Tevin's eyebrows lifted. "Truly?" he thought on that. "Strange."

She nodded. "Strange, indeed," she said. "I think in the end, however, he would have let us go. I believe he held some pity towards us."

Tevin wasn't sure what to say to that so he merely nodded, dropping his hands from her arms and clasping her hand in his big one. He began to walk again, taking her with him. He glanced around the enormous fortress, feeling more relaxed and settled than he had in weeks. Life was returning to a sense of normalcy and for that, he was grateful. For the first time in his life, he was genuinely looking forward to what the future may hold.

As Tevin kissed Cantia's hand, watching her smile happily at him, sentries began to take up the call on the walls. Tevin paused, listening to the chatter before calling up to the men to see what all the activity was about.

A rider was evidently approaching and Tevin remained safely back from the gatehouse with Cantia in his grip as the rider passed underneath the portcullis and was met by several armed guards. They pulled the man off his horse and stripped him of his weaponry before they allowed him to deliver his message. The man approached Tevin wearily.

"Dartford is under attack again, my lord," the man told him. "Lord Chafford is requesting your aide."

Lord Chafford was the baron currently in charge of Dartford Crossing, a local baron north of the crossing with a sizable fighting force loyal to Stephen of Blois. Tevin had discovered this the day he had returned with Cantia from her outlaw imprisonment and had already been in touch with the man, allowing him to hold fast the bridge with the Earl of East Anglia's considerable support. Chafford was closer to the bridge logistically so it made sense for him to control it. Now, East Anglia's support was being called upon.

"Who are the opposing forces?" Tevin asked.

The messenger appeared grim. "We are not sure, my lord," he said. "It could be Surrey."

Surrey was a sizable support network behind Matilda. More than that, it was the same force they had fought with when Brac had been killed. Tevin was already motioning to a few of the senior soldiers standing around him.

"Mount the men," he told them. "We ride within the hour."

As the men broke up to do the earl's bidding, Tevin quickly escorted Cantia back towards the keep. He turned to say something to her at the base of the stairs but the words caught in his throat when he saw that she was silently weeping. He put his arms around her.

"Why do you weep?" he asked gently, kissing her forehead.

Cantia drew in a deep, steadying breath. "Because I am a foolish woman," she tried to smile off her behavior. "You must hurry now. Your men are assembling."

Tevin opened his mouth to reply but stopped short when Myles came flying down the exterior stairs and Tevin informed the man of the situation. As Myles raced off to do Tevin's bidding, Tevin returned his attention to Cantia.

"Please tell me why you weep," he whispered.

Cantia was wiping at her cheeks, struggling to compose herself. "Please," she shook her head, not wanting to speak on her feelings. "You must go. I will see you when you return."

"I am not leaving until you tell me why you are crying."

Her brave façade wavered, clearly reluctant to speak. But she relented after a few moments of struggle.

"Because the last time there was a call to retake the bridge, Brac was killed," she whispered. Her gaze grew intense. "I cannot help but remember that moment he was brought to me with arrows sticking out of him. Tevin, if they were to return you to me in that condition, I swear I would be buried with you. I could not go on."

Tevin suspected the reason behind her tears and was prepared. He pulled her into a tight embrace, his face buried in the side of her head.

"That will not happen to me, not today," he assured her softly. "I have much to live for. I swear to you that I will return in good health."

She squeezed him tightly. "I believe you."

"Do you truly?"

"Aye."

Tevin pulled back to look her in the eye, just to make sure she wasn't lying to him. Seeing the luscious features gazing steadily back at him, he kissed her sweetly, twice, and gently directed her towards the stairs that led to the keep.

"Then go inside," he told her. "Make sure the keep is locked down. Admit no one until Myles and I return. Is that clear?"

"It is."

He blew a kiss at her. "I love you," he whispered as he turned to walk away. "Go inside now."

Cantia blew a kiss in return, mounting the steps to the keep as she watched Tevin head back towards the gatehouse. When he turned to look at her, she waved and took the steps quickly so he would not grow agitated with her. Once inside the keep, she and a male servant threw the heavy bolt across the door as ordered. Then, she went into the solar to wait out the men's return with Val.

It was a very long night, but Tevin returned whole and sound as he had promised.

CHAPTER NINETEEN

May, 1140 A.D.

CANTIA COULD FEEL TEVIN'S hand on her belly. Asleep or awake, his hands seemed to gravitate there, feeling the round firmness of her stomach and being rewarded on occasion with strong kicks. Even now, before dawn, they lay naked in each other's arms, burrowed beneath the covers on a cold May morning with his arms around her and his hand on her belly. Half-asleep, Cantia could feel the strong movements of the baby.

"He is very busy this morning," Tevin mumbled, his face against the side of her head. "How can you sleep through that?"

Cantia giggled. "I can sleep through it fine," she pretended to be irritated and rolled away from him. "It is your talking that keeps me awake."

Tevin's arms tightened when he realized she was trying to move away from him.

"Nay, lady," he muttered. "You'll not escape me."

Her laughter grew as he pulled her back against him, wedging himself between her legs as his hands stroked her belly and his lips nibbled sleepily on her ear. Eventually, he lifted her leg so that it was over his hip, his fingers seeking intimate places and listening to her groan softly with pleasure. When he withdrew his fingers and entered her from behind, very carefully, Cantia turned herself over to him completely.

This was a normal morning for them. Cantia would usually awake to Tevin making love to her. His powerful seed had taken root sometime back in the late fall, during that time when she was worried if she'd ever be able to conceive again. Their child was due in the summer and it was all Tevin could speak of. In his world, it was the most important thing that blinded his thoughts to all else.

The man had always been inordinately attentive and passionate, but with the event of the pregnancy, his attentiveness, concern and understand knew no bounds. He made it well known that there was no child ever born that had been more welcome, and Cantia was always made to feel that surely there was no woman more loved. He clearly adored her and she clearly adored him.

Even now as he filled her with proof of his desire, all Cantia could feel from him was his deep love and devotion to her. The fact that she was to give birth to his bastard didn't matter. To her, she was simply giving birth to the child of the man she loved and there was nothing more to it. No shame, no stigma. She had told Gillywiss once that she and Tevin were married in their hearts as much as any man and woman ever was, and it was the truth. She would give birth to this son, and then she would give birth to a dozen more just like him. The mighty Earl of East Anglia must have his legacy.

The physical changes had come over her fairly rapidly as her belly grew quickly. She felt fine most of the time except for occasional exhaustion, but her sexual appetite was enormous. Because of the way the child would sit in her belly, she experienced climaxes so powerful that Tevin had to put his hand over her mouth to keep her screams down and this morning was no exception. Cantia experienced a strong release that had her crying out in ecstasy. Tevin simply put his mouth over hers, kissing her passionately and trying to keep the noise down as he spent himself inside her. Never in his life had he known such desire or lust. It was beyond his wildest dreams.

"You," he admonished, his mouth still on hers, "must contain yourself, madam. One of these days your cries are going to raise the roof and I will have a good deal of explaining to do."

She grinned sleepily, satisfied, and wrapped her arms around his neck. "Are you complaining, my lord?"

He grinned devilishly. "Never," he kissed her again. "But I fear you are drawing the concern of Arabel. Her chamber is right below ours, you know. I think she heard you once because she asked me what you were screaming about. You know how I am when she asks me questions like that."

Cantia laughed softly. "You become tongue-tied and embarrassed," she teased. "The only things that can stump the mighty Earl of East Anglia are personal questions from his fifteen-year-old daughter."

He made a face at her, kissed her one last time, and climbed out of bed. It was still dark in the room, as it was just before sunrise, so he lit a fat taper with a flint and stone purely so he could see where he was walking. The massive wardrobe over by the wall was his destination and he opened the doors to a neat and tidy network of possessions, long cleared of Brac Penden's remnants.

"I have a conference in Thurrock this evening with Lord Chafford," he said, turning to glance at her. "You remember him, do you not?"

Cantia was sitting up in bed. She made a face. "Of course," she said, reaching for her dressing robe on the end of the bed. "A fat man with foul breath."

Tevin grinned as he pulled forth leather breeches. "That may be," he said, pulling on his breeches, "but the man commands a strong force that has held Dartford Crossing for months. It would seem that Stephen has been in touch with the man and wants to meet with us both, evidently. Lord Chafford and I need to discuss strategy for that meeting."

"Am I coming with you?"

"I would prefer that you did not. His stronghold is north of the Dartford Bridge and I must cross it in order to reach him. I do not want you on that bridge right now, not with all of the fighting that has gone on around it over the past several months."

She didn't like that answer. "Why cannot Lord Chafford come to Rochester? Why must you go to him?"

"Because he invited me."

"You are the earl, Tevin. You do not bow to another's summons. Tell him you will meet him at Rochester."

It was not a request or suggestion. It was a command. He fought off a grin. Cantia had been quite the tyrant as of late, unusual for the normally sweet and accommodating lady. He found the fire of pregnancy quite humorous at times, but he also had a healthy respect for it. If he didn't defer to her wishes in all things, there was often hell to pay. The powerful Earl of East Anglia was controlled by a lovely slip of a woman and he didn't give a lick about it. He loved it.

"If that is your wish, sweetheart, then I will send him word and tell him to come here tonight."

"Good," she nodded her head decisively. "Let that be the end of it."

"You will have to entertain him and be a party to his foul breath all evening, then."

She made a face at him. "I would rather suffer through it than have you away from me, even for a night."

He just smiled at her as he pulled a heavy linen tunic from the wardrobe. Cantia was on her feet, pulling the robe over her head as she moved for a second robe that was heavy brocade lined with lamb's wool.

"Why would Stephen want to meet with you both?" she wanted to know.

Tevin pulled a tunic over his head followed by another one of heavier wool. "Because I control the south side of the Dartford Bridge along with all of the roads from Gillingham to Wellhall. Moreover, East Anglia is my stronghold and I have ten thousand men at my disposal. I am more important to Stephen than most."

She fell silent as she sat down on the bed to pull on her doeskin boots, very warm in the cold morning.

"Rochester is far from East Anglia," she said softly. "When do you plan to return to Thunderbey Castle?"

He glanced over his shoulder to reply, noticing she was having difficulty pulling on her shoes. Her belly was already quite large and got in the way of normal activities. He went over to her, taking the boot and gently slipping it on her foot.

"Not until this baby is born," he said. "Many things have been put on hold because of him."

Cantia watched him pull on her shoe. "Like our trip to Saxony to seek Louisa's father?"

"Like that."

"I told you that I was fine to travel in the beginning. We could have been there and back again in these past several months."

He looked her in the eye, somewhat sternly. "I am not going to travel with my pregnant lady. I told *you* that."

"So we must wait until your son is born before we do anything to that regard?" she asked, growing pouty. "Then you will not travel with an infant, and neither will I. He will be several years old before we will be able to travel to Saxony, but what if we have more children? We will never go and we will never receive our annulment because I will never be able to travel."

"I could always send a missive, as I have suggested."

"And chance that it would not be received? A thousand things could happen to a lone messenger. Nay, we must all go together to ensure our request is received and approved."

Tevin wasn't about to suggest he could go alone. It would not be well met, at least not at this time, so he did what he usually did when she grew upset – he shifted the subject in an effort to both distract and comfort her.

"I am sure there are many different possibilities we can speak of at another time," he said quietly. "But in speaking of Thunderbey, to reiterate my position on the subject, I do not want to force you to travel over miles of open road in your condition, so we will wait until the child is born before I will as much as entertain the thought of returning home. Why would you ask such a question?"

Attention successfully diverted for the moment, she shrugged as she handed him the other boot and he slipped that one on as well.

"Rochester is my home," she said simply. "Hunt was born here and this child shall be born here. Do you not like it here?"

He nodded. "I like it very much," he reached down and carefully pulled her to her feet. "But, as you said, it is far from East Anglia. At some point, I must return home to my castle and to my people. I do not want to be gone overlong from my lands."

Her brow furrowed and he could see the pout coming. "I suppose," she said, doing a bad job of hiding her unhappiness. "But I do not want to travel with a new baby and if you must return to Thunderbey at some point soon, I am afraid you will go without us. I do not want you to go without us."

He kissed her forehead, hugging her gently. "I will never go anywhere without you," he assured her softly. "I have told you that before. I will never leave your side, Cantia, not ever."

"Promise?"

"Of course I do."

He appeased her somewhat and was in the process of kissing her again when he heard sentry shouts coming from the bailey. Going to the window, he pulled back the oilcloth to reveal an enormous bailey below, alive with the glow of dozens of torches. As Tevin watched the activity, Cantia came up behind him. Together, they watched the commotion on the walls.

"I wonder what the activity is about?" Cantia asked. "What could be happening so early in the morning?"

Tevin had his arm around her shoulders. He watched the increasing commotion for a moment longer before kissing her on the temple and releasing her. Returning to the open wardrobe, he pulled on a pair of woolen socks before sliding into his heavy leather boots.

"I will find out," he said. "I want you to stay to the keep until I know what is going on."

"But I have a meal to supervise."

"You may not go outside for any reason, at least not until I know what has my soldiers so excited."

She sighed and sat down beside him, watching him tie off the last boot. He leaned over and swiftly kissed her before rising from the bed and heading to the door.

"I will return shortly," he said.

Cantia blew him a kiss as he left the room, shutting the door softly behind him. With nothing to do and nowhere to go, she ended up lying back down on the bed and quickly fell back asleep.

When she dreamt, it was of copper-haired babies and summer weddings.

◌

TEVIN COULD HARDLY believe what he was seeing.

He actually looked at Myles, who was standing next to him, as if to confirm that the man was seeing the same thing. Myles looked surprised as well, so Tevin knew they were both envisioning the same thing. In the darkness of the new dawn, a group of weary and ragged people stood at the gatehouse of Rochester. Men in disheveled clothing, old weaponry, and one very old ox cart comprised the group, and at the head of it was Gillywiss.

Tevin had the gate guards raise the portcullis. When it lifted midway, he walked underneath it with Myles, John and Simon behind him. Although John and Simon did not know who Gillywiss was, as they'd never met the man, they could see that the appearance had Tevin surprised. With weapons drawn, they stood behind the earl as he engaged the ragtag leader of the group.

"What are you doing here?" Tevin asked the man. "What is so important that has you traveling in the darkness?"

Gillywiss was astride an old bay stallion. He wearily slid off the beast, coming to stand before Tevin with his usual wild-eyed look and toothy smile. In spite of his exhaustion, he bowed gallantly.

"My lord earl," he said. "I have brought you something that will make you forever remember my name."

Tevin cocked an eyebrow at the bold boast. "What do you mean?"

Gillywiss cocked a finger at him and began to walk back into his group of haggard travelers. "Come with me, my fine earl," he said. "I want you to see what I have for you."

As Tevin hesitantly followed, Myles, John and Simon fell in behind him with their weapons at the ready. The dirty, ragged group of men that had accompanied Gillywiss gave them a wide berth, unwilling to provoke the heavily armed knights. When the entire group reached the ox cart that was in horrific condition, Gillywiss tossed back the dirty canvas that covered the majority of the straw-covered bed. Upon it, in the darkness, lay a body.

"There," Gillywiss said proudly. "I did what I said I would do."

Tevin's brow furrowed as he gazed at the rolled-up corpse. It was so dark that he couldn't see very well. "What did you do?" he asked.

"I found her."

"Who?"

"Your wife."

Tevin's eyes widened as he stared at the pile. "You cannot be serious."

"Serious indeed. See for yourself."

Expression full of disbelief, Tevin hesitated a moment longer before snapping his gloved fingers at Myles.

"Bring me a torch," he hissed. "*Now.*"

Myles bellowed orders and someone came on the run out of the gatehouse bearing a searing torch, casting warm yellow light into the dark of the dawn. Myles grabbed it from the man, holding it high as Tevin reached into the cart to make clear the contents. He tried to stop his hands from shaking as he rolled the figure onto its back and peeled back the layers of musty, varmint-ridden material. As he tried to get a clear view, Gillywiss stood on the opposite side of the cart, watching intently.

"I told Lady Cantia I would find this woman," he said confidently. "I have many family members living in Paris, in the catacombs, and they know the streets. They know the people there. So I asked them if they knew Louisa of Hesse. Do you know what they told me?"

Tevin wasn't looking at him even as he shook his head. But that was the only reply Gillywiss received, so he continued in his usual theatrical fashion.

"They told me they might know of her," he went on, "but there are thousands of people living in the streets of Paris with no names and no history. I spent months in Paris, following clues that would lead me to nowhere or to women who claimed to be the wife of a great English lord but they could not tell me what your daughter's name was. That is how I tested them. I asked them to name the child they had abandoned. No one could tell me, but this one could. And she wept when she spoke of her."

He was pointing in the cart and by this time, Tevin had pulled away enough of the material so he could look at the face. Heart pounding, he had Myles hold the torch close so he could see the pale features. And what he saw shocked him to the bone.

"My… God," he breathed.

Myles was crowded beside him, equally electrified by the very pivotal moment. "Is it her, Tevin?"

Tevin just stared, unwilling or unable to reply for a moment. He just stared. Finally, he tilted the dirty face upward so he could see it from another angle. Then, he hissed.

"Louisa?" he shook the face gently. "Louisa, can you hear me?"

Gillywiss was watching the scene, rather proud of himself for doing what he set out to do. "She is a prostitute," he said as he watched Tevin try to rouse the woman. "I found her in a hovel of other prostitutes because I had been told a woman calling herself Princess Louisa lived there. When I told her I was looking for du Reims' wife, she wanted to know how Arabel was faring. She asked me to take a message to her daughter."

Tevin's head came up, his dark eyes intense in his pale face. "What was the message?"

"That she was sorry. And then she wept."

Tevin's gaze lingered on the man before returning it to the frail woman upon the straw. She was struggling to open her eyes.

"What is wrong with her?" Tevin asked. "Why is she collapsed like this?"

Gillywiss' gaze moved to the small figure. "She has the French disease," he said, his tone less grandiose. "Many prostitutes have it. It will destroy her mind and eventually kill her. She is not long for this world."

Tevin immediately removed his hands from the woman, as he certainly did not want to contract anything she might have. He pulled his gloves off as he looked at Gillywiss.

"Then why did you bring her here?" he hissed. "I do not want her infecting my entire castle."

Gillywiss shook his head. "You cannot catch her disease unless you bed her," he said. "That is why they call it the French disease."

"Nonetheless, I do not want her here. Cantia is pregnant and I do not want to risk her or the baby."

Gillywiss shrugged. "Can you tell for certain it is your wife?"

Tevin's gaze moved back to the lump on the straw. "I… I cannot say for certain," he said, sounding hesitant and strained. "It may be… but I cannot say for certain."

Gillywiss motioned to the men who were controlling the cart. Tevin and his men stood back as the cart began to move as if to turn around.

"I have done what I set out to do," Gillywiss said. "Your lady saved my sister's life, so I promised her that I would find the person that stood between her and her happiness, and I have done that. I have paid my debt. What you do with this woman is your own business."

Tevin's attention was divided between the cart and Gillywiss. It was clear he was still very shocked. He was also confused.

"Why would you do this?" He had to ask because he never believed the man had been sincere in his declaration to find Louisa. "Cantia is nothing to you, nor am I. I do not understand why you would do this."

Gillywiss' expression seemed to harden. He, too, was torn and attempting not to show it. "Because," he said, almost defiantly, "perhaps you will remember this day and you will be owing to me, and I can come to you when I need something and you will provide it."

"So you did it so I would be obliging to you?"

Gillywiss waved his arms at his men, who began to disband and move away. He followed them somewhat, like a shepherd moving sheep, waving his arms and casting Tevin and his men defiant yet triumphant expressions. The wild eyes were working steadily. But when the group moved a nominal distance down the road, Gillywiss suddenly rushed back in Tevin's direction with a finger thrust forward.

"I did it because your lady was kind to us," he was nearly whispering but the finger was shaking threateningly. "I did it because she and I have something in common, wanting things we can never have. I did it because she saved my sister's life. There are many reasons why I did this and you will not question me again."

Tevin gazed back at him steadily. He could tell the man was posturing for the sake of his comrades for his words did not match the angry actions.

"Not only do you seem to have a deep understanding of these dark times," he said quietly, "but it also appears that you are indeed a man of your word."

"I am."

"Come to see me again. We will discuss what I may do for you in return."

Gillywiss' gaze lingered on him as if trying to determine how serious he was. Then, the toothy grin made a bright return.

"Invite me to the wedding," he said rather saucily as he turned away. "Perhaps I will wear one of the fine garments your lady left behind. And if you do not understand what I mean, ask your lady. I believe she knows."

"She knows. She told me."

Gillywiss paused, an eyebrow cocked. "What did she tell you?"

"That you like her clothes more than she does, so she left them for you as a gift."

Gillywiss wasn't quite sure what to make of the statement so he laughed. Then he laughed again, that crazy wild-eyed laugh that he was so capable of. He was still laughing as he moved back down the road and mounted the weary bay stallion. The group closed in around him and they began to move off down the rocky road, into the dawn that was growing brighter by the moment. Tevin just stood there, staring at the fading figures, until Myles caught his attention.

"Tevin," he said quietly. "What do you want to do with her?"

Tevin turned around, seeing that Myles as well as John and Simon were clustered around the ox cart, gazing at the dusty, dirty figure on the bed. Tevin walked up beside Myles, gazing down at the unconscious woman, before replacing his gloves. Then, he rolled her onto her back so her face was fully in view. The more he looked at her, the more he knew the face.

"Simon?" he muttered. "You knew Louisa. Is this her?"

Simon sighed heavily as he gazed down at the slip of a woman. After several long moments, he nodded his head.

"I believe it is," he confirmed. "I can hardly believe it, but I believe it is."

Tevin took his hands off the woman, still staring at her. "God's Blood," he hissed. "This is something I never thought I would see again. After all of these years… and in such bizarre circumstances. It does not seem possible."

Simon could only shake his head, as stunned as his lord was, while Myles seemed a bit more logical about the entire thing. Unlike the others, he'd never met the woman and didn't have an over amount of emotional investment in the situation.

"I will ask the question again," he looked at Tevin. "What do you want to do with her?"

Tevin sighed heavily. "If she is ill, I will again reiterate that I do not want her infecting the entire castle."

"But if she has the French disease, it does not spread like the Plague. We can still bring her inside and keep her isolated."

Tevin was still resistant but he didn't have much choice. It wasn't as if they could leave the woman outside the walls, tucked away in the old ox cart, until they decided what to do with her. He looked at Simon.

"Have her brought inside and find a place where she can be kept well away from everyone," he ordered. "Have a couple of serving women clean her up and make her comfortable. Make sure they clean themselves after they have touched her, for I do not want her disease spread through them. Furthermore, have the physic exam her. I will speak with the man for his opinion on her condition when all of this is accomplished."

Simon nodded, already moving to carry out Tevin's orders. He was snapping his fingers at some of the soldiers lingering outside the gates to have them move the ox cart inside. As the old cart began to slowly move towards the gates, towed by a few soldiers, Myles turned to Tevin.

"What are you going to tell Cantia?" he asked quietly.

Tevin drew in a long, thoughtful breath. "For the moment, nothing," he said. "I am not sure at the moment. When this woman is in better spirits, I will speak with her to see what can be determined."

"And if it is Louisa?"

He lowered his gaze, contemplating his answer. After a moment, he shook his head. "Anything I say will sound harsh and ugly," he said, lifting his eyes to Myles. "The truth is that I am relieved. I am relieved if it is Louisa and the fact that she is very sick and more than likely dying. It means that she will soon no longer be an issue and I can marry Cantia as God and the laws of Nature intended. If that is a horrible statement, then I am horrible. I feel guilty for even thinking such things. But I will overcome that guilt the first time I take Cantia in my arms and call her my wife. Cruelty such as this will seem trivial."

Myles wriggled his eyebrows in sympathy. "I do not disagree," he replied. "But I should at least tell Val."

"Why?"

"Because she can read my mind. She has already learned this skill and we have only been married two months. If I do not tell her, she will beat it out of me."

Tevin gave him a half-grin. "Then it would be wise to tell her," he said. "Moreover, she knew Louisa. If anyone can confirm the woman's identity, Val can."

"I am not entirely sure I want my wife around a sick woman until we can determine whatever she has cannot be spread."

"Agreed. Make sure the physic examines her in short order so we know what we are dealing with."

Myles simply nodded and the pair of them watched the ox cart, which was now lumbering beneath the yawning portcullis as it made entrance into the enclosure of Rochester.

With wonder, disbelief, and perhaps some fear, they followed.

○₃

IT WAS NOON before the physic could be found and instructed to examine the woman in the cart, mostly because the castle physic of Rochester, although a knowledgeable man, was something of a drunk and it had taken that long to find the man sleeping off a binge in a muddy crevice of the castle.

Myles had manhandled the old surgeon to one of the unused smithy shacks where they had the woman called Louisa sequestered. Tucked away on a straw bed with a serving woman to watch over her, the surgeon took his time in examining the woman, struggling to shake off the after effects of too much drink with the big knight glaring daggers at him. The man felt her pulse, looked in her eyes and ears, and listened to her lungs. He also poked and prodded a good deal, and thumped her several times on the back and listened to the results.

Myles stood in the entry to the shack, watching, glancing over his shoulder now and again to make sure Val or Cantia weren't around to wonder why he was hanging around an old smithy shelter. Cantia was curious but Val was worse. She had the senses of a trained knight and he swore the woman could move like a phantom and read minds like a witch. He rather liked it, though. The past two months had been the best of his life.

Grinning when he thought of his lovely, strawberry-blond wife who was trying very hard to learn to be a good chatelaine, he refocused on the old surgeon as the man thoroughly examined the patient, who was by now becoming semi-lucid. Folding his arms across his big chest, Myles leaned against the door jamb, his mind wandering, when someone stuck a finger in his ear.

"Boo!"

Myles jumped as much from the finger in his ear as the voice, turning to see Val grinning back at him. He returned her smile as he turned his back on the door to block her view of the interior. Then he wrapped her up in his embrace.

"Greetings, wife," he kissed her sweetly.

Val put her arms around his neck, accepting his affection. "Greetings," she kissed him in return, savoring the gesture. "What are you doing?"

He shook his head, trying to distract her with sweet kisses and moving away from the shack at the same time. "Nothing of note," he said, trying not to lie to her. "More importantly, what are *you* doing?"

Val had her arms wrapped around his neck as he picked her up and began to walk off with her, her legs trailing down his long body. She giggled as he swung her around playfully.

"Walking with Arabel," she said, removing an arm and pointing over to her niece several feet away. "She wanted to come outside on this lovely day."

Myles smiled over at Arabel in her specially built chair with wheels on it, being tended by the two women who had raised her. She lifted a weak hand to wave at Myles and he waved back.

However, as Myles was smiling and waving, he was also quite frantic to move them both away from the old smithy shack. He couldn't believe he hadn't seen them coming. His mind must have been wandering more than he realized. But to take the blame off himself, he silently reiterated that his wife moved like a wraith and he was paying the price for it by being surprised at her appearance.

"Arabel," he called over to the girl. "I saw that a dog had a litter of puppies over in the stables. Do you want to see them?"

As he hoped, Arabel was properly distracted. She cried out gleefully. "Aye!" she clapped her hands. "Perhaps my father will allow me to have a dog like Hunt does!"

Myles grinned at her enthusiasm. "Perhaps," he said. "But do not tell him I told you about the puppies. He will berate me when he is unable to refuse you."

Arabel nodded happily and her women began to wheel her off in the direction of the stable. Just as Myles settled Val in beside him to follow, the physic emerged from the shanty and called out to him.

"My lord!"

Myles came to a halt, inwardly groaning as the physic made his way towards him. In fact, he was rather desperate to remove Val so he gently turned her in Arabel's direction.

"Go with Arabel," he said. "I will join you in a moment."

Val started to agree but the physic started talking before she could move out of earshot.

"My lord," the physic said again. "It would seem the woman has a disease of the lungs. I have seen it before. It is indeed contagious but should not create an issue if we keep her isolated and keep her mouth covered so she cannot breathe out her disease on others. I believe I can keep her contained."

Val heard him. She came to a halt, looking at the physic curiously even as Myles tried to turn her around.

"What woman?" she wanted to know, then looked at her husband with concern. "Do we have sickness at Rochester?"

Myles shook his head and started to reply to her, but the physic interrupted. "They call this disease *phithisis*," he said to them both. "The woman coughs up black blood. I can hear her chest laboring. She is far gone with the disease and will not live much longer."

Val looked very concerned as well as puzzled. "But I have not heard of anyone at Rochester being ill," she said to Myles. "Is this woman from the village?"

Myles sighed heavily, glancing at the physic and making a gesture for the man to vacate. As the old surgeon wandered back towards the shack, Myles turned his attention back to his wife. Gazing into her dark eyes, he knew he had to tell her. He could easily make up another story to satisfy her, but his conscience would not allow it. He had never lied to her before and wasn't about to start. Moreover, Tevin was sure Val could identify the woman if, in fact, it was Louisa. He put his arm around her shoulders and turned in the direction of the shack.

"Early this morning, we had visitors," he said quietly. "I must ask you now to keep this to yourself until Tevin informs Cantia. It is important."

Val nodded seriously. "Of course, Myles. What is it?"

Myles began to escort her towards the shanty. "Did Cantia or Tevin ever tell you about Gillywiss?"

Val nodded. "Cantia told me," she replied. "He was the outlaw who saved her from Dagan, was he not?"

Myles nodded. "Indeed," he said. "He also formed some kind of strange attachment to Cantia. He made her a promise."

"What do you mean? What promise?"

"That he would discover Louisa's fate so that Tevin and Cantia could be married."

Val's brow furrowed. "Why on earth would he do that?"

"As I said, he formed a strange attachment to Cantia. When he appeared this morning, he said that he did it because they had something in common, wanting things they could never have. He also did it because she saved his sister's life and he felt indebted to her."

Val came to a halt at the door to the shack, looking at him with an utterly baffled expression. "What did he do?"

Myles lifted his eyebrows at her. "I am hoping you can tell me."

He pushed the door open, exposing his wife to the dark and unsettling world inside. The physic and the serving woman were there, washing out some clothes in vinegar to put over the patient's mouth so she could not cough out her germs. Wary, Val stepped in with Myles behind her. He took her over to the straw mattress where a small figure lay, now with a cloth over her nose and mouth, and still swathed in jumbles of dirty blankets. She smelled like a sewer. Myles glanced over his shoulder at the physic.

"Remove the cloth on her mouth," he instructed. "I want to see her face."

The physic slid into the space between Val and the bed, peeling off the vinegar-soaked cloth. A very pale, very fair face came into view and the physic pulled back the blankets around the woman's head so her hair and features could be more plainly seen.

"Tell me who this is," Myles whispered to his wife.

Perplexed, Val bent over to gain a better look. She truly had no idea who she was looking at until the woman shifted and more of her features came into view. Then, an inkling of suspicion gripped her and Val peered more closely at the woman, drawing on distant memories to put a name to the face. When the woman sighed faintly in her sleep and a big dimple appeared on her chin, Val was seized with recognition. She grabbed Myles as if something had just terrified her.

"Louisa!" she gasped. "It... it is *Louisa*!"

Myles held on to his stricken wife. "Are you sure?"

Val nodded, so hard that her hair flopped over her cheeks. "My God," she breathed, blinking back tears. "I *knew* her. I thought we were friends. That is her, I swear it."

Myles pulled her away from the bed, gesturing to the physic, who went to his patient and covered her mouth and nose again with the soaked cloth. Meanwhile, Myles pulled his wife all the way to the door, kicking the panel open to get her out of the diseased hut. He had a strong grip on her because she was shaken and upset.

"Listen to me," he whispered. "You cannot tell Cantia. Tevin must tell her."

Val lost the battle against the tears. "It is not Cantia I am worried over," she wept. "Arabel will be devastated. All she knows of her mother was that she abandoned her and did not love her. Dear God, why is that woman here? What will we tell Arabel?"

Myles put his arms around her to comfort her. "You will tell her nothing," he said soothingly, steadily. "That is for Tevin to decide. I simply needed your confirmation that it is indeed Tevin's wife. You have done that. You must let your brother take care of the rest."

Val was wiping at her eyes with shaking hands. "That… that outlaw actually *found* her?" she was flabbergasted. "How did he find her?"

"He has family in Paris," Myles replied. "Since Paris was the last known location of Louisa, Gillywiss apparently went there looking for her. It took him months to track her down, but he did, finding her in a brothel. He brought her back because he promised Cantia he would."

Val was gazing at him with a wide-eyed expression, full of incredulity. "*Promised* her? But I simply do not understand. For what purpose?"

"I told you," he said patiently. "I can only surmise that it is so Cantia can know the woman's fate and, in knowing, pave the pathway for her and Tevin to be married. At least, that was the gist of what I understood."

It made some sense, but Val was still reeling. "I can hardly grasp all of this," she breathed. "Louisa has actually returned."

"Aye, she has."

She started to reply but the words caught in her throat and her expression changed from disbelief to one of sorrow. Her gaze moved to the mighty keep of Rochester soaring over their heads.

"I must speak with Tevin," she said, moving for the keep and pulling Myles with her. "He must know… my God, what must he be thinking of all of this? He must be astonished at the very least. The woman humiliated him, abandoned him, and now she is returned."

Myles took her hand to both slow her down and steady her. "Your brother can well handle his feelings, Val," he said softly. "I know you want to protect him, but he is a grown man. He can handle himself."

Val knew he was right but she didn't like his answer. Val had been watching out for Tevin for many years, as the younger sister to a powerful brother. There was something vulnerable about Tevin in her eyes and her protective instinct for him had only gotten worse when Louisa had deserted him and their month-old infant. She could feel her anger rise.

"You were not there when that… that woman discarded Tevin and Arabel like so much rubbish," she said, pointing angrily in the direction of the smithy shack. "She ran off with another knight, a man from her homeland. She never wanted to be married to Tevin but she went through with the marriage anyway, eventually leaving him with a sick baby and humiliating him. I know my brother can handle himself in any situation but it does not stop the sense of protection I have for him and for Arabel. I have tried very hard not to hate Louisa for what she did but right now, all I can feel is fury."

Myles was calm as he watched her. "Then what would you have me do with her?" he asked softly. "Do you want me to dump her in a church somewhere, with a charity where she will be cared for until she dies? Do you want me to send her away from Rochester to save your brother and Arabel's feelings?"

Some of Val's fury seemed to abate and she grew uncertain. "Tevin already knows she is here."

"He does, but he is not sure it is Louisa. He said you would know for sure. Would you lie to your brother and tell him it is not Louisa and we can simply rid her from Rochester?"

More of her fury took a dousing. After a moment, she shook herself, struggling to calm.

"Nay," she muttered, averting her gaze. "I would not lie to my brother, no matter how much I want to protect him. He should make the decision on what to do with Louisa."

"Then let us go and tell him the truth. Louisa has indeed returned."

Reluctantly, Val agreed.

CHAPTER TWENTY

T EVIN HAD TOLD HER not to go near the smithy shack, but Cantia wasn't so sure that she was inclined to obey him. After he had told her of Gillywiss' appearance and the subsequent unveiling of a dying Louisa, Cantia had moved from the realm of disbelief and shock to one of complete astonishment. She could hardly believe what she was hearing, torn between bewilderment and jealousy. But that didn't compare to what Tevin was feeling.

So she pushed aside her emotions to comfort Tevin, who seemed truly shaken and bordering on despondence. It wasn't so much for himself but for his daughter, and he and Cantia and Val had spent two solid hours attempting to determine how to tell the young woman that her mother, on her deathbed, had returned. It was a touchy and understandably emotional subject, with Tevin feeling quite protective of his daughter, wanting to shield her from the woman who had hurt her so badly. But he ultimately decided that he had to, in good conscience, tell her, and Tevin and Val went to Arabel's room to inform her of Louisa's arrival. That was the last Cantia had seen of them.

As the afternoon waned into shades of purple dusk, Cantia stood at the window overlooking the north portion of Rochester's bailey, her gaze on the smithy shacks all lined up against the outer wall. She knew Louisa was in one of them and, unlike the rest of the family, had no previous emotional investment in the woman. She was deeply curious.

Rubbing her belly as the baby kicked, she turned away from the window and headed down the steep spiral stairs to see how the evening meal was progressing. Clad in a rich, heavy brocade coat of emerald silk and a feather-soft shift the color of eggshells beneath it, she was warm and richly dressed, looking elegant and radiant, and every inch an earl's wife.

Cantia passed the level that contained Arabel and Hunt's chambers, pausing to peek into her son's room. Hunt was on the floor with the dog lying close by, playing with little toy soldiers made from sticks of wood. The past several months had been an adjustment for him with both his father and grandfather gone, but he had adapted.

All Hunt knew of Charles' absence was that his grandfather had gone on an extended journey and he had accepted the explanation as it had been carefully delivered by Tevin, but the truth was that he really wasn't particularly lonely. Now he had Arabel to play with and the two of them were very companionable. Arabel wasn't with him today, however, so he played alone. When he caught sight of his mother, he jumped up and ran to her.

"Mam," he grabbed her hand. "I am hungry. Isth it time to eat yet?"

She smiled at her little boy. "It is," she said. "Would you like to come with me to the kitchens?"

He nodded eagerly, pulling her from the chamber but easing up by the time they hit the stairs. He had been repeatedly reminded, and warned, of his mother's pregnancy and was properly careful, at least as much as a five year old could be. He ended up trying to help his mother down the last few steps, being a gentleman, but the moment she was off the stairs, he was yanking her from the keep.

Cantia fought off a grin as she allowed her eager son to tow her out into the yard. She found herself looking about, trying to catch a glimpse of Tevin or Val or even Myles, but everyone seemed to have vanished. Not particularly concerned, she returned her attention to Hunt only to catch a glimpse of the smithy shacks off to her right. They lingered in a cluster, run down, and somewhat foreboding. There was darkness there. Her curiosity had the better of her and she let go of Hunt's hand.

"Go into the kitchen and tell Cook that you would like some bread," she instructed. "Tell her I will be there in a moment."

Hunt cocked his head curiously. "Where are you going?"

Cantia answered indirectly. "I will be there shortly. Go, now. Do as

I say."

Hunt watched his mother head off towards a collection of seldom used stalls, but that was as far as his curiosity went. His rumbling belly had him turning for the kitchen and the alluring smell of fresh baked bread.

Cantia approached the shelters, her pace slowing. She grew more wary with each passing step, glancing around to make sure Tevin wasn't somewhere nearby. She knew he would become angry at her for disobeying him, but she felt an inexplicable pull to see the woman he had married. She understood clearly that the woman was dying and, in a small way, perhaps Cantia wanted to see for herself. She wanted to see this woman who had birthed Arabel and then had abandoned her family. Beyond that, she really wasn't sure why she wanted to see her, only that she did. Something strong and unseen was pulling her in that direction.

Two of the shacks were empty but she could hear movement in the third. Cantia paused, listening to the low hum of conversation, wondering if she should come back another time. As lady of Rochester, however, she had every right to know who was within her castle, or at least she told herself that. She had every right to be here. Squaring her shoulders, she opened the rickety old door.

The old physic was inside along with a serving woman from the kitchens. Cantia recognized her. Both of them turned to look at the lady of Rochester standing regally in the door opening.

"My lady," the physic greeted. "What are you doing here? You should not be jeopardizing the child so in the same room as a sick woman."

Cantia's eyes struggled to adjust to the darkness as she stepped into the doorway, her gaze moving across the dim chamber until she came to rest on a lumpy jumble in the corner. It smelled old and dank, mingling with the sharp scent of vinegar.

"I heard about this woman and came to see her," she said, wondering how much the physic knew about the identity of his patient. "Is she really dying?"

The physic glanced over his shoulder at the body in the corner. "She is," he replied. "A few days at most, maybe hours."

"Has she awakened? I was told she was unconscious."

The physic nodded. "She awakened a short time ago and we were able to feed her some broth," he replied, returning his attention to Cantia. "Does the earl know you are here? I cannot imagine he would let you come here and risk your health."

Cantia tore her gaze off the supine bundle, her eyes flashing as she looked at the physic.

"You will mind your own business," she snapped. "If you tell him I was here, I will make sure you are thrown out on your ear."

The physic lifted a hand in supplication and returned his attention to whatever he had been doing when she had entered the hut. Cantia, however, was unforgiving. She didn't want an audience for what she was about to do. She didn't want anyone witnessing what was likely to be a very emotional moment, gossip fodder to be spread throughout Rochester.

"Get out," she commanded. "Get out this instant."

The physic set his implements down and, without question, vacated the shack. The serving wench quickly followed. When the door swung shut behind them, Cantia returned her attention to the woman in the corner.

What am I doing here? The thought kept rolling around in Cantia's head as she approached the bed. She still didn't really know. As sunlight streamed in between the gaps in the walls, filtering in through the musty shadows, she came to a halt next to the straw mattress, gazing down at the partially-covered face.

The woman was breathing heavily. She could hear it. A wet cloth covered her nose and mouth, and Cantia reached down, gingerly took a corner, and pulled it off. The features of the woman were fair, if not somewhat plain, but she could see Arabel in the shape of the face. There was also a big dimple in the woman's chin, just like her daughter. Aye, the more Cantia stared, the more she could see the resemblance. Her heart began to pound.

"Louisa?" she whispered, paused, then whispered loudly. "Lady Louisa? Can you hear me?"

The woman twitched, drawing in a deep breath that brought rowels from her chest. Cantia stood back somewhat, not wanting to get too close, but she made sure she was close enough that the woman could see her. She tried again.

"Lady Louisa," she said in a normal speaking tone. "Can you hear me? Please awaken."

The woman twitched again. It took two more tries from Cantia to rouse the woman until, finally, the eyelids lifted. The eyes were only slightly open, however, and Cantia bent down so she could meet the woman's muddled gaze. Dark eyes finally fixed on her.

"Lady Louisa?" she said, more gently. "Are you Lady Louisa?"

The woman just stared at her. Then, she shifted slightly, trying to lift her head when she realized a very beautiful pregnant woman in fine garments was speaking to her. But she was so very, very weak, her life all but drained from her by the disease that was swiftly consuming her. All she could do was lay upon the straw and gaze, weakly, at the very fine lady.

"Qui vous est?" she rasped.

Who are you? Cantia replied to her in French. "My name is the Lady Cantia Penden," she replied. "I am the Lady of Rochester Castle, and you have been brought to us. Are you Louisa of Hesse?"

The woman continued to stare at her. Cantia waited, with bated breath, for a response, but none was immediately forthcoming. It was evident that the woman was too weak to carry on a conversation. Finally, the dark eyes closed. Cantia waited a nominal amount of time before realizing she might not receive an answer. As she debated on whether or not to leave, the woman spoke.

"*J'étais, une fois,*" she whispered. *I was, once.* She continued in French. "Now I am the wind. I will blow away until I exist no longer."

Cantia listened to the barely-audible words. "Do you know why you have been brought to Rochester?" she asked softly.

There was a very long pause. "I do not know. Men came to my home and took me away but they did not tell me why. I can only ask that you allow me to die in peace."

"No one has told you anything?"

"No."

Cantia considered what she would say next very carefully. "You have been brought to Rochester because your husband and daughter are here," she said quietly. "You were brought here as a favor to me."

The woman didn't react for a moment. Then, the eyes opened again, only this time, they opened wider. The woman actually appeared lucid. The pasty face registered an expression for the first time.

"My...?" she whispered. "My... child is here?"

Cantia lowered herself to sit on the ground so the woman wouldn't strain herself looking up at her. The conversation was difficult enough already. Several feet away, she sat on her bum in her fine surcoat and faced the woman.

"I want you to listen to me and listen carefully," she demanded. "Can you do this?"

The woman was hesitant at first but eventually nodded, as much as she could muster. "I can."

Cantia acknowledged the reply, wondering what, exactly, to say at this point. She wondered if she should be selective about what she told the woman but eventually opted for everything because she had come this far and there was no reason to hold back. For Tevin's sake, and hers, she would be forthcoming with the hope that the woman would be forthcoming as well.

"Long ago, you were married to Tevin du Reims," she finally said. "You are still married to him."

The woman's pale face registered even more shock. "How... how would you know this?"

Cantia tried to be careful. "I know this because he loves me and I love him," she whispered. "We cannot be married because he is still married to you. He did not know your fate, whether you were dead or alive, so a... a friend swore to find you so that we would know what had become of you. If you were alive, perhaps you would grant Tevin an annulment, but if you were dead... then at least we would know. I carry Tevin's child and we very much wish to be married but we cannot do that so long as... well, so long as you are still his wife."

The woman stared at her, shock turning to disbelief and, strangely, some understanding. "*That* is why... why...?"

Cantia simply nodded as the woman trailed off. Then she regarded her carefully for several long moments.

"Tell me why you left him," she said softly. "Tell me why you abandoned Tevin and Arabel."

The woman regarded her in return. She simply lay there and stared at her, some of the shock gone from her face as she came to understand why she had been brought to Rochester. With that understanding came defiance, and perhaps some self-preservation.

"He has brought me here to kill me," she finally muttered.

Cantia shook her head. "No one is going to kill you. But I would like to know why you left."

The woman didn't reply for a moment, but her expression didn't waver. When she finally spoke, it was with surprising strength.

"It was so long ago," she muttered. "Why does it matter now?"

"Because it does. Please tell me."

The woman hesitated for a brief moment before complying. She figured she had nothing to lose. She was dying anyway. What more could she say that wouldn't hasten that death?

"My name is Louisa Berthilde Solveig of the House of Hesse-Rheinfels," she said. "My father was Maurice the Bold of Hess-Rheinfels, the man who pledged me to Titus du Reims' son when I was still a very young girl. I had never met Tevin du Reims before the day we married, when I was still a child myself of fourteen years. I did not want to marry him, you see, because I was in love with my beautiful

Kael. We had fallen in love as children and were deeply devoted to each other. It was Kael who escorted me to my wedding with Tevin and watched the woman he loved marry another. He even stayed with me during my first year of marriage, as part of a contingent of soldiers my father left behind for my personal protection."

Cantia was listening intently to the stilted French with the heavy Germanic accent. Moreover, the woman spoke very softly and it was difficult to hear. But the story was essentially what Tevin had told her.

"If Kael was with you for so long, why did you wait until Arabel was born before leaving?" she wanted to know. "Why not leave right away?"

Louisa was exhausted from all of the talking but, somehow, she felt the increasing need to speak. She had not spoken of such things for fifteen years and in repeating the memories, she was reliving them. Visions of her beloved Kael were coming to mind and she could not help herself. From the dying woman's heart, the words were flowing forth.

"Since I am not long for this world, it does not matter what I say," she whispered. "You want to know and I will tell you."

"I just want to know the truth."

"But why?"

"For Tevin's sake. Please tell me the truth."

Louisa regarded her for a moment, the dark eyes glittering with the last embers of her life force. "What has he told you?"

"Just what you told me. He said you left him for another knight you were in love with from your homeland."

Louisa listened, digested, then took a deep breath. Her mind began to wander. "That is what my father told Tevin," she murmured. "But it was not the truth. Not entirely, anyway."

Cantia's brow furrowed. "What do you mean?"

Louisa's gaze grew distant. "My beautiful Kael was my love, my heart, my life," she said softly. "Tevin was never unkind. In fact, he was inordinately sensitive to my position. He seemed to understand I did not want to be married to him. I took advantage of that kindness. I was horrible to him."

"How?"

"Kael and I were lovers," she whispered, as if suddenly contrite after all of these years. "Tevin would share my bed at night and when he would leave to go about his duties, Kael would share it. Shortly after we were married, I... I became pregnant when Tevin went away. I knew he would more than likely send me away in disgrace at the very least if he knew the child was not his, so upon his return, I made sure to act as the attentive and affectionate wife, and we coupled. It was early enough in the pregnancy that I was able to tell Tevin the child was his, but I knew differently. When Arabel was born, she looked exactly like Kael. Terrified for my life, Kael convinced me to flee with him, so I did."

By this time, Cantia was gazing at the woman with shock. "*Kael* is Arabel's father?" she hissed. "Not Tevin?"

Louisa shook her head. "No."

Cantia's hand ended up over her mouth in an astonished gesture, hardly believing what she was hearing. "You are certain of this?"

"I am."

"Then... then you did not leave because she was crippled?"

Louisa sighed heavily. "I left because Kael convinced me that Tevin would kill me if he discovered the truth." She paused as a hint of a smile crossed her lips. "Kael and I lived together in Paris for three years until he left me for another woman. I was alone, with no money, so I contacted my father, who proceeded to inform me that he no longer had a daughter. He was ashamed of my behavior and disowned me. So I stayed in Paris and made money the only way I could. I was a prostitute."

Cantia was overwhelmingly astonished at the story. Her mouth was hanging open and she had to make a conscious effort to close it.

"Why did you not contact Tevin?" she pressed. "Perhaps... perhaps he would have taken you back."

Louisa shook her head. "And bring more humiliation towards him? To have a wife abandon you is bad enough, but to take her back... it would only make him look like a fool. I would not do that to him, for he was kind to me. I was simply a silly, foolish girl who made a very bad decision."

Cantia couldn't believe what she was hearing. Louisa's story rolled over and over in her mind until she was nearly giddy with it. After several long moments, she simply shook her head.

"I am sorry," she didn't know what else to say. "I am sorry a mistake cost you your entire life."

Louisa's dark eyes warmed. "It is better for Tevin and Arabel this way," she replied. Then, the eyes took on a wistful gaze. "My daughter is still alive, then?"

Cantia nodded. "She is frail but she is otherwise healthy," she said. "Tevin is devoted to her. She is beautiful and brilliant."

The dark eyes misted over and tears found their way onto Louisa's temple. "I had always wondered," she whispered. "I never stopped praying for her but I knew she was better off with Tevin. There was no life I could offer her. That is why I never returned for her."

Cantia began to mist up as well, thinking of Hunt, of the baby she carried, and so thankful that Louisa had that same mothering instinct in spite of the fact that she left her child. For Arabel's sake, she was glad. It was too little, too late, but at least the woman was showing remorse.

"Thank you," she finally whispered, tears verging. "Thank you for telling me your story."

Louisa merely closed her eyes, her mind moving to times past, of the knight she had been in love with and of the powerful husband she had betrayed because of that love. Her exhaustion overwhelmed her and her breathing began to grow heavy again. The emotions, the illness, were too much to bear.

It was clear the conversation was over. Cantia watched the woman for several minutes before struggling to her feet. As she silently turned for the door, Louisa stopped her.

"My lady," she said softly. "I have no right, but I would like to ask something of you."

Cantia paused. "Of course."

"I would like to see my daughter. If it is possible, I would be grateful."

Cantia could only nod. She could not give permission, as that was Tevin's decision. With a lingering glance at the frail woman on the mattress, she quit the shack and strolled out into the brisk air of the waning day.

CHAPTER TWENTY-ONE

"I TOLD YOU not to go near her," Tevin was livid. "Why did you disobey me, Cantia? Do you know what you have done? You have foolishly jeopardized your life and the life of the baby by going there. I did not believe you to be so foolish until now."

Cantia sat in the solar, her head lowered as Tevin raged. He was genuinely enraged, ever since he saw her walking across the bailey of Rochester and intercepted her. He had been glad to see her until he asked her where she had been and she had been truthful with him, mostly because she couldn't think of a lie fast enough. Now, he was furious and it was only growing worse.

"Well?" he barked. "What do you have to say for yourself?"

Cantia's head remained lowered and she shook her head. She didn't want to tell him about her visit to Louisa, not until he calmed down, so she kept her mouth shut. That only seemed to make him madder.

"You have nothing to say to me?" he put his hands on his hips, a sharp gesture. "Are you just going to sit there?"

She nodded. He threw up his hands and stomped around the solar, slamming the door in Myles' face when the man heard the shouting and peeked in to see what was going on. Infuriated, Tevin kicked a chair out of the way, breaking it, as he marched over to the lancet windows for a breath of cool air. He needed it before he broke more furniture.

"Foolish," he growled, his gaze moving out over the bailey. "Foolish, stupid and idiotic. Are those truly your qualities? I would have never guessed but today you have made me rethink that opinion."

His anger was starting to hurt, right though it was. For lack of a better response, and to force him to cool his anger sooner rather than later, she burst into quiet tears. He whirled away from the window when he heard the sobs. As Cantia knew, his anger took a dousing and he stared at her a moment, watching her heaving shoulders, before sighing heavily. All of the fight began to fizzle out of him.

"Do not weep," he told her softly, gruffly. "I was not trying to hurt you but... Cantia, why did you do it? I told you not to go there for a reason. I did not want you exposed to her disease."

Cantia only wept louder and turned away from him. "I do not want to talk to you right now," she sobbed. "Go away and leave me alone. You are hateful and mean."

He was starting to fold and trying not to. He began to make his way in her direction. "I am not leaving," he told her firmly but quietly. "I am sorry if I hurt your feelings, but you know what you did was wrong."

She put an arm on the back of the chair and lay her forehead upon it, sobbing. "You are nasty and terrible," she wept. "Go away."

"I am not going away."

"I am not going to talk to you."

"Then we shall make an odd stand-off."

She could hear him moving around behind her as he pulled up a chair and plopped down on it. She knew he wasn't about to leave but that had been her plan. He was calming down and that was all she wanted. To further speed that process, she stood up from the chair and rubbed at her belly, which always made Tevin want to rub it, too, because when she did it was usually when the baby was kicking and he didn't want to miss it. But he stayed on his chair, watching her, his hands clasped on his lap. Wiping at her eyes, she still made sure to sniffle and hiccup appropriately as she went to the lancet window and allowed the breeze to cool her warm cheeks.

Several minutes passed. Fifteen minutes passed and still, she said nothing. Tevin just watched her. Approaching the half-hour mark, he finally broke their stalemate.

"Are you ever going to speak to me?" he asked.

Cantia wasn't ready to fold. She wanted him to feel very bad about yelling at her so she turned away from the window and went to the solar door.

"I do not feel very well," she announced. "I am going to lie down for a while."

He was on his feet, moving towards her. "What is wrong?"

She opened the door. "I am exhausted from all of your yelling." She finally turned to him, tears gone and a spark of anger in her eye. "You could have simply asked me, quite calmly, what I had been doing rather than yelling at me and calling me foolish. You did not have to react that way."

His expression tightened up and he struggled not to feel remorse. "I am not going to apologize for becoming angry. I had every right."

She turned her nose up at him and went to the spiral stairs, carefully mounting them and disappearing to the upper floors as he stood there and watched. That lasted all of a few seconds before he hissed a curse and followed.

"Cantia," he followed her up the stairs. "Please wait."

She ignored him. "I want to lie down," she said again as she cleared the third floor landing and moved up to the fourth floor. "You have given me an aching head."

Tevin felt like the meanest man in the entire world as he followed her up to their chamber. He was a slave to her and he knew it, but he didn't care. Still, he didn't want to back down completely. He had a point to make.

When they reached the door to their chamber, he reached out to grasp her. She didn't resist but she was stiff in his arms as he pulled her against him and gazed down into her beautiful face. His expression was a mix between disapproval and repentance.

"I am sorry if I was harsh," he said softly. "But I asked you to stay away from her for your own good. Do you not understand that?"

She was having a difficult time resisting him. "I understand."

"I told you to stay away because I love you. I would be shattered if anything happened to you."

"I know."

"Will you at least forgive me for being hurtful?"

She thought a moment on the request, or at least she pretended to. But she eventually folded just like he did and wrapped her arms around his neck, hugging him. He swallowed her up in his big arms, thankful she wasn't holding a grudge. Then he kissed her on the forehead, on the cheek, and looked her in the eye.

"But from now on," he rumbled gently but sternly, "please stay away from her. It would destroy me if you contracted whatever disease she has. Agreed?"

Cantia regarded him, thinking on her conversation with Louisa. She remembered that the woman told her that Tevin had always been kind to her in spite of their circumstances and as she looked at him, she began to feel pangs of sympathy for him. He was such a wonderful man, sweet and wise and powerful, and her heart ached for him. *Arabel was not his child.* God, if she could only tell him. She wondered if she even should, if it would even matter after all this time. But she could not, in good conscience, withhold what Louisa had told her about Arabel. Tevin would never forgive her if he found out she knew and hadn't told him.

With a sigh, she laid her head against his chest and snuggled against him.

"Have you spoken with her at all?" she asked softly.

Tevin held her close. "Not yet," he said. "I have been occupied with Val and Arabel."

"How did Arabel take the news?"

"Better than I did. She is a wise and reasonable girl. She was quite calm about it. She wants to meet the woman but I am not sure that is a good idea."

Cantia looked up at him. "You must let her," she said. "We are speaking of her mother. No matter what you feel, you must let Arabel form her own opinion of the woman. She must be very curious so I would not forbid her from speaking to the woman. You may do more harm than good."

He lifted his dark eyebrows in resignation. "That is what Val said," he replied. "If both of you are telling me the same thing, then perhaps I should listen. I… I just do not want Arabel to be hurt or disappointed."

"She will be more hurt or disappointed if you do not permit her to meet her mother. Be present during the meeting if you must, but let your daughter come to terms with the woman who gave birth to her. This is a moment she never thought she would face and it is her right."

Tevin thought on that a moment before reluctantly agreeing. "As you say," he muttered. "But I will speak with the woman first, alone, before I allow Arabel near her."

Cantia could see the protective father, the humiliated husband, in his expression. She put a soft hand against his cheek.

"I spoke with her at some length," she said softly.

His brow furrowed. "How long were you with her?"

"Long enough," she said, eyeing him. "Tevin, I must speak with you before you go and see her. I must tell you what she told me."

He scratched at his head, intrigued, but unsure if he really wanted to hear all of it. After a moment, he simply shook his head.

"It was all so long ago," he said. "It does not matter any longer, whatever she has to say. I do not want to hear her excuses or explanations. My only communication with her will be where it pertains to my daughter."

My daughter. Cantia was feeling some apprehension for his reaction as she opened the door to their chamber and pulled him inside. When she quietly shut the door, she faced him.

"This *is* about your daughter," she said softly. "Sit down. I must tell you what she told me. It would not be fair to you if I did not."

He looked at her curiously but took the chair by the hearth and sat. Cantia went to him, standing before him, smiling when he put his hands on her belly purely out of habit.

"How is Talus today?" he asked.

She chuckled at the use of the baby's name, long before he was even born. They had spent a good deal of time haggling over names and

Tevin was very decisive in his wants. The child would be a boy, no matter what Cantia said, and his name would be Talus because Tevin had heard the name in a story his father had once told him. Talus had been a very strong man, immortal, and Tevin liked the name very much. It meant something to him.

"Your son is irritable and hungry," she teased, then sobered. "Tevin, we must speak of Louisa. I went to see her today because I wanted to know why she had abandoned you. I cannot imagine any woman being so cruel or callous towards her husband and child, and I feel so protective over you and Arabel that I simply needed to know. I did not go to see the woman purely to spite you. I did it because I love you."

He took his hands from her belly, gazing up into her lovely features. "Very well," he said steadily. "I am listening, then."

"You must promise to stay calm. Please, Tevin, I cannot take another rage."

"I will do my best, I swear."

Cantia sighed, turning her back on him as she paced a few feet away, gathering her thoughts. Then, she turned to him.

"When you were told she had run away with a knight from her homeland, that was only a very small portion of the truth," she said. "According to Louisa, she was very young when she married you and she had been in love with this knight for quite some time. I believe I know what it is like to be deeply in love. I believe you do, too."

He sighed. "Of course I do."

"If I was to marry another man, how would you feel?"

Tevin shrugged, averting his gaze. "I would kill him. I would not let that happen. I believe I have adequately demonstrated my devotion to you."

She nodded. "You have," she agreed. "So you can imagine what this young woman felt, being forced to marry a man she did not know and did not love."

"I can imagine."

Cantia continued. "Unfortunately, being so young, her judgment was also immature. After she married you, she and this knight continued to be lovers."

He looked at her. "Is that what she told you?"

"She told me that you would share her bed at night and he would fill it during the day."

"*After* we were married?"

Cantia nodded, seeing the hint of outrage on his face. She went to him, taking one of his big hands in hers and squeezing it tightly.

"She was young and foolish," she said softly. "She knows her behavior was terrible, but women in love do strange things."

"Do you make excuses for her, then?"

"Of course not. But bad behavior often has consequences."

"What consequences?"

Cantia knelt in front of him and he instinctively reached down to pick her up so she would not be close to the cold ground, but she resisted him. She held on to his hand tightly.

"Tevin, for Arabel's sake, I must tell you this before she speaks with her mother," she said softly. "I do not want to chance that you are caught off-guard by anything the woman says. She is on her deathbed and has nothing to lose. She may say many things and… I do not want you to be caught unaware."

Tevin's dark eyes flickered ominously. "Caught unaware by what?"

Cantia squeezed his hand sympathetically. "Louisa told me that you were away when she became pregnant with Arabel," she told him carefully. "She said that the pregnancy was early enough that when you returned, you performed as a husband should and she was able to convince you that you were the father. But she is certain that you are not Arabel's father."

Tevin stared at her, the color draining from his face. "She *told* you this madness?" he was both incredulous and outraged. "How is that…?"

Cantia continued quickly, cutting him off. "The knight she was in love with knew he was the father," she said. "He told Louisa that you would kill her if you discovered the truth and convinced her to flee with him. Being young, she didn't know what else to do, so she went. It was a horrible decision that cost her."

"It is not true!"

"It is, sweetheart. I swear this is what she told me."

Tevin was looking at her with an expression she had never seen before, something between utter astonishment and utter agony. Then, he leaned forward, collapsing, until he was resting his elbows on his knees, his gaze on the floor. He still held Cantia's hands tightly as if afraid to let her go. As Cantia gripped him, she could feel him tremble.

"Arabel...," he whispered. "Dear God... it cannot be true."

"I am so sorry, my dearest love," Cantia was close to tears on his behalf. "If I could have spared you the truth, I would have. But Louisa has no reason to lie about this. I did not sense that she was being deceitful in any way."

He groaned heavily, as if all of his strength had just left him. He struggled with his emotions, struggled to make sense out of it all. His mind, hurt yet analytical in searching for the truth, began to sort through the mess.

"I remember a man," he began after several long moments. "This knight was with her often, a man with blond hair and brown eyes. I remember this because his hair was very blond and... dear God, Arabel's hair is blond."

Cantia squeezed his hands, kissing his head to comfort him. She didn't know what else to do. She was afraid to say anything more as his mind struggled to come to terms with what she had told him. She could only imagine his pain, his shock.

"He was always with her," he repeated as if dredging up old memories, recalling snippets of the past. "Louisa's brother was always with her as well, and the two of them shadowed her nearly everywhere. She told me it was because she felt afraid in a strange land and she felt comforted by their presence and, wanting her to be comfortable, I allowed it. Now... it is starting to make sense. I never knew which knight she was in love with because when she fled, they all went with her, but now it is starting to make some sense. It must have been the blond knight who was always with her."

"Tevin," Cantia kissed his hands. "I would never presume to tell you what to think or how to deal with this matter, but I will say this – what happened occurred a long time ago. You said it yourself. In truth, it does not matter. I thought not to tell you what Louisa said about Arabel but I knew that I could not withhold such information from you. It is your right to know. But whatever the truth is, Arabel is innocent in all of this and she is very much your daughter. I would hope… hope that your love for her never changes, no matter what."

He looked at her, then. There was such sorrow in his eyes. "She *is* my daughter," he whispered, his eyes misting over. Then he sniffled loudly and wiped at his nose with the back of his hand. "Nothing will ever change that. But I… I am not sure…."

"Sure of what?"

"Sure if I should tell Arabel. Am I selfish not to want to tell her?"

Cantia kissed his hands again, his forehead. "If it was me, I would not tell her. Why should you? You are her father and she loves you. That is all she needs to know."

"That is all she will ever know, God willing," he said, regaining some of his composure. "All of this madness… we will forget about it. It will be our secret, you and me. I do not even want to tell Val."

"It will be our secret alone, I swear it." Cantia stroked his cheek. "You will go and speak with Louisa before Arabel does and tell her not to mention it. Tell her it does not matter, than none of it matters. I do not want Louisa to use Arabel like a confessional. The young girl need not hear all of her mother's sins because the woman is dying and feels the need to clear her conscience."

Tevin nodded in agreement before Cantia was even finished speaking. He whole-heartedly agreed. Kissing her hands reverently, and then her lips, he stood up and carefully pulled her up with him.

"I will see her now," he said, wiping his nose one last time as if to wipe away any emotion that was lingering. But he paused a moment, looking at Cantia with warmth in his eyes. "Thank you for being disobedient, sweetheart. I know your intentions were good. I… I think hearing this information from you was much better than if I heard it from Louisa. I am not entirely sure how well I would have received it. But coming from you… you gave me strength. I am grateful."

She smiled sweetly at him, accepting his tender kiss before he quit the room and shut the door softly behind him. Cantia's smile faded as she listened to his bootfalls fade down the stairs, thinking of the moment that lay ahead for him as he confronted the woman who humiliated and betrayed him, more than he could have ever imagined.

CHAPTER TWENTY-TWO

TEVIN STARED HARD at the woman, trying to see the young girl he had known so long ago. With the terrible aging and the progression of her disease, she looked like an old woman and she was only a little over thirty years of age. Life had been difficult for her, indeed.

Louisa regarded her husband, a very big man who had only grown more handsome over the years. She was quite astonished, actually. She had expected him to show up at some point, given her conversation with Lady Cantia, and she was prepared for his hatred and rage. Or, so she thought.

But Tevin did nothing more than stare at her for several moments, wondering how to start the conversation, when he finally gave up and simply shook his head.

"Long ago, I had imagined this moment and what I would say to you when the time came," he said. "Now that the moment is upon me, I do not know where to start. I suppose I could say that the only reason you are here is because I love another woman. You are here because of her and her alone."

Louisa had a difficult time understanding him, for she'd not spoken Middle English for quite some time. It was a confusing language.

"Me pardonner que mon anglais n'est pas très bon," she said softly.

Forgive that my English is not very good. Tevin took the hint, as he was fluent in three different languages. In this time of travel and trade, it was necessary. Additionally, if one had borrowed troops, it was necessary to be able to command them in a language they could understand. He shifted to French.

"You are here because of Lady Cantia," he said. "Do you comprehend?"

"Aye."

"I understand you had a conversation with her earlier."

"I did."

"She told me what you said about everything, including Arabel," he moved closer to the bed, his dark eyes intense. "Is this true?"

Louisa gazed up at the enormous knight, a man who was showing great restraint with his emotions. She could tell that he was struggling simply by his expression. Because she was so ill, she had no fear of the man. Death was coming for her, anyway. Tevin du Reims could not do anything more to her in that regard.

"I wish it was not," she said softly. "You were kind to me, my lord, but I was too young and foolish to realize it. All I knew was that I loved a man not my husband, and I wanted to be with him. I was, and I became pregnant. If your lady told you everything, then you also know that I fled because I was afraid you would discover the child was not yours and you would kill me for it. Perhaps you intend to now. But I go to God with a clear conscience."

Tevin listened to her quiet explanation, digesting it, before sighing heavily. Then, he shrugged.

"I cannot ask why you did it, because I know," he said. "I cannot pretend that I am hurt by your betrayal, because I am not. I was humiliated, that is true, but only as a man whose wife leaves him for another man. There was no personal emotion involved. You left Arabel with me and that was all I cared about. Even as I look at you now, the only emotions I feel are those pertaining to Arabel."

"I understand."

"What happened to the knight? The one you said is her true father?"

Louisa drew in a breath, coughing slightly when her chest roweled. Tevin stood well back as the woman covered her cough with a vinegar soaked cloth.

"He left me for another woman," she finally rasped. "I was seventeen years old. My father disowned me so I had no choice but to do what I could to survive."

"You are a prostitute."

Louisa simply nodded, closing her weary eyes. "Certainly not as I had planned for my life to happen," she said, opening her eyes and fixing on him. "I heard a few years ago that Arabel's father had been killed in a tavern fight. I also heard he had fathered several other children with different women. I suppose, in hindsight, I did not fall in love with a man of good character. But I was young... I did not know any better."

Tevin simply nodded. In truth, he had heard everything he wanted to hear and there was not much more to say. But he wanted to make one thing very clear.

"Arabel has asked to meet you and I have agreed," he said, his voice low. "Let me make it clear that you are not to tell her of your past indiscretions or of her true parentage. She does not need to know these things. Tell her of your family history, or of other meaningless things, but do not upset her with things she does not need to know. Do you comprehend?"

Louisa nodded weakly, but there was uncertainty to it. "She will want to know why I left," she said. "What would you have me tell her?"

Tevin averted his gaze, thinking on what his daughter knew of her mother's abandonment. "She believes you left because she was born crippled," he said quietly. "Perhaps... perhaps you should allow her to believe that and simply tell her that you are sorry for it."

"You would rather have her believe I abandoned her because she was deformed and not because she was her mother's bastard?"

He looked at her sharply. "She has already been hurt by what she believes to be the truth," he said. "If you tell her your real reasons, she will be hurt twice by your departure and betrayal. This I will not allow. No matter if she is truly not of my blood, I have raised her as my own and she *is* my daughter. I love her as much as I ever did and if you hurt her again, I swear to God that you shall not like my response. I am granting you the privilege of meeting this beautiful, young woman whom you gave birth to, who you are wholly unworthy of. Do not betray my good graces again."

Louisa's dark eyes were wide on him. After a moment, she simply nodded. "As you wish, my lord."

"If you have to tell her something, make it tales of glory that will make her feel good about herself, not like a worthless cripple whose mother abandoned her at birth. If you must say something to her, give her something to dream."

Louisa carefully regarded him. His words spoke of a very great love for Arabel, surprising when men were usually not the emotional sort. "I see you now as I saw you then. A man of great feeling," she said. "That is a rare thing, my lord."

Tevin's response was to shoot her a look of impatience before he turned for the door. As he put his hand on the panel, Louisa's soft voice stopped him.

"I *am* sorry, my lord," she said with as much strength as she could muster. "Please know how sorry I am for what I did. I am sorry we did not have the life together you had planned for."

Tevin looked at the woman. He couldn't muster the pity for her that Cantia had. "I suspect you are only sorry because your life did not turn out as you had hoped," he said frankly. "If you and your knight had lived a long and healthy life together, you would not be sorry in the least. You would consider Arabel and me a casualty of your decision and nothing more."

As he left the shack, Louisa came to realize he was right. He was right about something else, too.

Perhaps she should give Arabel something to dream.

◊

"FATHER, I DO NOT want you to go in with me," Arabel told Tevin as they crossed the bailey towards the smithy shacks. "I will speak to Lady Louisa alone."

Tevin was carrying his daughter in his arms. Her latest statement had his brow furrowing.

"You cannot go in alone," he said flatly.

"Why not?" Arabel demanded. "She cannot hurt me."

"Nay, she cannot hurt you, but the fact remains that I will be there."

"Why?"

"Because I will."

"But she may be afraid to speak if you are there," Arabel pointed out. "You are quite frightening when you want to be, Father."

"I will go in with her," Cantia said quietly, following the pair.

"Nay," Tevin said firmly, glancing at his lady. "I will go in. You may accompany us if you wish, but know that I am not comfortable with it. I wish you would simply stay out."

Cantia looked at him. "I am not going to stay out. If you go in, I go in."

Tevin rolled his eyes. "Stubborn woman," he muttered as they reached the shack. He stuck out a foot and pulled the door open. "Then stay close. If you get too close to her, I shall carry you out and spank you soundly."

Cantia fought off a grin at the threat, lowering her head because she did not want Tevin to see her face. He was edgy enough as it was and she didn't want to push him. Tevin was already moving into the dim, musty shack, keeping Arabel far from the figure lying in the shadows upon piles of fresh straw. He couldn't set Arabel down because there were no chairs in the room, so he stood several feet away from the bed and cleared his throat softly.

"Louisa," he said, his tone low as he deliberately left out "Lady". "We have arrived. Are you awake?"

The figure on the musty mattress stirred slightly. Bits of chaff blew up in the air as she moved, settling upon the uneven floor. Several long moments passed before a faint voice began to speak.

"In the fall, the trees will turn shades of orange and gold, soft strokes of the colors of sunset that appear vibrant against the deep blue sky." The voice from the bed was barely audible. "In the winter, the colors will disappear and the trees will be hidden by blankets of white snow, glistening and puffy pillows that look like clouds but melt to the touch. When I was a child, my brother and I used to run wild in the fields of shimmering snow that the old people would call Winter's Tears. We would make shapes in the snow. Have you ever seen snow, Arabel?"

Arabel was listening intently, mesmerized by the first sound of her mother's heavily accented French. It was a deep, raspy tone, not what she had imagined or expected.

"A few times," she replied softly. "But it usually melts and turns to mud. It never stays very long."

The vinegar-soaked rag came away from Louisa's face as she gazed at her daughter, nestled in her father's big arms. Arabel was several feet away but still, Louisa could see her delicate features. She was a beautiful woman, looking very much like her mother had at that age. Tears sprang to her eyes.

"In the spring, the show would melt and the streams would become great raging rivers," she continued hoarsely. "Yellow flowers would wake up from the frozen soil and the mountains would be covered with them. In the summertime, those same mountains would be overrun with families of rabbits and the entire valley would come alive with hopping, fuzzy creatures, all of them eating those pretty yellow flowers and growing fat and happy."

Arabel grinned at the visual description. "I like rabbits."

Louisa did something very surprising, then. She lifted her head and, extremely laboriously, pushed herself up so that she was resting on one elbow. It was as close as she could come to actually sitting up, but for her child, for this beautiful, young woman, she would make the attempt. She didn't want to speak to her lying down like a weakling. She wanted to show her daughter what she was made of.

"You come from strong and powerful people, Arabel," she continued softly. "My father was called Maurice the Bold because he was firm and strong, and everyone both respected and feared him. My brother was called Kurt the Brave, and he was indeed a very brave man. He once saved many people from a sinking ship by charging his horse out into the river and using his long beard as a rope for the drowning to cling to. It is true!"

Arabel giggled at the story of the man with the rope-beard, bringing a grin to Louisa's pale lips. "But the most respected and wise person in our family was my mother," she said, warmth and reflection glistening in her dark eyes. "You are named for her, in fact. Her name was Arabel Edeline Johanna von Karmann von Hassenpflug and was a direct descendent of the Valkyrie Sigdrifa, who was one of the chief Valkyries. Do you know who they are?"

Arabel was enthralled with the story. She shook her head. "Nay."

Louisa's smile grew. "Valkyries are the goddesses that choose who may live or die in a battle," she said, rather proudly. "They are in my blood. They are in your blood as well."

Arabel's eyes widened. "I am descended from *gods*?"

Louisa nodded. "Sigdrifa was known as the 'victory maker'. She brought luck to all men in battle. Perhaps that is why your father is such a great warrior – he has you to protect him. That is why you were meant to stay with him, you know. You have protected your father all of these years."

Arabel was astonished. She looked at her father, who was looking at Louisa with an odd sort of expression, something between disbelief and warmth. She had never seen that particular expression before. Rather speechless, she returned her attention to Louisa.

"But... but you left me," she said, sounding as if she was almost embarrassed to voice her thoughts after what she had just been told. "Why did you leave?"

Louisa's smile remained. "I never left you, Arabel," she murmured. "I gave you over to your father so that you could protect him while I was called away. We are Valkyries, you and I, and we are needed everywhere. I came back when I could but soon, I will be called away again."

Arabel cocked her head. "Where will you go?"

Louisa's strength was failing her. She had exerted herself all that she could. Carefully, she lay back down on the stiff and crunchy mattress, gazing up at her only child. She sighed faintly.

"Where all Valkyries go," she explained. "Walhalla. It is where all of the great warriors go when it is time for them to move on to another life. When it is time to die."

Arabel thought on that a moment. "Will I go there, too, when I die? I thought I would go to heaven. That is what the priests say."

Louisa could feel her life draining from her. Her arms and legs were growing very cold and she instinctively knew she was not long for this world. God had given her just enough time to reconcile with her child and now that it was done, there was no longer any reason for her to remain. It was time for her to go.

"Wherever you go, I shall see you there," she promised. "But for now, you must stay and continue to protect your father. That is what you were meant for."

She closed her eyes and faded off as Arabel, Tevin and Cantia watched. The hut grew excessively quiet, for not even the sounds of Louisa's heavy breathing filled the stale air. It was Cantia who finally went over to the woman and felt her pulse, realizing she was gone. She looked at Tevin with big eyes, implying the worst, and he took the hint. As he turned to leave, Arabel stopped him.

"Is she dead?"

Tevin nodded faintly. "She is, sweetheart."

He started to move again but she balked. "Please," she begged her father, "I… I just want to touch her. Can I please touch her?"

Tevin realized he was fighting off tears. He wasn't sure why, but he was. Perhaps it was because Louisa had done what he had asked and given Arabel a true sense of worth. Perhaps it was all fantasy, perhaps not. In any case, Arabel would forever remember the last words of her mother and cherish them. Louisa may have wronged both Tevin and Arabel once, but in the last few moments of her life, she made up for it. She gave Arabel the right to dream.

Silently, he took her over to her mother's body. Arabel wanted to be put down but there was no place to sit her, so he ended up putting her on her spindly knees as she sat next to the bed. When Cantia tried to move close again, he held out a hand to her and had her keep her distance. In fact, he moved back as well, going to stand with Cantia by the door as Arabel sat beside her mother's bed.

Arabel gazed at the face of the woman who gave birth to her, seeing her own features in the weathered reflection. Lifting a weak arm, she gently touched Louisa's hand, her wrist, feeling her still-warm flesh beneath her touch. Then, she reached up and pulled the blanket off the woman's head, revealing hair that had mostly fallen out. Louisa was almost completely bald. But Arabel gazed at the woman with some pity, some warmth, and stroked the sparse hair anyway. She was sad, but not terribly so. In fact, she felt rather comforted.

"If you are not in heaven when I get there, I will demand they take me to Walhalla," she whispered. "I will tell them I am a Valkyrie and they will have to let me go. But until that time, I promise I will continue to protect my father. Thank you for leaving me behind to protect him. I am glad you did."

Bending over, she kissed the woman's wrist and covered her head back up with the blanket. Then she turned to Tevin, who was standing near the door with Cantia in his arms and tears in his eyes. Cantia had her head turned but Arabel could see that the woman was crying. She smiled at the emotional pair, having no real idea why they were so weepy.

"Do not be sad," she said. "Look at her face. There is a smile on it. Do you think she was happy to have met me?"

Tevin blinked back his tears. "Of course she was," he said hoarsely. "She was very honored."

Arabel looked at the woman, somehow beautiful in death as she had not been in life. Her skinny fingers lingered on the woman's hand. "Will we bury her in the cathedral now?" she asked. "She is your wife, after all. That makes her a countess."

Tevin looked at Cantia, who was wiping the tears off her face. It was

Cantia who answered.

"She will be buried with the greatest of honors, as the wife of the Earl of East Anglia," she said softly. "But, more importantly, she was your mother. That affords her the greatest and most honorable funeral of all. Would you like that, sweetheart?"

Arabel nodded, lifting her arms to her father, who scooped her up off the floor. Thin arms wrapped around her father's neck, she gazed at Cantia.

"Did you know your mother, Cantia?" she asked.

Cantia's gaze moved to the dead woman, her attention lingering there for a moment. Thoughts of her own past hovered in her mind. "Nay," she looked away. "She died when I was very young. I do not remember her at all. In that respect, I think you were very fortunate to have met your mother. I wish I had."

Arabel reached out a bony hand to Cantia, who took it snuggly. "I think I was fortunate, too," she said, squeezing Cantia's hand. "She said that I am meant to protect my father. I think I shall protect you, too."

Cantia smiled gratefully as they moved to the doorway, opening the panel to reveal the brilliant sunset beyond. Streamers of orange and yellow brushed across the sky and they all paused, gazing up into the coming night because it was so beautiful.

"Soft strokes of the colors of sunset that appear vibrant against the deep blue sky," Arabel uttered softly, repeating the words her mother had spoken to her as she looked up at the brilliant night. "Father, do you think she meant to leave this sunset for us?"

Tevin followed his daughter's gaze. Then he kissed her cheek and managed to stroke Cantia's shoulder affectionately. He couldn't remember ever feeling so satisfied or so free.

"I do not think she meant it for all of us," he said softly. "I think she only meant it for you. It is the last gift she could give you."

Arabel liked that thought. As she looked up into the glistening clouds, somewhere, someway, she could see Louisa winking at her.

She winked back.

EPILOGUE

July 1156 A.D.

"**M**OTHER," THE YOUNG MAN was very serious. "I am quite capable with a sword. You must not worry."

Cantia was seated in the solar of Thunderbey Castle, gazing up at Talus and wondering when her little boy had grown up. At sixteen years of age, he was already as tall as his father although he lacked Tevin's bulk. That would come with time, she knew, but it was difficult for her to separate the young man from her little boy. She had already been forced to do that with Hunt before she was ready, as he was now the powerful Steward of Rochester at the young age of twenty-one years. He had Brac's good looks and sensibilities but Tevin's heart and soul. It was a wonderful combination.

Now, Talus was her second oldest, an extremely handsome young man with her lavender eyes and Tevin's features. He even had his father's long, copper colored hair. But she wasn't sure she was ready for him to grow up completely.

"Mother?" Talus said impatiently. "Did you hear me?"

Snapped from her daydreams, Cantia sighed heavily. "I heard you," she said. "Where is your father? What does he have to say to all of this?"

"He sent me here to tell you."

Cantia's eyes narrowed. "He did?" She set aside her sewing and stood up. "Where is he?"

Before Talus could reply, there was much chatter and laughter descending from the upper floors. The small solar was tucked back in the big, box-shaped keep of Thunderbey underneath the stairs, so any movement up and down the stairwell always tended to sound like a herd of cattle running about. Noise echoed.

Eleanor du Reims, the image of her gorgeous mother at fifteen years of age, was the first down the stairs with her siblings close behind. She held on to the youngest child, Kinnon, who was only four years of age, but Tarran, Tristen and Elizabetha were clustered in behind her, antagonizing each other. As children verging on young adulthood, they tended to be confrontational with each other. As Cantia listened to Tarran harass his younger sister, she called out to them.

"Tarran," she said in a threatening mother tone. "Stop pestering your sister. All of you come in here, please."

The gaggle of children wandered into the solar, Kinnon running to his mother and lifting his arms to her. Cantia picked up her youngest, a blond little boy who looked a great deal like Hunt had at that age. She looked at the group around her.

"Talus," she addressed her son. "Your father is taking an army to Wales and I am quite sure he did not ask you to join as a full-fledged warrior. I believe he is taking you and your brothers as squires."

Talus was grossly unhappy as Tarran and Tristen beamed. At thirteen and nine years of age, respectively, they had recently been called home from fostering at Pontefract Castle because it had been heavily besieged by the Scots twice in the past two years, and Cantia was frantic to bring her children home. Begrudgingly, Tevin had ridden north to bring the boys home, who weren't quite so sure what their mother was all worked up about. Their father said it was something about the irrational Scots. Now, with the prospect of accompanying their father to the Welsh border on behalf of King Henry I, they were thrilled. But Talus was jealous because his younger brothers had seen more war action than he had.

"But I have my own sword," Talus argued. "Father will not allow me to use it because he knows how upset you become. He…."

Talus' argument was cut off when the door to the keep opened and the grating of mail could be heard. Tevin made an appearance in the solar entry as Elizabetha and Tristen ran to him, both of them trying to talk to him at the same time. Tevin threw up his hands.

"I cannot understand more than one conversation at a time," he said, bending over to kiss Elizabetha on the forehead and putting a fatherly hand on Tristen's shoulder. "What is all the fuss about?"

"What is it ever about?" Cantia sighed. She went to her husband, kissing him. "Talus has informed me that he will be accompanying you as a warrior and not a squire to the Welsh Marches. Is there truth in this?"

Tevin looked at his tall son, wriggling his eyebrows at the lad. "I told him he could bring his weapon," he admitted as he looked at his wife. "Lord Marmion swore to me that Talus is already a very good warrior, and I must concur. I have seen Talus in practice and the lad has no equal."

Cantia lifted an impatient brow. "I realize he was the shining hero of Tamworth Castle when he fostered, but I also know that he is only sixteen years of age. I am not entirely sure he should be fighting Henry's wars. He is not even a full-fledged knight yet."

Tevin's gaze was a mixture of warmth and disappointment. "Do you not trust my judgment any more than that?"

Cantia sighed again and set Kinnon down, who was beginning to squirm. "Of course I do," she said, more gently. "But you are also a proud father and… Eleanor, why don't you take the children into the hall? The nooning meal should be ready."

Eleanor took Kinnon and Elizabetha, but the older boys seemed inclined to hang around until Tevin gave them a threatening glare and pointed to the door. Only then did Tristen and Tarran move, however slowly, with the other children. Talus, however, didn't seem to think the request pertained to him until Tevin literally grabbed the boy by the shoulder and pushed him towards the door. Unhappy, Talus followed the rest.

When they were finally alone in the solar, Tevin looked at his wife. Outside in the ward, he could hear the shouts of sentries, alerting the castle to an incoming rider, but he ignored the cries as he focused on his wife.

"I know you are unhappy about my going to the Marches," he said softly yet sternly. "You have made that clear, and I have made it equally clear that I must go. I am too important to the king's arsenal and he is determined to unite England and Wales, so I must do this. It is important."

Cantia didn't have a logical reply for him because she knew he was right, so she frowned verily and he put his arms around her, pulling her close.

"You are too old to be fighting," she protested weakly. "You must leave it to the younger men. You have already put in your time, Tevin. You fought for Stephen for years and now Henry. I do not want you on the front lines any longer. I want my husband home."

"And I *am* home," he chided gently. "You wanted Talus home, so I brought him home. Then you wanted Tristen and Tarran home because you were afraid for them, so I brought them home as well. Eleanor came home from Kenilworth when she was twelve because you could not bear to be away from her, and Elizabetha and Kinnon have yet to even foster and I am not entirely sure they ever will. We are all home with you, Cantia, and if it were up to you, we would be all bottled up safely in the bosom of Thunderbey for the rest of our lives."

Cantia was deeply frowning by now. "There is nothing wrong with wanting to have my children and husband safe and home. We have seen enough fighting and battles, you and I."

He kissed her forehead. "I know, sweetheart," he murmured. "But England is only safe so long as the next generation is prepared to defend and preserve her. Talus is ready to do that, as are Tarran and Tristen. You must let them grow up, and I must show them how. Will you please let me do that?"

Cantia tried not to let depression overwhelm her. So she simply hugged him, knowing she couldn't adequately voice her protests to the point where he would understand her. Not this time. He was right and they both knew it.

"Life seemed much simpler during the days of Rochester," she complained. "When did it become so complicated?"

Tevin laughed softly. "You mean the days of Charles and Gillywiss?"

Cantia smiled in spite of herself as she remembered the outlaw, from so long ago, who had changed the course of her life.

"I miss him," she admitted. "I miss his eccentric ways. Do you remember when he came to our wedding dressed as a woman? I would not have known it was him except he was wearing one of my old surcoats."

Tevin snorted. "I remember that Simon flirted with him and then nearly killed him when he found out he was a man."

That brought soft laughter from Cantia. "And Arabel," she added. "She was oddly attached to him after that."

"She knew he had brought her mother to her. It endeared him to her."

"It endeared him to us all."

"She told me that he had visited her at the abbey a few times. Did she mention that to you?"

Tevin nodded as he thought on his frail, intelligent daughter who had, at age eighteen, decided to pledge herself to holy servitude. It had seemed to be the right decision for her, but he missed her tremendously. What was it he had told Cantia? *You must let them grow up.* It was easier said than done.

Tevin sighed, his cheek against the top of Cantia's head. "Times did seem simpler back then but I know they were not. Time has a way of easing memories until all you can recall is the good."

Cantia was forced to agree but she was prevented from replying when Talus suddenly burst back into the room, holding something aloft in his hand.

"Father," he sounded eager. "A messenger just came from Lohrham Forest!"

Tevin looked startled for a moment, glancing at his wife. "Myles," he muttered, moving to his excited son and collecting the missive the young man held. He stared at it a moment before breaking the seal. "It must be about...."

Cantia was beside him, literally twitching with excitement and apprehension. "Oh, it *must* be," she said anxiously. "Hurry and read it. What does it say?"

Tevin had the missive unrolled. By this time, the other children had wandered back into the solar because they, too, had seen the messenger from their position in the great hall. Knowing they had all been awaiting news from Lohrham Forest, the small castle where Myles and Val had lived for many years, they were anxious as their parents were to hear the contents of the missive. Tevin could see his brood in his periphery but his gaze was fixed on the carefully scripted letters.

"I have prayed daily for them," he muttered, trying to bring the message into focus. His eyes weren't what they used to be. "Two stillborn children in the past sixteen years and now...."

Cantia was beside herself. "Now *what*?"

Tevin read slowly. He didn't want to get ahead of himself. Then, as Cantia watched his face, a smile gradually spread across his lips. She swore she saw the glint of tears in his eyes as he began to read aloud.

"My sister gave birth to a healthy boy four weeks ago," he announced. "They christened the child Christopher and he is doing very well. Myles says he has never seen a child eat so eagerly."

Cantia closed her eyes. "Thank God," she breathed, hugging her husband tightly. "Oh, thank God. They have waited for this child for so very long. Finally, a healthy son."

Tevin was beyond words at the moment. He was so thankful on behalf of his sister and of Myles that he was nearly weak with it. All he could do was wrap his arms around Cantia and thank God for his own blessings. He had been given so many that it was difficult to count them all. He knew, without a doubt, that he was the most fortunate man alive.

Tevin, Talus, Tarran and Tristen went to the Welsh Marches after all to assist Henry I of England in his quest to unite England and Wales. Although the battles, for the most part, were not successful, all four survived and the three young men, sons of the great Earl of East Anglia, went on to fight for Henry for many years while their father retired to Thunderbey Castle to live out the remainder of his life with his wife by his side.

Three years after the birth of Christopher, David de Lohr was born to Myles and Val. Christopher and David grew up to serve Richard the Lion Heart in The Levant, and eventually became two of the more powerful noblemen in the High Middle Ages. Christopher was granted the title Earl of Hereford and Worcester by King Richard, while David was eventually granted the title Earl of Canterbury when he married the heiress. Both men were strong supporters of the crown and major players in the annals of history.

Beautiful Eleanor Britton du Reims married the Earl of Newark, Geoffrey Hage, at seventeen years of age and gave birth to the first of four sons, Kieran, the very next year. Kieran Hage went on to become one of the more powerful knights in the arsenal of King Richard, serving in The Levant with his cousins Christopher and David de Lohr. He also ended up marrying a rather strange Irish heiress and returned to her homeland with her, forsaking the family honor and relinquishing the title of Earl of Newark to his younger brother, Sean. At least, that was how the Hage family recorded the event, but some scholars disputed that finding.

Finally, Huntington Penden became a powerful warlord in his own right as Steward of Rochester Castle and his own son, Brac, assumed the title upon the passing of his father. Arabel du Reims eventually became Mother Superior at Yaxley Nene Abbey in Leicestershire, devoting her life to the contemplation of heaven versus Walhalla and trying to find her answers within the word of God. She was relentless in her search for the truth and developed a reputation within the ecclesiastical community as a whip-smart scholar, a fair superior, and a strict task master.

When she finally discovered the verity to the great question that had driven her most of her life, her mother, indeed, was waiting for her.

She had her answer.

○3 THE END ○○

AUTHOR NOTE

While Angels Slept is a novel that was six years in the making. It was also a novel that took on a mind of its own and essentially wrote itself. What a wild adventure!

Tevin and Cantia are the ancestors of several other Le Veque characters, as noted at the end of the epilogue. Their daughter, Eleanor, is the mother of the great Kieran Hage, hero of *The Crusader* and *Kingdom Come*. Tevin's sister, Val, is the mother of two of Le Veque's greatest and most prolific characters, Christopher and David de Lohr, central characters in *Spectre of the Sword*, *Archangel*, *Dark Steel*, and *The Lion Heart* to name a few. They pretty much pop up everywhere. The tough part is knowing that Christopher and David's parents die when the boys are young, but Le Veque chooses not to write about that part. It is left to the reader's imagination. And in case you are wondering about Arabel's affliction, she was born with Spina Bifida, and Louisa died from tuberculosis.

Before everyone goes crazy with the fact that Valhalla, or Walhalla, is from Norse mythology and not German mythology, think again. Read about the intermingling of Norse, Germanic and European mythology and learn some interesting facts. It would seem that folks like to borrow each other's gods and heavens, and just change the name a little. It makes for interesting reading.

The Earls of East Anglia Series is related to the House of de Lohr and the House of Hage.

Tevin du Reims' sister, Val du Reims, marries a secondary character in this novel, Myles de Lohr. Myles and Val are the parents of Christopher and David de Lohr in Rise of the Defender.

Rise of the Defender

Tevin and Cantia's daughter, Eleanor, married Sir Jeffrey Hage, and became the mother of Kieran Hage, the main character in the novel The Crusader and Kingdom Come.

The Crusader

Kingdom Come

Of note: Kieran Hage #1 is the hero from THE CRUSADER and KINGDOM COME. If you recall in KINGDOM COME, which is a time-travel novel dealing with Rory and Kieran being back in Medieval Times, there's a big twist at the end of the book. Not want to blow this twist for those of you who haven't read it (and you MUST read it because it's a killer twist), Kieran 'disappears' from Medieval England at that point. He leaves behind his young son, Tevin, who was named after Tevin du Reims of WHILE ANGELS SLEPT, who was his mother's father (Kieran's grandfather). If you recall, Tevin from WHILE ANGELS SLEPT was the UNCLE of Christopher de Lohr because Tevin's sister,

Val, married Myles de Lohr, a knight. These two became parents to Christopher and David de Lohr, making Christopher and David distantly related to both Kieran Hages.

Kieran Hage #1, having left Medieval England at the end of KINGDOM COME, left behind his son, Tevin, who his brother Sean raised as his own. Tevin Hage was a great man, a powerful knight, and he was told that his father, Kieran, had been killed, as had his mother. Both of his parents are gone. Therefore, he knew his father was Kieran #1 and that Sean, even though he raised him, was his uncle. Sean then had three sons of his own that were younger than his nephew Tevin, and it was Sean's youngest son, Jeffrey (named for Kieran #1 and Sean's father) who had Kieran #2, named for Kieran #1. Kieran #2 is the Kieran who appears in The Wolfe and Serpent.

Therefore – Kieran #2 from THE WOLFE is Kieran #1's great-nephew.

For more information on other series and family groups, as well as a list of all of Kathryn's novels, please visit her website at www.kathrynleveque.com.

Bonus Chapters of the exciting Medieval Romance
RISE OF THE DEFENDER to follow.

1192 A.D. – Sir Christopher de Lohr is Richard the Lion Heart's champion, a man that the Muslims nicknamed "The Lion's Claw". Blond, battle-scarred and powerful, he is what all men fear. After the fall of Acre, Christopher makes a promise at the deathbed of a dying comrade to marry the man's incorrigible but wealthy daughter. Christopher returns home to marry the woman, but the only thing is interested in is her substantial dowry. He has no use for a wife and resents being forced into the marriage.

The Lady Dustin Barrington doesn't want a husband. Petite and beautiful, she is a goddess with the heart of a tomboy. When the enormous, seasoned warrior comes to Lioncross Abbey Castle to marry her, she savagely resists him. More than ever, Christopher regrets agreeing to marry the woman but as they are forced together in a contract marriage, something strange happens… somehow, someway, the animosity subsides and a gentle warmth takes its place. More and more, they come to care for one another but neither of them will admit it.

As the voyage of discovery begins, Christopher is distracted by a very important task entrusted to him by Richard. He has been sent back to England ahead of King Richard to assess the climate of the country and also to assess the activities of Richard's brother, Prince John. He leaves for London to put himself in the heart of the turmoil that is going on between Richard and John, and brings Dustin with him. The moment they arrive in London, an entirely new and dangerous world opens up to them.

Join Dustin and Christopher as they embark on the adventure of a lifetime. Evil princes, tournaments, politics, wars, and a threat to their relationship from deep inside Christopher's inner circle invade their loving and passionate world. When Christopher is reportedly killed in battle, Dustin must pick up the pieces of her shattered life and attempt to carry on. But don't count the Defender out just yet… can he make it back to Dustin in time to prevent catastrophe?

Become a part of the sweeping three-part saga in an epic Medieval Romance you won't soon forget.

CHAPTER ONE

Year of Our Lord 1192
The Month of September
Lioncross Abbey Castle
The Welsh Marches

Lady Dustin Barringdon bit at her full lower lip in concentration. Climbing trees was no easy feat, but climbing trees in a skirt was near impossible.

Her target was the nest of baby birds high in the old oak tree. Her cat, Caesar, had killed the mama bird earlier that day and now Dustin was determined to take the babies back to Lioncross and raise them. Her mother, of course, thought she was mad, but she still had to try. After all, if she hadn't spoiled and pampered Caesar then this might never have happened. Caesar had no discipline whatsoever.

She pushed her blond hair back out of her way for the tenth time; her hands kept snagging on it as she clutched the branch. But as soon as she pushed it away, it was back again and hanging all over her. She usually loved her buttock-length hair, reveled in it, but not today. Long and thick and straight. It glistened and shimmered like a banner of gold silk.

Her big, almond-shaped eyes watched the nest intently. But not just any eyes, they were of the most amazing shade of gray, like sunlight behind storm clouds. Surrounded by thick dark-blond lashes, they were stunning. With her full rosy lips set in a heart-shaped face, she was an incredible beauty.

Not that Dustin had any shortage of suitors. The list was long of the young men waiting for a chance to speak with her father upon his return. She truly didn't care one way or the other; men were a nuisance and a bore and she got along very well without them. Nothing was worse that a starry-eyed suitor who mooned over her like a love-sick pup. She had punched many idiots right in the eye in answer to a wink or a suggestive look.

"Can you reach it yet?" her friend, Rebecca, stood at the base of the tree, apprehensively watching.

"Not yet," Dustin called back, irritated at the distraction. "Almost."

Just another couple of feet and she would have it. Carefully, carefully, she crept along the branch, hoping it wouldn't give way.

"Dustin?" Rebecca called urgently.

Dustin paused in her quest. "What now?"

"Riders," Rebecca said with some panic, "coming this way."

Dustin lay down on the branch, straining to see the object of her friend's fear. Indeed, up on the rise of the road that led directly under the tree she was on, were incoming riders. A lot of them, from what she could see.

Her puzzlement grew. Who would be coming to Lioncross this time of day, this lazy afternoon in a long succession of lazy afternoons? The riders passed through a bank of trees and she could see them better.

She began to catch some of her friend's fear. There were soldiers, hundreds of them.

"Rebecca," she hissed. "Climb the tree. Hurry up."

With a shriek, Rebecca clumsily climbed onto the trunk and began slowly making her way up.

"Who are they?" she gasped.

Dustin shook her head. "I do not know," she replied. "The only time I have ever seen that many soldiers was when my father...." She suddenly sat up on the branch. "My *father!* Rebecca, climb down!"

Rebecca didn't share Dustin's excitement. "Why?" she exclaimed.

Dustin was already scooting back down, crashing into her friend. "It is my father, you ninny. He has returned!"

Rebecca, reluctantly, began to back down the scratchy oak branch. "How do you know that? Are they flying a banner?"

Dustin hadn't even looked. She didn't have to. "Who else would it be?" She was so excited she was beginning to shake.

The army was quickly approaching the ladies' position. Thunder filled the air, blotting out everything else. Now, they were upon them. Rebecca was down from the tree but Dustin was still descending.

Dust from the road swirled about as several large destriers kicked up grit with their massive hooves. They had come up amazingly fast and Dustin found herself paying more attention to the chargers than to what she was doing. As the knights reined their animals to a halt several feet from Rebecca's terrified form, Dustin tried to get a better look at them.

She was trying very hard to single out her father but her distraction cost her as she lost her grip on the branch. With a scream, she plummeted from the tree about ten feet overhead and landed heavily on her right side.

Rebecca gasped and dropped to Dustin's aid. "Dustin! My God, are you all right?"

Dustin rolled to her back, now oblivious to the knights and men that were watching her. All she knew was that she could not catch her breath and her chest was so hot it would soon explode. As Rebecca tried to get a look at her, one of the knights dismounted his steed and knelt beside her.

"Breathe easy," came a deep, soothing voice. "Where do you hurt?"

Dustin could not talk. She could only manage to lay there and gasp for air. The knight removed his gauntlets and flipped up the faceplate on his helmet.

"Take deep breaths," he told her, putting his plate-sized hand on her abdomen, just below her ribs. "Slowly, slowly. Come now, slow down. That's right."

As Dustin's shock wore off, tears of pain and shock began to roll down her temples and, for the first time, she opened her eyes and focused on the man with the kind voice. She was shocked to see how big and frightening he was. He gazed back at her impassively.

"Are you hurt?" he asked.

She shook her head unsteadily. "I do not think so," she choked out. "I can breathe a little better."

He silently extended a hand, carefully pulling her up to sit. The first thing Dustin noticed was how big his hands were as they closed around her own.

The knight continued to crouch next to her, his gaze still unreadable. Shaking the leaves out of her hair, Dustin gave him the once-over.

"Who are you?" she demanded softly. "Where is my father?"

"Who is your father?" he returned, ignoring her first question.

Dustin had a bad habit of speaking first and thinking later. If these men were her father's vassals, then they would have known her on sight.

"Why, Lord Barringdon, of course," she said, grabbing the ends of her hair and shaking them hard. "Where is he?"

For the first time the man showed emotion. His sky-blue eyes widened for a brief second and he abruptly stood up. She tried to look up at him, but he was so tall she had to lay her head back completely and she could not do that because her head was killing her. So she cocked her head at an odd angle, still looking up at him, as she struggled to her feet.

The man didn't help her rise, although he probably should have. He just kept staring at her.

"Lady Dustin Barringdon, I presume?" he asked after a moment.

His voice sounded queer. Dustin managed to stand on her own, putting out a hand to steady herself as the earth beneath her rocked. The knight reached out to balance her.

"Aye," she replied, pulling her hand away cautiously and taking a step toward Rebecca, who clutched at her. She eyed the man warily. "Who are you?"

She had no idea why the man's eyes were twinkling. His face held no expression, but she swore his eyes were twinkling.

"I am a friend of you father's," he said. "My name is Christopher de

Lohr."

"Where is my father?" Dustin demanded yet again, excited to hear this man was a friend.

The knight hesitated. "Is your mother home, my lady?" he asked. "I bring messages for her."

Dustin's excitement took a turn for the worse. She had asked the same question three times without an answer. She was coming to suspect why and her stomach lurched with anguish. *God, no!*

"*Where* is my father?"

"I will discuss that with your mother."

Dustin stared at him a long, long time. He gazed back at her, studying every inch of that beautiful, sensuous face. The gray orbs that met his blue suddenly went dark and stormy. She closed her eyes and turned away from him, beginning to walk back down the road. Rebecca, puzzled, yet not wanting to be left alone with a company of soldiers, ran after her.

Christopher watched her go, knowing she must suspect at least part of the reason why he had come. When he began to hear soft sobs, fading as she continued down the road, he knew that her fears were confirmed. She knew her father was dead.

He turned to his brother. "Get the men moving," he said, mounting his destrier, but his eyes were still on the lady.

Christ, but he was still reeling with surprise and pleasure at the discovery of Lady Dustin. She was beautiful. Damnation, he hadn't known what to expect. The entire trip home had been filled with dread and foreboding, but he could see his worries were for naught. Even if she was as stupid as a tree and as disagreeable as a mule, she was still beautiful. If he had to marry, she might as well be pleasant to look at. Any other qualities were superfluous.

Slowly, the army followed several paces behind her. Dustin had never known grief before and discovered it to be the most painful thing she had ever experienced. The knight wouldn't tell her where her father was and that in and of itself was confirmation of the worst. She wasn't a fool. Sorrow overwhelmed her and she suddenly could not breathe again. Her sobs grew into raspy puffs of air and the ground began to sway again. Dustin was aware of a blissful, floating feeling as a strange blackness swallowed her up.

Christopher saw her go down on the side of the road and he spurred his destrier forward. The animal came to a halt in a cloud of dust and he dismounted, pulling Lady Dustin's hysterical friend away from the crumpled form in the grass.

"What's the matter with her?" her friend cried. "She's dying. The fall will kill her!"

Christopher knelt down, noting the even breathing, steady pulse, but pale color. Mayhap the fall did contribute to this. He suddenly felt strangely protective, knowing that the woman was to be his wife. Wasn't it right for a husband to feel protective? It was the most peculiar sensation he'd ever experienced.

"What's your name, lass?" he asked the panting redhead.

"Rebecca," she replied, "Rebecca Comlynn."

Christopher nodded, turning back to the woman in the grass. "You will take us back to Lioncross, Mistress Rebecca. I will take care of Lady Dustin."

Rebecca started to protest but David grabbed her and seated her on his destrier before she could put up a fight. Christopher scooped up Dustin and managed to mount his own steed with surprising ease. She was light, this one, and small, too. Standing her full height she barely met his chest. She was little more than a child in his arms.

He stole a glance at her as he gathered his reins. Her lips moistly parted, she looked to be sleeping in his arms. Her hair, so incredibly long and silken, hung all over them both and he had to pull it free from the joints in his armor a couple of times. He could feel lust warming his veins. Spurring his great warhorse, they proceeded on to Lioncross Abbey.

Lioncross Abbey was so named because it was built on the sight of an ancient Roman house of worship and actually incorporated portions of two walls and part of the foundation. Additionally, Arthur Barringdon had christened it Lioncross after Richard and the quest. Prior to Arthur inheriting the keep from his father, it had been named Barringdon Abbey. Some older people in the region still referred to it as such.

The fortress sat atop a ridge overlooking a large lake and the deep purple mountains that marked the Welsh border could be seen in the distance. Thick banks of trees surrounded the fortress and made the region appear lush and fertile, even in the dead of winter.

Christopher took a good look at what was to be his new home, verily pleased. It was a fine fortress, easy to defend, with a small village about a half mile to the north. He found himself growing more and more satisfied with each passing step of his horse. Aye, he was worthy to be lord of this. He already found himself making mental notes about the structure, what needed improvement and reminding himself to ask questions about the revenues. As fine a warrior as he was, he was an equally fine scholar and knew what it would take to make Lioncross a profitable keep.

Dustin stirred in his arms and he was reminded of his burden. He looked down at her just in time to see her lids opening, slowly, as if a curtain rising. Again, he was entranced with the bright gray eyes and noted the thick lashes as she blinked. She was staring up at the sky as if trying to remember where in the world she was when her gaze fell on him. She blinked once, focused on his pale blue eyes, and then sat up so fast he had to throw his arm down on her to keep her from pitching herself right off of his horse.

"Put me down!" she hollered.

"Steady, my lady," he said. "We're almost back to your keep."

Her head snapped to the horizon where Lioncross indeed loomed. She began to struggle against him and he could not understand her panic, but he relented and let her slide to the ground.

She took off like a rabbit, her skirts up around her thighs as she pounded down the road. That incredible mane of hair waved behind her like a banner. Rebecca, not to be left behind, jumped from David's destrier and ran after her.

David reined his steed alongside his brother's, both of them watching the racing figures. "Now, what do you suppose that is all about?" David wondered aloud.

Christopher shook his head. "I have no idea," he replied, then grinned at his brother. "What think you of my new keep?"

David nodded his approval. "Exceptional. As is your new bride."

Christopher cocked a blond eyebrow. "I am surprised as well," he admitted. "Lady Dustin Barringdon looks nothing as I imagined."

"With a name like Dustin, I had no idea what to think," David snorted.

"Nor did I, little brother," Christopher agreed.

They entered the outskirts of the little village, passing an interested eye over the small buildings and tradesman's shacks. It smelled like sewage and livestock, and bits of dust kicked up in the occasional breeze. The road leading to Lioncross was a wide one and peasants scattered to stay clear of the approaching army. Christopher's horse accidentally crushed a chicken and sent a woman wailing, much to his displeasure.

Finally, the jewel of Lioncross loomed before them. The gates of the fortress yawned open before them and he halted the caravan with a raised arm.

"This will cease," he indicated the open gates. "With Wales so close, these people are fools to leave themselves vulnerable."

Beckoning David forward with him, he left the rest of his troops outside the gates. There was one bailey to Lioncross, a huge open thing used for a myriad of purposes. He studied it intently, already noting what needed changing as he and David rode for the massive double doors of the entry.

Sentries met them at the base of the front steps. Christopher announced himself and his purpose, and waited while one of the guards disappeared inside. He reappeared several minutes later followed by another man dressed in mail and portions of plate armor.

The knight studied Christopher with piercing dark eyes. He was not particularly tall, but Christopher could see the muscles on the man. He was a seasoned warrior. His face was severely angled with a sharp nose and a sharp mouth. Immediately, he sensed hostility.

"What is your business here?" the man demanded in a strong Germanic accent.

"I am Sir Christopher de Lohr," he repeated, matching the man's tone. "I bear a message for Lady Mary Barringdon from King Richard."

The man looked Christopher up and down, taking a step toward him. "Give it to me and I will see that it is delivered."

"I have been instructed by our king to deliver it personally," Christopher said evenly. "I would deliver it now."

The man didn't say anything but continued to glare until Christopher finally had enough of his animosity. Dismounting without permission, he removed two scrolls of parchment from his saddlebags and walked deliberately to the soldier, holding out one of the missives for him to see.

"Richard's seal," he stated in case the soldier was blind. "Twould be unwise of you to go against our king. Now move aside or escort me in; 'tis all the same to me."

The soldier stared at the seal, knowing it for what it was. He tore his eyes away and looked at Christopher again, but this time, with less hostility.

"You scared the devil out of Lady Dustin," he said in a low voice. "For that I should gut you right now, but because you bear the missives from our king, you shall be spared."

Christopher almost laughed. David, in fact, did, drawing the soldier's angry glare. The battle lines were already being drawn.

"What is your name?" Christopher demanded of the warrior.

"Sir Jeffrey Kessler," he replied. "I am captain of Lioncross while Lord Barringdon is away."

Arthur had made no mention of a captain but it was of no matter. Christopher would dismiss the man as soon as he wed the fair Lady

Dustin and put David in charge of the men.

"Gain us entrance, Sir Jeffrey," Christopher requested, but it sounded suspiciously like an order.

Jeffrey's gaze lingered on Christopher before complying, just long enough to emphasize he could not be ordered around by a stranger. Christopher followed, somewhat hesitantly, wondering if he shouldn't bring a contingent of men to protect him against any trickery from the Germanic knight.

He kept his hand on the hilt of his sword just in case as he followed the man into the dark and musty keep beyond.

ଓ

DUSTIN STOOD IN her mother's drawing room, pacing endlessly by the oilcloth-covered windows. Lady Mary, unflappable as always, continued to calmly work on a piece of needlework, ignoring her daughter's sighs and grunts of worry.

"Why do not you change your dress, dear?" her mother said calmly. "We have visitors."

Dustin glanced down at her surcoat. It wasn't even really a surcoat, it was just a dress made from faded brown linen, and a darker brown girdle that would have emphasized the magnificence of her breasts had the white linen blouse not been so over-sized. Dustin never gave any thought to her clothes, mostly concerned with the other aspects of her busy life. As long as they were clean and functional, it was all that mattered.

"Why?" she asked, rather clueless.

Her mother put the sewing down. "Because you look like a peasant waif," she said patiently. "Look at your slippers – they are dirty, as are your hose. Please change into something more appropriate.

"Appropriate for what?" Dustin wanted to know. "Appropriate to hear of father's death?"

"Do not raise your voice, please," her mother said quietly. She was a pale woman with black hair hidden beneath a wimple. She'd never been particularly well and had spent the majority of her life reclining one way or the other. It was a great contrast to Dustin's vigor. "You shame your father dressed as you are. Please go and change."

Dustin grunted in frustration and turned to her mother to argue until she realized the woman's hands were shaking. Her heart sank with despair for her mother's feelings. She knew how much the woman had loved her father. She forgot her own feelings as she focused on what her mother was surely feeling.

"I am sorry, Mother," she said, forcing down her lofty pride as she went to kneel by her chair. "I did not mean it. The truth is that the knight never actually said father was dead. I really do not know why he is here."

Mary stroked her daughter's blond head. "I know," she smiled gently. "Now, please, go change your clothes. That would please me."

"Is there anything else I can do for you? Wine, perhaps?"

"Nay, my dear. Hurry along now and do as you are told."

With a reluctant nod, Dustin rose and moved for the door. She crossed the threshold and turned the corner only to run headlong into a broad, armored body.

It was a strong impact. Dustin shrieked, jumping back as if she'd been burned as her eyes flew up to face her accoster. The same sky-blue eyes that she had seen earlier smoldered back at her, now with something more than mere politeness. Now, there was something appraising there.

"My apologies," Christopher said.

Dustin nodded unsteadily as Jeffrey led Christopher into the drawing room, leaving Dustin standing in the corridor with her hand on her throat, wondering how a mere gaze could make her feel so vulnerable. De Lohr's eyes were piercing and consuming, something she'd never experienced before. It was an odd sensation. Coming back to her senses, she rushed to her bedchamber to do her mother's bidding.

Ready or not, she wanted to hear what the man had to say.

CHAPTER TWO

Dressed in a soft blue surcoat that, even with its simplicity, was just about the nicest surcoat she owned, Dustin scurried back down to her mother's drawing room. The full blue skirt was fitted around her slim waist with a black girdle and a snug-fitting white blouse, much more flattering to her figure than the usual sloppy dresses she bound about in. Her cascading hair was pulled back to the nape of her neck and secured, revealing the sweetness of her face. But Dustin truly didn't care how she looked; she'd only cleaned herself up and changed clothes to please her mother.

Eager to get back to the center of action, she took the great stone stairs two at a time and nearly ran across the foyer and into the solar.

What she saw upon her arrival shocked her. Her mother, face in her white hand, was obviously crying. Jeffrey, pale and drawn, stood next to her. Anger flared in her chest and she turned accusingly to the strange knight.

But what confronted her unbalanced her completely. The knight had taken off his helmet, revealing a great crown of dark blond hair slicked back against his skull. His features were rugged and masculine, and a neatly trimmed beard and mustache embraced his square jaw. He was indeed handsome, in her opinion, but she angrily chased those thoughts away. The fact remained that this man had said something terrible to upset her mother.

"What goes on here?" she demanded.

Jeffrey attempted to answer but Mary cut him off. "Come in here, Dustin. Please sit."

Increasingly off-balance, Dustin took the indicated chair, which happened to be close to the knight. Mary sniffed daintily and dabbed at her eyes before speaking to her daughter.

"Dustin, I believe you have met Sir Christopher de Lohr. He served with your father and our king, Richard, in the Holy Land," she said softly. "As you suspected, my dear girl, the message he bore concerned your father's demise this past summer."

Dustin's eyes welled but she fought it. She did not want to cry with this knight staring at her.

"Oh, Mother," she sighed. "I am so very sorry."

Mary nodded, wiping her eyes again. "As am I," she replied quietly. "'Twill not be the same, knowing he will never return."

Christopher watched the two women in their grief. He was sorry for his friend's death, too, but it had been a long time ago. Furthermore, he had only delivered half of his message and he wasn't sure it would be such a good idea for Dustin to be in the room when he delivered the remainder. Yet it was of no consequence what the girl felt; she would do as she was ordered, just as he was.

He revealed the second missive and approached Lady Mary. "My lady, there is more from our king," he said as gently as he could. As shocking as the first missive would be, this one would be explosive. "This message is also from Richard."

Trying to maintain her composure, Mary graciously took the parchment and broke the seal. Christopher stood back, discreetly looking away as she read the contents. From what he had seen of Lady Mary, she was far more in control of her emotions than her daughter and he honestly expected no outbursts.

When Lady Mary finished, she calmly lay the vellum in her lap and stared at it for several long moments. Dustin watched her mother curiously until she could stand the silence no longer.

"What does the king say, Mother?" she asked.

Lady Mary lifted her eyes to her daughter. Christopher did turn and looked at the older woman, then, to see how she was about to handle this delicate subject with her unruly child. Mayhap it would give him insight as to how to handle her once she became his wife.

Mary was surprisingly firm. "It seems your father had a final wish upon his death bed, Dustin, and that was that you would be married to a man of his choosing."

Dustin stood up, her face suspicious. "Who?" she demanded. "We have been through this subject before. I do not wish to be married at all."

Lady Mary nodded patiently. "I know, dear, but what you want is of no concern to your father or the king," she said frankly. "Your father must do as he sees fit for you and for the future of Lioncross. You will, therefore, be married and your husband will become lord of Lioncross."

Dustin's lovely face darkened. She glared back at her mother a moment before finally averting her gaze.

"Has he selected someone?" she asked reluctantly, hoping beyond hope he had died before it was possible, failing to take into account that the king would have therefore made the choice in his stead.

"He has," Mary replied steadily.

Dustin's head snapped up, her jaw ticking. Hopefully the man was in the Holy Land with the king and it would be years before he returned. Mayhap by then she would be ready for marriage and duty.

Yet she also knew that it was useless to protest anything, her mother had been preparing her for this eventuality ever since her father left. She knew this time would eventually come, as distasteful as the idea was to her.

That was why her mother allowed young men to call on her, young men who came and were as quickly chased off by her quick temper and hard right-cross. Mary hoped that at least one young man would catch Dustin's eye, but alas, that had not happened.

"Who? Do I know him?" she asked after a moment.

Lady Mary turned to look at Christopher. Feeling himself the focus of attention, he straightened, looking from Lady Mary to her daughter as Dustin's gaze fixed on him. It was clear they were all expecting an answer. He actually felt a little nervous.

"You have met him, my lady," he cleared his throat.

She frowned at him. "Then who is it? And why am I asking you this question? Did Richard ask you to inform me?"

"Indirectly," Christopher admitted.

"Then who?" Dustin demanded in frustration.

Christopher slowly cocked a blond eyebrow. "Me."

It took a moment for the revelation to dawn on Dustin. At first she wasn't sure she heard correctly, mulling his words over and over. Then, as realization set in and she understood that her father, as well as the king, expected her to marry this massive, cold man, her mouth fell open.

"You?" she repeated. "I am to marry *you*?"

"Aye," he nodded.

She clamped her pretty mouth shut into a hard line. Lord only knew, she knew her duty well. It had been drilled into her ever since she had been old enough to understand that it was her duty to carry on the Barringdon line. And she was now looking at the man she would marry and breed with.

Dustin's first reaction was to scream and rant, but she knew it would be a waste of energy. Mayhap it would simply be easier all the way around if she gave in to the idea and came to grips with it. The best she could hope for was a quick marriage and then he would go and leave her in peace. Did he really plan to live here, with her? Lord, she knew nothing about the man. What if he intended to force her into a real marriage?

"We will be married immediately," he said decisively. "Today, if possible. Lady Mary, do you have a priest?"

Both Lady Mary and Dustin looked surprised. Jeffrey was positively red. Christopher ignored the soldier, focusing on the older woman and expecting an answer.

"Yes, my lord, we do," Lady Mary replied softly. "Father Jonah."

Christopher looked at Jeffrey then. "Fetch him. Now."

Jeffrey was near to burst a vein but obeyed silently. Christopher watched the man's stiff back, wondering if he were going to have to watch his own until he could kick the man out of the keep. Jeffrey did not like him; that was apparent.

Dustin stared at the knight. Her initial impressions of him had been those of indifferent arrogance. When he looked at her, she saw nothing but ice in those blue eyes and it frightened and angered her at the same time. Yet she knew one thing, she didn't want him and he didn't want her.

Christopher gathered his helmet and gauntlets. "If you ladies will excuse me, I have duties to attend to," he said politely. "I shall return shortly."

Dustin looked away from him as he strode past her and quit the room. As soon as he was clear of the door she whirled to her mother.

"I do not want to marry him," she snapped.

Mary knew this exchange was coming and was prepared. "I know, dear, but as I said, you have no choice. Your father selected the man he felt most capable to provide you your future."

"He is a stranger," Dustin said, snappish and frightened. "You have seen him look at me; he does not want me, either. I do not want anything to do with him!"

Mary opened her mouth when there was a sudden shadow cast into the room from the open doorway. Dustin turned to see Christopher looming in the arch.

His sky-blue eyes were riveted to her and she could feel the coldness. She stared back, wondering why he was looking at her like that.

"You may say whatever you wish about me, Lady Dustin," he said calmly. "But you will not speak to your mother in that manner ever again in my presence."

She stiffened. "It wasn't in your presence. You were out of the room," she pointed out. "And I will speak to my mother however I wish."

He stepped into the room and she fought the urge to step away from him. She wondered crazily if he were going to strike her. But, amazingly, he looked entirely calm.

"Before this day is finished, you will be my wife in the eyes of God and country," he said. "Even as we stand now, you are for all intent and purposes my wife. Therefore, you will obey me, as it is a wife's duty to obey her husband. I say you will speak to your mother respectfully at all times and you will comply. Am I making myself clear?"

Dustin was so angry she was shaking. But she met his gaze, clenching her fists until her nails bit into her palms.

"Perfectly, my lord," was all she could manage to squeeze out.

He nodded shortly, moving once again for the door and leaving the room without another word.

Dustin stared at the empty doorway, outraged and shaken. They were not even officially married yet and already he was giving her orders. She looked at her mother but dare not speak to her, afraid he was lingering in the hallway waiting for her to disobey him.

How could her father have selected this man for her husband? Her father loved her. How in the world could he have sentenced his only child to a life of misery with a man who was such a cold bastard? She shook her head, disoriented with the contents of the entire day. It was all too unbelievable.

"Dustin, dear, mayhap you should go and freshen up a bit before the priest arrives," her mother said softly.

Dustin looked hard at her mother. "And you will just accept this?" she demanded softly.

Mary rose wearily. "There is nothing to reject or accept, Dustin. 'Tis simply the way of things." Her daughter turned away in disgust and Mary sighed. "Think of the positive, dear. Sir Christopher is as fine and tall and strong a man as I have ever seen, and I am sure he will protect Lioncross admirably. The fortress will be in capable hands."

"But what about me?" Dustin whispered, appalled that she was on the verge of angry tears. "What will happen to me?"

Mary put her thin hands on Dustin's shoulders. "Pray treat him well, daughter. Ye shall reap as ye sow."

Dustin rolled her eyes and turned to face her mother. "I do not want to marry anyone. I am only nineteen and I...."

Mary shook her head, "You should have been married two years ago. You know that as well as I." She dropped the hands from her daughter's shoulders. "Now, I am exceedingly weary and wish to rest a bit before attending your wedding."

Dustin gazed at her delicate mother, her heart once again aching for the loss of her father. She could only imagine the pain her mother was feeling. She had loved him so. For the moment, she forgot her own torment. Her mother was right; there was nothing she could do and the sooner she accepted that, the better. But she still could not swallow the thought of being married to that monstrous man.

"I shall come with you, Mother," she said softly.

There was nothing more to say.

☙

OUTSIDE IN THE BAILEY, Edward and David had everything under control. Edward, his dark hair plastered with perspiration, approached Christopher as the man emerged from the keep.

"Well? How did it go?" he demanded with restrained humor.

Christopher looked at his friend and flashed a brief look of distaste. "I am marrying the lady as soon as the priest arrives."

Edward grinned full-on, deep dimples in each cheek. "Congratulations, old man. And do not look so displeased. She is quite lovely."

Christopher shook his head, not wanting to discuss Lady Dustin further. His mind was already racing ahead, thinking on his return trip to London.

"When we return to London, I wish to leave my own men in charge. I do not trust nor do I like their Germanic captain. I would establish Lioncross as my own from the start."

"Agreed," Edward nodded, but did not volunteer to stay behind.

Christopher eyed him. "One of my own knights, I said."

Edward avoided his gaze. "Understood, my lord. But I wish to accompany you to London. Leave David here."

"David will wish to accompany me as well," Christopher reminded him. "And he is my brother."

Edward let out a heavy sigh and shrugged. "Aye, my lord," he answered grudgingly. "I will stay."

Christopher slapped a heavy hand on Edward s shoulder. "I knew you would see things my way."

Edward nodded in resignation as he followed Christopher across the compound. Christopher studied every inch of his keep critically, seeing things he had not seen in his first sweep. There were sections of the battlements that were missing stone and great holes in the bailey in spots. Everything needed to be smoothed out and resurfaced, and the keep needed work. Still, it was worth it. The prize was still mighty.

They met up with David near the squat and sturdy gatehouse, discussing everything from the upcoming wedding to Prince John in London. Christopher knew Edward was terribly disappointed that he would not be able to accompany him to London, but Christopher truly needed his trusted man here. When Edward was called away by one of the men-at-arms, David faced his brother.

"You could use him, Chris," he said softly. "Lioncross will do well with your men-at-arms establishing themselves here. Your presence will be known to all.

"I need no one with me in London, even you," Christopher replied. "Richard asked this task of me and me alone."

"What Richard asked was for you to keep an eye on his brother and report back to him," David hissed. "For all purposes, Christopher, you are a spy, a royal plant. Should John discover this, he will execute you as an enemy of the crown."

Christopher snorted. "He cannot. He has not the authority."

"You saw how he has established himself in London," David persisted, at a loss to understand his brother's attitude. "He has done everything but declared himself king. He rules England, not Richard."

Christopher's eyes flashed at his brother. "Richard is our king," he said slowly. "Whatever I do in London, I do it for our sovereign lord.

John has no power over me. My orders come directly from Richard."

David shook his head faintly, not knowing what else to say. "As you say, Lion's Claw. I can only hope that you are not the one to be gored."

Christopher looked at his brother a long moment. Then he smiled. "You worry like an old woman, little brother."

David shrugged. "I do not know why I even bother. You always do what you want to, anyway."

Christopher's jocularity faded. "Not in this case," he glanced at Lioncross. "To obtain this mighty fortress, I must do something I most definitely do not want to do."

"Marry Lady Dustin?" David smiled. "Why not, Chris? Jesus Christ, she's beautiful. Big tits, too."

Christopher cocked an eyebrow. "Does she? I didn't notice. In fact, I can't seem to get past all that hair. She's got enough hair for three women."

David nodded seductively. "Think about it, Chris, all of that hair flowing over you as she mounts you."

Christopher waved his brother off. "I get the picture. She's so damn small that I will probably tear her asunder. Not the most auspicious way to begin a marriage."

David laughed heartily and Christopher joined him for a few moments, chuckling at Dustin's expense.

"On second thought, Chris, maybe I will stay here," David snickered. "'Twill be a pleasure to watch after my brother's wife, the poor lonely woman."

Christopher's amusement vanished. "You will not touch her. Is that clear?"

David was taken aback by the tone and by the deadly flicker in his brother's eye. He was suddenly very curious about the sudden burst of husbandly protectiveness. The only person Christopher was passionate about was Richard, and himself. Strange that his new bride would provoke that kind of a response.

"Aye, verily," he said. "It was only a jest."

Christopher was embarrassed for his outburst and looked away, wondering why in the hell he had done it. He was a reasonable man and deduced that he was naturally protective of Lady Dustin for obvious reasons. Firstly, she was his chattel. Secondly, she was a weaker female and fell under the category of knightly chivalry. Any other reason disturbed him too much.

"You could always take her to London with you and keep an eye on her yourself," David suggested, goading his brother to see what other responses he could get. "John would go mad for such a lovely woman."

Christopher shook his head. "I'd spend all of my time fighting the prince off her," he said, but in faith, did not think the suggestion to be a bad one. After all, he could keep an eye on her and get to know her better. There was no knowing how long he would be staying in London, and if he left Dustin here, he would be just as much a stranger upon his return.

As he mulled over the possibilities, there was a shout from high atop the wall. Riders had been sighted and were rapidly approaching the village. There were only three, riding fast for Lioncross.

The gates were open and Christopher positioned himself dead center, his huge serrated broadsword in his left hand. David and Edward joined him, a grim welcoming party for the intruders.

As Christopher watched the three knights approach, he was aware of his protective feelings towards Lioncross, as well. He hadn't been at the fortress for an hour and already he was ready and willing to die for it. It was his, already under his skin. It took him a moment to realize he had finally come home.

The riders reined their great destriers to within several feet of the drawbridge, the horses dancing and kicking up dust. Christopher waited, ready to spring into action and cut off a head should it be so required. He was as coiled as a spring.

The rider in the middle suddenly began to laugh, a curiously familiar laugh. Ripping off his helmet, he continued to laugh heartily.

"So the rumors were true, Lion's Claw," he said, dismounting his steed.

Christopher went limp with relief. He knew the face and he knew the man. "Leeton de Shera," he hissed. "How in the hell did you find me?"

Leeton just laughed as he approached and the other two knights tore off their helmets as well, joining in the laughter.

"Christ on his Mighty Throne," Christopher muttered a curse, gazing at the others. "You brought the devil twins with you. Max and Anthony de Velt."

The de Velt twins were mirror images of each other, of average height but built like the mighty mountains of the north, with long dark hair and brown-eyes. Leeton, however, was as blond as Christopher and more so; even his eyelashes and eyebrows were white. He was tall and well-built, and had been Christopher's close friend since they had fostered together in Derby. He had not chosen to crusade with Richard, instead, remaining as captain for the Earl of Derby. Christopher wondered what he was doing so far from his fortress.

"Why aren't you at Derby?" Christopher demanded, taking Leeton's outstretched hand and shaking it.

Leeton shrugged. "I still am, on occasion. But no longer as captain."

Christopher grew serious. Leeton was by far one of the best knights he had ever seen and he was puzzled as well as concerned.

"Why not?" he asked.

Leeton's face grew sad, soft, as he released Christopher's hand. "Do you remember the earl's daughter, Rachel?"

Christopher nodded. "Of course, Leeton I knew her well."

"I married her," Leeton replied quietly, but Christopher could read the tremendous grief in his friend's eyes. "Two years ago. Last year, she bore me a son. She died three hours later."

Christopher was stunned. Aye, he had known the fair Rachel, and he knew Leeton had always been sweet on her. For them to marry was not a surprise, but he was deeply saddened by Rachel's death. He could see that Leeton was still having trouble coming to terms with it.

"Please accept my condolences," he said softly. "But your son was healthy?"

"Aye, Richard is magnificent," Leeton nodded. "He lives with the earl and his wife. I, however, cannot bear to stay at the keep because it was where I met my wife and where she died. So I have spent a great deal of time in Worcester, and in Nottingham, on errands for the earl. I see Richard when I can."

Christopher sighed heavily, feeling the man's anguish. "If I had a son, I would not let him out of my sight," he murmured. "How can you be apart from him?"

Leeton cleared his throat and lowered his gaze. "He is the image of Rachel, Chris," he said softly. "Every time I look at him, I see her, and my grief is fresh."

Christopher understood. With silent sympathy, he clapped his friend on the shoulder and the two of them turned back to the others, now engaged in lively conversation with Edward and David.

"Chris, what's this I hear that you are to be married?" Max asked loudly.

Christopher nodded coolly. "Unfortunately, in order to gain this magnificent keep, I have to marry the heiress," he said. "I have only met her today, and today we will be married. You will all attend the ceremony, of course."

"You are getting married?" Leeton was shocked. "Jesus, Chris, what a hell of a surprise. How on earth did this happen?"

Christopher didn't want to go into that at the moment. He gave Leeton a wry smirk. "By decree of our illustrious Richard," he said, rather grandiose. "He commands and I obey."

Leeton could see the reluctance, the humor, and it was difficult not to tease Christopher because of it.

"Your devotion to our king is indeed limitless," he said dryly. "So what does this woman look like? Twisted and old? Medusa in the flesh?"

Before Christopher could answer, David's gaze suddenly moved to the keep and he found himself following his brother's focus. On a second floor window overlooking the bailey, a small figure in blue silk and flowing blond hair stood watching the knights. When Dustin noticed she had been sighted, she abruptly disappeared back into the castle.

"That," Christopher said, "is she."

None of the knights said a word, looking up at the window as if she were still standing there. The de Velt twins' mouths were hanging open. All jesting faded as the shock of the lady's appearance settled.

"*That* is Medusa in the flesh?" Leeton asked in disbelief. "God, Chris, you failed to mention she was absolutely beautiful. I feel like an arse."

Christopher shrugged noncommittally. "The fact that she is easy on the eyes will only make the marriage a bit more palatable," he said. "But I have come to see that she is exceedingly stubborn and disrespectful."

"Who cares? The two traits can be changed," Leeton insisted. "You cannot do a thing about her looks, but her manners can be molded. She can make you a fine wife."

Christopher shrugged carelessly again, his only answer. The conversation turned back to the king, the prince, and the crusade, and Christopher whole-heartedly joined in. But in the back of his mind, the small woman with the incredible hair kept appearing and try as he might, he could not shake her.

Read the rest of **RISE OF THE DEFENDER** in eBook or in paperback.

About Kathryn Le Veque

Medieval Just Got Real.

KATHRYN LE VEQUE is a USA TODAY Bestselling author, an Amazon All-Star author, and a #1 bestselling, award-winning, multi-published author in Medieval Historical Romance and Historical Fiction. She has been featured in the NEW YORK TIMES and on USA TODAY's HEA blog. In March 2015, Kathryn was the featured cover story for the March issue of InD'Tale Magazine, the premier Indie author magazine. She was also a quadruple nominee (a record!) for the prestigious RONE awards for 2015.

Kathryn's Medieval Romance novels have been called 'detailed', 'highly romantic', and 'character-rich'. She crafts great adventures of love, battles, passion, and romance in the High Middle Ages. More than that, she writes for both women AND men – an unusual crossover for a romance author – and Kathryn has many male readers who enjoy her stories because of the male perspective, the action, and the adventure.

On October 29, 2015, Amazon launched Kathryn's Kindle Worlds Fan Fiction site WORLD OF DE WOLFE PACK. Please visit Kindle Worlds for Kathryn Le Veque's World of de Wolfe Pack and find many action-packed adventures written by some of the top authors in their genre using Kathryn's characters from the de Wolfe Pack series. As Kindle World's FIRST Historical Romance fan fiction world, Kathryn Le Veque's World of de Wolfe Pack will contain all of the great storytelling you have come to expect.

Kathryn loves to hear from her readers. Please find Kathryn on Facebook at Kathryn Le Veque, Author, or join her on Twitter @kathrynleveque, and don't forget to visit her website at www.kathrynleveque.com.

Printed in Great Britain
by Amazon